The Family Holiday

ELIZABETH NOBLE

PENGUIN BOOKS

PENGUIN BOOKS

UK | USA | Canada | Ireland | Australia
India | New Zealand | South Africa

Penguin Books is part of the Penguin Random House group of companies
whose addresses can be found at global.penguinrandomhouse.com.

Penguin
Random House
UK

First published 2020

001

Copyright © Elizabeth Noble, 2020

The moral right of the author has been asserted

Extract from *To Kill a Mockingbird* by Harper Lee.
Published by William Heinemann.
Reprinted by permission of The Random House Group Limited. © 2018

Set in 12.5/14.75 pt Garamond MT Std
Typeset by Jouve (UK), Milton Keynes
Printed and bound in Great Britain by Clays Ltd, Elcograf S.p.A.

A CIP catalogue record for this book is available from the British Library

ISBN: 978–1–405–93454–1

www.greenpenguin.co.uk

For my very own wonderful, beloved family

Out of the crooked timber of humanity
no straight thing was ever made.

Immanuel Kant

I

CANDLEWOOD FARM

Luxury rural retreat
  Ideal for families or groups (no hens or stags)
  A charming Cotswold manor house, plus a group of sympathetically restored outbuildings to provide characterful additional accommodation: sleeps 16 in 8 bedrooms (cots available)
  Outdoor swimming pool, tennis court, croquet lawn
  Outside catering optional
  Pets welcome

The photographs in Charlie's smart, glossy brochure seemed to have been taken in high summer. The kind of high summer England collectively dreamt of but hardly ever seemed to experience, of the vivid pinks, lilacs and oranges of a flowerbed, the cobalt of a cloudless sky, and shimmering heat. Charlie wondered how long they'd had to wait to shoot the pictures. Years, maybe. Or perhaps the photos hadn't really looked like that at all, and they'd laid fancy filters and special effects over the top, like the kids did with the endless pictures of themselves they seemed to take, these days. It looked completely idyllic. Which was, incidentally, the word used most often in the brochure.

The house was pleasingly symmetrical, built of warm

Cotswold stone, clad in a flowering wisteria (first trick: wisteria bloomed in the spring). The garden was classic country – seasonally correct, this time – with manicured hornbeam hedges and deep beds of lupins, delphiniums and dahlias. Blowsy full roses curled around metal arbours set along a path down to a small blue lozenge of a swimming-pool with teak sun-loungers and a tiny pastel-coloured summerhouse for changing into your costume. It was the sort of garden Charlie had been trying to grow all his adult life, and here it was. There was a smart tennis court, with a high green fence, and a croquet set.

Small 'lifestyle' photographs interspersed the more informative ones – a jug of icy Pimm's and some glasses, pretty pottery bowls full of tomatoes and strawberries you just knew were still warm from the sunshine under which they had been picked. Or, at least, that was how it looked. It all seemed to be saying, 'Everything is soft-focus perfect here. Your life could be this way too, if only you'd come . . .' Selling a fantasy. And Charlie was buying.

There'd been no glossy, professional brochure twelve years ago, when Daphne had seen an advertisement in the back pages of one of the women's magazines she pored over every month. She'd neatly sliced out the ad, with the special little cutter he'd bought her one Christmas to do just that. Kept it in what she called her file of dreams and schemes, which was one of those paper concertina things, tied with a ribbon. Daphne's was pink flowers and a yellow ribbon, bought from WHSmith on the high street years ago. It had lived, and still did, on the bookshelf in the kitchen, with her old cookbooks. It was all still there.

She'd annotated most of the cookbooks – adjustments to recipes, notes on temperatures – and he couldn't bear to throw them away, though he hadn't used them once since he'd been on his own. He'd got away with it, too. Convention, friends and his well-meaning children had contrived to remove most of her physical presence from the house in the years after she'd died. Her clothes and handbags had gone to charity shops, and their wardrobe hadn't smelt of her in years. Her jewellery, such as it was, had been spread among the family according to her wishes, expressed on a note left in its box. But no one seemed to have noticed that he hoarded the cookbooks. He could open one at random, run his finger over her big, round handwriting, and summon her up, stirring a pan on the stove in her apron, sipping a glass of wine as she squinted to read an instruction. He'd kept the file as well. That, too, could bring her back to him, as if she was still here, for a moment.

Knitting patterns, places to visit and reviews of books she ought to read. He could see her sitting at the table with the little plastic device. He'd found it in there, the ad, crumpled between a guide to spending forty-eight hours in Copenhagen, and an article on French *brocante* markets in easy reach of Calais. They hadn't made it to the flea markets, but they had spent a lovely weekend strolling past the colourful houses of Nyhavn and listening to classical concerts in the twinkling Tivoli gardens in the Danish capital, just a few summers before she died.

He'd booked the house for his eightieth birthday on his seventy-ninth, almost a year ago. Even then the kindly woman he'd spoken to on the telephone had told him he was lucky to get it. She'd already had bookings for July 2020, she said. It was highly desirable, she told him, and he felt very pleased with himself, grateful to Daphne, too, and the file of dreams and schemes. Without it, he might not have known where to start. Ten days. High season. It would have had to be two weeks, a period of enforced togetherness that even Daphne would probably have balked at, but they had a wedding party booked in for a long weekend, Lucy said, so ten days would work. For twelve people. Seven thousand pounds. It was a fortune. A frankly ludicrous amount. His first car had cost him two hundred quid. Their first home, his and Daphne's, three thousand five hundred, that itself an unimaginable sum to his parents, who'd never owned a home of their own. This was just a holiday, for crying out loud. The deposit had been an even thousand, transferred online. The balance for the accommodation had come due six months ago, and been paid in the same way. The catering he'd organized and some other extras would be settled after the event on the credit card he'd used to secure the booking.

And Daphne's voice had been in his ear the whole time. Still. He'd long since recognized that she'd been the impetus behind everything that was any good in his life. He thought he'd appreciated it while she was alive, but the full impact didn't strike him until she was gone. She had been the light of his life. It was a cliché, but it was true. He missed every single thing about her but, forced to say what he missed most, he'd say laughter. Whole days passed now, in his world, without it. Barely an hour had passed without a laugh while she'd been alive, even in the tougher times.

She'd brought to his life the colour and the laughter, the fun and the adventure – the joy – and she'd given him all the people he loved most. A daughter and two sons. Four grandchildren now. Ethan, whom she had met and adored, Bea, Delilah and Arthur, whom she hadn't, although he knew she'd have adored them just as much. It had all come from Daphne. Hers was such a habit of lightness that somehow it persisted from beyond the grave. Of course he knew she wasn't speaking to him. He wasn't senile. It was just that he had heard her so often and for so long that he knew, just knew, what she would have had to say about, well, everything, really. And she would have been pleased about this. She'd have said, 'Bugger the cost. You planning on taking it with you, you old skinflint?' But there'd have been a twinkle in her eye, a fond smile, and a warm hand on his arm so he'd know she was mostly joking, and he'd do it.

So he'd done it.

He'd meant to tell the kids, meant to invite them out loud, face to face. Maybe it was cowardly to do it this way. The truth was, for all his bluster and front (that was what Daphne would have called it), he had been afraid of the expressions that might pass across their faces before they rearranged them politely. He knew exactly what he was asking of them all, and he was asking anyway. He suspected it would mean far less to them than it did to him, and of all the good fights he'd fought in the years since Daphne had died, the hardest one was not to seem needy. He hated the very idea. So he was, in truth, a bit scared of asking them, even as he acknowledged she'd have snorted if he'd said so to her. He'd do it by post. In front of him now were three large brown envelopes, one addressed to each of his children. To his eldest, Laura, and his sons, Scott and Nick. He slid a brochure into each, with the notes he'd handwritten. Each just a little bit different because they were. Each outlining his singular desire to spend his eightieth birthday surrounded by the people he loved, in a beautiful place.

They'd laugh at the possibility that he might be frightened of them. The family myth was the other way around. He was the formidable one. The disciplinarian. The curmudgeon. The trouble was, that shtick had worked when he'd been half of a double act – the tough cop to Daphne's soft one. It had never been true, just how they'd managed it. It was one of a million reasons he'd been lost since she died. One of a million reasons he'd been faking it since she died. Willing them to notice. Which they seemed not to have done. Hoping they didn't all at the same time. They were absorbed, God knew, in their own lives, and comfortable with the family myths. Scott had said to him, about three years after Daphne died, that he'd expected his father to marry again. To be married again already, in fact. Charlie remembered registering that, amazed that his son knew him so little. That, he could never, ever have done. She had been it, for him. Unforgettable. Irreplaceable.

It was only partly true, he knew, that this was about what he wanted. It was about them, too, and their families. Without Daphne as the link, he was further from them now than he had ever thought he would be. And yet close enough to see how much they still needed and missed their mother. Especially Nick. But Laura too. All was not well there. And Scott – he barely understood Scott, these days. He felt almost tearful, suddenly, at his own inadequacy, certain that if his wife had been there, she'd know exactly what to do, how to help, how to make things better. He should have paid more attention to the way she did it. Been less quick to hand her the phone whenever any of them rang. 'I'll get your mother.' He wanted to be better with them than he was. Almost tearful was an all-too-frequent occurrence, these days. He hated not knowing what to do. But he was determined to try. For her.

2

The sound of the alarm shattered the peace. Laura reached out and felt around on the bedside table, smashing her target with the flat of her palm, more violently than was strictly necessary. She opened her eyes and turned her head on the pillow with a groan: the bright sunshine streaming in around the edges of the blackout blind was an assault. Seven thirty a.m. It wasn't too early, unless you'd been tossing and turning until three, and only dropped off again near dawn so you didn't wake refreshed, but from twenty thousand leagues under the murky sea of deep sleep. She lay still for a moment, waiting to remember all the stuff she'd managed to forget for a few hours, and taking her emotional temperature. Yep. Still alone. Still angry.

Laura couldn't remember the last time she hadn't been angry. It felt to her as if her rage was part of her now. It was her best friend and her bitterest enemy. The strength in her spine and the tremble in her gut. It was rage that woke her every morning and powered her through her day, and the same rage deflated her like a balloon at night, sending her into a deep and instantaneous sleep from which it capriciously roused her at two, three or four o'clock. It started, with consciousness, deep in her core, and travelled, like pins and needles, to the tips of her fingers. It wasn't a red mist: mist was too light, too permeable.

It was a crimson blanket, and it smothered her daily. But without it she'd have had nothing at all.

She threw back the duvet and moved to sit on the edge of the bed, rubbing her eyes. She could see herself in the dressing-table mirror. Pasty legs beneath a scruffy nightshirt. Baggy, crêpy eyes. Wild hair. Christ. She registered the thought that she hadn't heard Ethan moving about the house and almost shouted his name, then immediately remembered: he wasn't there. He'd stayed with his father last night. Ouch. The little stab, the tiny sting. Every time. And he'd been doing it more and more lately . . .

She wasn't supposed to make him feel bad about it. She honestly tried not to. She wasn't even supposed to see it as a betrayal, but she did. In her heart, to her shame, she wanted him to reject Alex, to hate him for what he'd done, because he'd done it to both of them, not just to her.

Having an affair – cheating – he'd done to her and her alone. She was the one he'd made vows to. But the rest he'd done to them both. He'd shattered their family, altered for ever the shape of their lives.

And still Ethan wanted to go there. Why the hell wouldn't he? A shiny new apartment. A happy father. A shiny new girlfriend, too, eager to impress him. Fewer rules. And no Laura.

It wasn't fair. Alex simply hadn't put in the effort. Whatever excuses he might make, however he might reinvent their history, he knew, she knew, and one day Ethan would recognize, he just hadn't given it the time. He hadn't thrown and caught a million tennis balls in the garden, or changed a thousand nappies, or sat for hours in

9

the middle of the night in a steamy bathroom while Ethan had croup – a dozen times before he was three.

Downstairs in the kitchen, Laura made a large mug of tea, filling the cat's bowl while it brewed. Not that the cat was anywhere to be seen. Perhaps he'd found his way to Alex's new flat, too, forgetting who'd emptied his litter tray and filled his food bowl every day for the last eight years. She flicked on the radio, but found herself immediately irritated by the voices, and switched it off again. In the front hall, there was a small pile of envelopes. The post had gone from being quite boring (bills, pizza-delivery flyers, dental appointments) to being quite alarming: she and Alex did most of their communicating through lawyers now, while accountants and financial advisers, too, were getting in on the action of dissecting their lives. She didn't open things straight away any more. She left official-looking letters until the evening, after she'd drunk a vodka and tonic.

This morning there was an envelope with her dad's writing on it. That, she could risk opening with tea. She padded back to the kitchen table and opened it with her finger, pulling out the glossy brochure and the letter inside.

My darling girl,

I would love you three, along with your brothers and their families, to join me here for the first ten days of August this year: as you know, I reach the grand old age of eighty then, and I can't think of a better way to celebrate than by having all of you around me. I know it would have made your mum happy.

I thought, when I last saw you, that a decent holiday would do you good, my love, and I hope you'll come and let me spoil you.

Dad xox

Shit. Alex had moved out four months ago and she hadn't told her dad yet. She hadn't really told anyone. People knew, of course – that stuff filtered out and spread like wildfire. But she hadn't said it to anyone except a couple of old mates and the cast of professionals poring over the detail of their lives. He'd left on Boxing Day, with a leather holdall, a cardboard box, and a new place already lined up. They'd limped through the pre-Christmas parties and events, together but not really. People didn't notice, once they'd had a couple of glasses of mulled wine, that you'd arrived together but hadn't spent one whole minute side by side until you left. Christmas Day had been torture. Long silences, too many vodkas and a turkey dinner it had been hard to swallow. After lunch, Ethan had begged to go to his girlfriend's. Alex had told her then. Somewhere between the *EastEnders* episode and the Bond film. And then, of course, winter got quiet and dull and hibernate-y anyway. She'd seen her dad once, for lunch at a garden centre halfway between their homes. They'd eaten quiche, then wandered among the dead-looking February plants searching out hellebores for his borders, chatting about Ethan's exams, the heavy rainfall of the last week and Jeremy Corbyn. And she hadn't lied about her and Alex. She just hadn't said anything because it was too hard. The note implied he'd noticed something was slightly off, but he hadn't asked.

Now she'd have to tell him that Alex had left her for another woman. That she was a single mother to Ethan. That her husband didn't love her any more.

But not just now. She didn't have to tell him this morning. Ethan wasn't here. It would be Alex nagging him to get out of bed, to put his breakfast things into the dishwasher, and answering the usual questions about football socks. If he bothered to do any of those things. She could go back to bed, pull the duvet over her head, and stay there for as long as she wanted . . .

3

It was lunchtime when Heather called. Scott was in New York, six hours ahead. She called on her way home from the gym or the school run, almost always from the car, on speakerphone. Scott hated speakerphone. Heather shouted at him, broke off from shouting at him to shout at other motorists, and went back to shouting at him. Heather was a Jersey girl – New Jersey, that was, not the island next to Guernsey, and never more so than while she was driving when she could, and frequently did, 'go full-on hoodlum', as she called it, at the slightest provocation. He loved his wife, God knew he did, but he did not like being shouted at. Or other people being shouted at in his presence. Even when every sentence ended in 'honey' or 'sweetie', pronounced 'sweedy', it still set him on edge.

He'd been an Englishman in New York. She'd been a Jersey girl in Surrey. A pair of aliens. An odd couple. At forty-three, Scott was still almost surprised on a daily basis to find himself married, a stepfather to her two daughters, an 'instant-family' man, although it had been more than a year now. That his wife and stepdaughters were American was nothing short of stupefying. He'd been travelling between his firm's offices in London and New York for almost twenty years, spending up to five days at a time in the Big Apple, sleeping in a nondescript hotel in Midtown, working long days in a behemoth of an office at 39th and Lexington, and Heather was the first American girl to show him the vaguest interest. He'd been taken aback – neither his teeth nor his hair fitted the New York aesthetic, the former being uneven, overlapping in places and more ivory than bright white, and the latter crawling slowly but inexorably back towards the top of his head.

She'd gone for him. As predatory as a big cat. That was what his New York colleague Matthew had told him one evening after work in a crowded Irish bar, with characteristic bluntness. He'd known it before Matthew had said so, although he appreciated the concern. He'd known it, and he'd absolutely let it happen.

He was lonely. She was pretty, in a wholesome, obvious way – all blonde waves and blue eyes – and she'd seemed kind, and if it was a gamble to assume that this was the real her, not just the act of a calculating, mercenary female, then he reasoned the gamble was worth it. He'd made a pretty successful career of gambling. Was this so different?

'So there's a big fat envelope here addressed to you, Scottie. Should I open it?'

No one else called him Scottie. He wouldn't let them. Even with her, it had taken a while to get used to. Now he liked the way it sounded – 'Scoddie' – all *d*s, no *t*s – in her husky, warm voice. 'Go for it.' He heard the tearing of paper.

'It's a brochure . . . for a holiday place. Looks like the Cotswolds. Hold on . . . there's a note. It's from your dad.'

Scott was genuinely surprised. 'What does he say?'

'Hang on, I'll read it . . .'

Scott and Heather,

I would so love it if you and the girls would join me and the rest of the family at this place in August to celebrate my eightieth birthday. I've chosen somewhere that hopefully has enough stuff to keep teenagers amused and, of course, Ethan will be there, I hope, so they shouldn't get too bored. You can even walk into the village, where there's a bit to do. It would be very good to have the opportunity to get to know Heather, Hailey and Meredith better. I know it's probably rather short notice for you, but I shall keep my fingers crossed you can make the time work. Let me know.

With love,
Dad xx

'Below his name and the kisses he's written something else. It's in a different pen, like an afterthought. It says, "Your mum would want us all to be together. She'd want it to have happened far more than it has. Maybe that's my fault. It would mean a lot to me if you would come, son."'

'Bless him, that's sweet.'

'He spelt "Hayley" with an *i*.'

'Heather . . .'

'I know. I don't mind. At least, I mind less than I mind that we're supposed to be going to Mykonos in August . . .'

'Have we booked?' By which, of course, he meant had Heather booked. She had a black Amex card now and she knew how to use it. She was, in fact, really, really good at using it. Not that he minded. There was plenty of money, and it made him happy to see her happy. There had never seemed much point in having it before.

'No. But I had the most darling place all lined up. I was

going to show you when you got back tomorrow. It's in Condé Nast *Traveller* magazine's top-ten places in Greece. It's pretty much carved into this rocky cliff. But you can walk to the town. Which has shops, restaurants, bars . . . There are only about thirty rooms, and a gorgeous restaurant.' Her voice dropped an octave, into the sexy range of which she was a mistress. 'And every room has its own pool . . .'

He didn't doubt its gorgeousness for a moment. And Scott had absolutely no problem with a little pool attached to every room. There'd been one at their honeymoon hotel in the Maldives, and Heather had shagged him in it at least once every day of the ten they were there. Which had been more than worth the sunburn he'd got on the small bald patch at the top of his head.

'Can't we go after? Or before?'

'We could. The girls start school at the very beginning of September.'

'So?'

'Are you sure you'll be able to take the time off for two holidays in August?'

'Definitely.' He wasn't sure but he'd worry about that later.

'Promise?'

'I promise. We should go.'

'Do you think it will be fun?'

'I didn't say that. I said we should go.'

'I hardly know your family.'

'Dad's point exactly. This is your chance to charm them all like you've charmed me, darling.'

'Flatterer.'

'Truth-teller.'

'Do we have to go for the full ten days?'

'We can say yes to the full ten days. And I can invent an excuse to get us out of there after a few if it's a nightmare.'

'You're a genius.'

'That's why you love me.'

'It's one of the reasons.'

And he believed her, though he knew others might not.

Afterwards, while he ran his usual 7.5 kilometres on the treadmill at the gym near the office, facing screens showing Bloomberg, Scott tried to remember the last time he'd been on holiday with his brother and sister, Laura and Nick. And he really couldn't.

They'd never fallen out. No big *Jeremy Kyle*-style fights – no great wrongs done. He'd drifted away and, untethered, they either hadn't noticed or hadn't minded. They were siblings, not friends. Laura and Nick were friends. He'd always been different. Always felt left out. They'd made him feel dull and wrong when they were all young. It was easier to drift. Maybe it was time . . .

4

Nick's left arm was going to sleep. As was he. *Room on the Broom* was spread on his chest, unfinished. He knew its rhymes and cadences by heart now, and didn't need to read, but the children loved the pictures, followed the words on the page, and knew if he skipped a spread.

All the running on blustery Primrose Hill this afternoon had done its work. Delilah and Arthur had gone floppy and heavy within his embrace well before the end of the story. Across from the small bed the three of them were lying on, Bea, his big girl, was already spark out on her own, duvet kicked back as per normal, arms above her head in surrender pose. Nick eased his arm out from under the children, and picked Arthur up, laid him gently in his cot, then turned back to Delilah. He lifted her legs, pulled the cover back and over her, deftly and quickly, so as not to rouse her. He made a token effort to extract her thumb from her mouth, but at that, she resumed the strong rhythmic suck that would keep it there a while longer, and he smiled. Stubborn even while sleeping. Arthur yawned noisily, and turned onto his stomach, raising his bottom and scooting his knees up to under his chin. He kissed his elder daughter's warm cheek, smoothing her curls. Then he stood still in the middle of the room, and waited a minute, gazing at his babies, before he bent down and switched off the light by Delilah's bed. The room was still illuminated, by two small nightlights plugged in at the skirting, and by the neon stars stuck to the ceiling in a pattern approximating the solar system.

This was Bea's room. Delilah's, slightly larger, was next door, and Arthur's was the box room across the landing. Bea's had been the first to be decorated when they'd moved in – sunny yellow with bright primary-coloured furniture and a rainbow rug. Delilah had crawled defiantly in the direction of pink and sparkly the minute she'd graduated from the nursery so her room was an unabashed temple to girliness. And the nursery had been repainted sky blue in the excitement post-scan when they'd found out Carrie was carrying a boy.

The rest of the house was a symphony of tasteful greys and soft accent colours – almost out of a magazine in its compliance with trend and fashion. But Carrie had gone to town in the kids' rooms and they were characterful, vivid and fun.

Moving them all in together had seemed the right thing to do, after their mum had died. His friend Fran had suggested it. Carrie had met her in a yoga class when she was pregnant with Bea, and Fran with Fred. She'd been the first person outside family to ring the doorbell after it had happened, laden with casseroles and toilet rolls, and pretty much pushed her way in, because she had loved Carrie too, and keeping busy helped, and because she knew that Carrie would have wanted her to brush the tangles out of Bea's hair and Dettox the kitchen surfaces.

In the first strange, wretched days, Carrie's parents had been there, white-faced and zombied by grief, but at least there'd been three of them at bedtime. One to settle each distraught child. When they'd gone, as they'd had to, back to their farm in Cumbria, Nick had moved between the rooms, running on empty, soothing and holding his babies in turn. The plaintive sound of one, heard in the background to the sobs of another, tortured him. Fran had helped him move Arthur's cot and Delilah's tiny bed in there, shifting the displaced doll's house and toy shop into the space vacated in Delilah's room. It had worked, too. They'd started sleeping, comforted, somehow, by the presence of each other. He'd wanted to sleep in there with them. Had done, in fact, for a few weeks. Not that he'd slept. He'd lain on a flimsy air mattress for a few hours at a time, not sleeping. Fran had put a stop to that. She'd deflated it and forced him back into his own bed, where she'd also changed the sheets and removed Carrie's hand creams and eye serums from her bedside table.

Downstairs now, he poured a glass of wine and put Muse on the speaker, quieter than he'd have liked so he could hear the kids if they called. He unloaded the dishwasher and, checking a laminated sheet of A4 paper fixed to the fridge door with magnets, took Bea's PE bag from a hook in the utility room and checked that her shorts and polo shirt were in it, along with a pair of black plimsolls. He put it by the front door and, while he was there, collected the small pile of post from the brass basket attached to the letterbox. Interiors catalogues. For months he'd been cutting out the small address boxes on the back pages of these, all addressed to his wife, and returning them, but still they came, interiors catalogues, with their embroidered cushions and their seed-pod chandeliers and their carefully curated accessories. She'd call them her porn, poring over them with a huge mug of mint tea, the paper tab of the teabag dangling over the side, sitting at the kitchen table. He'd given up on the cutting and posting. He had less energy, it seemed, than he had done in the beginning. Now the catalogues made the journey from brass cage to paper recycling without anyone daydreaming about owning anything in them. The brown A4 envelope almost did, too, but Nick saved it at the last minute.

Nick,

This is booked, paid for, and happening. I've invited Laura and Scott, and their families. We'll be a gang. A dysfunctional, not entirely simpatico gang, maybe, but a gang nonetheless. So please, please bring B, D and A with you and just come. Be with us. We all love you so much, you know. I haven't seen nearly enough of you since it all happened. I know I'm not your mum, and she'd know better than me how to help you, but I do care so very much. And it's my birthday, so you can't say no, really. It may be blackmail, but there it is . . .

Dad xoxo

Nick smiled, and flicked through the brochure, with its sunny, stylish pictures, not so very different from all the damn catalogues. And then he cried. It wasn't unusual. He cried most nights. It was just as much a part of his routine as checking Fran's laminated lists, and flossing his teeth.

5

Scott was the first to confirm. Charlie imagined himself on a neat to-do list, being ticked off.

'Crikey. Whatever time is it there?'

Scott paused for a moment, checking his screen. 'Six a.m.'

'And you're up?'

Up, done five km on the static bike, showered, dressed and in the office, Scott wanted to say, but he didn't. Mum used to say the hours required by his work were ridiculous. 'It's all machismo,' she would exclaim incredulously. 'It can't possibly be necessary. You'll all die young,' she'd pronounce, in consternation. Dad would let her rant, then nod his understanding at Scott. Dad had been a country solicitor. Maybe never once at his desk at six a.m., in truth, but it suited him to indicate that he understood. It was a curious thing, having a child so successful he eclipsed anything you had achieved professionally, engendering a mix of pride and something like embarrassment. Silly. You should choose it that way. Nevertheless . . .

'There's a nor'-easter forecast for this afternoon. Might shut the whole damn place down. Thought I'd be in early and see what I can get done before the chaos starts.'

'But it's meant to be spring!'

'I know. Late. Happens, though . . . They're predicting up to a foot of snow.'

'I thought New Yorkers took that in their stride.'

'They do, more or less. I mean, I fly home in three days and I'm not worried about the flight. They'll have cleared it all up by then. It's just today . . .'

Weather talk. Along with cricket, rugby and football, the safest territory known to Englishmen.

Scott cleared his throat. He needed to get on. 'So, Dad. We got your invitation.'

'Oh, yes?' Charlie was holding his breath.

'And we'd love to come. It's really very generous of you.'

Always that slightly formal tone. It made Charlie sad. He ignored it and injected as much bonhomie as he could into his response. 'Oh, I am glad. All of you? Heather, Hayley, Meredith?'

'Yes, all of us.'

'I was worried you might have made bookings already.'

'No. You caught us in time. We will have a holiday, the four of us, and no doubt Heather will bring the girls over here to catch up with family at some point. She couldn't do Easter, with Hayley's exams, but those ten days work for us. We'll be there.'

'That's brilliant.'

'Have you heard from Laura and Nick?'

'No. You're the first.'

That wasn't quite true. Laura had sent him an email, asking to meet him for lunch. They were seeing each other the next day. She hadn't said, in the two lines, whether she, Alex and Ethan would come.

23

'Well, I so hope they can make it too.'

That wasn't quite true, either, Scott thought. But it was the right thing to say.

Charlie arrived first, and took an empty table in the café. He saw Laura coming from about a hundred yards away, before she'd put on her game face. He was shocked at her appearance. She'd lost a load of weight in the long gap since the last time they'd met, and she was pale and drawn, beneath slightly too much makeup, which wasn't her style. She was a handsome woman, his only daughter: she looked like her mum, and she didn't usually fuss much with makeup. Her colouring – dark hair, almost olive skin, doe eyes with long dark lashes – didn't require it, any more than her natural curls needed to be artfully arranged. Today, though, she was wearing blusher, and reminded him of Aunt Susan from *Worzel Gummidge*. She looked anxious and exhausted. As she got to the café door, she stood up straighter, tucked her hair behind her ears, and rearranged her features into a smile, and that shocked him too: she was preparing to put on an act for him. But no amount of acting could disguise the dark circles under her eyes or the way her cardigan hung from her shoulders.

'Hi, Dad.' He hugged her, feeling her ribs. She'd never been one for physical affection, even when she was tiny. Nick would lie on your lap all day, and even Scott didn't mind a bit of a hug, but Laura would squirm and wriggle out of an embrace. Today, though, she practically collapsed in his arms, became almost heavier, so he held her, gently patting her bony shoulder, and wondered what the hell was wrong.

After a long moment, she pulled away, and sank into the chair opposite him. When he took his seat, and looked at her, wondering how much small-talk lay between now and when he might find out what was going on, her eyes filled with tears.

'Oh, Dad.'

He laid his hand across hers on the table. A smiley waitress approached with her pad and pencil. He raised a hand, surreptitiously, and she backed away, nodding understanding.

'Darling. What is it?'

He never needed Daphne more than at moments like this. Laura needed her mum. As she had for every scraped knee and wounded heart of her childhood and adolescence. And he needed her to tell him what to do.

For a few minutes, Laura patently couldn't speak. She was trying to control sobs. Charlie went to the counter, and ordered two English Breakfast teas and a large slice of carrot cake with two forks. Cake seemed a good idea, in the absence of any better ones. Daphne always fed sad people. Or happy ones. Or worried ones. He grabbed a fistful of paper napkins from the stack by the till, and when he got back to the table, he pressed them into Laura's hand. Then he sat, and waited for her to calm down, blow her nose and be able to speak. While Laura got herself together, the smiley waitress, no longer quite as smiley but empathetic and kind, came with their order, leaving it silently and swiftly, studiously avoiding eye contact with Laura. He would tip her well.

'Alex has left me. Left us.'

Charlie inhaled sharply, then exhaled slowly through

blown-out cheeks. Experienced a sheer rush of relief that she wasn't ill. That Ethan wasn't ill. Because nothing could be as bad as that. He realized that, after all, he wasn't surprised. Buying time. He could hear Daphne, knew exactly what she'd say. Not to Laura, of course – but afterwards, to him.

To Laura, he was infinitely gentle. 'Oh, my poor love. When?'

'Christmas.'

A stab. Months ago. She hadn't said. Maybe he hadn't given her the opportunity. 'Why didn't you tell me?'

'I haven't really told anybody.'

'But why not?'

'Humiliation, pride, hurt . . . and anger. I'm so bloody angry, Dad.'

'Is there . . . ?' Charlie didn't know how to phrase the obvious question. Thankfully, Laura didn't need him to.

Her tone was bitter. 'Someone else? Of course there sodding is. Isn't there always? He's such a fucking cliché.'

He always fucking was, Charlie wanted to say, but he didn't. He didn't swear like that, although if any situation might make him this would be it. He poured tea from the pot into the two mugs, then refilled the pot with the hot water the waitress had brought. And stirred sugar into both mugs, even though neither of them took it normally.

'A younger woman, who works with him. I mean, for God's sake. Genevieve.' She said the name slowly and deliberately.

'Has he moved out?'

She nodded. 'To some swanky new flat he's renting, for now.'

'But you and Ethan are still – I mean you'll still be able –'

'To stay in the house? No. He's way ahead of the game. Been to see solicitors. Got it all sorted. Wants to be divorced as soon as possible. Sell the house.'

'Can he do that?'

'Course he can. Fifty/fifty, everything we have. The house is a huge share of that.'

'Plus maintenance for Ethan, surely?'

'Yeah. He'll have to pay maintenance until Ethan's eighteen, then education, all of that. But he wants a completely clean break from me.'

'So you'll have to put the house on the market?'

'He wants that done in time for the spring market. That's now, more or less.'

'Can he make you do that?'

She nodded despondently. 'I think so.'

'Bastard.' Charlie spoke under his breath, but he wanted her to hear him.

'Bastard is right.'

'Have you been to a solicitor?'

'Solicitor, accountant . . . I've had to. I think that's why I'm so angry. It's only because I'm furious that I can get through a single conversation, let alone a meeting, without doing' – she gestured with her hands at the pile of napkins now in front of her – 'this.'

'I wish you'd told me.'

'I'm sorry, Dad.'

'Don't be. You've nothing to be sorry for. I just wish I could have helped you.'

'I don't think you can, Dad. It's not your job.'

'It will always be my job.'

She smiled.

'Won't it always be yours, to help Ethan?'

Tears welled again.

'How is Ethan?'

'I don't know. Quiet. Shell-shocked. Or not bothered. It's hard to tell. Uncommunicative. There's a girl. It all seems to be very intense, you know. He spends most of his time with her at the moment.'

'Is he still seeing his dad?'

Laura nodded. 'He has keys to the bachelor pad. Welcome anytime, Alex says.' Her voice was sarcastic.

'And he goes?'

'Why wouldn't he? No rules there, I'm pretty sure. And I'm probably the worst company in the world.'

'I'm sure he doesn't think that.'

Laura laughed bitterly. 'I'm pretty sure he does, Dad. I can't even stand to be around myself.'

'That's nonsense. You're still you.'

'I don't even know who that is any more.'

They sat quietly for a moment. Charlie picked up a cake fork and slipped it into Laura's hand. She stared at it and gave a very small laugh. 'Cake's the answer, is it?'

'If the question is, what shall I eat right now, then, yes, cake is the answer.'

The laugh got a little bit louder, but was still, he knew, perilously close to a sob.

Laura broke off a piece of the carrot cake, and ate it.

'I don't know the answers, my love. But I do know that you're not alone. You mustn't try to do this on your own. I'm here for you. I want to help.'

'Thank you, Dad. I appreciate that.'

'Don't just appreciate it. Believe it.'

She smiled gratefully.

'You'll come on holiday, will you?'

She nodded. 'That'd be lovely. Of course. And thank you for fixing it all, for organizing, for making me come. It'll just be me and Ethan. No Alex, obviously.'

Charlie wondered if he dared risk it. Decided he would. 'Thank fuck for that.'

Which was exactly what Daphne would have said.

And Nick, last as ever, sent an email. Brief, not unfriendly: *Thanks, Dad. That sounds great. Count us in.* He had done a lot by email since Carrie. He was busy, Charlie knew. Time poor. But it wasn't just that. He liked the remoteness and the one-sidedness of it. No need for conversation. No questions. No break in his voice to try to disguise.

But he had said yes. Charlie felt relieved. Everyone had said yes. Daphne would be bloody delighted. They were all coming. Dysfunctional, disjointed, distant. All with the baggage of their own messy lives. And all coming except her. God help him.

6

Heather's was the first face Scott saw once he'd cleared Customs. She was leaning over the rail at Heathrow Terminal 5, jewel-like among the drab, dour drivers with their A4 name signs and their bored expressions. And she was smiling her broad, dazzlingly white smile. And it was for him. It was before eight a.m., and she must have been up and out of the house well before seven to get here, park, and order the two Costa coffees she was now holding, but she had full makeup on. No last-minute Lycra for her – she wore gym gear only to the gym, and was more than slightly judgemental about women who called their gym gear athleisure wear and wore it everywhere, particularly if they looked like they never went anywhere near a gym. She was wearing dark skinny jeans and a vivid fuchsia silk blouse. And heeled sandals. At home he knew the emperor bed would be neatly made, and there'd be no toast crumbs on the marble kitchen island. Not that she ate toast, of course. This woman, his wife, had her act together, which was, he acknowledged, wonderful to come home to.

He felt the frisson of pride he'd eventually grown used to feeling when he saw her. With a delightful after-shudder of lust. The surprise that accompanied both sensations was gradually wearing off, and he was grateful for that. He'd stopped pinching himself.

She couldn't put her arm around him, because of the coffee cups. He took her face in both hands, and kissed her deeply, drinking in the clean, sweet smell and the familiar taste of her. A man on her right stared. Scott didn't care.

'Hello, darling.'

'Hey, babe. How was the flight?'

'It was fine. Uneventful. Fast.'

'D'you eat?'

'In the terminal, before I boarded. Slept through breakfast.'

'I grabbed you a croissant.'

'Mmm. Sounds good.' They were walking towards the lift. He took a coffee with one hand, and put the other on her waist, feeling the delightful wiggle of her bum just beneath. 'I missed you.'

She winked at him. 'Damn straight you did, Scottie.'

Inside the car, unencumbered by coffee cups and briefcases, he took her in his arms and kissed her again, more hungrily now that they were alone.

'How's traffic?'

'It was fine on the way up. It's rush-hour now, though. It's probably crappy.'

'Damn.'

'Have you got to work?' It wasn't unusual for him to get back from a red eye, shower, dress, and spend five or six hours at the desk at home. Such was the nature of the beast that paid for the Audi Q7 they were sitting in, and the five-en-suite-bedroom house with a tennis court they were heading back to. And the shimmering trio of long diamond and platinum necklaces that were glinting

31

at her neck and into the amazing cleavage just below the fuchsia silk.

'Nope. Schedule says "at leisure in Haslemere".' This he whispered lasciviously in her ear, and she giggled. 'Girls at school?'

She nodded. 'And they have sport after. It's Wednesday.' Raised an eyebrow coquettishly.

'What are you waiting for? Let's do battle with the A3.'

All the sex. All the lovely, married, daylight, any-room-in-the-house-you-like sex. Thank you, God and Goldman Sachs.

Heather drove onto the M25, where, predictably enough, they slowed almost immediately to a frustrating 20 m.p.h. Scott drank his coffee and ate the pastry she'd bought him.

'How has it been here?'

'Busy.'

'Good busy?'

'Great busy. I've gotten lots done.' He didn't doubt it for a second. She sounded buzzy and he was pleased. He wasn't entirely convinced that Heather wouldn't get bored buried in the country. Which was really only an extension of the worry that she would get bored with him at some point and bolt.

He'd been gone almost a week, which was a little longer than normal. He tried not to be away now for more than two or three nights, but this trip had been extended to five nights, and he'd missed her. Really missed her.

The house was still a novelty – bought after they'd married. Home before that (and home was stretching it a bit) had been a smart, cool one-bed flat in a converted warehouse in Shoreditch. All bare brick and 50-inch plasma screen. He'd paid a designer to make it look like he was stylish and modern. He'd never turned the oven on. Now it was an Arts and Crafts country house in three-quarters of an acre in a quiet Surrey town. He didn't know Haslemere at all. He'd never even been there until the Saturday Heather had produced a plastic wallet with the details of seven potential houses and brought him down. He'd asked for a maximum hour's commute, and a relatively straightforward airport run, then left the decision to her. She'd been delighted by the look of the place – 'This is what Americans dream England looks like' – with its quaint high street, and easy access to rolling hills. It also had a good school for the girls, which was key, he knew, to Heather's decision.

He kept the Shoreditch place, grateful that he could afford both. The mortgage he'd started with in London had been paid off with bonuses long since, and he could pay cash for Haslemere too. He wanted to be ready with exciting romantic mini breaks when and if the time came to dazzle her. The girls' school offered flexi-boarding so they could stay a night or two.

So far, she hadn't seemed to miss the bright lights. There'd been an extensive refurbishment to micro-manage, though, so her life had been a whirl of fabric swatches and paint charts and what she called 'antiquing'. Walls had been knocked down, so the Lutyens-style exterior now gave way to a very American aesthetic inside, all light and airy and spacious. He thought it worked. It shouldn't but it did. A bit like him and Heather. The kitchen now rejoiced in a four-oven Aga she adored for its Englishness but never cooked on, along with a wall of Wolf appliances and a six-ring gas hob that boasted a pot boiler – a tap that came out from above the hob, with the exclusive purpose of filling pots, as the name suggested – embedded in the herring-boned tiles behind. To Heather it was the ultimate status symbol. She'd babysat for an affluent family in Montclair one summer before college and they'd had one, and she'd dreamt of owning one ever since, apparently. The Haslemere plumber was mildly baffled at the request, but happy to oblige. She was easy on the eye, was Mrs Chamberlain, and grateful, and she gave him real coffee, not instant.

Scott knew nothing about antiques or pot boilers or fabric-covered walls, and if he occasionally balked at an invoice that crossed his desk, and wondered what his mother and father, who had told tales of furniture bought on the never-never, might have had to say about it, he honestly loved the end results. The house, which had previously been in one family, untouched, for thirty years, had been transformed into a stylish, calming, seriously good-looking home where the everyday ovens were turned on most days. It was a ridiculous notion, and one he would never share, but, owning this now, it was almost as if he felt like a grown-up for the first time.

The goal at work had always been to succeed, to make money, to win, to climb the ladder, all the clichés. Since Heather, that had shifted. He still had the hunger – you couldn't be there if you didn't have it – but the end game had changed. There was a reason for all of it that there hadn't been before. It felt infinitely healthier.

'The girls? How are they doing?'

'Hayley is all about the studying. They've got them so wired about the exams. The GCSEs. Thank God she's only doing five. Did you know they mostly do, like, ten? Eleven, some of them! Crazy. And Mere made it from the Cs to the Bs in netball, which she was wildly happy about.'

'Good for her. All that practice paid off.' He had spent hours with Meredith the weekend before this last trip, throwing the ball, passing, googling the rules. Meredith had been the easier nut to crack. She'd been younger, when he'd come into her life. They'd bonded over *The Simpsons*, a love of burgers, and his willingness to spend hours throwing balls in the garden – baseballs, at first. She'd seemed happy he was there, almost from the start. They'd been walking to get doughnuts one weekend morning, before he'd started 'sleeping over', when he'd spend the evening with Heather, drive her home, go back to work, then to his hotel alone, and drive back for breakfast, and Meredith had slipped her hand into his. He hadn't made a big deal of it, but he'd found it so moving he'd almost cried.

Hayley had been harder. That bit older, nearer to adolescence. Already testing her mother a bit, she'd viewed him with something like suspicion, something like fascination. Her frank, appraising gaze made him anxious. Maybe he'd pushed a bit too hard at first, trying to establish his credentials, pretending to know more than he actually did about Jay-Z and Beyoncé.

Heather stroked the back of his hand. 'You star. When you're twelve, in an English school, that's apparently like winning the lottery.'

'And work? How's work?' he asked. She threw him a sly

glance to see if he was making fun. He sort of was, although in the gentlest, fondest way. It didn't really seem much like work to him.

This latest project was only a month or so old. The house was finished. The last tradesman – the landscape gardener and his team – had left a few weeks ago. Heather had been looking for her next challenge. Her words. He was pretty sure that, at some point, he'd constituted one. He didn't mind. More than didn't mind. Was profoundly grateful to have been a challenge Heather had taken on. But she needed a new one. And then she'd hit on it. She would be, she announced to him, in all seriousness, an Insta-influencer and lifestyle blogger. This, she informed him, was a huge sphere. A brave new world. And right up her alley. If he suspected that it was a new spin on why excessive shopping was justifiable he was smart enough to keep that thought to himself.

Once, at work, when he'd hardly known her except to form the somewhat inappropriate opinion that she was the best-looking woman in the place, he'd expressed surprise and delight that an admin task he'd thought would fill days had taken her just one. She'd smiled at him, her head on one side, and said, 'I find that the best way to get something done is to just get on with it.' Never had a phrase so succinctly captured a personality. The laser beam of her diligent attention had moved now from his filing system to him, to relocation, refurbishment and now to the latest project. She was all about the hashtags, the flatlays, the Insta-stories and the artful shots of everything from flowers to food to sunlit corners of their home. Not him. He'd ruled himself out. He had no doubt that she'd grow her modest couple of hundred followers to many thousands of disciples before too long. Whatever that meant.

She spoke for two junctions of the M25 about it. About some new post series she was planning, and a great contact she'd made online. He didn't so much listen as let her voice wash over him. He was tired. He'd slept as badly as a six-foot-four man usually did on an overnight flight, even in business class. He murmured approval when it seemed appropriate. She didn't mind.

Then, when they'd turned onto the A3, she asked, 'Did you speak to your dad? About the birthday thing? Tell him yes?'

'I did.' He looked at her but she had her eyes firmly on the road. 'Is that okay?'

'I said so, didn't I?' But she sounded benevolent, not irritated. 'I can absolutely roll with it. Was he happy to hear it?'

'Delighted.'

'Did the others say yes too?'

'Apparently. Dad sent me an email saying they were all coming. We'll be a full contingent of Chamberlains. All together. For ten days. In an English summer.'

'That's good, right?' She was choosing to ignore the sarcasm. He loved her all-American optimism. The whole have-a-great-day thing. The broad toothy smile. The can-do attitude. All stereotypes, he knew. All true as well. Just a little infectious. A sunny yin to his instinctively cautious yang.

She'd only met them all en masse twice. At their wedding reception, and at Carrie's funeral. Both distinctly different, of course, but similar in their 'best behaviour' social mores. She didn't have a clue what she was dealing with. But then again, he reasoned, neither did they. His siblings hadn't come up yet against her relentless, energetic cheerfulness, or her endless capacity to see the best in everyone and everything. She'd blow through them like a tuberose-scented breeze. It was almost exciting to think of it.

He brightened. They'd left the A road, and were less than a mile from home. 'I'm sure it'll be a blast, as you say, darling.'

Home was reassuringly as he'd left it. Scott dumped his suit-carrier gratefully in the front hall, and shrugged off his jacket, throwing it over the newel post.

Heather put both arms around him and held him for a moment. He rested his chin on top of her head.

'Welcome home, babe.' Her voice was at its softest.

'I need a shower.'

She pulled away to look at him, and he knew at once what was on her mind. 'May I join you?'

'You look clean to me.' Raised eyebrows. So un-English. But he'd taken her by the hand and was walking towards the stairs.

She let herself be led, although it was all her idea. 'Well, maybe I'd like to get dirty again.'

7

When the phone rang in the hall, Nick always jumped. It happened so seldom. People had called Carrie at home. They didn't call him, which was fine. He'd never much liked people's disembodied voices. He liked to see faces when he spoke to them. Carrie had laughed at him about it when they were first together. She'd goaded him into calling her, and at first, to him, their chats had felt stilted, awkward. He couldn't shake the fear that this gorgeous girl must have better things to do than talk on the phone to him. Within weeks they'd been talking for hours, the receiver held between his ear and his shoulder while he cooked, or moved clothes from the washing-machine to the tumble dryer, or just lay on his bed staring at the ceiling. Those long, meandering, getting-to-know-you conversations where they'd found out all about each other. But that had just been Carrie.

'Nick?' It was Ed, Carrie's dad. 'How are you?'

'I'm okay. You?'

'We're doing well. You know . . .'

He did. They were doing as well as they ever would, was what he'd meant. 'Farm in good shape?'

The question was essentially pointless. Nick knew next to nothing about the farm, except that, beautiful as it undoubtedly was, it was incredibly hard work, and that, although Carrie had left it for university at eighteen, seeking bright lights, big city, she still felt, in some ways, that it was home. He'd always felt just a little out of place there: his own upbringing had been resolutely suburban.

'Yes, yes. All good. Thank you. Lambing's pretty much done. Didn't lose any.'

Carrie would have been there for that, if she could have made it work. She couldn't get enough of it. She'd gone with Bea last year and taken an amazing photograph of her, sitting down holding a new lamb, all shiny and slimy, her face alive with joy as she looked up at her mother in wonder. It was one of his favourites. 'That's great.'

It was always a bit laboured and unnatural now. Like they were both afraid of the huge weight of what they wouldn't say.

'And how are the kids?'

He scanned his brain for details to share. 'Bea lost a tooth. First one.'

Ed chuckled. 'That's great. Bless her. Did the Tooth Fairy come?'

'Sort of.' He'd remembered at three a.m. Texted Fran at six to get the going rate. Slid two pound coins under Bea's pillow just before she woke up. Didn't find the tiny milk tooth until he stripped the bed a week later to wash the sheets. He'd placed it in a small box, in his bedside drawer, next to the velvet pouch where he'd put Carrie's engagement and wedding rings.

'Delilah? Arthur?'

'They're well. I mean, the normal snuffles and stuff but, yeah, they're fine.'

Ed paused, small-talk apparently over. Nick heard him exhale. Then it was Maureen's voice. 'Hi, Nick.'

'Hi, Maureen.'

'We were . . . we were just wondering, I mean wanting to ask . . . have you had any thoughts about sorting out some childcare?'

So that was it. The purpose of the call. This again.

'Maureen . . .'

His mother-in-law's voice grew a little sterner. He could see her, in his mind's eye, drawing herself up. She adopted a particular posture when she felt she'd held her tongue long enough. He'd seen it first over wedding planning, once more over breastfeeding, again about potty-training. She seldom held her tongue as long as Nick, and even Carrie, wished she would: they both knew her motives were pure and kind, but still . . .

The childcare thing was none of her business.

Except it was, of course. If not theirs, then whose? He grudgingly acknowledged, just to himself, that his own mother would have been saying very similar things, had she still been around. Dad didn't – it had never been his style: he dreaded interfering above all things, however much he would probably have agreed with Mum.

He knew things couldn't go on like this. He was killing himself.

Work had been fantastic, to start with. Everyone was incredibly shocked and sorry and, yes, of course, he could take as long as he needed to get himself sorted out. But they didn't mean that. No one realistically could. People rallied around, all good intentions and kind impulses, and the hastily appointed person covering for him at work did the best they could. No one was indispensable. But some people were more indispensable than others and, a few

41

months in, it became clear he was one of them. His role as head of graphic design at a trendy, next-big-thing advertising and marketing consultancy couldn't be handled indefinitely by his team. He had client relationships, and he was a key player in pitches and meetings. Comments were made. It became clear, eventually, that he had a choice to make. Come back to work, or leave.

He needed to work. The mortgage had to be paid. Carrie hadn't been working when she died, but all their sums had been predicated on the fact that she would want to, once Arthur was at school. What they owed on the house was eye-watering, and he had shoes to buy. Every few weeks, it turned out.

And he might very well have gone completely mad if he hadn't gone back to work. But leaving the children had been an extraordinary wrench, and he hadn't yet managed to do it properly. He worked from home most of the time, at a computer set up on an IKEA trestle table in the front room, where he and Carrie used to watch TV, drink red wine and fool around after the kids had gone to bed. He tried to push everything else away when he sat there, be incredibly efficient, but he didn't always succeed. He was surrounded by his memories. Arthur went to the childminder, two streets away. Delilah was at a nursery a five-minute drive from home, and Bea at the local primary school five minutes beyond that.

Nick worked frantically in the hours they were out of the house, getting up to shove loads of laundry into the washing-machine, and far more, once they were in bed.

He felt he failed all the time. At work, he dropped balls. People were still being kind as they tried to catch them, but just a tiny bit less so, and the irritation in their voices was less well disguised when it happened. At home, he was racked constantly by guilt. Had he spent enough time with them? Had he cuddled them for long enough? Had he read enough? Was he enough?

He knew Ed and Maureen were right when they said it was unsustainable. He needed proper help. He needed a substitute mother. A stand-in wife. At least, that was how it felt when he tried to think about it.

The last time they'd come down, they'd tried to open a conversation about getting some full-time, live-in help, about him going back to work properly. He'd tried to listen, and be reasonable, but he'd ended up shouting at them that they had no idea how he felt, and that it was none of their business how he chose to make this new, awful, life work, and the visit had ended badly, although Maureen had held him briefly when she left, and Ed had had tears in his eyes when he'd shaken Nick's hand.

He'd felt dreadful immediately they'd gone. They'd lost their daughter. He knew they only wanted to help him. Worst of all, he knew they were right.

'Now, Nick. Please don't get angry. We're sorry about the way we handled things, when we were with you.'

'Maureen . . .'

'No, I need to say this, love. You need to know that we're only ever trying to help you.'

'I do know, Maureen.'

'Carrie would be furious if we fell out.'

'We're not going to fall out, Maureen.'

'No, we're bloody not.'

He laughed at the defiance in her voice, so typical of

her. She laughed too, and it broke the tension. They'd always been friends. An easy, warm relationship had existed between them since he'd first got to know them as a young man. It had been part of the charm of a life with Carrie – that understanding. It had deepened, with marriage, and then again, wonderfully, as he and Carrie became parents themselves, and made Ed and Maureen grandparents. Layers of love. He'd always been proud of it. His mates moaned over pints at the pub about domineering fathers-in-law and manipulative mothers-in-law, and he never had shocking anecdotes to share. Maureen even got on with Daphne, for God's sake.

'We wanted to tell you we think you've done a brilliant job, since – since she went. We're very proud of how you've handled yourself. She would have been too. You know that, right?'

God, he hoped so. 'Thank you, Maureen.'

'But it's okay to accept help. You know that too, right? You don't have to do it all on your own.'

'It's hard.'

'We know.' Her voice broke. 'We *do* know. It's hard for all of us.'

'Maureen . . .' He heard her sniff, pull herself together. 'I will think about it, about getting some more regular help. Something permanent. At home. I promise. Okay?'

'If you mean it, and aren't just saying it.'

'I mean it.'

'That's good enough for us, then.' She was obviously relieved. 'For you and for them.'

Nick wanted to change the subject before she demanded details and a timeframe. 'Ed says the lambing went well.'

44

Maureen admitted defeat, and let herself be led away from the childcare issue. 'Very well. The weather's been kind too. Unusually mild. The kids would have loved it. I'll never forget Bea's face last time, bless her. Just like Carrie used to look. When d'you think you might be able to bring them up, for a proper stay? You could leave them for a few days. Ed would come down and get them.'

He knew how sincerely the offer was made. He just couldn't imagine leaving them. Not yet. 'I was thinking maybe Easter? We could come up for two or three nights?'

'Three nights?' Granny-hearing, rounding up. 'That'd be grand. Good Friday to Easter Monday?'

He let himself be swept along. 'That sounds great. If you're sure.'

'Don't be daft. Course we are.' She sounded excited, and he felt guilt, his usual companion, that he hadn't been up for ages. 'We'd love it. I can do an Easter egg hunt.'

8

Stepping out of the car into the chilly day, Laura forced her shoulders down from their habitual hunch by her ears, pushed her shoulders back and took deep, deep breaths of the fresh air. She stretched out her arms, parallel to the ground, then raised them slowly, her palms touching in prayer above her head.

'What *are* you doing?'

Her friend Mel – her very best friend – had been bent over on the other side of the car, tying the laces of her walking boots. She straightened and looked at Laura with amusement.

'Being mindful.'

'Oh, Jeez. Not you as well. Everyone's at it.'

'At what?'

'Mindfulness. They've just introduced an after-school club in it.'

'And?'

'And!' Mel scoffed in reply. She was a semi-professional scoffer, often indignant about something, but there was never spite or malice in it.

'Well, peace, sister, to you too.' Laura smirked.

'It's not the stretching I object to. It's the new name for it. Mindfulness. What the heck? If you tell me you've discovered the calming power of colouring in, this walk is not going to go well.'

Laura laughed. That was why she was here. The mindless or mindful yomp, the fresh air, and the cake with tea that would certainly follow were just fringe benefits. She was here because Mel made her laugh. She always had.

They'd been friends since they'd met in their local NCT class. They'd waddled into a community centre in Tooting one dark, drizzly evening all those years ago, six and a half months pregnant with Ethan and Mel's son Jack, and within the first hour had recognized in each other a kindred, irreverent spirit. The other expectant parents had been a serious and sober lot, taking careful notes and asking detailed questions, Mel and Laura the only gigglers in the room, the only ones, apparently, attuned to the silliness of a room full of pregnant women and anxious men. And the only ones without husbands in tow on that first occasion. It had been fairly obvious, even before they sloped off to the pub next door, while the others enjoyed a cup of tea and a biscuit in the centre's foyer, that they would be friends. And so it was.

Mel's husband, Rick, had been in the army, on a posting. Alex had been at work. He'd had the NCT class in his diary for ages, but when he'd phoned Laura half an hour before it was due to start, saying he was stuck in a client meeting, she wasn't surprised. She loved him. But even then he'd been hopeless at the practical stuff. Ethan was 'planned', in the sense that they'd talked about trying to fall pregnant, and she'd stopped taking the pill and started taking folic acid, but Alex had seemed bewildered and sometimes even overwhelmed by the whole experience. She wasn't convinced he was going to be all that helpful.

She hadn't really minded that because she felt so entirely

ready for the baby, and considered Alex's inadequacies even less after she'd met Mel. They became, very quickly, each other's support system. Their mutual state fast-tracked intimacy. It was Mel she shopped with for car seats, muslin squares and breast pads, Mel she called when her Braxton Hicks were so strong she couldn't believe (and didn't want to) that it wasn't real labour. Rick was delighted. Alex was relieved.

Mel was the first person Laura had met in a long time who genuinely didn't care what anyone thought of her. 'Other people's opinions of me are none of my business,' she would say, and actually meant it. Laura had always envied her that trait, maybe tried (and probably failed) to emulate it. It seemed to her that the older they'd got, the greater the difference between them. They'd looked similar when they'd met, pregnant with their babies, glowing, with clear young skin. Laura knew she had grown thinner and more brittle, Mel rounder and even more 'not giving a toss'. But, to Laura's occasional surprise, the friendship had endured, rooted in the births of their children but sustained by affection for each other. Jack was born first, when Laura was thirty-eight weeks pregnant. It was the wrong way around: Jack was due several weeks later, but he came early. Rick wasn't there and couldn't get back in time, Mel's mum lived in Spain, so she'd called Laura, at four a.m., and Laura had been with her, push by painful push, when Jack was born five hours later. That tied you to a person with strong rope.

When Laura's time came a few weeks later, she had her amazing mum with her, and she'd never been more grateful for their relationship. Daphne had driven up, with

Charlie, when Laura's waters had broken, and hadn't left her side, laser beam focused on Laura's contractions even as Alex made endless unnecessary trips to the vending machine and to check his phone for messages. But Mel had been Ethan's first visitor, sweeping in with Jack in a pram, and scooping Ethan out of his plastic crib, her eyes full of happy tears.

They'd been each other's lifeline through those first extraordinary months, comparing notes and empathizing along the steep learning curve of motherhood. Then overseas postings, and life, had taken Mel out of Laura's everyday world as the boys toddled towards nursery school, and both had been bereft, texting and speaking several times a day until they built new lives around the hole each had left in the other's world. To their relief, the ties remained, and the shorthand communication they'd developed stayed the same.

When Rick and Mel had divorced, the boys were still quite young. It had been Mel's idea, but she had stayed in the West Country, where Rick's last posting had been, and had a perfectly amicable relationship with him and his new wife, Clare. Jack had two half-sisters, and spent alternate weekends with his other family, with seemingly minimal angst and aggravation. For the last six or seven years Mel had been living above a pub in a Wiltshire village with a straightforward, jolly man called Cliff, who thought the sun shone out of her.

Maybe that was the difference between them. Mel basked and relaxed, warmed by the rays of Cliff's adoration. Laura had desiccated and grown husk-like from Alex's neglect. Mel made everything look relatively easy – even the traditionally tough stuff – and Laura felt she made heavy weather out of it all.

Mel had been the first person she'd called after Alex had turned everything upside-down. She was still pretty much the only person Laura could really talk to about it. Mel had the knack of making space for Laura to talk into but equally easily filling it if that seemed better.

'Come on. Let's yomp. Mindfully.' She unclipped Hector, her Irish setter, from his lead. He bounded off excitedly. Mel put her arm through Laura's, and marched off in his general direction.

She fixed Laura with a penetrating stare. 'So, apart from you not sleeping and, clearly, not really eating either, what's new with you?'

'Is it that obvious?'

Mel squeezed her arm. 'Only to me.'

'Bollocks. I look like death warmed up, I know.'

'You've looked more radiant. Not gonna lie. Jack says that all the time. That he's not gonna lie. Does Ethan do that? Like there's no presumption of honesty in our relationship, and he needs to qualify every bloody thing that comes out of his mouth.'

Laura laughed. 'All the time.'

'Idiots.'

The first part of the walk was quite steep. They concentrated, in silence, as they climbed. Laura felt her lungs tighten. God, she was unfit. She stopped as the ground flattened, staring through the trees at the horizon. Mel stopped too, picking up and throwing a stick for Hector.

'And, speaking of idiots, how is Alex?'

Laura snorted. She loved that. No pussy-footing around.

Absolutely no attempt at even-handedness. It was glorious to have someone 100 per cent on your side. 'He's an arsehole.'

'No argument there. What's he up to?'

'Oh, nothing new . . .' She paused. 'Winning Ethan.'

'What do you mean?'

'It's like . . . He's got this new place, and it's all cool and I don't think there are any fucking rules there at all, and Ethan wants to be there. Of course he does. Why wouldn't he?'

'Has he moved out?'

A wry laugh. 'God, no. I'd like to see Alex's face, if Ethan suggested that. I'm still doing all the damn washing and form-filling and homework-nagging. It's just that he'll go there any chance he gets. Alex bought him an Xbox, for fuck's sake.'

Mel took a deep breath. 'You're not to take that personally, Laur. Honestly. Jack would sell me for a bag of chips, let alone an Xbox. They're teenage boys. All the blood's rushed to their groins. They grow about an inch an hour. They're completely unreliable. They're lumbering through the torture of their adolescence like lanky, spotty, slightly smelly and very clumsy Bambis, and they have absolutely no idea whatsoever of the finer feelings of their parents. None of them. Let alone being able to conceive of how to hurt them deliberately. Honestly. Trust me.'

'Okay. Wow. I wouldn't go into teenager PR if I were you.'

Mel laughed. 'Oh, they're great too. If Jack takes the bins out without me asking, I practically weep with joy. He told me I looked knackered the other day and made me a cup of almost drinkable tea. I nearly bought him a car, I was so excited and proud.'

She beamed at Laura, then wagged a finger at her. 'And then he produced a letter from school saying he was in detention all week for some transgression. He only showed me because I had to sign the thing. Amazed he didn't try to forge my signature.'

'Ethan makes me tea.'

'See? Be pitifully grateful for that. He's not trying to hurt you. He's just trying to get through.'

'I know it's unfair to mind.'

'Ah, it's inevitable, lovely. I get it. But it's Alex who deserves your anger.'

'Trust me, Alex's quota of my anger is not a worry.'

'And how are you channelling it, that anger?' Here came the challenge. 'Got a forensic accountant yet?'

Laura shook her head.

'I've told you, you need to stay mad, at least where he's concerned, at least when you're talking to him or his lawyers. He's counting on your being broken. He needs you to be weak and weepy when all this is negotiated. That's what they do. Be broken inside. Be broken with me. And your family. But you be coldly, furiously, productively enraged with him, and you let him get away with nothing.'

'Your divorce wasn't like that.'

'So I'm the exception. I actually left a nice guy. My bad. Trust me, you never know a guy until you've met him in court.'

'Isn't it "You've never known a woman until you've met her in court"? I think Norman Mailer said it.'

'Yeah, well, he was absolving men. Hell hath no fury

and all that. *Plus ça change* ... I'm more Ivana Trump, "Don't get mad, get everything!"' She rubbed her hands together. 'Except that you only get everything by BEING MAD and STAYING MAD.'

'Is this daytime-TV wisdom?'

'Rude.' Mel put her hands on her hips indignantly. Then she smirked. 'Some of it. Girlfriends. Lots of girl-friends getting divorced from shits. Books. Life. You need to listen to me.'

'Easy for you to say.'

'I know it is. And it's hard for you to hear.'

Laura smiled ruefully. 'Will you come with me? To the next lawyer's meeting?'

'You know I will.' Mel mimed an undercut punch.

Laura did. She could almost feel sorry for Alex, con-fronted by this energy and will, and she felt a sudden rush of love for her friend.

They'd been walking the whole time, and they were suddenly at the top of the hill. The trees had given way to a clearing, and the view was distractingly wide and far. Laura stared out at it, and breathed.

Next to her, Mel nodded decisively. 'Okay. End of ser-mon. Back to the car or down the next hill to the teashop. More walking, but with cake.'

'Cake. Definitely cake.'

'You have to have some too. You can't just watch me eat it. Promise.'

'If they've got lemon drizzle.'

Mel smiled. 'Oh, they will. Come on.' She strode off confidently, yelling for Hector.

9

He was going to be late for the childminder. Again. He never meant to be. He set an alarm on his watch and on his laptop. He started every day with the best of intentions. It was just that stuff came up when you were trying to be all things to all people. You couldn't just drop everything in the middle. Important phone calls and deadlines mattered, and they took precious little account of the fact that Arthur had to be collected from the childminder before Delilah and Bea from nursery and school, or that if he wasn't, the entire routine was shot, and Nick would collapse on the sofa, or back at his desk when the last of them fell asleep, and feel that he'd completely and utterly failed. Today it was a pernickety client, making changes and tweaks for the sake of it, demanding to see a finished piece of artwork now when tomorrow would almost certainly have been fine. Nick had made two, three, four changes, each one, in his opinion, detrimental, each one bringing him perilously closer to his deadline for leaving the house. No fight left in him for what looked best, he pressed send on the final version, and switched on his out-of-office reply angrily. He was going to be late.

Karen was kind, and he knew she was incredibly sympathetic to his plight. He didn't necessarily enjoy being the subject of her pity, but it was helpful sometimes. It was Karen's retired and omnipresent husband, James, who often stood behind her at the door, with a countenance that said he shouldn't play the young-widower card, at least not on Karen's time. Fran had helped him find Karen in the dreadful weeks after Carrie's death. Carrie would have liked her, she said, and the way she ran things. Karen had raised three kids of her own, fostered a handful more, and was unflappable and competent but, far more importantly, fun as well. He still felt as if he was abandoning Arthur, the first time he handed him over, although Arthur, oblivious, had beamed at Karen and immediately started trying to gnaw at the large amber beads she wore around her neck.

He would always be oblivious, baby Arthur, to the tragedy of losing his mother so very young. Bea had clear and definite memories of her. Delilah would think she had, her subconscious weaving together fragments of what was real with photographs and pieces of video. Arthur could barely even pretend to remember her. It was crazy – what they had shared, in those brief weeks and months after his birth, was entirely central to his very being: she had delivered him, fed him, rocked him against her chest at dead of night. And he wouldn't have any recollection of her at all. The sadness he felt for himself was sometimes dwarfed by the sadness he felt for his poor motherless children. He'd had her for years and years, Arthur for no time at all, really.

If it wasn't for Carrie's intensive campaign, there'd have been no Arthur. Nick had been very happy with his two girls. A colleague at work had said something in passing about two kids being manageable and three tipping him over the edge, and another knew someone who'd gone for just one more and fallen pregnant with twins. There was so much that could go wrong. He'd been ignorant of all that stuff the first time, then sleep-deprived and unaware of the risks at the second. Now he felt wide awake to them. What if something went wrong? What if it was twins?

Carrie wasn't done, she said. She knew she had one more baby in her. Nothing would go wrong, she promised. She was still only thirty-four, fit as a flea. Two straightforward pregnancies and two perfectly healthy babies. Far from agreeing with him that these were two good reasons not to push their luck, she saw it as proof that they were lucky and that the luck would hold for one more baby. She didn't need it to be a son, she claimed, when he took that tack. She just knew that their family wasn't complete yet. One more baby. She'd seduced him when his guard was down, and fallen pregnant almost at once. She'd taken a test before she was technically supposed to, but he already knew – something softened in the curve of her face almost on conception, and she'd started to look just like she had when she was carrying Bea and Delilah. Her complete joy had swept away his reservations, because it would have been churlish not to let it do so. One more baby.

That one more baby was making life very complicated. Karen answered the door almost simultaneously with his knock, ready. Mercifully James was elsewhere this afternoon. He apologized as usual, even though she always told him it was all right, grabbed Arthur and his changing bag, and bundled him into the car seat without interacting with him beyond a quick, dry kiss on the top of his precious head. He thanked God, not for the first time, that Arthur was such a genial and easy-going baby. He chuntered away incoherently in the back. There were interminable three-way temporary traffic lights on his usual route. If the car in front of him had just gone a tiny bit quicker, they wouldn't have changed to red, he'd have got through and he wouldn't have been late for Delilah. Nick smashed the steering wheel with an open hand, much harder than he'd meant to, and caught the horn unintentionally. It blared, loud and unnecessary, harmonizing with his mood, so that two mothers pushing buggies alongside the traffic jumped in fear, and turned to glare at him. He shrugged his apology. In the back Arthur, who had his limits, scrunched his face, ready to cry at the discordant sound.

'Sorry, mate. I'm sorry. Don't cry.'

It was too late. Arthur whimpered pitifully. Still in neutral, Nick reached around to squeeze Arthur's foot, murmuring to him that it was all right. He suddenly remembered Carrie, when Bea was so small that he was actually frightened of holding her, murmuring to him that babies could feel what you felt, so when you touched them, you had to be calm and relaxed so that you didn't communicate negative emotions to the child. He let go of Arthur's foot. He wanted to cry himself.

Ed and Maureen were right. Daphne would no doubt agree. He needed help. He couldn't do this. He wasn't good enough to do this by himself.

IO

Heather sat up in the middle of the massive bed, her back against the upholstered headboard, and arranged the soft white sheet around herself. The cup of black coffee Scott had made her before he left, and put gently on the side so as not to wake her, was still warm, and she cupped the mug in her hands. The bed faced two large windows onto the garden at the back of the house, and the sunrise was just beginning outside, black giving way to a delicate coral pink, the trees at the back of the plot silhouetted dramatically. It was still early – Scott typically left, silently, for his train at around six, and she needn't get up for the girls until seven or so. It was six twenty now. The next thirty or forty minutes were hers. In her Insta-life, the one she shared, she would probably call it meditating. Mindfulness. Maybe yoga. But in truth, and in private, this was Heather's 'pinch me' time.

Everything about being here surprised her. Being married to Scott, being in England, in this extraordinary home, being comfortable . . . it was all so new. Most of all, it was being safe and feeling secure that dazzled her.

For so much of her life, she hadn't been. She'd been born to an angry father, who drank too much, and a mother who lived in fear of his drunken tempers, in a rented home, where money was usually in short supply, seldom spent on shoes and heating, more often on booze and all too brief treats to make up for the booze. Heather's childhood had been shadowed by anxiety.

None of it had been dramatic. There was never anything to alert the teachers, the authorities or the neighbours so no help ever came. There was no one to see that it might be needed. Her parents never had any friends, and the neighbours were wary. It was a solitary, strangely quiet childhood. Her father growled rather than shouted; her mother used silence as a weapon against him. And Heather was mostly irrelevant. She wasn't starving. If she was sometimes hungry, it was because, often, no one bothered to cook, not because there wasn't any food in the cupboard. That was why she had learnt, balancing on a chair in front of the stove, when she was seven or eight. No one ever hit her, barely threatened to, but they didn't hug her either. That was why she'd started having sex with boys when she was sixteen. She was smart enough, always, to recognize and understand that sex wasn't love, and that those boys didn't care about her. But the exchange was worth it to her for the brief moments of contact: the sensation of being held, of being important, at the centre of things. You could tell yourself almost anything in those moments, and believe it.

She went to school in clean clothes, even if they weren't often new or ever ironed, but no one read her report card, or helped her with a science project, or made her a costume for a play. That was why she'd worked so hard, wanting to believe that doing better might change things. And always, always dreaming of getting out. Before she even knew where and what out was. As she grew older, she realized that New York was where 'out' was. Like it had been for Melanie Griffith in *Working Girl*, the Hudson river seemed to separate miserable mediocrity from gilded happiness and opportunity.

She knew what she had going for her. Chiefly, an evangelical determination to have a different life. Second, an unshakeable faith in the qualities she possessed and could use to make that happen. She knew, although her parents had never told her, that she was pretty. Pretty enough for girls to be catty towards her. When girls were quite pretty, other girls wanted to buddy up with them. When they were really pretty, they hated them. She knew she was sexy. The rolled-back eyes, quivering spines and moans of more than a dozen boys had shown her that. She was more sharp than clever, more quick than intellectual. She could organize, and she could get people – men – to do things she wanted them to do, and that was maybe the biggest skill of all.

She crossed the Hudson the minute she could, and she didn't look back. She rented a tiny room in a dive apartment in Midtown East and she went to work, temping in offices and teaching herself business software packages and basic accounting in the evenings, specializing in going the extra mile, until she found a permanent job. Another company, another rung up the ladder, evening classes and diplomas, a bigger room in a less dive-y apartment, it was always less about success and ambition than safety. She saved her pay, the cushion making it easier to sleep. And she dreamt.

The girls' father was a mistake from the start. A blip. That was how she thought of him. She'd let herself be distracted. Fooled, even. She'd got them. She could never quite reconcile the joy of their existence with the misery of her marriage to their dad. She couldn't wish she'd never met him because without him there'd have been no them, but despite that he remained the biggest mistake of her life. She'd been pregnant when they married at City Hall. Pregnant again before Hayley was walking. She'd had a warm home, and enough money for food, their clothes and shoes, and for a while she'd tried to pretend to herself it was enough. That for a girl like her it should be enough. But it wasn't.

He was a lousy husband. Controlling, mean-spirited, selfish. And, just like at home, there'd been no outward sign. He'd never laid a finger on her in anger. Or the girls. She'd have killed him for that with her bare hands. He wasn't even cruel. But there was nothing about him that sustained her. He wasn't supportive, or kind, or proud. He didn't seem to know her, or to mind that he didn't. Like 'wife and kids' had been a box he'd thought he was ready to tick.

And when he'd ticked it he'd lost interest.

When she'd finally caught him out in infidelity, she was almost grateful. As hard as it was to raise the two girls, work a full-time job and keep all the balls in the air, she vowed she wouldn't be fooled again, even if it meant she was alone for ever.

It wasn't money with Scott, whatever anyone said. There were plenty of guys in New York with money, obscene amounts of it. It was kindness, and manners, and the respect with which she saw him treating people in the office – everyone from the mailroom boy with the metal cart to the receptionist and the boss. He had a gentleness about him and for ages she'd confused it with Britishness. That wasn't it. One day he'd overtaken her on the sidewalk between the revolving door of the office and the steps down to the subway. She was carrying a large bag of groceries. At first she hoped he hadn't seen it was her – she tried hard to keep her home life away from work – but the bag was heavy, and she was hot, and tired. Like Melanie Griffith. She'd changed into sneakers, her court shoes on top of the food in her bag. He was walking much faster than her, with his long legs, unencumbered by shopping. He was on his cell phone. But he'd noticed her. He stopped, turned and smiled uncertainly, took a few steps back in her direction. 'Heather? May I help you with that? It looks heavy.' And he'd taken the bag before she'd agreed.

She knew what people thought of her. Gold-digger. Airhead. Opportunist. She didn't care. All this loveliness – the home, the holidays, the handbags and the diamonds – this was frosting. She wouldn't pretend she didn't like it, because she did. She really did. For the first time in maybe for ever, she had exhaled, and she didn't wake up worried at three a.m., and who wouldn't want that? But whatever they thought, any of them – colleagues, family – she knew Scott was the cake.

11

'Ethan? That you?'

The front door closed. Laura was in the kitchen, standing in front of the open fridge, wondering what to make for dinner. She was a good cook, or at least she had been once – experimental, enthusiastic – but food was uninteresting to her now. Ethan seemed just as happy with a short rotation of nursery meals – spag bol, gammon, chips and eggs, breaded chicken – as he had ever been with her more varied and adventurous efforts. He'd been an Annabel Karmel baby – she'd put every fruit and veg you could think of through the Mouli and then into a thousand little ice-cube trays, and she'd congratulated herself on a job well done until he'd turned two and begun ruling out flavours one by one. By the time he was three he was eating an almost completely beige diet.

'Oh, give it up, Laur,' Mel had scoffed down the phone. 'Jack is eighty-five per cent chicken nugget, he's on the umpteenth centile and hasn't missed a day of nursery this year.'

This unimaginative repertoire suited Ethan perfectly. Things you could eat with just a fork, leaving one hand free for whatever electronic device you were using – a teenage dream. At this point, her spice drawer probably had cobwebs.

He hadn't answered. Probably had his headphones on.

She slammed the fridge door shut and shuffled into the hall, right into Alex.

He shouldn't do that. Shouldn't just come in. This wasn't where he lived any more. Acutely aware of her messy hair, and her not-quite-fresh baggy cardigan, which she now pulled around herself defensively, Laura felt her heart race, and hated him for it.

'Sorry.' He wasn't. 'Didn't mean to scare you.'

'Where's Ethan?'

'He went straight up. Some physics homework or something.'

That felt bloody disloyal of Ethan. Making it seem like he wasn't bothered about seeing her. He'd been gone all weekend. She tried to channel Mel, and not mind. 'What do you want, Alex?' She knew she sounded testy. She should have challenged him on just bowling in, instead of giving him this crotchety-old-woman impression.

Alex had the audacity to look taken aback at her tone. 'I wanted to talk to you about the summer.'

'Oh.'

'Is this a good time?'

So polite. So considerate. So fucking fake. She mumbled that it was fine, and stood aside so he could walk into the kitchen. He looked around, then leant against the counter opposite the French windows.

They'd spent years in this kitchen. Cooking, eating, bickering, laughing. They'd fought here, kissed here, fed their baby in his high chair here. She'd folded a million pairs of his socks in this room, Jenni Murray for company. And he'd stood right there, near the windows, when he'd told her he was going and not coming back. How dare he lean there now, like he still belonged? Like this was his home still.

There was no rulebook for this stuff, no code of etiquette for how to talk to someone you'd loved and lived with, had a baby with and now regularly fantasized about kicking until they begged you to stop, but whom you had to talk to because they were the other parent to that baby, who had gone straight to his room.

She folded her arms across her chest and stared at the floor. There was a row of crumbs along the skirting.

'We'd like to take Ethan to Greece.'

And there it was. The 'We'. Innocuous word. Did he do it deliberately or unconsciously? It was a red-hot poker either way.

'It's a week. A flotilla holiday. Lots of boats, sailing together.'

'I know what a flotilla holiday is.' She'd rather have died than admit she didn't.

'Of course.' He was on his best behaviour.

'He gets seasick.'

Alex laughed dismissively. 'He did. When he was small. Surely he's grown out of it by now.'

She didn't know. She remembered a cross-Channel ferry, a whole pack of wet wipes, a green toddler.

'There'll be other young people. He'll love it.'

'Have you told him?' She corrected herself. 'Asked him?'

'No. I wanted to talk to you first.'

'When is this holiday?'

'First two weeks of August.'

'No.'

That shocked him. 'No. That's it?'

'No. He's with me then.'

'What are you doing?'

There was a note – a tiny note you'd probably have to have spent half your life with him to hear – that said, 'What could you possibly be doing that would be better than what I'm proposing?' The merest, faintest sneer in his question. You might say, if you didn't know, that she was paranoid and neurotic. If you didn't know.

She wanted to say it was none of his business. 'It's a family holiday. All of us. For my dad's eightieth.'

'Gosh. He's eighty already. Of course. Sounds lovely. Well, perhaps we should ask him, Ethan, I mean, ask him what he'd rather do.'

She wished she could be sure of what Ethan would say. She wished she'd already mentioned his grandfather's birthday celebration to him. She'd been waiting. She didn't even know why. Maybe because she suspected he wouldn't want to go.

'Don't you dare. Don't you dare put him in that position.'

Alex raised his hands in a way that said he thought she was unhinged and he couldn't talk to her while she was in this frame of mind. 'Look, Laura –'

'No, Alex. You look. I've said yes already for both of us. We're going. It's important. You need to change your dates.'

He shook his head. 'There are lots of people involved.'

'Well, then, perhaps you'll have to go without him.' She imbued the 'you' with all the weight his 'we' had carried.

'He's not a pawn, Laura.'

'I'd like you to go now.'

'That's not very grown-up, is it? It's been months. We should be moving on. We should be able to be civilized. We need to be able to talk about these things without every conversation degenerating into a slanging match.'

She knew he was right. And she knew she wasn't ready. 'I'm sorry I'm not moving at the speed you want, Alex.' She heard sarcasm dripping from her words. It was a struggle to keep her voice quiet. She wanted to scream.

Ethan's heavy footfall on the stairs drew their eyes to the doorway. He still had his headphones on – those stupid big Beats. He glanced from one parent to the other as he pushed them off his ears onto the back of his neck. He looked discomforted, and she hated that they were doing this to him. 'Didn't know you were still here, Dad.'

'I was talking to your mum about the summer.'

'Right. Okay. Me and my mates have been doing exactly that as well. There's a festival in Croatia we were talking about going to. And Reading, of course. Everyone's going to that.'

Laura fixed Alex with an expression she hoped was defiant, but must have been imploring. His appetite for the fight had clearly passed.

'You know, it's late – you've got that homework to finish. No hurry. Let's talk about this next week, huh?'

Ethan had his head in the fridge now, foraging. 'Sure.'

'You take care, okay?'

'See you, Dad.'

Alex didn't look at Laura as he left, and when she turned back from closing the front door, leaning weakly against it, Ethan was halfway up the stairs, headphones back on. She wished he would stay downstairs, take the headphones off and talk to her. She knew there was a girl-friend, Saskia. She didn't know how serious it was. She didn't know what to do. Buy him condoms? She couldn't bear the thought of it – her baby. And sex in general. It was so far from her consciousness. She might never have sex again. The thought of her beautiful boy . . . She shook her head. No wonder he didn't want to talk to her.

12

The counsellor had said they should have lots of pictures of Carrie. As many as they wanted. There she was, framed in most rooms of the house, smiling out at them from windowsills and chests of drawers. The kids had those montage frames with dozens of Carries. Bea often spoke to her as she passed them in the morning, and sometimes she kissed one.

Nick had the pictures out because the counsellor had said he should. One day they might not hurt. They still did now, though. Mostly he tried not to look at them, not when he was trying to get through the business of the day. Looking at them was for wallowing and, most of the time, he couldn't let himself do that.

He was carrying a load of small-people laundry upstairs when the pink sparkly dress snared him.

Carrie in a pink sparkly dress, cut low in the front, with little flouncy sleeves on her shoulders. He'd met her at that party, back when he'd liked parties. Well, back when he hadn't hated parties. It was the summer between his second and third year at university, and he was interning all week with a local law firm, his dad's idea, and going to twenty-firsts almost every weekend, criss-crossing the country by train, coach or cadged lift to don black tie (slightly oversized, purchased at Oxfam, to his mother's dismay) and drink lukewarm wine in a white nylon marquee.

They were a shoal in black wool, him and his mates. Saturday travel, Sunday hangover, repeat. He'd almost missed this one – Cumbria was bloody miles away, and even with his railcard, the train fare had felt eye-watering. A weekend at home, sleeping all day, had seemed more appealing. His mate Simon had persuaded him, found him a seat in a beaten-up Fiat, and an actual bed in another mate's house only a few miles from where Steve's party was taking place. Supposing he hadn't?

Occasionally, long after he and Carrie were together, he'd be gripped by a weird retrospective fear of something that hadn't happened. What if he hadn't gone? What if he'd missed her? What if, having skipped the twenty-first, he was somehow still invited to Steve's wedding, six or seven years later, had met her there, and it was too late, because she was with someone else, and maybe he was too. Would you know, instantly, what a mistake those two other relationships had been? Would you know she was the one you were supposed to be with? Or would you just smile at her in passing, think what a pretty girl Steve's kid sister was, have a casual chat on the edge of the dancefloor and go on with your life?

It seemed unimaginable. He had gone, thought Cumbria was staggeringly beautiful. Changed in a pub toilet, been handed a glass of something alcoholic. And there she was.

He'd never thought he'd be one of those blokes, the kind who are struck by a thunderbolt young and don't look anywhere else. Who just know: This is my person. A year before, one of his more laddish mates had done exactly that – come back from Interrailing with a soppy grin and a suddenly serious girlfriend. Nick had been nonplussed by his transformation. Judged him, a little.

He'd been having a sort of a fling with a girl at uni. Nothing serious for either of them. Certainly no declarations or promises had been made. She wasn't invited to this party, and neither of them had minded that or fretted about absences or separations. He liked her well enough, and he certainly liked sleeping with her, but he didn't think about her when he wasn't with her. The last fling had been like that, too, and the several before that. It had always been thus. Most had petered out without scenes or recriminations. There'd been remarkably little drama.

This was different. Instantly, inexplicably, vastly different. He suddenly sensed all the drama in the air. He thought immediately of the friend he'd judged last summer and wanted to ring him, say he was sorry, that he got it now.

For at least an hour, he just watched her. His mates came and went, and he half paid attention to what they were saying, moving around the room so that he could always see her. It was everything about her and nothing in particular. It was her smile. The way she moved in her pink sparkly dress. The ease with which she chatted to everyone. Her dancing – face tilted upwards, eyes closed, hands high above her head, like she was alone in her bedroom. It was the peculiar, unfamiliar sureness that she was there for him.

'Are you ever gonna talk to me or are you just gonna stare at me, d'you think?'

She had her hands on her hips, her head on one side. Nick had no idea where she had come from, and where his mates had faded away to, but she was right in front of him. He could feel his cheeks colour, betraying him.

'You make me sound like a weirdo.'

'Are you a weirdo?'

'Nope.' He racked his brain for witty banter. He was good at it. Except with her, apparently.

'Steve says you're Nick.'

'You asked him?'

Did she wink? 'Caught me.' Her confidence was audacious.

'Really?'

'Yeah. I said, "Steve, who's that weirdo staring at me so I can get Dad to chuck him out?"'

Nick must have glanced over her shoulder, looking for the dad, just for a moment, but it was long enough for her to win the point. She laughed. It was a glorious sound. He'd been watching her laugh for an hour but now he could hear it too, and it was even better than he'd been imagining. If you hadn't felt like this, it sounded ludicrous and fanciful. But if you had, you knew. That was it. He never questioned it, not once, after that night. He was going to be with Carrie.

When he'd got home, twenty-four hours later, he'd hugged his mum in the kitchen, harder than normal. She'd wrinkled her nose, told him he smelt like a brewery in a farmyard, but hugged him back, of course. Then she'd drawn away to study him. 'You look very happy, son.'

'I am.'

'Good night?' She'd done that clever thing she always did – turned slightly away from him, busying herself making a cup of tea – so it was somehow easier for him to speak.

72

'Amazing night.' He saw her mouth curl into a smile, and an eyebrow rose just slightly.

'That sounds like a girl.'

And he realized he was busting to tell someone. 'Not *a* girl, Mum. *The* girl.'

'Oh, really? *The* girl.'

'I met my wife yesterday.' He felt the blush rise, hot and red. What a dick. Who said that?

She hadn't laughed at him, hadn't fobbed him off. She'd put the two mugs on the table, with a plate of toast, and sat down.

'You're not going to tell me I'm an idiot?'

'No. I don't think you're an idiot, darling.' She smiled conspiratorially.

'Was that how it was with you?' Nick willed her to say yes.

'No. Not really.'

Nick bit into the toast, partly hungry and partly to create a diversion.

Daphne hadn't finished. 'But I think you'd find that was how it was with your dad. If you were to ask him. And if he were to admit it.'

'Really?'

'Well, it makes me sound bloody conceited but, yes, I think so.'

'Did he tell you?'

She laughed. 'God, no. I'd have thought he was a weirdo.'

Nick remembered Carrie's teasing question. 'But he told you eventually?'

'Yes. Ages afterwards. When I was a done deal.'

'So Dad thought he'd met his wife, and you thought . . . what?'

'I thought he had potential.'

'Wow. Potential. That's harsh, Mum.'

'What does she think? Your wife.' Her tone was gently teasing.

'God knows. Probably that I'm a weirdo.' Daphne laughed, then sipped her tea. 'Actually, maybe she thinks I might have . . . potential . . .'

Daphne had put her hand over Nick's, on the handle of his mug of tea. 'Well, she sounds like a good girl to me. She's right about that, at least.'

Now Nick held his breath, then ran one finger across Carrie's cheek in the photograph. 'All right, weirdo.'

13

Scott had stepchildren. Two teenage stepdaughters. He had a photograph in his wallet, for God's sake, of the four of them.

'Pancakes! Ready!' Scott shouted in the hallway, directing his voice at the upstairs landing. They weren't pancakes as he knew them – the crêpe style Daphne had made for them when they were young, eaten as a treat in front of the television, with lemon juice and as much sugar as you could get away with sprinkling on them before she caught you. These were – like his whole family now – an American import. Small, thick and dry, eaten with bacon and maple syrup, they were a weekend ritual. He'd learnt how to make them from scratch, and now a stack was waiting on the warming plate of the Aga.

Saturday mornings had never been like this. They'd been for errands, dry cleaner's, hair trims. For long workouts and admin catch-ups. Not now. Now they were for long breakfasts, the prelude to sports fixtures, cinema visits, party drop-offs and country walks ending in pub roasts. These weekends were better – they were actually rather wonderful.

The girls appeared, summoned by the smell of pancakes, one by one, bed soft, and clad in their brightly coloured Abercrombie & Fitch sweatpants, with their mother's blonde wavy hair, and her face shape – the heart with the endlessly appealing, slightly jutting chin. As sisters, they were completely different. Hayley, the older of the two, was more serious and studious, conscientious and organized, like Heather. Meredith was the more rambunctious, with a chaotic streak that probably ought to have irritated him, but which he found enchanting. Hayley was a lark, Meredith a night owl, who practically had to be Semtexed out of bed in the mornings, unless, of course, a stack of pancakes was waiting. It *was* ten a.m. He'd been up since seven, and that constituted a lie-in. The peace of the early part of the day was good, but by nine, he was itching to make the batter with which he could lure them from their respective pits to join him.

For some people, Heather's daughters might have seemed like baggage. For Scott, who hadn't even known what was missing from his life, the girls were a bonus. He'd assumed, before he knew her, and he didn't really know why, that she was single and childless.

She'd told him almost straight away. If he had noted brief surprise at his own reaction – that it made her more interesting to him – he hadn't questioned it. But she'd waited months to introduce them, until she was sure of him, he reasoned, and he understood. He remembered being nervous. He'd made up his mind about Heather by then. He needed them to like him. He wanted to like them. They'd gone to Rye Playland, one late-spring Sunday – an amusement park upstate from Manhattan, by the sea, where the rollercoasters and cotton candy were ready distractions. Sitting at the top of one steep swoop, Heather and Hayley in the car in front, Meredith beside him, she'd slid under his arm for comfort, and he'd felt such a jolt, such a rush of something he couldn't quite name.

His brother Nick was a born father, so at ease with and delighted by his children that he looked like that was what he'd been put on earth to do. Laura was a completely devoted mother. They'd been raised by Daphne, the most passionate, adoring, fiercely supportive and protective mother. But Scott had never really thought about parenthood for himself – about whether having children was important to him, a priority, or whether not having children was a mistake he'd regret in later life. He'd never had a girlfriend serious enough to make him think about it. If he'd had a biological clock, he'd never heard it ticking. Marriage, mortgages, children – that had been the stuff other people did. He'd always imagined someone would push over the first domino for him and trigger the change. No one had. Through his twenties there'd been girls – one or two had even tried to goad him into things, but he'd found it relatively easy to resist: no woman had moved him, not really. He was a logical man. Seismic shifts were caused by earthquakes, not tremors.

Laura had asked him about them, back when he'd been just getting to know them, as surprised, perhaps, as he was that he was suddenly a stepfather. He'd defined them to his sister: Hayley, he'd said, was like a cat, more aloof and less obviously affectionate, circumspect and careful, while Meredith was a puppy, boisterous, playful, desperate to love and be loved. Meredith might have been easier to win over, but that made his victories with Hayley far more valuable.

And now here they were, his three girls, sitting around

the kitchen table, their knees up, eating pancakes with just a fork. If he thought sometimes that his mum would have loved them, he had to concede she might not be so wild about their table manners.

'Delicious.' Meredith pushed her plate away and rubbed her belly.

'Not as good as toast with Marmite,' Scott teased.

'Ew! Yuck! Don't even say Marmite.' Meredith groaned. 'Disgusting.'

'Better Marmite than "yeast spread",' was Hayley's sarcastic rejoinder. She arched an eyebrow, and Scott laughed.

Heather, sexy in tight jeans and a white blouse, had taken the family calendar off the wall and was going through it, a pen in one hand, a mug of black coffee in the other. Hayley read dates off her phone for her mother to write down. Matches, speech day, exam timetable. Meredith rolled her eyes at Scott, who gurned back.

'Okay. It'll be over soon, baby.'

Hayley sighed. 'It'll never be over.'

Scott laughed. 'I remember that feeling. It will. I promise. And, believe me, the freedom, once you push back the chair after that last exam, it's the best. You're going to have the best summer.'

'You sound American.' This was Meredith, teasing. 'We always say everything is "the best".'

Scott pushed her arm playfully, and it slipped off the edge of the table. A rogue piece of pancake fell onto the table. Heather frowned. Scott grabbed and ate it. Meredith giggled.

'It is *the best* feeling.'

'Speaking of summer . . .' Heather attempted to bring the chaos to order. 'We've had a lovely invitation.'

'To where?' both girls asked simultaneously, Hayley sounding sceptical, Meredith excited.

'To spend some time with Scottie's family.'

Hayley's eyes narrowed. 'Where?'

'It's in England. A beautiful country house . . .'

Hayley pushed her chair back from the table, visibly disgruntled. 'Ugh. English summer weather.' Last summer hadn't covered itself with glory. There'd been so much rain. So much. There had been a lot of black humour about webbed feet and building an ark. When Heather had come home – unironically – with one of those SAD lamps, for people who couldn't cope without sunlight, and confessed she was pining for the New Jersey shore, Scott had booked a holiday in Turkey. The day they left, a ten-day heatwave started. It had ended the day they flew home.

'Come on, now . . .'

'Like last summer?'

'It might not be. It isn't always raining, you know.' Scott smiled.

Hayley wasn't convinced. 'Yeah, right.'

'Well, it means a lot to Scott that we're there.' Heather's tone was decisive.

'Who else will be going?'

'Well, it's Charlie's birthday. He'll be eighty.'

'Great. An octogenarian's birthday celebration.' But Hayley's expression wasn't quite as truculent as her tone. Scott winked at her.

Heather missed the wink and ploughed on. 'Laura will

79

be there, and that means Ethan. You remember Ethan, from our wedding? And Nick, with all the children.'

'Aw. Cute.' This was Meredith's first pronouncement.

'Exactly.'

Hayley persisted: 'What'll we do? Apart from babysit?'

'Who said anything about babysitting?'

'I really *want* to babysit. Do you think Nick would let me?' Meredith directed her question to Scott, since her mother was glaring at her sister.

'I'm sure he'd love some help with the little ones. There's a tennis court, and a swimming-pool . . .'

'Wetsuits provided?' But Hayley was almost smiling now.

'Hayley!'

'Mum! Scott was just talking about how amazing the summer was going to be. You know those kids from school have invited me to the Reading Festival. And I really, really want to go.'

'You said. Several times. This isn't then. This is before that.' But Hayley was Heather's daughter, a good negotiator.

'So can I go?'

And Heather knew blackmail when she heard it.

And Scott could only marvel at the mistresses of negotiation going head to head. No boardroom he'd ever been in stood up to the kitchen table right now.

14

Ethan wished there was someone he could talk to. He didn't know what to do with all his feelings. His soul or his heart or whatever part of him it was – a part he'd only really been aware of in the last little while – felt like it was too big for his brain, too big for his body. He felt a ball of something pressing on his lungs, his stomach, his mind, like he might burst with it all.

Life was bad enough, hard enough. The exams weighed on him like a heart attack. So many balls in the air: Shakespeare and the periodic table and irregular French verbs and ox-bow lakes and equations. Everyone's expectations of him were high – Mum and Dad's, his teachers' – and it felt suffocating sometimes.

He didn't sleep a lot. Not when he was supposed to be asleep. He watched one a.m., two a.m., three a.m. on the ceiling, projected there by the clock, his mind and heart racing. At eleven a.m. all he wanted to do was put his head on the desk, like they used to in Kindergarten, and close his eyes.

He was often tearful, and he hadn't cried since he was a little kid. It made him feel ashamed and furious. He cried in bed at night alone. Snotty, harsh, sobbing tears under the duvet. Hated himself for doing it, for the weakness it showed.

Even if there was someone he could talk to, what the

hell would he say? He couldn't even order the thoughts to himself.

He was angry. Mostly, that was it. Angry and sad. Angry with his mum and dad. Especially Dad. They said kids were the selfish ones. He couldn't think of anything more selfish than what his father had done. What a fucking awful year to make this particular decision – to blow the family life wide apart. He had exams. He had big decisions to make. Even he knew he needed stability, for Christ's sake. Stuff happened – he knew that too. A mate of his from football, who was in the year above, had had all this crap going on in his GCSE year because his mum had breast cancer. Someone else's dad had lost his job, and that had messed everything up – they'd had to move house and stuff. But *his* dad could have bloody waited.

He told himself it was Mum Dad didn't want any more. Sometimes he whispered to himself that she'd asked for it – she could be such a grumpy bitch. Then he was horrified at his own disloyalty. And he knew that it was both of them Dad couldn't be bothered with now. Mum and him. He felt abandoned.

And then flattered. When he did see Dad, he treated him more like a mate, bent all the rules Ethan had known all his life, granted freedoms and liberties. But in darker moments, Ethan knew it to be disinterest, disengagement. Dad couldn't be bothered to apply all the usual guidelines and consequences. He didn't want to be his father.

His protectiveness of his mother sat uncomfortably alongside his weird and messed-up feelings about Dad's new girlfriend. She had small, high tits, and she wore tight jeans with high-heeled boots, and he didn't know where to look when she was there – aroused and repulsed in equal measure. He was painfully aware that his father was having sex with her, hideously embarrassed because she was too young.

This happened to other people. Loads of them. He had mates it had happened to. Why didn't they seem so messed up by it? Were they all crying, like babies, in bed, and wanting to punch windows and walls the whole time, or was it just him?

His limbs were too long for his brain to control them adequately. He felt clumsy everywhere. He was still plagued by spots but he had stubble too. He stank if he didn't shower. His hair wouldn't lie the way he wanted it to, and he was still wearing the retainer the orthodontist had prescribed once he'd taken off his train-track braces last year.

He couldn't drink as much as his mates did without puking, and cigarettes made him feel sick, although he refused to let that stop him smoking.

He didn't know what to do with this self-loathing, and he couldn't imagine an end to it. How he would ever be okay with it all – how he would get through the exams, and even if he did, there were A levels, then UCAS, then uni, then a job hunt. Life lay ahead like a series of opportunities to fuck up. How Mum would ever stop being so destroyed by Dad going. How he would ever stop getting an erection when Genevieve bent over to put something on the lower shelf of Dad's fridge.

And then, when he thought he was just about as low as he could go, as irredeemably, miserably, unreachably a mess, she'd just happened. That was precisely, almost to the day, when Saskia had slid into the seat next to him on the coach to the last geography field trip, a day visit to windswept and freezing Chesil Beach.

She'd moved to his school at the start of year ten, and they'd never really spoken. She was in a few of his classes, but the cliques were formed, and the battle lines between the sexes pretty well drawn by then, so there'd been no real chance. She was dark blonde, and pretty, but in a very quiet way – not the orange-tinted, eyeliner flicking, go-on-I-dare-you way the really popular girls were. He wasn't sure she wore makeup at all. She had a nose stud, a tiny sparkly one, and he'd always thought it seemed intriguingly out of character, speaking of a wild streak that had, outwardly, no other signs.

She'd smiled at him, and for some reason – vestiges of politeness, maybe – he'd felt obliged to push off his headphones. She'd asked him what he was listening to, and he'd said Oasis, and instead of scoffing at his old-school tastes, she'd turned out to know all the words to 'Wonderwall', although she preferred Pulp and Blur, she'd said. And just like that, maybe, she was going to be the one to save him, he thought.

15

Yoga helped. It actually did. Who could have predicted that? Laura had spent a lifetime avoiding strenuous exercise, believing herself to have been born without the endorphins other people always talked about. There'd been netball at school, and hideous hockey, of course, and she'd briefly flirted with university rowing, mainly because of the social life to which it offered access. But for its own sake, for its positive benefit on one's body, let alone on one's mind, she'd had a lifelong cynicism about exercise. She'd even been a bit judgemental – shock, horror – about other people's devotion to it. Her brother Scott's daily gym visit, his new wife Heather's insistence that reformer Pilates had completely changed her life. Even Nick, jogging in ancient, holey shorts and a T-shirt. They all seemed to her, well, just a bit self-absorbed. Naturally and effortlessly slim, she'd never seen a reason or felt an urge to start. Sometime around their collective mid-thirties, mothers at the school gates had gone from wanting to meet for coffee and cake to charging off to boot camp on the common, beginning their King Canute attempt to hold back time, and she'd felt bewildered by it, when coffee and cake was so much nicer, and time's winged chariot was unstoppable anyway. Then even Mel had betrayed her, insisting she try yoga, with her typically blunt brand of advice: 'It'll help suppress your inner bitch, Laur.'

So she'd gone, because her inner bitch was far more worrying to her than any spare tyre or aching hip flexors could ever have been. And it had been hard and hateful to start with. She didn't have the right gear, and her T-shirt kept riding up and exposing her bra, and her neglected feet looked awful even to her on the mat when she'd discovered you had to take your socks off to do even the simplest manoeuvre, which had seemed difficult at the beginning. Downward dog made her head feel congested and achy, child's pose was vulnerable, and full-sun salutation required more arm strength than she possessed. Plus you had to breathe in and out on the motions in the right way, and that felt very much like rubbing your belly and patting your head in synchronicity – impossible to maintain.

But the teacher had been beautifully patient and kind, as well as firm and insistent, which turned out to be a potent combination. She would stand behind Laura and coax her limbs into places her mind really thought they couldn't go, and her soft voice and example made the correct breathing come naturally in time.

And the very best part was the *shavasana* at the end, when you lay perfectly still for a few minutes, covered with a soft blanket, and a bean bag infused with geranium across your eyes. 'When thoughts come, do not engage with them,' the teacher said, and while Laura might have scoffed in weeks one and two, by week three, she was getting better at pushing them away. Now, those few minutes, two or three times a week, suffused her with the most welcome sense of calm and tranquillity, like a natural high. She might even describe herself as evangelical about her yoga.

She tackled paperwork on yoga days, banking the peacefulness and eking it out on dealing with the crap her divorce generated. For years, she hadn't done administrative stuff. She'd stopped work when Ethan was born. She might not have done, if she'd loved what she was doing, but she remembered feeling uninspired, stagnant even. In truth, pregnancy and early motherhood offered a way out. Not very PR or girl power, but there you go. Alex had wanted her to, and she'd been happy to comply, besotted with her baby, and feeling lucky that they didn't require her salary to survive. He'd dealt with the household bills, financial advisers, pensions and savings. She'd handled all things Ethan – school paperwork, holiday bookings, that sort of thing – and all the domestic stuff. Alex had changed precious few nappies, and cooked dinner once in a blue moon. Only when she was ill, come to think of it. He couldn't have named more than a couple of Ethan's teachers, or his little friends, and wouldn't have had a clue whether Ethan had been given the MMR as a combined vaccination or as three separate shots, or if he'd had chickenpox.

How had that happened? How had she let that happen to herself? To each other. When had they stopped being an equal partnership? When they'd met, she'd been competent, capable and confident. She'd been bloody good at what she did – practice manager at a firm of architects in the city. He'd fallen in love with someone and gradually, knowingly, turned her into someone else, then been surprised when he suddenly didn't love her any more. Wasn't that the stupidest thing you'd ever heard? And she'd let him. Which was even stupider. What had she been thinking? Had she been thinking at all? Had she taken the easiest, laziest route through life and did that make it her fault? Why hadn't she gone back to work, even part-time – had something for herself? Her own money, clothes in the wardrobe that didn't go in the washing-machine, something to talk about at dinner besides their child.

He'd been a good cook when they'd met. He'd done a course at Leith's. And a season at a chalet in Méribel, cooking three courses plus hors d'oeuvres for posh ski-ers. He'd seduced her with food in his flat near Balham tube – prawns in garlic butter, a perfectly cooked steak, a chocolate fondant – and she'd thanked her lucky stars she'd found him. Now he barely knew how to switch on the oven.

She had to find a way out of the hole she was in. She didn't want him back, even if she sometimes fantasized about him begging her forgiveness. She didn't wish him well – she wanted to see him fall on his face with Gene-vieve, wanted the silly girl to wake up to the fact that the man she'd fallen in love with had walked away from eight-een years of marriage and a child to be with her. Or just to realize that he would be old too soon. She wanted Ethan not to forgive him, even if she felt slightly ashamed at the selfishness of that. And, yes, she wanted him to pay. So Mel was right: she needed to buck her ideas up, reawaken the part of her brain that understood numbers and legal speak, and not let him screw her over. Know her rights. Be more angry than sad. More aggressor than victim. Not keep making the same mistake she'd made for too long.

Be less Alex's wife, Ethan's mother, and be more Laura. Whoever Laura was. She'd been interesting, hadn't she? Funny, sometimes. She'd had lots of mates. She'd sung in karaoke bars, learnt to speak Italian at evening class because it sounded so lovely, and gone abseiling to celebrate turning thirty. She was still Laura. She had to be.

16

Nick texted Fran just before he put the kids into the car: *Got time for a coffee after drop-off?*

Her reply pinged onto his screen just as he finished doing up the various seatbelts and slid into the driver's seat. *Absolutely. Nelly's at 8.45? Gets me out of boot camp. Xx*

He smiled. *I could do 9.45 if you want to do the class?*

Instant response. *Coffee.* An emoji of a steaming cup. Then a tick. A blonde in an aerobics leotard. A poo. A yellow crying, laughing face.

He sent back a thumbs-up.

Miraculously, despite delivering the children in reverse order to his afternoon routine – Bea first, then Delilah, and Arthur with Karen last – he was at Nelly's first. He ordered two lattes and a *pain au raisin*, and took his tray to the table in the window, choosing the ancient wing-backed armchair facing the park. Fran burst in a minute later, dressed in leggings, trainers, and an ancient grey sweatshirt that swamped her, her hair piled on her head.

'Do you ever actually go to that boot camp?' Nick smiled at her.

Fran laughed, then took a large bite out of his *pain au raisin*. 'Almost never.'

'Oy! That was mine. I'll get you your own.'

'Only wanted a taste . . .'

He pointedly moved his plate to the other side of the mug.

'Boot-camp clothes are basically just the acceptable version of pyjamas. I once tucked a nightie into some trackies to do the school run, and your wife said I'd crossed the slummy-mummy line, then shared with me the genius of athleisure wear. She used air quotes and a ham American accent when she said it. "No one knows whether you've just been exercising, are just heading to exercise or don't intend to get any more exercise than chewing a pastry."'

'Genius.'

She reached for the *pain au raisin* again. Nick handed the plate to her.

'So what's up?'

'Need more free advice.'

'My speciality.'

'Need a nanny.'

Fran picked up her cup, and held it in both hands, taking a slow sip, waiting for him to expand. He felt embarrassed, although he knew he needn't. 'I'm . . . not coping very well. Ed and Maureen have been on at me, for the sake of the kids, to get some full-time, live-in help. I can't seem to do it all by myself. Work is piling up. I need to go back to the office, really. Or think about doing something else. They've given me a long rope, but they're getting fed up with me being absent. And I think the kids are being short-changed. I am just about managing, Fran. But that's it.'

'So it's a good idea, right?'

He rubbed his hand across his face. 'It feels . . .'

'Feels what?'

'It feels like I'm trying to replace her. It feels disloyal, somehow.'

'Well, that's ridiculous.'

'And I feel like I've failed.'

'And that's even more bloomin' ridiculous. Where are you getting this crap?'

He smiled. 'Say what you think, why don't you?'

'All right. I will.' Fran sat forward in her chair, and rested her elbows on the table. The sleeves of her enormous sweatshirt completely covered her hands. 'I think it's the most sensible suggestion you've made in a while. Everyone needs help, you big idiot. This shit is hard. You've got three children under the age of six and a full-time job, and you're trying to do it all on your own. Before you even start to deal with the grief that the four of you feel, which is actually a bit of a full-time job in itself. You get someone in who can help you with the practical stuff. You probably should have done it ages ago. You get your arse back to work, where the people are. Then when you're with the kids, you can be properly with them, instead of trying to do ten things at once. And you'll have a moment to catch your bloody breath.'

'Okay.' He smiled weakly at her. 'Done?'

'I'm not, actually. This disloyalty crap. What do you think Carrie would say about that, Nick, if she heard it?'

He shrugged.

'I'll tell you what she'd say. She'd say get your head out of your arse.'

He laughed. 'That's exactly what she'd say. You knew her so well.'

'She'd say hire the best nanny you can find, get her in as soon as possible, go back to work, stop feeling inadequate –'

'Okay, okay. I get it.' Nick sipped his coffee.

'Then she'd probably say, on second thoughts, make it a manny. Or at least an ugly girl with a flat arse.'

Nick snorted into his coffee. For a second he could see her precious face, nose wrinkled in thought, eyes sparkling with her own joke, saying exactly that. He'd got the summer holidays sorted. Cobbled together. Just about. He promised himself he'd bite the bullet and sort it out properly for September. Promised Carrie too.

17

It hadn't been like her dad Rupert had said. Not at all.
He'd completely twisted it. Up in his room, lying on the
bed he was almost too long for now, Ethan kicked against
the pine footboard until his toes hurt. He wanted to hit
something so hard that he'd skin his knuckles. He was
embarrassed, humiliated, furious and frightened. He
wanted to climb out of his own skin and disappear. This
was a nightmare.

He'd thought they were all right, Claudia and Rupert.
He thought they'd thought he was too. Most of his conversations with Claudia had been about food, and his
apparent hollow legs, and most with Rupert about football, which Ethan didn't know much about. Still, they'd
been okay. Strict. Maybe like his own mum might have
been if she hadn't been so distracted, but probably a bit
more so. She had all these rules, Sas, when she was allowed
to text, curfews, stuff like that. Her mum always had to
ring the mum of a kid who was having a gathering or a
party to find out whether there'd be adults present, what
the booze policy was. Saskia hated that. Ethan and she
weren't allowed in her room, and when they were in the
TV room, Claudia was always making excuses to come
in, and always left the door open when she went out again.
Trying to be casual.

He'd hardly recognized the bug-eyed loon Rupert had

been downstairs just now. His angry red face, his puffed-up chest. He'd come up close to him, trying to make himself as tall as Ethan, although he was still at least four inches shorter, and Ethan had seen the strings of spittle on his lips, felt his breath on his face before Claudia pulled him away. For a moment, Ethan thought he was going to hit him. His hands were balled into tight fists by his sides. Ethan had brought his hands up to protect himself. Mum had been screeching that he'd better not dare. 'God, Rupe. No. No.' That had been Claudia, who was crying noisily. It was all so completely messed up.

He didn't know how they'd all got there. It didn't make sense to him. He'd wanted to talk to Saskia, although it had been made abundantly clear that that wasn't going to happen any time soon. He wondered if he'd ever see her again. They'd been going out for five months. Girlfriend and boyfriend. And they'd been 'a thing' before that, for a few weeks. His mates who'd had sex with girls had done it much sooner. Or said so. He and Saskia had waited. They'd talked. They'd talked about waiting, for Christ's sake. They'd messed about, of course, done other stuff. But not that. They had resisted. It all felt grown-up. Saskia had gone to the doctor on her own and got the pill – the doctors weren't allowed to tell Claudia, she'd told him.

He knew they'd lied. Saskia to her parents, him to his. It had been easier for Ethan – they'd gone to his dad's. Mum hadn't known his dad was away. And Dad hadn't exactly known he was there. But he'd given him a key, hadn't he, to his new place? Given him a brief, manly hug and told him he was welcome anytime. Ethan hadn't believed him – he knew Dad didn't really want him hanging around at his new place, not when he was there, but his conscience had been pretty clear about letting himself in when he knew Dad was away, shagging Genevieve in a swanky country hotel.

He didn't even have his own room at his dad's. He'd been glad, as he led Sas up the wide staircase to the guest room. It was like a hotel, with a wide, smart bed, and a bathroom of its own. Nothing like his room at home. No posters of Cheryl Cole or class photos from primary school. No worn Man United duvet cover and toast crumbs, definitely no sticky tissues – and God knew there'd been a lot, with all the resisting. She'd loved it – exclaimed over the white orchid on the bedside table, and the grey silky bedspread. Some of the chat had been nerves, he knew. He felt them too. They'd gone quite far – as far as they dared – at parties and in their living rooms, quick fumbles between parental interruptions. This was entirely, completely different.

And he'd taken a bottle of wine from the rack in Dad's kitchen, screw top, so he didn't have to mess about with a corkscrew, and, yes, they'd *both* had a glass, quite a big one, but she hadn't been drunk, and neither had he. It took more than that. Much more for him. Rupert said he'd 'plied her with alcohol'. Made him sound like some creepy bloke in a club. He'd hated that. Anger had given him a rush of courage, and he'd tried to sound cool. 'For Christ's sake,' he'd said, 'it was Rioja, not Rohypnol.' That was when he'd thought Rupert Reed was most likely to hit him.

He knew it had been smart. He was trying to save face. As wretched as Mum and Dad splitting up had been, this, her parents showing up and accusing him like that, was the single worst thing that had ever happened. Since Saskia, the anger had receded. But here it was, flooding back, bringing with it the self-loathing. They were determined he'd done something wrong. Something very wrong.

They thought he'd committed rape. The horrifying thought that Saskia might have accused him of it exploded in his brain, white bright. It wasn't true. He knew that. How frightened of this awful man would she have had to be to lie about it? He couldn't believe she'd do that. It was her father, her shitty father. He'd twisted it. He'd warped it.

But it hadn't been. How could it have been? They loved each other, didn't they? They'd done everything right. He'd been gentle and careful and thoughtful. And it had been beautiful. Wasn't that what they were supposed to want for her?

Downstairs, he heard more angry, hissing voices. Heard the front door slam. 'You haven't heard the end of this,' Saskia's dad was saying. He couldn't hear what his mother said in response. Outside, a car pulled out and seemed to speed away. Even the car sounded angry. He waited for his mum to come up, but she didn't.

Long, long minutes later, he crept out of his room to the landing. He could see his mum sitting on the stairs. She'd retreated from the closed front door, backed up a few yards, and was sitting, her head in her hands. She looked . . . defeated.

'Mum?' His voice sounded choked. He took the first few steps down towards her. 'I'm sorry, Mum.'

She turned her head, and he could see that she had

been crying. 'Oh. My love.' She stood up, and opened her arms wide. He flew down the last stairs into her embrace. She put her arms around him so tightly it was almost painful.

'I'm so sorry, Mum.'

And then they both just cried, and held each other, in the quiet hallway. Neither of them quite knew which one was holding up the other.

18

The day Carrie died had started like any other. That was the way all of the day-they-died stories started, wasn't it? Because, of course, they did, and, of course, it had. Because if you knew how that particular day ended, you'd do almost every tiny thing differently. You'd hold her in the middle of the bed, where the two of you always woke, back to back, but still touching. You'd forgo the familiar comforting bum-bump routine you'd developed to make sure you'd both heard the alarm or the baby, whichever was first. A lazy hand swung backwards to pat whichever part of the other person was nearest before you threw off the covers and forced yourself to sit up and rub your eyes, the better to greet an ordinary day.

You wouldn't shout semi-crossly when she asked a question you couldn't possibly be expected to hear because the shower was running and the radio was set five clicks higher than you'd ever set it. You'd eat at the table, not standing at the island, spooning Cheerios in with the urgency of a man with places to be and the manners of a Neanderthal. You'd tell her things. Say things. Important things. No one ever said important things at a weekday breakfast unless they were domestically important – did you put the bins out? Is the Sky guy coming today? Have you remembered it's parents' evening tonight? Did you pick up my dry cleaning, honey? That was his important thing that morning. She was his wife, the mother of his children. A clever, funny, fiercely bright, amazing woman. And *that* was his important thing that day.

She had, of course, collected his dry cleaning. It was hanging on the back of the coat-cupboard door. Had he registered irritation that it hadn't made its way upstairs, where he'd wasted a few seconds looking for it? Would he have dared to be irritated about that? He might have been, because he didn't know what day it was.

How would you say goodbye to someone if you knew it really was goodbye? How would you ever let go? You'd do every tiny thing differently. And you'd never give her the bloody car keys.

At first he'd thought he'd lost them all. When he took the call, he'd thought his whole family was gone. No one would tell him. No one knew. So he'd felt the strangest sense of relief, even in the first dreadful moments of knowing he'd lost her, that he hadn't lost them all. The relief was a chink of light in the crushing darkness of that knowledge, and it was brief, and then it was gone.

It was 6 August. Arthur had turned one a month or so earlier. Bea was four, and Delilah was two and a half. They'd just been away for the first time as a family of five. He'd only been back at work for a day or two. It had been a great week in a hotel in Newquay. Nothing too ambitious. The weather had been unusually good, and they had filled their time with sandcastles, rockpools and ice creams. The hotel had been one of those clever places totally geared up for young families, with waffle machines in the dining room and baby listeners in the bedrooms.

Several times he'd taken the three children to breakfast on his own, and left Carrie to sleep. He'd known he'd be all right – it was a safe-space dining room, with patient, non-judgemental staff happy to help. He was supposed to be an equal parent, confident and competent, but in truth the three of them and just him still scared him a bit. The noise, the potential for mess and the infinite possibilities of domestic disaster. It was okay here – lots of new-men dads all in the same boat. And the lie-ins had paid off. Arthur was the worst sleeper of the three children, and Nick's work meant Carrie had borne the brunt of it while she was on maternity leave. She was due back at work in September and was tired in her bones: he'd wanted to let her sleep until she was woken by her own body clock, not someone else's. She relaxed, and was revived. She laughed a lot, and looked at him in the way he loved most.

Their room had had a small balcony that faced the sea, and all three children had slept better than ever before, exhausted by playing in the fresh air. After they'd passed out, impossibly adorable, Nick and Carrie had drunk a little on that balcony. Carrie had just discovered Aperol Spritz, and he'd packed the wherewithal to make it for her in the room: she'd have two after dinner, and be tipsy, and remind him very much of the Carrie he'd married. Golden from the sun, where he was just pink.

And so, after that lovely week, he'd been a little bit resentful of going back to work. A little bit grouchy. After he'd tracked down his clean shirt, and shovelled in some

Cheerios, he'd kissed her forehead. Not her mouth. And he'd gone to work, where he was instantly buried in backed-up emails. He hadn't thought about her again. Until he'd got the call.

Afterwards, he couldn't really remember the journey to the hospital. How he'd staggered out of his office, said something – what? – to the nearest colleague, left the building. He must have hailed a cab. Maybe someone had followed him out and done it for him. He couldn't remember what he'd said. Just that the taxi driver – a burly Asian, with a neat row of photographs of his own kids taped to the roof of the cab – didn't let him pay for the ride. Called him 'mate', and wished him well. And that random empathy had nearly made him sob.

There'd been a queue at the desk in A and E. A young woman with a bandaged hand. A milky-eyed old man in carpet slippers. They were both directed to the chairs by the window, with the vending machine and the three-year-old copies of *National Geographic*. He'd felt a stab of envy at their waiting-room status as he was ushered immediately beyond the desk. They were waiting because they could.

Carrie had been driving. Less than five miles from home. She was a good driver. Slower than him. Careful. It didn't matter, though, any of that, if the person in the other car was none of those.

She hadn't told him she was dropping Arthur off with a friend so she could take the girls to soft play for a couple of hours. It was minutiae. Tiny detail. No need for him to know. She hadn't even known when she'd said goodbye. She'd been speaking to her friend Susie on the phone after he'd left – Susie had said she'd have Arthur while Carrie took the girls: soft play was impossible with a baby in tow, and it was such a wet day, and they loved it so . . . They'd have talked about it later. How it smelt of feet and how Bea had helped Delilah climb a rope net, and how the soft-play centre charged five pounds for a cup of chips because they had a captive audience.

They'd blue-lit her to the hospital. But she'd been dead when they arrived. She might have been when they put her into the ambulance. Maybe it was important to try, or just to be seen to try, when it was a young mother, like Carrie. Or maybe there had been a chance. If the crash had happened a mile closer to the hospital, or at five miles per hour slower, if the doctor had been less tired or just a better doctor. If, if, if. Ifs tortured him with their possibilities. With their different endings.

But there was just this one ending.

Another driver had hit Carrie's car on a junction. He wasn't drunk. He was late. He knew the road, but he misjudged the lights, and didn't have time to slow down. The front of his car hit the side of theirs where the driver sat, far too fast. He killed Carrie. He didn't kill Bea or Delilah. Just their mother. Catastrophic internal injuries.

The other driver had killed himself too: he was declared dead at the scene. Consolation? Frustration? Neither. Totally irrelevant. His survival would maybe have meant a charge, a trial, a devastatingly light sentence: someone to be angry with. Sometimes Nick longed for that complication, because it would have been somewhere to channel rage. More often he felt no rage at all. Just sadness.

At the hospital, he didn't have to make heart-rending decisions about which bed to sit beside. There was no long wait, no time to pray or weep. Carrie was dead and the children were fine, physically at least. Bea and Delilah were fine. They'd evidently both been asleep. The motion of the car had always worked like magic: he'd spent hours driving around when they were small, at night, lulling them to sleep in third gear. Their bodies hadn't braced for the impact, and their high-tech car seats had saved them from so much as a scratch. The first people on the scene had taken them out, away from their mother, held them and cooed while the ambulance came. They didn't know anything about Arthur. There was no baby. No car seat. For a couple of minutes, Nick's mind raced with the unbearable ifs.

It was Bea who'd solved the mystery, pale with shock, and so small on a gurney meant for an adult. 'Arthur went to play at Susie's.'

Carrie's phone was in her handbag: 25 per cent battery charge, which was typical of her. He'd bought her a power-bank recently, and there was a cable permanently in the car, but she didn't always remember to use it. Recent calls. Susie. He didn't really know Susie. They'd met a handful of times at drinks or dinner. He'd had to call her and tell her. She was the first person he'd said it out loud to. Carrie's dead. Before Carrie's parents, even. 'Carrie's dead. Will you please bring Arthur to the hospital?' And Carrie had looked fine, lying like Sleeping Beauty from the Disney film of a hundred sleepy Sunday mornings, peaceful, still and beautiful. This time he'd kissed her mouth, not her forehead.

Surreal. It all had been surreal. He'd called them next, Ed and Maureen. Then Charlie. He'd asked Charlie to call Laura and Scott. Then he'd called Fran, because he truly didn't know what to do next. And that was his life now. Knowing what to do next – or, rather, *not* knowing what to do next – had become an everyday state of being for him.

19

Coming home at the end of a long day, when signalling failures at Waterloo had meant a crowded train with standing room only, even in first class, Scott registered more shopping than normal cluttering the hall. There was a pile of boxes just inside the front door.

Heather came towards him with a crystal tumbler of malt whisky. She did this most days when she was at home, with only a touch of irony. She called it her *Mad Men* move, or her *Good Housekeeping* circa 1960 technique. He rather liked it.

'This is a lot of packages, even for you.' He gestured at the pile.

'Hold on – I didn't order some of them. Most of them, actually. Maybe even none of them.' She considered.

'Who did, then? Have the girls got to my Amex?'

'They're gifts, hon. Hashtag gifted.'

'Gifted from whom?'

She adopted a patient tone. She'd explained this. 'Companies who want me to promote their products to my followers.'

'Always makes me want to laugh when you say "followers". Like you're some cult leader.'

'It isn't funny. It's a job.'

'Is it, though?' He cocked his head to one side.

She punched his nearest arm playfully, then gestured expansively in the direction of the boxes. 'Free stuff.'

'We so need more stuff! And is it free if you have to post something about it?'

She parroted back the line he'd heard before: 'All endorsements are genuine. All opinions are my own. I have to protect my brand.'

He resisted rolling his eyes at the mention of her brand. 'How many followers are we talking now?'

She drew herself up proudly. 'Fifteen thousand last count. And new ones every day.'

He was secretly impressed. 'How the hell . . . ?'

'Other people recommend your page . . . stuff like that. People get to know what you're about.'

'So you're all in on it?'

'I suppose. It's a very supportive community.'

'Is it, though?'

'Stop saying that.' She imitated him, her head cocked just like his. '"Is it, though?" You cynic.'

He loosened his tie and undid his top button. 'So what's in all of these?'

'Not sure yet.' She sat down on the floor, cross-legged. He hadn't noticed she had a pair of scissors. 'Wanna open them with me?'

He couldn't resist her. She made things fun, and it felt good. He kicked off his shoes, and sat beside her on the floor. 'It's like Christmas. Or a wedding list.'

'Ah, we didn't register for our wedding.' She made a mock-angry face. 'Call this making up for that.'

'We didn't need to register for our wedding. We already had most stuff. We weren't kids. And, besides, we weren't American.'

'You guys have wedding registers.'

'I know. God knows I know. I must have bought a hundred bloody toasters in my time for couples I barely even know.'

Heather giggled. 'So you're the guy who buys the toasters? I always wondered who did.'

'What does that mean?'

'Well, a toaster doesn't exactly scream imagination and romance, now does it?'

He poked her in the stomach. 'I'm sorry. Should I have bought the satin sheets and furry handcuffs?'

She grabbed his hand, laughing now. 'Whose weddings were you going to?'

'Besides, toasters can be very romantic. If they're used to make breakfast in bed . . .'

'I see what you did there.' She slid one blade of the scissors along a strip of tape, and pulled back the cardboard edges.

'Exactly – imaginative and romantic. That's why they pay me the big bucks.'

'And how many times, since our wedding, when no one bought us a toaster because we didn't register –'

'Because I already had a four-slice stainless-steel Dualit toaster,' he interrupted.

'– since our wedding, have you made me breakfast in bed, mister?' She'd put the scissors down now, and scooted across the floor the short distance between them. He put his arm around her and pulled her to him.

'Ah, trick question. You don't like crumbs in the sheets.'

'You got me. Can't stand them.'

He tipped her face upwards and kissed her, the boxes forgotten.

Theirs had been a small wedding. Laura and Alex's had been a Hugh Grant-worthy affair – village church, marquee in the garden, Mum in a state of high excitement for nine months, and a vast hat for nine minutes, after which she'd promptly removed it because she said she couldn't properly kiss people, and there were a lot of people who needed kissing. Dad choked up all day, terrified about giving his speech. Nick and Carrie had done a similar thing in Cumbria, with their own bohemian spin on it. Carrie had worn Converse All Stars under her cobwebby lace dress and danced all night in a circle of friends. Scott had been an usher at both, in morning dress for Laura, and a brown suit with drainpipe trousers that matched the other attendants' at Nick's, and he'd been equally uncomfortable in both, not quite at home in his outfits or in the saccharine soft focus of the days.

He and Heather had married at Chelsea Register Office at midday on a Tuesday. Just the two of them, Nick and Carrie, heavily pregnant with Arthur, Laura and Alex, Ethan, Charlie, Meredith and Hayley. Nick and Laura had acted as witnesses, and Carrie had collected petals to shower them with on the steps. Heather had worn a white trouser suit, declaring herself to be channelling Bianca Jagger, and he'd let himself be talked into a suit in a blue far nearer to cobalt than navy. The wedding had cost about thirty quid, the whole thing, and it took about ten minutes.

It got considerably more expensive afterwards, when they went to Claridges in a series of limos for a five-course lunch with a wine flight. He'd made a short but sincere speech, which he'd found surprisingly easy to write, in which he said he'd never entirely understood love until he'd met Heather, who held his hand, her eyes bright with tears throughout. And then they'd stayed the night in a vast art-deco suite, with the girls down the hallway in a slightly less vast twin room, ordering room service and watching movies. Laura had offered to take them with her but Heather had wanted to keep them near, and he hadn't minded. He understood already how it worked. The girls came first. They always would.

It had been a lovely day.

It had threatened, briefly, not to be. The phone call giving the family two weeks' notice of the wedding was literally the first any of them had heard about Heather. Until he'd had something concrete to offer, he hadn't known how to tell them, which he knew was pathetic, but also understood was just how he was. He'd never really told them stuff. Less so, even, since Mum had died. She had had a way of getting him to spill beans – a knack that his dad didn't have or seem to want to learn. Apparently it was weird. That was what Laura had said to him, anyway. She seemed excessively irritated by it – he remembered not understanding that at all. Nick was rueful, and Charlie made no attempt to hide his naked hurt. Scott had meant it to be a nice thing, having them all there, and it had seemed anything but. He wondered if they should have eloped, said their vows on a Maldivian beach instead.

They'd rallied, of course. Carrie's warmth had permeated the day, as it always did. She was an unstoppably energetic, radiating force of goodness, who brooked no nonsense, and seemed incapable of negativity. Nick was a lucky man. At least, he had been. Scott had always seen what Nick saw in Carrie. Alex he got less. There had always been something almost sneering about him, even as a young, unproven man with a shaving rash and a florid complexion. And he was a vicious drunk, always had been, and that was a red flag to Scott. There were too many of those guys in the City. Guys whose human suit slipped off when they were in drink and revealed a reptilian underneath. He understood Laura's extreme reaction more, now he knew she and Alex had been having problems. And Heather had explained to him how that would have impacted on how she behaved and how she felt about their getting married.

Perhaps he'd suspected their questions about Heather. Maybe that was why he'd presented her as a *fait accompli*, all dressed up and ready to marry. Perhaps that, too, was just how he was.

It wasn't fair on Heather. They barely knew her. Since the wedding, they'd only been together as a family once, at Carrie's funeral – that most dreadful, unspeakably sad of days – so it hardly counted. None of them could speak properly: that day had been a series of murmurs and choked sobs.

Now, suddenly, among the freebies, he was worried about her. 'Are you nervous about the holiday?'

She had returned to the packaging, but she paused, scissors in mid-air, her face confused. 'Should I be?'

'No. Of course not. I just mean . . . you don't know them very well, my family. And they don't know you.'

'So, that'll change, right?'

He chuckled. 'I guess it will. Ten days in close quarters.'

'How come you make it sound like a jail sentence, not a holiday?'

'I don't mean to.'

'Are they crazy?'

'Aren't all families a bit crazy?'

'Sure. I know mine was.' That was how she always spoke about them, in the past tense, although as far as he was aware they were alive and well and living in New Jersey. She'd never wanted to talk about them, and she'd never offered to take him there to meet them; they were compartmentalized in her past, the door firmly closed. 'Sounds like you're more worried about spending time with them than I am.'

'It'll be strange, is all. We haven't done anything like this, without my mum.'

'When was the last time?'

'Oh, God. Years ago. After Laura married Alex, and Ethan was born. Carrie and Nick were going out, I think, but she wasn't there . . . They weren't that established. Mum and Dad rented a villa with a pool – Portugal.' He couldn't remember the year. 'Ethan was just a toddler.'

'And how was that?'

'Good, I think. Okay. We played golf.'

'Really?' She sounded incredulous. He never played golf.

'Yeah. Me, Nick, Dad. Maybe even Alex. Mum and Laura stayed at the villa with Ethan, who was obsessed with the pool, as I remember.'

'Sounds nice.'

'All different now, though, isn't it? Mum's not here.' He contemplated. 'I'm just not sure how we work as a group without her.'

Heather had her head on one side, listening.

'She ran the show. Everything. Not just the practical

stuff, although she did that too. She was the fixer . . . the glue. None of us have much in common apart from parentage.'

'You grew up together.'

'Of course. But as adults we've got such different lives. Such different views. Politics, even. We have that shared history, of course, but it recedes, doesn't it, when you're older? She was the common thread.'

'And your dad?'

'I kind of think he's been lost without her. Just treading water.'

'It matters to him, though, this holiday. Why do you think he's done it?'

'It's his birthday.'

'I know that. But when did you last spend his birthday with him? All of you?'

Scott closed his eyes, scanning through the years. 'Seventy.' He could see Charlie – there must be a photograph – standing against a colourful border in his garden at home, sheepishly holding two gold helium balloons – a 7 and a 0. Ethan, aged six, was clutching one of his legs. Daphne was stage left, her hands clasped under her chin, beaming at them both.

'Before you lost your mum?'

'Would have been the same year. She got ill that autumn, at least. She died in the winter. January.'

'And not since?'

'Weddings, christenings, funerals.'

'Just the formal stuff?'

He nodded.

'So this is a big deal. For him.'

'I suppose it must be.'

'So we all have a responsibility. To make it a good one for him. For your mum.' She laid a hand on his leg, and squeezed gently. He felt a moment of profound gratitude for her. He felt she was adding layers of perception to his life, to his relationships. She had changed everything – all his perspectives, all his priorities. He was a lucky man. 'God. You are good.' He put his arms around her. 'So good. And wise. Did I mention wise?'

'Oh, keep going!' She laughed, the sound muffled against his chest.

'And smart. You make me more good.'

'Oh, you were already pretty good when I met you. I could see that.'

Thank God she had. He changed his tone, made it lighter. 'Can I be one of your followers? Can I, please? Can you *influence* me? I'm very suggestible . . .'

She brought one hand around from his back to prod him in the ribs. 'You can certainly make a follow request. I'll consider it.'

'Oh, you'll consider it? If it's good for your brand!' He flipped her over in a single movement, and lay on top of her on the floor, his arm behind her head to cushion it against the hard surface.

She laughed with delight. 'Oh, yeah, baby, only if it's good for my brand . . .'

20

Ethan didn't want to talk to his father without her. Dad had to be told, but he wanted the two of them to do it together. Even in the midst of her fear and anxiety, Laura registered that as a good thing for her relationship with her son. He was hers, still hers.

She didn't want to do it at home. But she didn't want to meet in a public place. She texted him that she needed to speak to him, and that she and Ethan wanted to come on a Saturday morning. She hoped she needn't make the point that Genevieve had better not be there, but in the car on the way over, she rehearsed asking her to leave if she was. They hadn't met yet, and she was in no hurry for that – and now was most definitely not the time. This was about *her* family, and Genevieve had no part in it.

She'd dressed carefully, pulling smarter clothes than normal from the back of the wardrobe – a pair of black cigarette pants and a silk shirt. The trousers were loose around her waist, but if she tucked the shirt in and bagged it out, they didn't look too bad.

She dried her hair, curling it under with the brush, rather than scraping it into a ponytail, and put on light makeup.

Then she stood and looked at herself in the mirror. Older, more tired, ever so slightly scrawny, but she recognized herself from the days when dressing well and being groomed were part of her armour for battles she won more often than lost. Today she needed Alex to be an ally, not an adversary.

In the car Ethan barely spoke. He was pale and looked very young, hunched in the passenger seat beside her. She knew he wasn't sleeping either – she'd heard him in his room on several nights, moving about. He had dark circles around his eyes, and there was a fresh crop of sore red spots across his cheeks and chin.

She'd made him talk, the first night, after Saskia's parents had gone. Once he'd finished crying, and the adrenalin had subsided enough for her to stop shaking, she'd made hot chocolate and pancakes, the comfort food of his childhood, mostly so she could face the stove and keep busy for a few moments. They'd sat at the kitchen table. He didn't eat or drink. She'd poured a heavy measure of whisky into her mug when he wasn't looking. She had a million questions, but she sensed it would be better for the information to come out of him in his way. He took some time to process, and then, through ugly, angry tears, he spoke. Every few minutes he rubbed snot on the sleeve of his plaid shirt, and he kept squeezing his eyes and wiping tears. She wanted to hold him again, but when she took his hand on the table, he pulled it away.

Shock had seemingly removed whatever sense of privacy Ethan might have had, and fear made him speak. He was animated by the need to explain. He'd told her everything, she thought. It had been his first time, he said, that first time with Saskia, and she believed him. He told her that the two of them had talked about it before it happened. That Saskia had gone to the doctor, that he'd bought condoms anyway, from the chemist.

The word *rape* hung in the air, ugly and stark. He said it several times, in stunned disbelief. Laura was amazed by how comprehensive his understanding of the word was.

'Rape is some poor girl getting hijacked by an Uber driver and taken into the woods and having a knife held to her throat. Rape is some shithead thinking he can do whatever he wants cos a girl is out of it. Rape is having sex with someone who says no. Whether that person is your wife or your girlfriend or some randomer. Whether you've had sex with them before or not. Whether you're drunk or not. I get it. It's 2019. You've banged on about it often enough. I know about "no", for fuck's sake. That's not what this was. How can he say that? How dare he say that?'

That was the bit she didn't understand. 'Could she . . . I mean might she —'

His voice crescendoed: 'No. No.' He was horrified. 'She wouldn't do that.'

New and terrifying information spilt out of him. She couldn't believe she had been ignorant of it. She should have realized. Most of his mates were sixteen. Why hadn't she realized — been ahead of it? She was instantly afraid she knew the answer. She'd been consumed by her own pain. She'd stopped parenting. Not the practical stuff. She'd cleaved to domesticity — his socks were washed, the fridge was full, school forms were signed. But for the real stuff, the stuff that matters, she'd been sleepwalking. Apparently all his mates had done it. If not all, then most, he promised. At parties, in the back of cars, in tents at festivals. Some with girlfriends, more with relative strangers whose names they might not even have bothered to learn. Boys he knew – hell, boys she knew, boys she'd watched grow up, boys whose mothers she spent time with – were treating girls like dirt. 'Stats don't have faces,' Ethan said. That was what one of them had said. A frightening number seemed to be off their heads on those ghastly alcopop VKs or, worse, on weed or MDMA while they were doing it. At least one had caught something and had had to take antibiotics.

Five minutes ago those boys were playing *Minecraft* and watching football. Their mothers believed they were raising them with morality, with respect for women. Every generation pushed the envelope, she knew. Social mores changed. Kids were almost obliged to do things that perplexed and, yes, horrified their parents. But this – this was bewilderingly out of sync with what she had thought. Had she just been colossally naïve? Did everyone else's mother know this stuff was going on? Did they think it was okay?

He was incandescent at the injustice of it. He'd done it right. And he was the one who was going to get into serious trouble. It made no sense to him at all. And she couldn't tell him it did to her.

Concern for their son defused Laura. Alex smiled easily enough when he opened the door. Genevieve wasn't there. She might have been curious about the flat, some other time, might have taken in the fashionable glass furniture and statement cushions that Alex would probably have dismissed had she suggested they buy them for their house. In the clinically clean and white kitchen, he made mugs of coffee in his fancy machine.

'So what's this all about?'

Ethan looked at Laura.

'Do you want me to explain?'

He nodded.

She'd been tempted to ring Alex and give him the basic facts before they came, a heads-up, but something had stopped her. She'd needed to see his face. 'I'm not sure whether you're aware that Ethan and his girlfriend Saskia were sleeping together.'

Alex gave a rather sharp intake of breath. 'I –'

'Here.' She tried to keep the blame out of her voice. Tried very hard.

He looked down at the table. 'I see.'

Laura shook her head. 'Anyway. They were. They are. They've been going out for a while. It's all been consensual, exclusive, all that . . .'

Alex nodded, clearly uncomfortable.

'But Saskia isn't sixteen. Not for a few weeks. She's fifteen.' She waited for the penny to drop, but Alex still didn't say anything.

She sighed. 'And it seems, and we're not sure yet how, but it seems her parents have found out about the two of them. And they're furious. The other night they came to the house and started shouting the odds. Well, her father was, at least.'

Ethan made a small strangled sound. This time he let her put her hand on his arm. He couldn't meet his father's eye.

'That seems a bit OTT.' Alex wasn't grasping the seriousness of the situation.

'He's saying it's statutory rape because Saskia is under age. He's saying he's going to the police.'

'They won't want to know, surely?'

'They have to take it seriously. If Saskia's parents make an accusation.'

'And?'

Why didn't he know any of this? He hadn't sat through the excruciating sex chat at school. He hadn't thought about it. He'd been too busy with his own selfish sex life. It wasn't a kind thought, and maybe it wasn't fair, but the yoga mantra wasn't working right now, and her mind entertained it.

'And if it goes like it could, that's a conviction on his record. That's the sex offenders' register. For years.' She spoke slowly and deliberately.

At last the seriousness of it was beginning to dawn on him. 'But that's ridiculous. He's barely sixteen himself.'

She couldn't protect Ethan from knowing the full implications of Saskia's father's thoughts. He knew already.

'They're both kids.'

'Not in the eyes of the law. Not about this. One is capable of informed consent. One isn't.'

He was opening and closing his mouth, like a guppy, searching for the right thing to say, the most important question to ask. 'What does Saskia have to say about that?'

'We don't know. They must have taken her phone. Ethan and Saskia's year isn't at school at the moment. They're on study leave. So he hasn't spoken to her. And there's no way they'll let him see her. Saskia's father just came around, shouted the place down, made his threats and left.'

'So you don't know if he's been to the police?'

'No. You know what we know now.'

'Christ.' Alex ran his hands through his hair, and held his breath, then blew it out through his mouth.

'I'm sorry, Dad.'

Laura turned to him, and heard her voice, fierce. 'Don't do that. You don't need to be sorry.' She looked at Alex.

For the first time in a long time, he didn't disappoint her. The colour had drained from his face. He shuffled his chair awkwardly around the table, and put his arm around Ethan's shoulders. 'Oh, my poor boy. I'm sorry. I'm so sorry.' Ethan laid his head on the table, and Alex laid his beside his son's and they stayed like that for a short while. Ethan was crying quietly. Laura squeezed his knee.

When Alex raised his head, he looked at her across their son's prone, stricken form, and gave a grim, tight-lipped smile. 'We're going to sort this out, I promise you. I'm so glad you've both told me. And we're going to sort it out. Okay.'

She didn't know how or even if that was possible. Or how long it was since she had seen him standing along-side them, on their side, on her side. Or how long it was since she had felt gratitude towards her husband. But she felt it now.

21

Nick was catching up on emails, the ten o'clock news in the background, when Bea appeared in the kitchen doorway, rubbing her eyes. He went straight to her and picked her up, holding her tightly. She was bed-warm, and smelt like fabric softener and sleep. 'What's the matter, my love?'

'Can't sleep.'

It was a weirdly adult expression, like something she'd heard someone else say. And it was patently not true. She'd been asleep. He'd checked on them all at around half past nine. And she looked so sleepy, here in the kitchen, her eyes half closed against the light. 'Warm milk?'

She nodded, and nestled into his neck. He held her on his hip while he filled a small mug with milk from the fridge, and blasted it once, then twice, in the microwave. He stuck a finger in it to make sure it wasn't too hot, then went into the living room holding his daughter and the mug, and settled himself and her in an armchair. Bea rearranged herself to lie on his chest, and he stroked her hair for a few moments.

She sat up, pushed her hair back from her face, and reached for the milk, drinking it and looking at him.

'Better?'

She smiled. 'But I don't want to go back to bed yet.'

'Okay.'

'I want to stay with you for a bit.'

'Okay.'

'You're doing work.' She'd seen the open computer on the kitchen table.

'Nothing important. Not as important as you, anyway.' Nick winked at her. 'We could read a story?'

Bea shook her head. 'Tell me about Mummy.'

Nick's guts twisted. This had happened a few times now. The counsellor said it was perfectly normal. Healthy, even. Keeping Carrie alive for the children was important. As long as you let them bring it to you, not the other way around. Only Bea did it. She seemed to know instinctively only to do it when they were on their own, never in front of her siblings. This nocturnal encounter of theirs was almost a regular thing now. Delilah was too young to pose the question, although she looked at pictures of Carrie, and Arthur, of course, would have barely any memory of her.

'What do you want me to tell you about?'

'Tell me about when I was in Mummy's tummy.'

'Ah. You in Mummy's tummy!' He ruffled her hair. 'Would you like to see a picture?'

Bea nodded. Nick took his phone out of his shirt pocket, and scrolled quickly through the photos. 'Here's one.' It was the obligatory scan picture. Bea's spine, her heart, her face in eerily accurate detail. Bea glanced at it, but shook her head. 'I want to see Mummy.'

He swiped. 'Okay. This is that same day. This is Mummy the day they took that picture of you in her tummy.' Carrie, looking rueful, standing by a water-cooler, drinking from a plastic cup. Trying to achieve the required balance of a sufficiently full bladder that you weren't completely desperate to empty, as required by the sonographer.

But Bea didn't seem satisfied. Nick caught her drift. She wanted full on Moby-Dick. Which was, he almost smiled, exactly the way Carrie had always described herself in the third trimester.

He moved forward a few months. And found what he wanted. A picture of Carrie taken in early May 2013. About two weeks before Bea's due date. In the garden, on an unseasonably warm day, feet up on a stool, hands clasped under the belly the better to show its huge swell. Her face a bit rounder than normal, smiling excitedly. 'There you are.'

'Mummy looks happy.'

'She was. We were. We couldn't wait to meet you.'

'Was I born soon after this?'

'Yes. Very soon. Mummy had already packed her suitcase to take to the hospital. She had put it by the front door, because she knew otherwise I'd forget it.'

Bea giggled. 'Like swimming kit.'

Nick nodded, mock-sad. 'Yes, like swimming kit.'

'Why did she need a suitcase?'

'She needed some pretty things for you to wear to come home.' He scrolled quickly past all the shots from the delivery room. Found one of the three of them the midwife had taken – Carrie all neat and cleaned up, smiling triumphantly in a fresh nightie. Him shell-shocked and delighted. Bea in their arms, tiny and wrinkled and swollen-eyed.

'I look funny.'

'You look gorgeous.'

'My Babygro isn't pink.'

'No. We didn't know whether you were a boy or a girl until we met you.'

'Really?' This thought intrigued her.

'Nope. Mummy wanted a surprise.' He remembered how badly he hadn't wanted a surprise. But Carrie had insisted. He remembered going out and buying an armful of pink stuff the first chance he'd got, so completely chuffed with his daughter.

Carrie had been ready. Calm, joyous and competent. He hadn't. Not if he was honest. Not until the second he'd held her in his arms. He'd been playing the part of expectant father, scared stiff. He'd done every single thing that was expected of him but he'd lain wide awake, almost every night, next to Carrie and her ever-expanding form, wondering if he was ready.

She'd set the pace for almost everything in their life, and she'd done that with this too. He trusted her completely. He just didn't necessarily trust himself as much.

'Were you glad I was a girl, Daddy?'

He squeezed her. 'Oh, yes. Of course. I always thought you were. I thought Lila was a girl too, and I had a funny little feeling that Arthur was a boy.'

'Why?'

'He kicked Mummy a lot more than you two did.'

Again the chuckle. He felt rewarded by it. 'Naughty Arthur.'

'Not naughty. He didn't know, did he? He was just in a hurry to get out and play football.'

He could hear Carrie, moaning beside him, in their bed. Arthur had been the heaviest of their babies – a whopping nine pounds two ounces to Bea's tiny seven pounds four.

'I remember that!' She sounded delighted. 'You could see his feet in her tummy.'

'That's right.'

Sometimes when they'd been talking like this, Bea would bring herself to the present and say she missed her mum. Other times, she seemed happiest to dwell in the past. Tonight was the latter, so that it was almost like the two of them were pretending Carrie was in another room, attending to Arthur, maybe, or folding laundry in the kitchen. It was as comforting as life got, these days, and Nick went willingly along with Bea's unspoken fantasy.

Eventually, Bea laid her head on his chest again, and put her thumb into her mouth. Nick laid his own head back against the sofa. Quite soon he felt Bea get heavy, and her breathing slowed. The weight of her, and her peace felt good, so he lingered there awhile before taking her back to bed and returning to his laptop.

In some respects he'd come a long way from that callow youth in the delivery room, wondering if he would cope with a family, in others no distance at all. He'd always taken strength from Carrie, aped her confidence, her fake-it-till-you-make-it attitude towards everything new and untried, and, God, he was still trying to now.

22

Laura got to town far too early and parked higher than she normally would in the multi-storey, so that she had further to walk to where she had agreed to meet Claudia. Her legs were disconcertingly jellylike. She had felt almost disoriented with anxiety since she'd received the text from Saskia's mother last night, asking if she would please meet her after work the next day, to talk, she'd said. Just the two of them. The mothers. She'd called Alex to ask if it was a good idea, surprised at how easily she'd slipped back to consulting him when it came to Ethan. He'd said, yes, he thought so, but warned her not to admit anything or apologize, as though what had happened was a fender-bender at a roundabout. She'd fought the urge to remind him that 'Never apologize, never explain' was more his mantra than hers, and promised to report back on what happened. They didn't, by mutual agreement, want to tell Ethan. Until they knew what Claudia's agenda was, it would only pile on stress, and he was already buckling. Alex volunteered to take him out for a pizza or a curry. Ethan didn't like curry. But she acquiesced: he'd go to his dad's after work, and it meant he needn't know she wasn't at home, where he always, always found her at five thirty. Somehow, work didn't seem a barrier to Alex's doing this, and she tried not to mind that, in a crisis, he could find time, when so often, without one, he hadn't made any.

She hadn't even told Mel what was going on. Or Dad. Too much of a maelstrom was swirling. Their broken little family had coalesced around Ethan and what was happening to him. It was discombobulating – a Daphne word from her childhood. It had probably never been more appropriate.

She had no idea what Claudia wanted. She hoped that, in choosing a public place, she was signalling there wouldn't be any shouting. It was late in the day. The after-school crowd had gone home, and the after-work one was in the pub, not the café. One of the staff was already washing the floor and putting chairs on the tables. The other was clearly irritated by her ordering a pot of English breakfast tea, although they didn't actually close for another half-hour.

Rupert had been making all the noise, when they'd shown up late that evening at Laura's house. She might not have known Claudia if she'd passed her on the street. She was, however, the only woman in the café – the other customer was a scruffy old man – and her expression, as Laura entered, told Laura she remembered her very well. She was a slight woman, Laura's age or maybe older. What Daphne would have called well preserved. She'd been very pretty once, you could tell, and her blue eyes were still very blue. She was wearing an Hermès scarf at her neck, tied in the immaculate, fancy way Laura never quite managed to pull off, and she had an old-fashioned hand-bag, like the Queen always carried. Based on appearances, at least, they were from different tribes.

After the briefest of pleasantries, oddly given and received, Laura busied herself for a moment with the tea-pot and small milk jug. She had to get up again to retrieve a spoon, then stir the water vigorously to produce tea with any colour at all. It meant she needn't look at Claudia, who was clearly trying to speak, and struggling to know where to start.

'I got your number from Saskia. Rupert doesn't know I'm here. I hope it's okay that I messaged you.'

There was no anger in this person. Laura felt flooded with relief.

'How is she?'

Claudia smiled weakly at the concern. 'She's in bits. How's Ethan doing?'

Laura felt protective. 'He's a total mess. He's incredibly upset at what he's being accused of.'

Claudia stared at her hands in her lap. 'Of course he is.'

'I know you know him.'

Claudia knew Ethan better than Laura knew Saskia. To be honest, she'd been in no state, the last few months, to play nice with Ethan's girlfriend. She'd been glad he seemed happy. She had spent little time with them, and that arrangement had seemed to suit them all. They'd slept together at Alex's, but it could just have easily have been at hers, and she would probably have had no idea. It was one of the facts she had castigated herself about in the last few days. Another reason to feel shitty. Ethan had reported that Claudia and Rupert seemed okay, Saskia's mum a bit easier than her dad, and lots of rules he deemed petty and childish. But he'd eaten dinner with them a few times. Watched a match or two with Rupert. It had all seemed cool, he said.

She'd quite liked the little she'd learnt about Saskia. She seemed bright and sweet. And fond of Ethan. They'd laughed a lot, the two of them, at little in-jokes that didn't seem remotely funny.

'I do, a little. And I think he's a nice boy, Laura. I honestly do.'

'Then you have to know what nonsense this is.'

Her cheeks pinked up. 'My husband is very angry.'

'Believe me, so is mine.'

'I'm sure he is. I've told Rupert we need to sit down, the four of us, and talk about it.'

'How about the six of us? They're not kids.' Even as she said it, she couldn't quite imagine it. But it seemed wrong to exclude Ethan and Saskia. It was probably the least appropriate moment to treat them like little kids.

'She is. To him, at any rate. He can't bear – just can't stand – the idea of her being . . . you know . . .'

'Sexually active?' Laura couldn't be doing with Claudia's prudishness.

'That. And in love. Maybe the love part more than the sex. He just wasn't ready.'

'It isn't really about whether he was ready, though, is it?'

'I know.' She squirmed in her chair. 'Look. Let me try to explain.' She took a deep breath, and Laura could tell she was about to launch into something she'd rehearsed to herself before she came. 'Rupert is an older father. We met rather later in life, to be truthful. I was already thirty-nine when we married. He's ten years older. We thought we couldn't have children. We started trying right away. It just wasn't happening. And then it was. I got pregnant naturally before we had a chance to go the IVF route. It never happened again. Well, I did get pregnant. Once more, when Sas was four. But I miscarried, early on.'

She knew she was digressing. She shook herself back to her point. 'Anyway, she was all we had. He was besotted, right from the start. I know a lot of men aren't that interested, are they, when the children are babies, before they can talk? Not Rupert. She was the centre of his universe, from day one.' The slight sadness of her own demotion was obvious. 'It's all been about her, about protecting her, giving her the best. We were living abroad, with his work, but she's the reason we came back: he wanted her to finish her education in England, and he couldn't bear to send her to boarding school. He went, you know, when he was seven. His father was in the forces . . .' Another detour. She was so desperate to explain his behaviour. To try to make him seem sympathetic.

'When we first came home she had a hard time. Girls can be so – so cliquey and cruel. She wasn't very happy, not very settled. We wondered whether we'd done the wrong thing – whether we should have stayed where we were. I know he blamed himself. And then she and Ethan got together and it was like the light came back on. She was happy. I was worried they might be a bit, you know, obsessive. But I was incredibly glad she had him . . . I just didn't realize – I suppose I didn't want to think . . .'

'That they were sleeping together?'

'Did you know?'

Laura couldn't lie. 'No. Not specifically. I hadn't thought about it. I should have done.'

Claudia's eyes had filled with tears. 'I found the pills. She'd been to the doctor and not told me.'

Laura could feel her hurt. 'At least she was being sensible.'

'It still hurt. It was a jolt. She'd gone from being a kid who told me everything to being a young woman who'd take herself off to the doctor and – and I'd – I'd just missed it.'

'I think maybe we all miss it.'

'Even though we never stop looking?'

Laura laughed. 'Yeah. Even though we never stop looking.'

They smiled at each other, both understanding.

Laura wanted to offer something. 'I don't know whether Ethan said, or maybe Saskia, my marriage ended recently. I've been . . . coping with that. Not coping with it, really . . .'

'I'm so sorry.' She didn't say whether she'd known or not. It didn't really matter.

They sat for a moment. They weren't so different after all.

'When I told Rupert he went mad. Started raving about how young she was. How she was too young. I don't know where all that legal stuff came from.'

'Is he going to pursue it? The legal stuff?'

'He hasn't decided, he says.'

'And you?'

Her face softened. 'I don't want him to. It wouldn't change anything.'

Again, the anger rose. It was so very close to the surface. 'It would change everything for my son.'

Claudia raised her hand. 'I'm sorry. I didn't mean that. I understand what it would mean for Ethan. What it could mean. What I meant was that it wouldn't undo what's happened.'

'But it could ruin his life.'

She leant forward, spoke quickly. 'And I know he doesn't deserve that.'

'Damn right he doesn't.'

'Believe me, I hear you.'

'He loves her. I know they're kids. But he really believes he loves her. I don't think he would ever have done anything that would hurt her. I don't actually think he has it in him to hurt anyone. He's never been like that. But her . . . her least of all.' Now she thought she might cry. Perhaps she should.

'I know that.'

'What happened between them might have happened sooner than any of us would like, but it happened consensually, it happened somewhere safe and warm, and I'm certain it happened in a loving way. You have no idea – and neither, apparently, did I – how few kids that holds true for. No idea at all . . .'

'I do. Saskia says all of that.'

'To just you or to both of you?'

'He . . . Rupert hasn't actually sat down with her yet. He wants to calm down.'

'That's ridiculous.' Laura couldn't help herself.

'It's how he is.' Said as a fact, not as a defence. Everything about her made clear that he wasn't an easy man to live with.

Laura snorted derisively. 'You've got to stop your husband going to the police. To do so would be entirely wrong.' Alex might have tried to stop her talking to Claudia in that way, from coercing, but Laura could see hope. Claudia didn't believe Ethan deserved to be in trouble for what had happened. Claudia was her route to Rupert. She almost trusted her, sitting in that café.

Claudia nodded. 'I'm going to try.' There was something alarming in the way she said it. Rupert was clearly impossible to manage. He sounded awful. Like all of this was about him, not Saskia.

'Please.' She was begging now, for Ethan, her sweet, beautiful boy. 'Please.'

23

Nick couldn't stop thinking about the Micky Flanagan sketch where the comedian talked about the difference between going out and going out-out. He'd barely been out after dark since Carrie. Let alone out-out. This, however, was definitely out-out. Fran had insisted. She'd told him if he didn't call Ed and Maureen and ask them to look after the kids she would.

'It isn't easy for them, with the farm.'

'Bollocks. Don't give me the farm excuse. I've never heard them give it. You know they'd drop everything. They have people to take over from them. It's just an evening.'

'It's two at least. It's a bloody long drive. I can't ask them to do it on back-to-back days.'

'So they'll stay two or three nights at yours. And you'll let them. The kids will love it. It'll make them happy. You'll get a break. It's. All. Good.'

Things had been strained between him and his parents-in-law since The Conversation, so he emailed, like a coward, instead of calling. Stay a night or two. Three even. Just like Fran had said. The response was almost instantaneous. They'd be delighted. They'd sleep over. They'd missed the children, they said, which made him feel guilty. Fran had offered him a choice of activities: dinner, cinema, bowling.

'Bowling?'

'Why not?'

'Sticky carpet. Smelly shoes. For a start.'

'Okay, funster. Just a suggestion. I happen to be very good at bowling.'

'Another reason not to go.'

He'd chosen dinner. Discovered, in that instant, a latent craving for Asian food – he hadn't had any in for ever. In the weeks and months after Carrie died, food had come almost entirely from the freezer in Tupperware labelled by concerned friends. Endless casseroles, lasagnes, pies. He was grateful, of course. There was not an ethnic ingredient in any of it, but it was suitably heavy on the comfort and the carbs. He hadn't faded away physically since Carrie died: instead he'd developed love handles.

Since the sympathy catering had dropped away, and their new domestic normality had established itself, he'd stuck to a small, simple and distinctly unexotic repertoire of things he knew the kids ate. They weren't big fans of flavour, it seemed. Carrie had tried, God knows, making vegetable faces and fruit in funny shapes and hiding courgettes and carrots in bolognese, but without Carrie, he'd taken the line of least resistance to full tummies, and given up coaxing them into avocado and broad beans. He occasionally looked at plates of fish fingers and pasta shapes that were a culinary Dulux paint chart, and heard her gently admonish him.

He wasn't any better with himself. Mostly he'd picked from their unfinished plates, fish fingers and chicken nuggets eaten at the sink. And who ordered takeaway for one? Sad bastard. Suddenly, surprisingly, with Fran's invitation, his mouth almost watered at the thought of a chilli prawn or a green curry. So, no to bowling, but a big yes to a spicy meal eaten sitting down where other people were. It was almost – just almost – exciting.

Maureen hugged him hard when he opened the front door to the pair of them. Delilah and Arthur were in bed, but Bea was still up, and she ran into Ed's arms. Her grandfather picked her up and held her tight. More than the others, Bea looked like her mum – exactly like the photograph of Carrie, taken when she was the same age, that Ed and Maureen had on the mantelpiece at home. Note to self, Nick thought. More grandparents, more often. Something about his grief made him possessive of his kids, but it wasn't fair.

'You look handsome.' Maureen smiled, touching his shirt collar briefly. 'I like this.'

He looked down at himself. It wasn't a new shirt. She must have seen it before. 'Thanks.' He smiled at her.

They hadn't asked him where he was going. Christ – did they think he was on a date? The thought was bizarre. He heard himself blurting out, 'It's just supper with an old friend of ours. I won't be late.'

Maureen nodded, unquestioning. 'You have a good time. Don't hurry home. Enjoy yourself.'

'Thank you,' Nick mumbled. He knelt down, and held Bea's tiny body tightly. 'You okay, monkey?'

'I'm going to read to Granddad. Aren't I, Granddad?'

'You are, my love.' Ed put his big hand on her head affectionately.

'I'll see you later.'

Bea kissed his cheek, then took Ed's hand, her attention already elsewhere. 'Bye, Dad.'

On the other side of the front door, Nick leant against

it. It was still hard to leave them: that was what Carrie had done. Kissed Arthur goodbye and left him. It was easier with work: he understood that their lives must go on. Easier at the school gate too. This was different. He didn't have to go. He had his house key in one hand – he pushed the edge into the palm until it almost hurt, because physical pain, he'd discovered, running so fast and so far that only the agony in his chest made him stop, was the fastest distraction from the emotional kind – and set off.

Fran was already at the table when he arrived, with a large glass of wine in front of her. He bent and kissed her cheek briefly. She smiled.

'Am I late?'

She shook her head. 'I was early. Mad keen babysitter three doors down. Saving up to backpack around South East Asia. Offered to do bath and bed, which I obviously leapt at, slummy-mummy that I am.'

'You look nice. Didn't recognize you without the athleisure.' This was true.

Fran narrowed her eyes, then smiled. 'Flatterer.'

The waiter approached the table with two menus.

'Bottle? What is that?'

'Sauvignon Blanc. Why not?'

'A bottle of that, please,' Nick said. 'And some prawn crackers while we choose . . .'

He drank the first glass very fast. They ordered and did parent small-talk for a few minutes. This was safe territory – they did it in each of their houses and at the school gates. It was easy enough to do it in a restaurant. Not too weird. They'd done it, the four of them, him and

Carrie, Fran and Craig. But usually it would be Fran and Carrie in a maternal huddle, him and Craig talking football. They'd never been as close as the girls. They'd never have been mates without them. But they understood that the strength of the bond between their wives made it compulsory for them to rub along together, so they did. As long as they didn't talk about politics, it was tolerable. Carrie once said she wasn't sure what Fran had ever seen in Craig, but they hadn't talked much about it beyond that. He'd have joked – something about not all women being as lucky as Carrie was – some naff, stupid joke, the kind he made all the time and not any more. He'd been busy being happy in his family cocoon. He liked Fran a lot, and he knew Carrie adored her. But he was also sort of ambiguous about her. Craig too. In the nicest possible way, politely disinterested.

He could never have known how much she would come to mean to him in the months since he'd lost Carrie. How much he relied on her. How grateful he was for her.

'You're off on holiday soon, aren't you?'

Nick nodded. 'Dreading it slightly.'

'It'll be fine. Safety in numbers, Nick. Didn't you say your brother and sister both had kids?'

'That's right. Stepkids, in my brother's case. Girls. Teenagers. My sister Laura has a boy, Ethan.'

'Well, teenage girls will love your tinies. You'll probably hardly see them. You could do with a rest.'

Nick hadn't conceived of the ten days as even potentially restful. It was a seductive thought.

'Take a few books. Let the others help with the kids. Hang out.'

'Yes, Fran.' He smirked at her.

'Where is it again?'

'Cotswolds.'

'Not far from us, then. We'll overlap.'

'Really?'

'I think so. Where exactly are you?'

He checked on his phone. Fran opened her diary and read out her own destination.

'I don't think yours is that far away from ours.'

'But you'll be living it up in some swanky country mansion courtesy of your dad, and we'll be slumming it in tents. Sorry – yurts, if you please.'

'Really?'

'Yes. See? Yours is looking better every minute, right?'

'Can't see you in a yurt, Frannie. Isn't glamping just fairy lights around your compost toilet?'

'Don't you dare laugh at me, you bastard.'

'Who's laughing?' But they both were now.

'It's the very fanciest of tents, I'll have you know. With a proper bed, allegedly. Besides, I'm adaptable.'

'I'm sure you are. Are there . . . showers?'

Fran snorted now, and put her head into her hands in mock-despair. 'I bloody hope so.'

'What about Craig? Has he got a Bear Grylls side?'

Fran's mirth subsided, and her expression changed.

'Fran?' For a dreadful moment he thought she was going to cry and he didn't think he could cope with someone else's tears, especially hers. 'Fran? What is it?'

'I want to tell you something, and I've been really scared about telling you.'

'What could you be scared of telling me, for Christ's

sake? Oh, fuck – you're not moving, are you?' Nick felt a stab of genuine fear. 'You can't.'

'No. No. Well . . .' Fran wasn't looking at him now. She was staring hard at her hands in her lap. Turning her napkin over and over into a fan.

'Come on. Spit it out.'

'Me and Craig. We're splitting up.' She spoke fast.

Nick was shocked. 'What? Divorcing?'

Fran shook her head. 'Separating for now. But, yes, probably divorce at some point. I haven't got that far.'

'Oh, my God. What happened?'

'Nothing happened.'

'What's his problem?'

'It's not his problem, Nick. It's mine.'

'I don't understand.' Nick was trying to remember the last time he'd seen the two of them together, but he couldn't remember when that was. Ages ago.

'I don't want to be married any more. Not to him.'

Nick didn't speak. He waited. He'd got better at doing that.

Fran took a very deep breath. 'I don't love him any more. I haven't for ages. Sometimes I'm not sure I ever really did. Not properly. Not like . . .' For a second he swore she was going to say 'like you and Carrie', but maybe that was just him. Her voice trailed off. 'Not like I should have done.'

'Why didn't you want to tell me?'

'It seems so – so ungrateful, when you . . .'

Nick put up his hand to stop her. 'Don't do that.' He hated it. He'd been very aware of it over the last year. At work. Around. People felt they needed to minimize their own shit because yours was so much worse. Did your spouse die in a car accident? No? Then what have you got, really, to complain about? But that was them, not him. He hated the weirdness it put into all his real conversations. He hated Fran doing it now. 'I'm sorry I didn't know.'

She laughed, but the sound was hollow. 'For Christ's sake, Nick. Don't be stupid.'

'How long?'

She shrugged. 'Have I been feeling like this?'

He nodded.

'Months.' She curled her lip. 'Years.'

'God. Did Carrie know?'

'Some.'

'I'm glad you told her.'

'Do you remember that time we went into town and had cocktails? Her first big night out after Arthur?'

He remembered it well. Arthur had wailed all evening, refusing to take breast milk from a bottle. Carrie had come home a bit tipsy (although she hadn't drunk much) and fed him, and he'd gone straight to sleep, and she'd joked about being the worst mother in the world, and he'd joked that she should be more worried about being the worst wife in the world. It was the first time they'd made love since the baby, because two big glasses of wine made it easier than it might have been without. The memory hit him in the face, all senses blaring. Her laughter, and her hand pulling him towards the stairs.

'That was when I told her I didn't think I could stay with him.'

Carrie hadn't said a thing.

142

'It was so long ago.'

'I know. I tried. God knows I tried. When Carrie died . . .'

She struggled to articulate what she meant, but he thought perhaps he understood nonetheless. Just as he also understood that you couldn't stay married to a person you weren't happy with just because someone else had lost the person they *were* happy with. Like a weird, messed-up tribute to marriage.

He put his hand in the middle of the table, beckoning for hers. She took one out of her lap and let him hold it in his own. Squeeze. 'I'm sorry.'

'I'm sorry too. You have no idea how much I wish he was a total pig. You know?' She was laugh-crying. 'A serial cheat, or a bully. Or a weirdo.'

'No, you don't. He's still the kids' dad.'

'You're right. Okay. I wish he was dumping me. He didn't believe me. Not at first.'

'And now?'

'I think he does.'

'And the kids? Do they know?'

'I figure it won't be real for them until he actually moves out.'

'And is that going to happen?'

'He's rented a flat in town. From the beginning of July. I'll start talking to them about it nearer the time. I think that's best.'

Nick didn't know what to tell her. 'I'm sure you're right.' He wasn't sure. Kids were extraordinary little emotional weathervanes. He'd learnt that much from Bea and Delilah since Carrie.

*

They finished the evening, but the light tone of earlier had disappeared. Nick felt inadequate. And sad.

He paid their bill while Fran was in the loo. When she came out, he could see that she'd been crying, and he wished he'd known more what to say.

His car was parked outside the restaurant. Had he imagined he'd be sober enough to drive it home? He pulled out his phone and tapped onto the Uber app. 'I'm calling you a cab.'

'Can I drop you at home?'

Nick shook his head. 'I'm going to walk.'

She nodded slowly. 'Can I get a hug?'

'Of course.' He wished he'd offered. Not treated her like she was brittle. He knew better. Nick opened his arms and Fran stepped into them. He closed them around her, and they stood on the pavement together. She'd hugged him before – lots of times, casual, quick embraces – but this felt different. She was taller than Carrie. Thinner. And she clung to him now. For the first time he felt her breasts squashed against his chest. Her arms around his waist, where the new love handles were. Her breath was coming fast, and her chest heaved. Nick adjusted his stance. This was the closest he'd been to another human being – except his small, precious children – in so long. He could smell her hair. He wanted . . . he didn't know what he wanted.

Fran pulled back a fraction, and he felt her ragged breath on his neck. Suddenly, he just needed it to stop. He moved his hands to the tops of her arms, and deliberately stepped back, putting air between them.

A car pulled up. The driver wound down the window. 'Chamberlain.'

Fran gave a small laugh. 'Saved by the Uber.'

'Fran.' He knew he needed to say something. He just didn't know what.

She raised her hand to stop him. 'Night, Nick.'

24

Charlie silently thanked Daphne and the universe that 30 July dawned bright and sunny. Arriving in good weather seemed far preferable to any alternative scenario and more portentous of a happy time. The forecast on his iPhone wasn't bad either – the temperatures were pretty consistently predicted to be in the low twenties and there was a row of defiant yellow suns for the next ten days, bar one day midweek, which currently showed rain. He resolutely ignored it.

He was up early, keen to be the first to arrive, too excited (or anxious) to sleep well. He'd packed the car last night. Daphne would have packed the night before. Their honeymoon was the last time he'd ever packed a suitcase for himself, before he'd lost her. They'd come from different houses, of course. Their suitcases were dropped off at the pub where their reception was held, then stowed in the boot of the car to which his best man had tied tin cans. It was great, seeing all their mates in the pub, but, God, they'd been in a hurry to get away. To start married life. Sleep together. They'd driven to their Devon hotel without stopping, been shown to their room by a rotund, smiling woman, who talked too much, then gone to bed and stayed there for about eighteen hours straight. Eventually, he had lain on pillows and watched her unpack, teasing him for what he had and hadn't brought, and when he'd complained, she'd climbed back onto the bed, sat across his lap and promised him he'd never have to pack his own suitcase again. He'd joked about that alone being a good reason to marry her, even though she'd given him so many better ones. And he never had.

She'd have packed for both of them, and thus his linen shirts and casual trousers would have arrived looking smoother and fresher than they would today, but he'd done his best, at least, to match tops and bottoms as she would have done. She'd complained, with some justification, that, left to his own devices, he'd only wear beige, navy and grey. Without her, his ultra-neutral instinct prevailed most of the time, but he'd tried to pack from what he thought of as her end of his shirt rail where the stripes, pastels, and – whisper it – the odd floral print she'd bought him, or made him buy for himself, still hung. He'd closed the case and put it by the front door before he remembered swimming trunks, which took some finding, and then he'd added trainers, he wasn't sure why.

The rest of the boot he'd filled with booze and his camera equipment – including the big tripod he'd had to rummage in the loft to find. Daphne would have demanded a group shot. They'd be eleven, he'd realized. More than they'd ever been before. They'd been an uneasy eight in the last family photograph – the one she'd had framed and hung in the hallway. Him and Daphne. Alex and Laura, with a toddling Ethan, Nick and Carrie, and Scott. It had been taken at Nick's wedding. It wasn't a conventional posed picture – there was nothing formal or organized about the day Nick and Carrie had planned for themselves – but at some point the photographer must have gathered them together so casually they hadn't even known he was doing it, and snapped them laughing at something, Charlie couldn't remember what. The women were sitting on hay bales, clucking over Carrie in the middle, ethereally lovely in her lacy slip of a dress, and the men grouped behind them facing in different directions, beer glasses in hands, while Ethan was at the front, captured in a hip-thrusting, arm-waving dance move. It was a gloriously happy photograph. Even Alex and Scott looked relaxed.

And now Daphne, Alex and Carrie would be missing. Big people-shaped holes in the fabric of his family. But Bea, Delilah and Arthur might dance. Heather, Hayley and Meredith would add their American health and orthodontically enhanced smiles. Could he take a picture where they'd look as happy? Could he make it happy?

The M40 was as benevolent as the weather, and Charlie pulled in half an hour before he was due to meet the woman, Lucy Moore, he'd been speaking to on the phone for so long. There was a red Fiat parked on the gravel, and as he pulled in beside it, a young woman in a pretty flowery dress came out of the house, smiling broadly. She bounded over to the driver's door and opened it for him. 'You must be Mr Chamberlain.'

He nodded. 'Please, call me Charlie. And you're Lucy?'

She pumped his hand enthusiastically. 'I am. Lovely to meet you. Welcome.'

Her enthusiasm was contagious. She quizzed him about his journey, almost took credit for the clement weather, and insisted on giving him the tour. And the house was as good as it had looked in the pictures. Charlie was relieved. The kitchen was enormous, dominated by a long scrubbed-pine table, with a racing green Aga at one end, and a separate oven and a hob. Lucy knew her stuff, and talked incessantly, pointing out the main fridge – 'And that's the drinks fridge. There's a small chest freezer, too' – a larder cupboard, 'Nice and cool for cheese and things', and a door that led to the utility room, although she insisted on calling it the flower and boot room, 'because who comes on holiday to do washing?' She was far more charming than irritating, though. Her obvious pride in the house and all its thoughtful extras was very appealing.

There was a chintzy living room, with nice squashy sofas, lots of books, magazines and board games, then a games room, with a pool table, table tennis, and a small card table with a chessboard. She explained it used to be the dining room, but 'Who wants one of those, these days, hey?' Besides, she added, there was a small kitchen and a dining area down by the pool – that was where the caterers would set up and serve his special birthday dinner.

Outside, a wide patio had loads of wicker seating, a couple of umbrellas and a fancy-looking barbecue. A path on one side led down to the large chalet-type building that housed the swimming-pool, behind bifold glass doors that pushed all the way back 'so it feels like you're actually swimming outside, on lovely days', and the fence of the tennis court was visible down a path that ran along the other edge of the house. Lucy waved expansively at the rest of the garden. 'There's loads of places to explore or get lost . . .'

Upstairs, on the first floor, there were large, beautifully decorated bedrooms for him, Laura, and Heather and Scott, each having an en-suite with a roll-top bath, plus two other bedrooms, one set up for Nick's three children, and one a double, with a shared bathroom. They all had large, dark pieces of furniture, but bright modern curtains, and soft furnishings.

The final two bedrooms were on the top floor, in the eaves of the house – two twin rooms sharing a bathroom.

Back down on the first-floor landing, tour evidently over, Lucy asked, 'Are you deciding who goes where?'

'God, no. I'll let them duke it out among themselves, once they get here.' Charlie laughed. He'd carried a bag up the stairs on his first trip up. He picked it up. 'I'm bagsing this one, though.' He headed for a bedroom.

He'd chosen the smallest of the three, of course. Heather and Scott were the only couple, and he wanted Laura to have a nice room. He'd be more than fine in the smallest.

'Fantastic. Good for you.' Lucy laughed her jolly laugh. 'Right. Well, I'll leave you to it. Hopefully the rest of the family won't be far behind.' And she was off, mentioning for the third or fourth time that she was just next door, and that he wasn't to hesitate if he needed anything, anything at all. 'Have the most glorious, wonderful time!'

Charlie was out in the garden, confirming what he had read about the utter safety of the swimming-pool – a code keypad, and one of those clever covers that you could apparently float a hippo on – when he heard cars. Stupidly, his heart beat faster. They were here.

They'd managed to arrive together – well, Laura and Nick had. He'd warned his sons, in the vaguest of terms, that Laura would be alone, so Nick didn't express surprise at seeing Ethan in the front seat of her beaten-up Volvo and no Alex. As Charlie emerged through the hall that ran from front to back of the house, he saw Nick shaking Ethan's hand, then relenting and ruffling his hair, although he had to reach up to do it. Laura had obviously taken Arthur out of his car seat, and she was holding him on her hip while bending over to kiss Bea and Delilah.

'You're here.' He held open his arms expansively.

'Granddad!' The little girls charged at him, squealing. He managed to pick them both up, but only for long enough to squeeze them to him, and plant kisses on their gorgeous necks, before he set them down. Laura next. He registered that she looked tired. And thin. Arthur reached out, and clung to him, a human bridge between him and his daughter. Then Ethan, too old and too tall for squealing or clinging, but fond enough to submit to a manly hug. And Nick, his baby boy. The sight of him made Charlie want to cry old-man tears. His beautiful baby boy.

Scott and Heather weren't far behind. 'We'd have been on time, Dad, but there was this blasted conference call as well . . .'

'Isn't there always?' Eye-roll. 'We had to pull over on the M4.' That was Heather, immaculate and warm . . .

It wasn't quite true, although there had been a conference. Somewhere between home and the Cotswolds, Hayley had spotted a sign for Reading and the whole festival thing had reared its controversial head again. The teen who'd climbed into the car in a reasonable mood, scrolling on her phone and bobbing her head to the personal soundtrack in her ears, instantly changed.

'When are you gonna agree to let me go? Really agree. Everyone else is making plans.'

'You've got a ticket, haven't you?' There was indeed a ticket, purchased as an end-of-exams gift.

But Hayley wasn't mollified. She knew that her mother was still not certain that she would let her use it. 'Not the same thing.'

Meredith sighed dramatically, and put on her own headphones. This was a row she'd heard before, more than once.

Heather angled herself in the passenger seat so she could see Hayley. Scott tried to make eye contact, but she avoided his gaze.

'Listen, Hayley. I just don't feel good about it.'

Hayley started to speak, but Heather raised a hand to stop her. 'It's my job to protect you.' She corrected herself. 'Our job. There's a hundred things that could go wrong.'

'You're exaggerating. Hundreds of thousands of kids go. Every year.' Hayley's tone was derisory.

'And something dreadful happens *every year*.' Hayley snorted. Heather counted off hazards on her fingers. 'Drink, drugs, sex –'

'What do you even mean, sex?' Hayley interrupted, incredulous.

Scott wished he had headphones.

'I mean I need you to be safe. Can't you understand that?'

'And I will be. You did a good job, raising me. I'm sensible. I'm not an idiot.'

'It's not you I don't trust, darling. It's other people.'

Hayley tugged at her hair dramatically. 'That's just so stupid.'

'Help me out here, Scottie,' his wife implored.

Scott took a deep breath, and paused just a second too long.

'See, even Scott thinks you're crazy!' Hayley leapt into the space he'd foolishly left.

'Hey, Hayley, that's not true.' Scott sensed danger.

It was the one piece of unsolicited advice Dad had given him after a few glasses of wine at his and Heather's wedding. Always present a united front: that's the secret with teenagers. 'If I disagreed with your mother, I'd tell her in private. Never in front of you lot. Never.'

'Your mum is looking out for you.' He'd already told her that he thought it would be fine. That he thought Hayley deserved it, and that he thought it would be unkind, under the circumstances, to separate her from her new friends.

'But you'd let me go, wouldn't you?' She'd make a great lawyer, his stepdaughter.

She was hectoring the witness now. 'I'd be in a big group. Kitty's brother – and he's twenty-one – he's going, with a gang of mates, and they've told her mother they'll pitch tents with us, so there'll be blokes around to "protect us".'

Heather snorted.

He tried to defuse the situation. 'Good use of blokes there, Hayls.' It didn't work.

'We'll have phones . . .' Her voice trailed off in frustration. She sounded like she might cry.

After a period of silence, she tried again.

'I'll be the only one who isn't there?'

'The only one? Really?'

'The only one of my friends.'

Heather looked at Scott. He put his hand on her knee.

'It's taken me long enough to get in with them. You have no idea how hard it is to break in when you're late starting. No idea . . . I'm finally in. I have real friends. And you want to make me different again.'

Heather was quiet.

'That's cruel. Don't you think?'

Scott squeezed her knee.

The car spoke next: *Your destination is ahead on the left.*

Saved by the sat nav.

'Shall we shelve this for now?' He didn't want to arrive mid-row. 'We're very nearly there.'

Heather put her hand across his on her knee and squeezed back, then turned to Hayley and took a deep breath. 'You can go.'

'Really?'

'You promise me – you promise me you'll be careful?'

'I promise. You're serious, right? This is amazing.'

Heather smiled. 'Serious.'

Then she shook herself. 'Right. Game faces on. We're there.'

When Heather hugged Charlie, he smelt gardenia, powder and health. She was wearing a sleeveless pink top, and he thought her biceps, smooth and golden, were probably bigger than his.

He deliberated about kissing Hayley and Meredith,

decided to go with one on each cheek, no body contact. Daphne would have folded them into her ample bosom, complimenting, relating and loving. But he wasn't Daphne.

Everyone, even the girls, exclaimed gratifyingly, at once, about the house. Except Arthur, who whinged gently. 'He's just woken up. He's always grumpy, when a nap gets cut short,' Nick explained, as he reclaimed him.

'Him and me both,' Charlie joked.

'So quaint.' This, of course, was Heather. Only Americans described Georgian houses as quaint.

'You going to give us the tour, Dad?' Laura asked.

They filed in through the sage green front door with its brass bee knocker, luggage forgotten for now, leaving Charlie to bring up the rear. His heart felt full. They were here. They were all here. Almost all here. The someone who was missing was still his everything, her absence, still, always, a gaping hole.

25

They needed organizing but so far so good. They seemed to like it.

'Oh, my God! This place is spectacular!' Heather was the most vocal, and Scott slapped his back. 'Good job, Dad.'

Bea and Delilah pulled at Nick's arms. 'We wanna see the pool, Daddy.'

'Yes, pool, pool, pool! I brought my armbands. Are you gonna come swimming, Granddad?' Delilah couldn't stand still, but bounced from one foot to the other in excitement.

Meredith had crouched down to Arthur's level, and been rewarded by the chubby arms around her neck, so she had him proudly on one hip as they all followed Charlie around the ground floor.

'That fabric is darling!' Heather exclaimed, over a sofa in the sitting room. Laura rolled her eyes. Scott caught it and raised an eyebrow in warning. Nick saw the eyebrow and gurned at his sister. Heather remained oblivious. 'I just love the ticking, too.'

Charlie didn't know what ticking was. But he was glad she loved it.

Outside, the group split – Nick and Meredith succumbing to the children's squeals and heading to the pool, the others beyond it to the tennis court.

'Wow. This is great!'

'Full-sized and floodlights! Amazing!'

Charlie flicked the switch proudly. When one light failed to come on he felt a sense of personal failure.

Upstairs, the bedrooms were, as he had hoped, more or less self-explanatory. Heather had murmured appreciatively at hers, and more specifically at its bathroom's reassuring-looking plumbing. Cases were unloaded from cars and carried upstairs, and someone made tea.

And then it became clear that they needed organizing. This would have fallen to Daphne, and she'd have done it so stealthily that no one would realize they'd been organized, just let themselves be suffused with her calm certainty that everything was running smoothly. Meals would appear as if by magic. The car would have been full of brownies and fruit cakes and piped meringue nests. For years he had laughed at her, setting off on self-catering holidays with jars of spices. How he missed it. Charlie had arranged for caterers to come in and serve two dinners, one on his birthday, the other on the last night. He'd done his best, and all his children could see how much the holiday meant to him. But there were eleven people to feed, breakfast and lunch and supper, for a week, and the charming Fortnum's welcome hamper provided just Earl Grey teabags, rose petal jam, biscuits for cheese, some shortbread and a bottle of claret.

Someone needed to go to the supermarket.

'I'll go.' Laura hadn't grasped how quiet her life had been lately. The kitchen was cacophonous, and suddenly a potentially quiet Sainsbury's seemed quite appealing.

'I'll come with you.' Nick plonked Arthur into Charlie's arms. 'If someone can watch my kids . . .'

Meredith practically bounced. She already had Delilah's hand in hers, and Bea was hovering nearby. 'Me. I can. I will.'

Heather nodded at him, letting him know that Meredith might *think* she was in sole charge but she wasn't, and he smiled gratefully at her.

'Do we need a kitty?'

Scott shook his head. 'Just keep the receipts. We can sort it out afterwards.'

'Are we going to take turns to make a dinner?'

'Yeah, that's fair on Nick. Arthur can peel the veggies.'

'Good point. All hands on deck, then.'

Scott opened the back door. 'Sounds good. Is there a barbecue? I'm good with fire.' He pounded his chest with his fists, Tarzan-like. This was a lighter, funnier Scott, Charlie thought, which augured well for the week. He seemed more like his siblings than he had done in ages. Or, at least, more like they had been before . . .

'There's a huge one. Very superior-looking, round there on the terrace,' Charlie told him.

'Great.'

'I made brownies.' Heather was holding several large Tupperware containers. She opened the larder cupboard and put them down. She reminded him, in that moment, of Daphne. A pair of feeders. The thought made him smile.

'There's a fruit cake in this hamper.' Ethan had burrowed through the packaging and emerged with it held aloft.

'Right. Eat cake. Make tea. Oh, have you got milk?'

'Yeah. In those old-fashioned bottles in the fridge – it's

really cute. And I think it's organic. Must be from a local farm.'

'Okay. Good. We'll be back with the wherewithal to cook tonight and all day tomorrow. I can't think further ahead right now.'

'Get ice cream.' This was Bea, but Ethan nodded enthusiastically.

'Ooh, and those pod things for coffee – there's a machine.'

Hayley tutted, with all the sanctimoniousness of youth. 'They are *so* bad for the environment.'

'Not as bad for the environment as your mum is if she doesn't get a strong mug of coffee in the morning.' Scott slung an arm around Heather's shoulders, and kissed her cheek.

'Hey!' She fake-slapped him.

Hayley conceded. 'He's right. Bring capsules. Lots of them.'

'I did already.' Heather was triumphant. 'I have a case of them in the car. I saw the machine in the brochure.' Daphne again. Organized. Efficient.

After the noise in the house, it was wonderfully quiet in the car. For the first five minutes, by unspoken agreement, neither Nick nor Laura spoke much beyond the simple decisions on which way to go. The metallic voice of the sat nav sent them left out of the driveway, then three miles on the straight before the next turn. Nick drove country-lane slowly, and Laura forced herself not to want him to speed up. She was always in so much of a hurry, so quickly frustrated or enraged by other road-users. And

Nick could drive as slowly as he wanted, she reminded herself. If what had happened to him had happened to her she might never have sat in a car again.

When Nick began a conversation, there was a hint of forced gaiety. 'Bit of a turn-around, huh? You and me on our own, Scott playing happy families.'

'I'm glad for him.' The enormity of Nick's aloneness was not easy to make light of, if you weren't Nick, and no one would have believed him if he'd tried.

'Me too. It's just weird . . .'

'I know what you mean.'

Nick took his eyes off the road to glance at his sister. 'How come you didn't tell me yourself about Alex?'

Laura shrugged. She'd been half expecting the question. She assumed he knew the answer – shame, embarrassment, humiliation, exhaustion, the inability to talk without sobbing or hissing . . .

'Have I been so far up my own arse that you couldn't tell me?' There was a note of genuine hurt in his question. They'd always been the closest of the three, more alike than they were to Scott. Ripples of damage – things like this caused small waves of ever-diluting pain around everyone involved, however peripherally. The collateral damage of pursuing your own happiness without regard for the happiness of other people. Selfish, selfish bastard.

She smiled weakly. 'No. Of course not. Not that you aren't completely allowed to be, by the way. I've been that much up my own.'

'I'm really sorry about it.'

'Are you?' She didn't mean to sound so arch. She wondered what Dad had told him, how much detail he knew.

'Shouldn't I be?' Nick wasn't pulling any punches.

Laura sighed. 'I don't know.' Which was honest at least.

Another mile of silence. She knew Nick was giving her room to speak, but she had nothing to say.

Changing the subject, at last, she asked, 'How are you doing?'

'Don't you do that.'

'Ask how you are?'

'Ask how I am in *that* voice. The one dripping with pity.'

She punched his arm. 'It's dripping with sympathy.'

'Is that significantly different? Really?'

'I think so, yeah.'

'Then I'm doing okay, thanks.'

'Don't *you* do that.' She smiled sideways at him. 'Are you okay-okay or okay-shitty really?'

Nick blew out his cheeks out and exhaled slowly. 'Depends on the day, Sis. Or the time of day.'

She nodded understanding. It was like that, grief. Tidal. Seasonal. 'The kids look fab.'

He laughed grimly. 'Oh, I've mastered the hair and co-ordinating outfits. You could check behind their ears and you wouldn't find dirt. They brush their teeth for two minutes too. I have an egg-timer in the bathroom. I can even do plaits.' Fran had taught him, early on. She'd used the long macramé strings from a hippie-ish dreamcatcher Carrie had loved and he had gently mocked, when she'd bought it to hang in Delilah's nursery. Over a bottle of red, Fran had taught him patiently how to pull the strands over each other until he could do something resembling the styles Carrie used to create for Bea each morning before school. They still weren't great, but they were plaits. A piece of simple mechanical continuity for Bea, who couldn't see the wonky results, just felt his brush and his hands in her hair in the morning.

'That stuff matters.'

'I don't know if it does.'

'It does. Routine does. They're not just neat, Nick, your babies. That's not what I meant. They seem good. They're . . . smiley.'

She would never forget the tiny pale faces of Bea and Delilah, when it had first happened. They hadn't come to the funeral. She remembered that he'd worried himself sick about whether they should be there or not – read conflicting advice, canvassed opinion. In the end, he didn't take them for the one simple dreadful reason that he didn't trust himself not to weep, and he couldn't bear them to see that. Almost went back for them once or twice. They'd stayed with a coterie of kind, appalled mothers from school, who'd brought their own children around to cocoon them in something approximating normal. But, tiny as they were, they knew it wasn't.

Today's little girls had been in better shape than that, much better, wonky plaits notwithstanding.

'They're wildly excited to be here.'

'And you?'

'Truth: I'm not wildly excited by anything any more. But I know I could use the break from all the single-parenting. Keeping all the balls in the air because I'm so bloody terrified of dropping one. I'm knackered. Deep-down-in-my-bones tired. The idea of having some help with the kids . . .'

'I get it. I could sleep for a week.' It was a different kind of grief, and there was the fear, too, about Ethan. She couldn't tell him, and she'd never compare, but she understood. The net result was evidently the same. A fatigue so profound it couldn't really be described. 'Do you think anyone would mind?' She laughed.

'With Heather chuntering on, it's possible no one would notice.' Nick sniggered.

Laura was glad to move on to a lighter subject. 'Still not quite sure what to make of her . . . She's so shiny.'

'Do you think we'll get to see her without hair and makeup this week?'

'I reckon she sleeps in it.'

'Nah. There'll be, like, a twelve-step cleansing routine. And flossing. Lots of flossing.'

'Oh, we're horrid. Are we so small-minded that we can't get our heads around Scott being married after all these years? Or a stepfather. Or are we just jingoistic? Is it because she's a *foreigner*?'

'No. God, no. We're not *those* people. I think it's because we don't entirely trust her motives.'

'Where do we get the nerve? That means we don't trust Scott to make smart decisions. He's spent his life making smart decisions. Unlike me.'

'Didn't mean that.'

'Well, it's true, isn't it? None of you ever really liked Alex.'

Nick took a moment to speak. 'That's not fair.'

Laura glared at him, and he squirmed, then conceded. 'Okay. Not a lot.'

'I gave up work, all my independence, everything when I married him.'

'Oh, come on. You make that sound unusual. Millions of people do it. And millions of people get divorced.'

'You never would have done, would you?'

Nick pursed his lips. 'No. I don't think so.'

'Sorry.'

'It's fine. You don't have to treat me like I'm breakable. I'm still here, so I can't be. So, you've split up. I'm a widower. Net results the same. Us, alone. Scott, loved up. He can't keep his hands off her – did you see?'

'Ew. Maybe we're just jealous.'

'Oh, I'll hold my hand up to that. I'm so, so, so bloody jealous.'

'Do you hate being alone?'

'I hate being without her. I don't know if that's the same thing.' Nick thought, very briefly, of Fran, and how she'd felt in his arms outside the restaurant.

He banged the steering wheel. 'Enough! Enough of this maudlin crap. The sun is shining. Let's not do this now. Let's put the radio on and pretend we're happy.'

Laura fumbled with the knobs, unfamiliar with Nick's car. She hit the right one, and music filled the car. Nineties Queen. They spontaneously started shouting along, windows down, pretending.

26

Meredith and Heather had taken Nick's three to the climbing frame in the garden. Scott and Charlie were fiddling with the barbecue. Nick and his mum weren't back from the supermarket yet. Upstairs, Ethan lay on the narrow single bed in the twin room he'd been allocated, his hands behind his head. He'd thrown his bag onto the other bed. They were meant for kids, the beds. Little kids – his feet were almost hanging off the end. The duvet cover was kiddish too – bright stripes, like a deckchair – and there were hooks on the back of the door like dog tails. The floor below, where everyone else was sleeping, was for the grown-ups. He was sentenced to what he thought of as the nursery floor. He could hear the little kids through the window, and the low murmur of his granddad speaking with Scott. It was incredibly quiet here. They were miles from anywhere. His room was at the top of the house, and the ceiling sloped so he could stand upright only in part of the room. Scott's stepdaughters were in an almost identical room opposite, and there was a bathroom between the two. That meant sharing, a thought he didn't relish. He'd barely even met them. Now he had to share a bloody toilet with them.

They'd both said he had to come, Mum and Dad. He didn't know where to put himself, so he might as well put himself here. Mum had had to come – she'd promised

Granddad. And Dad was away with Genevieve on some fancy Italian holiday. The subtext was that they wouldn't dream of leaving him home by himself. So here he was.

My wild summer, he thought ruefully. Stuck in the middle of nowhere with a bunch of babies and relatives. Woo-hoo. Home for results. The Reading Festival was 'under discussion', whatever that meant. He had a ticket – he'd bought it before everything had gone off. He just didn't know if they were going to let him use it.

The exams had gone by in a weird blur, in the end. You thought they'd never be over and then they just were. God only knew what he was going to get. Study leave had been self-imposed exile. His mates had suggested getting together to run through flashcards or, more likely, to play *Call of Duty*. He never told his mum anyone invited him anywhere, and he'd lied to his mates, telling them she was being a total bitch and not letting him go out at all. They'd more or less stopped asking. She didn't want him studying alone up in his bedroom so they'd made half of the kitchen table a desk he didn't have to clear at the end of the day, and he'd worked there. Sat there, at least. She'd fed him endless snacks. She'd kissed the top of his head nearly every time she walked past, and although he often brushed the kiss away, like swatting a fly, he was glad of it. He was her project again. He knew how worried and protective she was, and while on one level he was sorry he was putting her through that, he secretly liked the feeling of being at the centre of her universe again. It was comforting and familiar.

She and Dad were getting on better, too. He didn't think they'd get back together or anything like that, but they were talking. They were Team Ethan. More like it used to be.

He hadn't seen Saskia that whole time, in real life, or on social media. He'd been blocked on all her accounts. He imagined Rupert standing over her, foaming at the mouth, making her delete him over and over again. No Facebook, no Instagram, no Snapchat. He hadn't heard her voice. He had videos of her on his phone. Zooming in and out on her face, laughing. In one she blew him a kiss, sunlight making her squint. He had watched them all incessantly at first. Now he could hardly bear to.

He'd probably stuffed up the exams. Mum kept saying it was okay. That he'd be fine. That, even if he wasn't fine, if he got five A–C grades he could just move on to his A levels and put them behind him. He wasn't sure he believed she and Dad really wouldn't lose their minds if he got five Cs. He'd been predicted a mix of As and Bs. Like, ten of them. Maybe some A*s on a good day, some of his teachers had said, in the final parents' evening before study leave. Not that he hadn't tried. There'd been whole days when he'd buried himself deeply in revision. Just to distract himself.

Saskia was cleverer than him, maybe way cleverer. She was – she had been – talking about Oxbridge, or Durham. Her dad had been at Oxford, and she knew he wanted her to apply to his old college, if she had the grades. But she said if she went at all, she'd be more likely to choose Cambridge, and make somewhere just hers, not a family thing. She knew what she wanted to do – political sciences, something like that. She listened to Radio 4 and read her dad's copy of the *Spectator*. Ethan had joked that he got smarter just being with her.

They'd been at some of the same exams. Seeing her walk in had been a jolt. She'd had loads cut off her hair, and it sat just on her shoulders now. She'd smiled at him, a pinched, regretful smile, but he couldn't read anything more in her face. She looked pale and worried. But her mum had driven her to all of them, and come back to collect her. His mum had offered, but he'd said no, that the fresh air and short walk would clear his head before and after a paper. Maybe he'd hoped he'd get to see her, to talk even. But Claudia was there, hovering in her estate car, and Saskia came in just before the exam started, and scuttled off the moment the papers were collected. She always sat behind him in the rows of desks lined up in the sports hall, near the exit, because of their surnames, and he was glad about that. He wouldn't have been able to concentrate if he'd been able to look at her. He always spun around, the moment the invigilator took his paper off his desk, but she was always gone.

He missed her. He missed the way she smelt, and felt, and sounded. In bed, at night, when he couldn't sleep, he went over conversations the two of them had had, played his memories of her in his head, tried not to feel resentment towards her for following her parents' diktats so faithfully.

He might have stayed in the room all afternoon, but hunger moved him. He and Mum had stopped at Chieveley Services for sandwiches and coffee, but that had been ages ago. In the kitchen the welcome pack yielded a box of shortbread: he took three, and wandered onto the back patio, squinting at the sun like a nocturnal animal.

Outside, Hayley, his sort-of cousin, was swinging on a

chair on the patio, reading a book. Every other swing, she let her toes catch on the paving, then pushed herself off again. Her toenails were neon green, and her legs were very brown. She looked at him over the top of the paperback as he walked past, and threw himself down onto a second swing chair. He nodded to her, but didn't take off his headphones. He tried to keep his chair still, but it resisted him.

After a minute or two, Hayley laid her book on her stomach and looked at him purposefully, so he slid the headphones onto his neck.

'What are you listening to?'

'Oasis.'

She wrinkled her nose. 'Aren't they old?'

'They're brilliant.'

She raised a cynical eyebrow, but didn't argue.

It was his turn to ask a question. She was sort of waiting for him to say something. 'What do you like, then?'

'All kinds of stuff. Grime. R&B. Ariana Grande . . .'

'You're kidding, right?'

She smirked. 'Just testing. Not Ariana Grande.'

'Thank fuck for that.'

'I wouldn't let Mere hear you say that. Major fan.'

Ethan grimaced. 'What you reading, then?'

Hayley picked up the book, held it out towards him. '*To Kill a Mockingbird*. Do you know it?'

'"You never really understand a person until you consider things from his point of view – until you climb inside of his skin and walk around in it . . ."'

Hayley sat forward excitedly. 'Wow! You do know it.'

'Yes.' He was glad of it, too. He knew Hayley and her

sister were at a fancy private school in Surrey. At their mum's wedding to his uncle, he'd thought he'd got a touch of smug arrogance off them – he couldn't have pinpointed what or how, but he knew enough kids like that to recognize it. It might have been shyness, he supposed.

'Did you do it for GCSE this summer?' She'd realized, and Ethan felt deflated. He'd quite liked her being impressed.

'Yeah. But I'd read it before.' This was not true, but definitely impossible to prove.

'Me too.' This, he suspected, was the truth.

'And you're reading it again?'

'I like rereading. And this is my favourite. I'm going to call my daughter Scout. If I have one . . .'

Even in his soppiest thoughts about Saskia, or their dopiest conversations, they had not covered baby names. 'Cool.'

'How'd you do, do you think?'

Ethan shrugged. 'Really trying not to think about it.'

'Me too.' He didn't believe that. She looked clever. Private-school kids got spoon-fed everything, didn't they? Off a silver spoon.

'Which question did you do?'

God. He wished he hadn't started, but now he had to finish. The excruciating conversation about which question they'd both answered lasted a few minutes, then petered out, mercifully.

Ethan wondered if it would be rude to put his headphones back on.

Hayley carried on swinging. 'Have you got a girlfriend?'

He eyed her suspiciously. Did she know? But she didn't

look sly. Just nosy. And did he? He supposed not. 'Not right now, not really . . . You?'

'Girls' school.'

Which was not really an answer.

He was about to slip his headphones back on and put them both out of their misery when he heard his mother shouting from inside the house for help to unload the car. He nodded at Hayley, not sure they had made much progress, and escaped.

27

In the kitchen, Heather had definitely taken charge. The boys had carried the shopping in, and now Scott was loading tonic water, white wine and Diet Coke into a drinks fridge in the corner by the window. Nick and Dad were nowhere to be seen, and Ethan had made himself scarce too.

'I see gender roles are very much alive and well in my family.' Laura hadn't meant it to sound quite so snippy.

Heather smiled at her, but it was brief and not entirely genuine. 'Or maybe they thought it would be too crowded in here.' She'd made Laura feel petty.

To show she didn't really mind, Laura grabbed a few boxes of cereal from the table in the centre of the room where the boys had left them, and began to put them into an empty cupboard.

'Oh, Laura, I think it might actually work better if we just, you know, left the cereals out on that dresser – where the gap is? That way everyone can help themselves in the morning and not get in the way of the kettle and the coffee machine, right?'

She might very well be right. But she was annoying as well.

'What *would* you like me to do?' And this time Laura *had* meant her voice to sound just a tiny bit sarcastic. If Heather heard it, and Scott certainly did – he stiffened – but, then, he'd been hearing it for more than forty years, she chose to ignore it, flashing a megawatt smile at Laura.

'You know what, Laura, you're just so sweet. But I'm fine to do this. Honestly. I'm all unpacked upstairs. You haven't had a chance. Let me do this.'

She'd brought an apron – a chalky white linen apron, the kind like a pinafore. An apron. She unfolded it, slipped her arms through the straps and smoothed it down. 'If you want to do something, maybe you could make us all a nice cuppa.' It sounded odd in her accent. Very Dick Van Dyke in *Mary Poppins*.

Scott coughed. Laura wasn't sure which one of them was getting a warning.

She took a deep breath and picked up the kettle, wonderfully uncrowded by cereal boxes. 'Great idea.'

It might be a very long ten days.

In the late afternoon, groceries put away, Laura took a long bath, which she never did at home. She hadn't been very good at keeping still lately. Buzzed around like a demented fly. She tried to read a book but couldn't concentrate. An interiors magazine she'd found downstairs in the sitting room didn't interest her either. Her attention span was pathetically short. She threw it onto the bath mat and lay back in the hot water, her eyes closed, concentrating on breathing slowly in and out. Not engaging with the thoughts.

The water had been too hot, and the air outside was still very warm. She couldn't be bothered to dress up. She ran a brush through her hair, and pulled on a linen shift that she should have hung up when she unpacked, but she didn't bother with makeup or jewellery, although she would undoubtedly feel dowdy next to Heather. And old next to Hayley. She didn't really care.

Ethan was in his room at the top of the house. She'd tried to coax him out, but he said he'd come down when the food was ready, and his face was set in a way she knew made it pointless to argue. Poor angry, lost kid. She wanted to hug him. All the time. And she had to stop herself.

Downstairs, in the kitchen, Charlie was pouring gin and tonic, taking the business of slicing lemons and adding a sprig of rosemary to the glass very seriously. He held up the bottle. It was Homebrew 2. Laura smiled, and put her arm around his shoulders briefly.

'Mixologist!'

'Trust me – they taste great. I meant to bring some juniper berries too.' They clinked glasses and Laura sipped.

'Where is everyone?'

Charlie shushed and pointed at the sitting room. Laura stuck her head around the door and saw Nick's kids sprawled across Meredith, thumbs in, in front of the television, watching *Frozen*.

'I think Heather and Hayley are still on the tennis court.'

'God. So keen.' But she tried not to sound judgemental. She didn't want to rock any boats.

'And your brothers are having a testosterone-off at the barbecue. Why do you think I'm making so busy with the gin?'

Outside, too many cooks were definitely spoiling the broth. Or, at least, worrying the fire. They'd always been this way, her brothers. She'd been born almost exactly between the two of them, and had played referee over and over throughout their childhood. Scott was clever, Nick dogged and determined. They both seemed pretty certain they knew best about the damn barbecue, although the bickering sounded more good-natured than snarky.

She left them to it and came back inside. Then, having made her contribution by artfully pouring gourmet salad from a plastic bag into a large glass bowl, searching out a breadboard and a serrated knife for the four French sticks, she poured herself a second large gin and tonic, which might or might not have been a good idea, and snuck away. She walked past the climbing frame to the bottom of the garden, where there was a gate. The pool and the tennis court were the other way, so no one had explored in this direction. She could hear tennis balls being thwacked, and Heather offering enthusiastic encouragement. She looked back to see if she'd been missed, but she hadn't. Before she'd wandered outside, Charlie had taken his gin to the sofa, where Bea was earnestly explaining to him who Olaf and Anna were looking for. Opening the gate, she wandered through and, skirting the edge of a small field, made her way to what was obviously the vegetable garden the brochure had boasted of. There was an old-style green-house, and a load of neat raised beds formed from railway sleepers. It was all very Marie Antoinette, and she wondered who ate the produce. Maybe they were supposed to, and the bagged salad from the supermarket was an affront.

There was a mossy Lutyens bench bathed in the last of the apricot evening sunshine. Laura plonked herself down in the middle of it, drew her legs up underneath her dress to sit comfortably cross-legged, and rested her cool glass against her sternum, letting the sun warm her face, her eyes closed. Being still.

When she opened them again, it was because she had sensed that someone else was there. She saw the shadow of a man, at first, and then he came fully into view. He was smiling. 'I'm sorry. I didn't mean to disturb you. You look very peaceful.'

She uncrossed her legs, and sat upright, feeling self-conscious. 'It's fine.' She hadn't meant to sound so brittle. She forced a smile.

'Are you staying at the house?'

She wondered if she wasn't supposed to be there. 'Yes. Sorry. I arrived earlier. I'm with the Chamberlain family.' She sounded foolishly formal.

He walked towards her with his hand outstretched. She moved forward to shake it. Just before she took it, he looked at it, wiped it against the shorts he was wearing. 'Sorry. Sorry. I'm filthy.'

'It's fine.' She smiled, and they shook hands.

'That's two fines and two sorrys so far. We must both be English.'

He was laughing at her, his voice full of amusement. 'Sorry.' Now they both laughed.

'I'm Joe.'

He was nice-looking. Handsome. Mel might even have said he was a 'phwoar out of ten', which was a favourite expression of hers. Not crazily younger than her, but a bit, maybe. It was harder to tell with blokes. Life was a bit less cruel to them on the looks front. He had a deep tan, but white lines around his eyes – from squinting without sunglasses on, or maybe from smiling. There was blond hair on his chest – it was sprouting out from the V of his T-shirt. He was good-looking enough, she realized, to make her very slightly regret not blow-drying her hair and slicking on mascara.

'Laura.'

'It's good to meet you, Laura. Enjoying everything so far?'

She nodded enthusiastically, endlessly polite. 'Absolutely. It's a beautiful place.'

'Yes, it is.'

'Do you . . . ?' She didn't want to ask him if he worked there. Which was ridiculous. God, she was bad at small-talk. Casual conversation. It wasn't rocket science. She felt awkward.

'Do I work here? Yes. Among other things.' He apparently didn't find it a strange question at all.

She nodded. That was a bit enigmatic. But he wasn't weird – if her radar was still at all reliable. He was one of those quietly confident people she rather envied. Daphne would have described him as comfortable in his skin. You could just tell, right away.

'I live over there,' He gestured behind him. 'On the farm. Looking after this garden is a sideline, really. I do it because I enjoy it.'

'I can tell. It's great.'

'You're a gardener?'

She shook her head. 'I kill stuff. Houseplants, mainly.' She shrugged ruefully. 'But I like to see a beautiful garden. My dad grew a few veggies, when we were kids, but nothing like this. It's fantastic.'

'Ah, it's going over a bit now. Looked its best in June.'

She couldn't think of an interesting response.

'Have you come in search of something for supper?'

'Well . . .'

'There's some chard that's just right. Lovely in a salad. Some tomatoes too – come on.'

She followed him. 'Sounds amazing.'

'Tastes better than what you can buy in plastic.'

Laura thought guiltily of the bagged leaves.

'I didn't bring anything to put things in . . . Stupid.' She might as well go along with his suggestion that she had been foraging. Better that, perhaps, than aimlessly wandering. Or hiding.

Again, he was amused by her. His eyes twinkled. 'No problem. I'll find you a trug. Hang on.'

He disappeared briefly into the greenhouse, emerging with a small basket. 'Here you go.' She took it and walked behind him – the path here was too narrow to go side by side.

He didn't talk much while they harvested the food. The tomatoes smelt amazing, their red skins still warm. She liked that he was quiet. It didn't feel weird: he just wasn't one of those people who needed to fill every space with inanities.

When they'd finished filling the trug, he stood up and back. 'There. That looks good.'

'It looks delicious. Thank you.'

He gave a small bow, an old-fashioned gesture. 'You're very welcome. Enjoy.'

She took two steps backwards from him, then slowly turned and made her way towards the gate that led to the others.

'Will I see you down here again?'

She spun around. He was standing on the path, watching her. 'We're here for ten days.'

'So, yes.' He smiled, and the white lines disappeared into his tan. 'I'll look forward to it.'

She turned back towards her family. She was through the gate before she realized she was smiling.

28

It was dark outside, with an unpolluted starry sky. Dinner had been eaten and cleared away, many hands making light work. The others were still congregated around the large wicker table on the patio, but Nick was upstairs, watching his babies. They'd fallen immediately to sleep. He'd been happy to relax the routine and abandon bedtime, but they'd had other ideas, exhausted by swimming and running around the lawn, so enormous compared to theirs at home. So he'd brought them up, and made them all brush their teeth, and now they were in his king-size bed, duvet thrown back, thumbs in. He'd lift them later, and carry them to the room next door. It was ironic. They'd been split up at home, and now here they were reunited – the two rooms were joined by double doors, open now – there was a single day bed in the corner of the other space, with a trundle pulled out and made up for the girls, and an ornate metal cot for Arthur. He supposed for visitors with fewer children, this served as a sort of private sitting room. Now, within just a few hours, it looked like a post-rummage jumble sale. Meredith had supervised the retrieval of swimwear, and then pyjamas. Everything else he'd packed for the week appeared to be strewn across the floor between the two spaces. He'd have to move everything to close the doors.

So, yet again, they'd all be together. He wondered what Fran would say.

Fran.

They hadn't spoken since the dinner.

Busying himself with preparations to come away, frantically trying to get up to date with work so he needn't do any over the next ten days, trying to remember what they'd all need while they were here, and what had to happen at home while they weren't was a kind of multi-tasking he wasn't used to. He hadn't realized it had been a while since he and Fran were in touch. Longer, probably, than they'd gone without speaking since Carrie died. Except he sort of had known. He'd probably been avoiding her. It had been weird and awkward outside the restaurant, and he didn't know how to erase that bit and get back to what they were before it had happened. He'd half hoped she would do that for them both. He was used to her fixing things. But she hadn't called him. And now he felt a bit of a shit about it.

Guilt pricked at him.

He picked up his mobile, searched for her name among his contacts. His finger hovered above the call button, and then he made himself press it.

She didn't answer. Four rings and then he went to voicemail. He wasn't ready to leave a message – he hadn't known what he was going to say when he heard her voice, so he certainly wasn't prepared to converse with the synthesized one speaking to him now.

'Ah. Um. Um. Hi, Fran. It's me. Nick . . .' He hit himself on the forehead. Awkward bugger. Like she wouldn't know it was him. 'All settled in here. The kids have lapsed into a coma. Must be the country air. Just . . . checking in . . . Think you're off yourself, sometime.' He didn't know how to end the message. 'So . . . um . . . if I haven't missed you, have a great time. Call me back. Or not. Um. Yep. Talk soon. Lots of love.'

God. Ridiculous. He switched the phone to silent so it wouldn't wake the kids.

He heard the murmur of chat wafting up from downstairs. He ought to go back. He wasn't sure he could face it. The kids looked so cosy. He leant back against the headboard and closed his eyes for a moment. Fatal. Perhaps he could leave them there, and just bed down in the truckle. He was tired. But he hadn't said goodnight to everyone, and he didn't want to be rude. He went to the loo, then splashed some cold water on his face, determined to manage another half-hour at least.

When he came out, his phone screen was silently lit. Fran. He took the handset back into the bathroom, gently pushed the door closed, and perched on the edge of the roll-top bath. 'Fran?'

'Nick. Hi! Did you just call me?'

She sounded perfectly normal. 'Yeah. Sorry. Did I disturb?'

'Absolutely. Thank God. How are you?'

Her voice was happy and light. Possibly even very slightly slurred.

'Good. Here in the sunny Cotswolds . . .'

'Snap.'

'Oh. You're away too. I thought it was nowish . . .'

'Yep. Yurt me up, Scotty. Got here yesterday.'

'How is it?'

'Honestly? Not as basic as I'd feared. More basic than I'd have chosen.'

He laughed.

'Much as I'd like to think I'm a roughing-it, back-to-nature girl, I think I may just have to admit to being a power-shower four-hundred-thread-count-as-long-as-I-don't-have-to-iron-the-sheets kinda girl.'

'You're not in an actual tent, are you?'

'Well. Yes and no. It's glamping, darling. So it's a tent, but not Bear Grylls-style. It's sort of shabby chic. Shabby chic meets gap year in India . . .'

'I kind of get it.'

'You know who'd love it? Carrie would have loved it.'

He got the feeling she'd invoked her on purpose. Inserted her for the normality of it. But she was probably right. Sounded straight up Carrie's alley. 'Are there lots of like-minded people around, at least?'

'Bit soon to tell. How about yours?'

'Well, the people are all family. The house is quite grand.'

'Shut up. You've got four-hundred-thread-count sheets, haven't you, you jammy bugger?'

He laughed again. 'Very possibly. I've also got to worry about the kids scratching antiques and drawing on fancy-wallpaper walls, though.'

'*Quelle horreur.* My heart bleeds.'

He'd missed her. Missed the banter. She always brought him up a level, from the depths he felt himself fighting not to sink into. She got to ignore the huge Carrie-shaped elephant in his room because she knew – better than almost anyone – just how big it was. And that normality mattered to him. It was probably why the weird physical thing – whatever it was – that had happened between them had freaked him out so much. He couldn't risk losing her by getting things confused, by messing them up. She was too important to him.

'I'm over here drinking wine from a box. From an actual box. With a spout, Nick. And you're over there playing at Lord Grantham in *Downton Abbey*. What is wrong with this picture?'

'We should meet up.' He'd said it before he'd thought. He wanted to see her.

'Really?'

'With the kids.' For the avoidance of confusion. For a moment she didn't answer, and he wondered if she was trying to come up with an excuse not to. 'Why not?' he dared her.

She hesitated for just a second. Then he heard the smile in her voice. 'Yeah. Why not? That'd be fun.'

'Okay. Let's, then. Why don't you text me the details of where you're staying? I'll figure out what might work – try to find somewhere the kids would like, halfway between us.'

'You sure?'

'Yeah. I'll gift the other adults here a kid-free afternoon. A lot of highbrow paperbacks got splashed around the pool this afternoon.'

'You just had to get the pool in, didn't you?' But she was still smiling. He could hear it. 'You do that, Nick. I gotta go. I've had to walk to the edge of a field to get a good signal. Better get back to the yurt and make sure the kids haven't been stolen by dingos.'

'Leave it with me. Talk to you tomorrow. Don't fall into the fire on your way to the toilet block in the middle of the night.'

'Piss off.'

Normal service, apparently, resumed. Thank God.

29

Charlie was surprised to realize he'd slept very well. That didn't happen often any more. He seemed to sleep lightly, waking at small sounds and changes in light, to go to the loo once or twice, or plagued by restless legs and cramping toes. Sometimes he was awake for two or three hours, listening to the World Service, and then he'd fall into a deep sleep from which he awoke, almost hung-over, after nine, which felt lazy. Maybe it was the country air, or the relief of everyone having arrived safely and relatively happily, or the three or four drinks he'd had last night, two or three more than he was used to. It was nine thirty. He stretched at the window, and enjoyed the gentle breeze on his skin, before showering and dressing. The others might appear in pyjamas or tracksuits but he was from a generation that needed to be dressed to face the world.

Lucy had told Charlie she lived with her husband Col in a cottage on the edge of the grounds. She'd said he could pop round, if he needed anything. He had telephone numbers – a landline and a mobile – but since she'd offered, and since he fancied a walk, Charlie strolled over to ask about the floodlights on the tennis court. He might carry on to the village, to the newsagent, to buy a pile of papers. Everyone seemed to read them on their phones now, but he preferred a paper. He wasn't sure which they took. You couldn't tell, could you, when they studied their phones? He amused himself by reckoning the *FT* for Scott, the *Mail* for Heather, *The Times* for Laura and the *Guardian* for Nick. But he might be wrong. He wouldn't like to voice the guesses aloud. He liked the rustle, and the browsability of newsprint, and he really didn't like constantly pushing buttons on his phone with his thumbs. His family wouldn't either, if they knew anything about arthritis. And they were going to know about arthritis, the way they carried on – the kids especially – their thumbs constantly working the keys of their damn devices.

He could hear church bells – a sound he'd always loved, but realized he didn't hear much, these days. Daphne had arranged for a ring of them, a full glorious forty-five minutes, on the morning of their wedding all those years ago. She hadn't told him – it had been a wonderful surprise. She'd even tried to persuade him to try campanology. He'd chosen home-brewing instead, much to her chagrin, back in the days before craft beer, when it meant a hoppy smell emanating from plastic vats in the bathroom and a vile yet potent result. A couple of years before she died, Scott had given him 'a gin experience' for his birthday: he and Daphne had mixed botanicals in a smart London hotel, overseen by an exuberant gin-maker, producing his own bespoke spirit that Daphne had christened Homebrew 2, the gin they had been drinking last night.

The bells were lovely. He felt light and cheerful as he strolled. So far, so good. Things had seemed easy enough yesterday when everyone had arrived – jolly, even. They had all mucked in. The kids were a great help, distractingly noisy and demanding. The bigger kids had even been chatting – he'd seen them.

Lucy's cottage was as appealing as the bigger house but in a completely different way. The latter was solid and even quite grand. This one was utterly pretty. They were both lovely places in this very lovely part of the world, where there were still bells. The garden was the star of the show here – it was clearly a real labour of love. Daphne would have been enchanted by it: she had loved cottage gardens. Butterflies fluttered in swathes of buddleia in front of towering sunflowers, and a bed of vividly coloured dahlias was immaculately staked and pruned. There were galvanized metal and terracotta pots of geraniums, pinks and zinnias by the front door, and the knocker was a brass bee, like the one at the main house. The effect was gloriously old-fashioned and welcoming.

Lucy answered the door in a blue linen sundress, her hair piled on her head and contained by a colourful scarf. She was as warm and friendly as she had been the day before. She seemed unperturbed by his intrusion, apologizing unnecessarily for the floodlight issue, and promising to call the electrician first thing on Monday. She was just making tea, she said – her husband Col was mowing the lawn – would he like to join them? Something about her open face made him say yes – it didn't feel as if she was just being polite. Why not?

Col, it seemed, was just like her in temperament, if not in physicality – he was a big bear of a man, with a shock of salt-and-pepper hair. He abandoned the mower gratefully when Charlie and Lucy rounded the corner with a tea tray, and came over to the shaded patio, smiling broadly. He shook Charlie's hand warmly, apologizing for his sweaty, dishevelled appearance, and took a seat, stretching his back and crossing his arms behind his head, tilting his face towards the sun. Lucy lightly stroked his arm as she passed him – the affectionate gesture touched Charlie.

'Is everything all right up at the house?'

'It's wonderful. Living up to expectations and some.'

'Glad to hear it. It's a fantastic old place. They did a beautiful job, too, renovating it.'

Charlie nodded agreement. 'Who actually owns it?'

'It's a couple. They have a small chain of clothing shops in London, the south-east. As far as Cheltenham, actually. This was a bit of a project for them. I think she likes renovations, to be honest. They bought this off the old boy who'd lived here for ever about five years ago. He couldn't cope with it – the place was getting quite dilapidated. He went into a home, to be nearer to one of his kids.'

'I'm sorry.' That was probably Charlie's greatest fear, the dreaded care home.

Col smiled and nodded. 'He died quite soon – really soon – afterwards. Which was probably what he would have chosen. His wife had died. He'd had enough.'

Charlie knew exactly what he meant.

Lucy looked slightly anxious, keen to change the subject. 'One of the floodlights isn't working,' she said.

'Oh, no.' Col sat forward. 'Want me to come and have a look at it?'

'No, no. No need. Certainly isn't urgent. I absolutely don't want to disrupt your weekend.'

'I'll call Ben in the morning.' Lucy smiled. 'I'm sure he can sort it.'

Col nodded. 'Ben's a great guy. Knows what he's doing. Have you got keen players?'

'My daughter-in-law, Heather, is, I think. She's very keen for her daughters to play too, although I'm not sure they're quite as gung-ho.'

Col grinned. 'Got you. Teenagers, are they?'

'They most certainly are.' This wasn't entirely fair on Meredith, who was being Mary Poppins to the smaller children as he spoke, but he reasoned they didn't need to hear the minutiae of his family dynamics.

They talked easily for a while longer. Col was an accountant at a practice in Cheltenham. He was evidently a few years older than Lucy. He'd bought the cottage before he'd met her several years ago, and she'd moved in with him before she'd got the job as manager at the house. 'Not that it looked much like this, before she arrived, inside or out. Classic bachelor pad.' His pride in her was evident.

'It's a beautiful home.'

'The bones were always there, but I'd never had the time, the inclination or the vision to make it look like it should – like it does now. That's where this one came in.' He gestured towards Lucy, who beamed at the compliment.

'So it all worked out beautifully.' She smiled lovingly at Col. 'Dream man, dream house.'

Col groaned theatrically. 'Oh, God. Cringe.' But his face said otherwise. 'Sorry, Charlie. I'm well aware that we're nauseatingly happy.'

'Why would you apologize for that? I was nauseatingly happy with my wife. It's rather nice to be in the orbit of nauseatingly happy, just for a while.'

For a moment or two the three of them sat in the pretty garden, each looking out at the bucolic scene, sipping their tea. Charlie hoped the silence wasn't uncomfortable. He hadn't meant to make it so.

Lucy broke the quiet by asking if he'd like his tea topped up. What would the English do without their tea and their tea talk? He didn't want any more, really, but it was easier to acquiesce and let her fuss with the teapot and milk jug.

'Lucy says you're with your family for the week.'

'That's right. Ten days, actually.'

'So who is with you?'

'All three of my kids with their families.'

Col waited, seeming to want to hear more. Perhaps they were interested in the minutiae after all. 'My eldest son, Scott. He married rather late, found himself with an instant family.'

'The tennis players?' Lucy was back now, and had obviously been paying attention, when he introduced them all yesterday.

'Exactly. Heather is American.' This was apropos of nothing. Charlie realized he probably needn't have mentioned it. It made him sound quite old and rather parochial. 'My other son, Nick – he's the youngest. He's the father of the three small people – he lost his wife, Carrie, a year ago. He's a widower.' It was a bloody awful word.

'Oh, God. That's awful.' Lucy's hand flew to her mouth, her shock real. There was nothing you could really say. 'I'm so sorry.'

'Thank you.' He'd said that a lot. What else might fit the moment? Every time he'd said it in the twelve months since it had happened, the shock and horror of it was reflected back at him from the face of whoever heard it, and each time it reverberated with him anew.

He moved along. And then remembered that now, newly, he had to explain Laura's family too. 'And Laura, my daughter – she's separated from her husband.' It was obvious Col and Lucy didn't know what to say to this catalogue of misfortune. He tried to explain. 'Part of why I booked the house – I'm trying to help them all. And I'm not much good at it, really. Not good at it at all. That was very much my wife's department. She was the fixer in our family. But I have to try. I figured, I don't know, proximity . . . time, space, somewhere neutral, maybe that would be a start.'

He was startled by Lucy putting a hand on his arm. She looked tearful. He hadn't come for this. He didn't know these people, whose idyllic Sunday he'd invaded. He put his hand across Lucy's, patted it, then sat forward on his chair, readying himself to stand, to leave.

'So, yes, don't ever apologize for your nauseating happiness.' He gave a small laugh, hoping to make it less awkward, drawing things to a close as graciously and elegantly as he could manage.

'I think they're lucky to have you.'

He wanted to correct her: they were lucky to have had their mum, that's for sure.

Desperate to change the subject, and to escape now, he scanned for a safe subject. 'Everything okay for the dinner – the caterer – tomorrow?'

Lucy let him move on. Perhaps she was even relieved. 'Yes, yes. All good. I spoke with Jen on Friday. She's fantastic. Calm, organized. And a brilliant cook. She'll pitch up about five, I think, to get everything ready. Is that okay?'

'Sounds perfect. Thank you, Lucy. Now I'll leave you to your lawn and the rest of your Sunday. Thank you for the tea.'

'It was a pleasure.'

'Good to meet you, Charlie.' Col pumped his hand sincerely.

At the side gate, Lucy hugged him. It was a surprising gesture, but a welcome one. Human contact. 'It's a lovely thing you're doing, Charlie. I think so, anyway. I'm sure they do too.'

He felt tearful. He looked at the roses, assiduously dead-headed and already full of new buds. 'Gertrude Jekyll, right?' He gestured towards a vibrant pink climber.

Lucy nodded.

'A favourite of my wife's. A great favourite.'

This was entirely familiar to him, these days: his rheumy old eyes filled with quick, easy tears far more often. These weren't so much sad as emotional. Also normal. All his feelings were so much nearer the surface than they had been during the rest of his adult life. He'd have expected to feel embarrassed but he didn't. Maybe it was easier to talk to strangers, especially kind, gentle ones, in a beautiful garden on a sunny summer's day. Maybe he was just too old to feel embarrassed any more.

30

Unaccustomed to waking up naturally, Nick had come to with a jolt, followed by a flash of panic, sending adrenalin coursing through him, negating the benefits of the longer sleep in an instant. The children's beds were deserted. His panic – swimming-pool – vanished when he remembered the locked door with the digital keypad. His second comforting thought was that he could hear all three of them. They were just outside the door, which was wide open, still in their pyjamas, on the landing with Meredith, giggling. She looked at him anxiously. 'I hope you don't mind. Bea came to our room, and she said it would be okay to get Arthur.'

'So you could have a lie-in, Daddy.'

'It's so okay, Meredith. Thank you.' Nick got up and went to them, bent and ruffled their heads.

'We've even had our breakfast. We had Kraves.'

'Terrific. Who brought those? That's crack for preschoolers, basically, right?'

'Laura.' Meredith looked sheepish.

'That figures. When we were kids, Laura always begged for those multi-packs of cereal when we were on holiday, then ate all the Frosties. She's the pusher.'

Now he ruffled Meredith's hair, too, so she'd know he wasn't angry.

The children weren't that interested in him. He wondered

if Heather might let him keep Meredith for ever, and wandered down in search of coffee.

In the kitchen Heather was busy arranging a tableau on the table. She had laid a hardback book Nick recognized from the window of Waterstone's as a recent award-winner across a linen placemat. There was a silver bookmark with a blue silk tassel about a third of the way through it, but she had been reading a David Baldacci paperback by the pool yesterday – Arthur had soaked it, staggering along the side of the water in his armbands. Next to it there was a tiny white milk-bottle-type vase, with an equally tiny spray of cottage-garden flowers arranged in it, then a small bowl of yoghurt, on which raspberries, blueberries and strawberries had been arranged with military precision, and topped with a scattering of seeds and a mint leaf. It was all achingly photogenic, which was obviously why Heather felt the need to be standing on a kitchen chair, taking a photograph of it, rather than eating it.

She gazed down at him as he came in and smiled her wide white smile, totally devoid of the embarrassment Nick might have assumed she would feel having been caught in this odd activity. He felt scruffy in his ancient plaid pyjama bottoms and last night's T-shirt, and ran his hand through his bed hair. Heather was already dressed and ready for the day. All tight jeans and pink lipstick, with hair that, without looking stiff, never seemed to be out of place. Where did she find linen that didn't crease? When he wore a linen shirt he looked like an unmade bed. She looked . . . pristine. He concluded that the linen wouldn't dare wrinkle. Carrie would have found her fascinating. He imagined that he and she might have been whispering about Heather at night behind the closed door of their bedroom. In a way that, if not quite unkind, they would prefer no one else to hear. He wished he'd looked in the mirror, or at least sucked a bit of toothpaste out of the mangled tube upstairs, before he'd appeared.

'Hi, Nick. How you doing?'

'Hi, Heather. Good. I'm good. You?'

'I'm fantastic. It's a gorgeous day.'

She went back to her phone, taking a few more pictures.

'What are you up to?' She might not feel that this was strange, but he did, a bit.

'Flatlay.'

'Excuse me?'

'This – when you photograph stuff from above. It's called a flatlay.'

He was completely familiar with flatlay, of course, but it didn't seem necessary or kind to say so.

'It's for my Instagram.'

'Ah.' He tried to sound like he understood. 'Can I get you a coffee?' He busied himself with the machine.

'I'm great, thanks. Just had one.' He thought perhaps she'd had more than one, to have this much apparent energy so early on a holiday Sunday.

She had climbed down now or, rather, jumped down, like a mountain goat, and was staring at her phone. 'Just gonna edit this . . .'

He hadn't asked, but he supposed she just assumed he was interested. Or that she was one of those people who needed to fill silences with chatter, but he liked her voice, her accent, so he didn't mind. 'Where is everyone?'

She didn't look up from her screen. 'Laura, Ethan and Hayley are still sleeping, I assume. We may not see them for a while.' Was it snide, to include Laura with the teenagers? He couldn't see her face, so he couldn't be sure. 'I saw your father heading off thataway', she stuck her thumb over her shoulder, 'a while back, so I assume he's gone for a walk. Scott is cycling. And I think Meredith is playing with your kids somewhere.' She didn't miss much.

'There!' She pushed a button decisively, and set the phone on the table, then sat, took the bowl out of its place and started to eat the berries, gingerly, with her fingers.

Nick plonked down beside her with his mug of black coffee. 'Meredith, by the way, is a doll. My kids completely adore her.' He had learnt the power of complimenting other people's children at the nursery door. It was a highly successful social lubricant.

'I think the feeling is completely mutual. It's cute, right?'

Nick continued, 'She has a lovely way with them.'

'I'm glad you're happy for her to spend time with them. It makes her feel very grown-up, taking care of them.' He'd expected her to say something nauseating about her daughter. Like how empathetic she was, or how her kindness was a gift. This he found reassuringly low key and normal.

'Well, she seems very grown-up. And it got me an extra couple of hours in bed, so I'm very much a grateful dad.'

'They're gorgeous kids, Nick. Adorable.' Her turn.

'Thanks.'

She was looking at him appraisingly, but if she was about to say something, she thought better of it, and he was happy to divert her. He'd grown used to people trying to find the right things to say to him, about Carrie, and about the kids, and, frankly, he'd sooner not have the set conversation. He didn't know Heather, not really – they'd only met at her wedding and Carrie's funeral, for God's sake. She'd arrived in their life abruptly, without them having the chance to size her up. He didn't know if it was fair to assume that Heather would deal in platitudes, but he was exhausted by them, and short-fused about it.

'So, this flatlay business. Say what?' He scratched his head, Stan Laurel-style, which was only slightly disingenuous.

Heather giggled. 'It's a thing I'm trying.'

'A business thing?'

'Kind of a business. It can be a business, if you get good at it.'

'Right?'

'It's using social media to promote things, basically. Selling a lifestyle. You post stuff, you influence other people.'

Nick knew vaguely what she was talking about because he didn't live under a rock. She was the first of this new ilk of salesperson he'd met, though. It wasn't hugely interesting to him, to be honest. He'd never been quite clear how it generated an income but was aware it did for some people because others were suggestible. The thought that she hardly needed an income now she'd married his deeply solvent brother seemed uncharitable, and Carrie, with her firm feminist principles, would have been horrified by him saying so. It might, in the imaginary under-the-covers whispered conversation they'd have been having, have earned him a playful swipe. Carrie was all about the sisterhood.

'I see. Well, good for you!' Nick rather hoped that drew a line under the conversation he rather wished he hadn't started now.

'That reminds me, how do you feel about pictures of your kids online?'

'What do you mean?'

'Well, some people won't show their kids' faces or use their names, others do. Where do you stand on that?'

He stood some distance away from whatever the hell she was going on about. 'I don't really do Instagram or Facebook, all that stuff.'

'But if someone else were to post them?'

Nick felt like he was being ambushed. 'What did you have in mind?'

Heather shook her head dismissively. 'Oh, nothing specific. I just mean, well, I'm going to be blogging and gramming a bit this week – it's all so lovely here, it would be ridiculous not to. It's an amazing opportunity. I'm just asking how you'd feel about your gorgeous babies appearing in some of my posts.'

'I don't know.' He really didn't.

Heather raised a hand. 'No worries. No need to decide right now. I won't post without your approval, okay?'

At that moment, Scott opened the front door, clacked in noisily on his shiny studded shoes, undoing his helmet and unzipping his Lycra suit.

'Wow.' Nick laughed. 'All the gear and no idea!'

'Up yours.'

'You look like Mark bloody Cavendish, mate. Is that a padded crotch or are you pleased to see me?'

'You can scoff, you slob, but I've just cycled . . .' Scott sat down on a kitchen chair, and fiddled with his Apple watch '. . . thirty miles, and I've got the heartrate of a napping toddler.'

That wasn't entirely true – his florid complexion betrayed him, and Nick smirked. 'I'm just jealous.'

Scott widened his eyes at his brother. 'Well, we've probably got the same size feet, Nick – always used to, didn't we? You are so welcome to borrow the bike.'

Nick snorted. 'No, you're all right, cheers.'

Heather, at the sink now, filling a big glass with water for Scott, giggled. 'I won't go with him either. Terrifying. Once your feet are in the pedals, you can't get 'em out, right? Want to play tennis, later?'

'I might actually be more frightened of going up against you on the tennis court than I am of Scott's bike, Heather.' She looked pleased. 'I'm more of a slow-jog kind of a guy. And there's been precious little of that lately.'

'Offer stands, mate.'

'Mine too.' Heather had a hand on Scott's shoulder while he downed the glass.

The weird conversation about the kids had passed, for now, without him having to answer her. He really wasn't quite sure what he thought about her, but looking at his brother now, he felt, as he had yesterday, a stab of pure envy so sharp it was almost like a physical blow. The casual touch. The easy intimacy. It hurt to watch it.

31

There was a missed call and a text from Alex's number when she woke up: *Please call me.* Laura had switched her phone to silent before she'd gone to sleep, left it face down on the mahogany chest across the room from the bed. Everyone – almost everyone – she loved was here: surely she could stand down.

Apparently not.

She had only two bars on her phone in the house. Out in the garden it rose to four. She looked towards the vegetable garden, remembering Joe from last night.

She dialled Alex's number. The dialling tone was the kind that meant the phone you were calling was abroad. He was on the Amalfi coast with the pert, bikini-clad Genevieve, no doubt sitting with her, sipping the first champagne of the day, in some swanky old-school hotel with waiters in cream jackets and black bow-ties. She and Alex had been there together, years earlier, for a tenth-anniversary trip. Ethan had stayed with his grandparents for a week, the longest they'd been apart from him since he'd been born. They'd hired a car in Naples and driven on the crazy winding roads to the staggeringly pictur-esque towns that clung to the rocks by the coast. She'd been carsick, and that had irritated Alex. She'd missed Ethan and that had, too. He'd accused her of being too attached to their son. When it started raining on day

201

three, that had also pissed him off, but even he couldn't find a way to blame that on her.

From the small balcony of the hotel they were staying in, you could watch weddings taking place in a small garden: she remembered seeing one get spectacularly rained off, the bride being hurried away under large umbrellas and the guests getting soaked by rivulets running off the hastily erected tarpaulin that wasn't up to the task, while Alex lay, ignoring her, in the middle of their large romantic bed, watching a Premier League match on Sky. It was what she remembered most about the whole week, the bride's peals of laughter, her joy undiminished by the weather, the groom's tender care: watching that wedding disaster and contemplating her own marriage.

She wondered if he'd taken Genevieve to the same places, and whether Genevieve knew he'd already been there with her.

'Laura?'

'It's me.'

An uneasy peace had broken out between them, unspoken. Ethan came first. Concern for her child – their child – suppressed resentment and rage, just for now.

'Have you heard anything?'

No preamble. He was always like that. It was as if he was too important, too time poor, for the normal pleasantries. How are you? How's Ethan?

'No. If I had, I'd have told you.' She bit back the sullen 'wouldn't I?' And 'idiot'.

'I'm in and out of mobile service. And Wi-Fi. It's a nightmare.'

She realized, with a jolt, that she didn't envy Genevieve,

for all the Negronis, the truffle tagliatelle and stripy sun-loungers facing the ocean the girl was experiencing.

Alex hated not being in control. And none of them was in control. Since the conversation in the café, when she'd begged Claudia to persuade her husband not to report Ethan to the police, they'd been in a hideous limbo. Claudia had made no promises. She clearly wasn't in any position to do so: Rupert so obviously made the decisions in their household. Ethan hadn't seen Saskia – at least, not to talk to. None of them had any clue whether Saskia's parents were going to take it further or not. It was torturing all of them. As time passed, Laura let herself feel slightly more hopeful that nothing would happen – that his threats had been rage talking, that once he'd calmed down and thought it through, he would see that Ethan had no real charge to answer. That it wouldn't be fair for Ethan to be punished for something that his own daughter had willingly, happily, participated in. Ethan wouldn't talk about it. His misery was almost palpable. She wasn't entirely sure he'd grasped the seriousness – the potential danger – and she couldn't see why constantly going over it with him would be a good idea. There'd be time enough. She'd warned him of the importance of staying away from Saskia, since that was what her parents wanted. He'd heeded the warning. She was proud of the way he'd got through the exams. God knew what the results would be, but he'd stuck with it.

Alex saw it differently. He wanted to fix it. He loved his son: Laura knew he did. He wanted to protect him, and he was angry on his behalf at the accusation that had been levelled at him. But there was more to it than that: he wanted to win. It frustrated him that he couldn't exert any influence. Make it go away.

He'd gone straight to his solicitor. He'd made Laura tell him everything but he hadn't taken her with him. He'd been frustrated by that visit – his lawyer had basically told him there was nothing Alex could do but wait: it could make it worse for Ethan if he reached out to Saskia's parents. That the police might prefer not to press charges but that if her parents insisted they would have no choice, and that, yes, all the implications were real and possible if that happened.

Now all he could do, all any of them could do, was wait, with other people holding their son's future in their hands, and there was nothing they could do about it. They all hated it, but he hated it more than anyone else.

'How is he doing?' He'd remembered that it was all about Ethan.

She softened then, a little. 'He's still quiet. He's chatting a bit, with Heather's daughters, but he's pretty withdrawn, you know. I sort of have to drag him out of his room.'

'Poor kid.'

'I've got him.'

'I know.' Long pause. 'You're a good mother, Laura. You always were.'

She was shocked. She hadn't expected that. She couldn't cope with kindness, not from him.

Immediately tearful, she didn't quite trust herself to answer. She made a strangled sound that might have been thanks and rang off.

32

Charlie nearly escaped. Glorious as it was to be sur-rounded by his progeny, it was noisier than he was used to, and a peaceful walk once, or perhaps twice, a day was, he thought, the antidote. He'd gone back to his room for his hat, Daphne's constant protestation that he must keep the midday sun off his head ringing in his ears, or he might have got out before Heather had stopped him.

'Where are you off to?'

'I thought I'd head to the village.'

'I was going myself, maybe grab a coffee. Lucy said there were a couple of interesting shops, and a café or two. I could go with you. I mean, I was gonna drive . . .'

Why Heather would need to go in search of expen-sively produced coffee when she had stocked the kitchen with about three hundred capsules, Charlie didn't know. Why he felt vaguely afraid of being alone with his daughter-in-law, he also didn't quite understand. His peaceful stroll had been hijacked into a four-wheel-drive outing. Daphne would say he should go.

'Sounds lovely.' He smiled at Heather, as sincere a smile as he could muster. Scott was watching.

They parked in the middle of the village, Heather effortlessly reversing her frankly enormous beast of a car into a space that he wouldn't have thought was big enough for it.

'American driver,' she offered in explanation, although he hadn't said anything. 'This is actually pretty small. I used to drive a Buick Enclave, which is basically a tank.'

'And you're so little.' He wondered, as soon as he'd said it, whether he was allowed to say things like that in 2020. She didn't seem to mind.

'Power steering!'

Once she'd fed the machine and put a ticket on the dashboard, she put her arm through his, and steered him in the direction she wanted to go. 'Lucy told me there's a great florist, and I want to get some things for tomorrow.'

He supposed she meant his birthday. But he discovered he was happy enough to be led. Daphne might have called it a Ready Brek glow. It was one of her phrases, and it applied to this sunny, sweet-natured daughter-in-law she would never meet, with her ready laugh and her unbridled enthusiasm. She brought with her a . . . a lightness. He liked it. She was quite fun to be with, exclaiming over this and that. She bought a round, old-fashioned wicker basket in one of the first shops they came across, and proceeded to fill it with some cheese from a cheesemonger ('How do you say it – *mong*er? I never heard that before'), paper bags of fudge ('Don't tell my cardiologist – this is basically sugar, right?') and an armful of bright blooms from the florist ('You haven't seen these, Charlie. They're a surprise'). When she had eventually exhausted the charming but admittedly limited array of independent shops on the main drag, she plonked the pair of them into chairs at a coffee shop, where they ordered tea and a tea-cake for Charlie, cappuccino for Heather. 'Nothing to eat, thanks. I'm gonna demolish that fudge later.'

When the drinks had come, and the waiter had gone, she put her elbows on the small table, and rested her face on her hands, leaning forward towards him. 'I wanted to thank you, Charlie, for this holiday. It is incredibly generous and kind of you.'

He was touched that she would make a point of saying so, especially so early on. 'You're welcome. I was just so glad everyone could make it.'

'To celebrate your big day? How could we not?'

'Ah, that's sweet.'

'And I'm glad – really glad – to have the chance to get to know everyone better. Well, at all!' She laughed. It was a nice sound. 'I know Scottie kinda sprung me on you all. And I came with some baggage, I appreciate.'

'That's no way to talk about your beautiful girls.' He was teasing, but her face was suddenly quite serious.

'You know what I mean, though, right? Must have been a shocker for you all.'

'It was a surprise. I'll grant you that. He hadn't said much.'

'He hadn't said a word. Secretive little bugger, your son, hey?'

The way she said 'bugger' was funny – a quintessentially English pronunciation in the middle of her New Jersey drawl. He found it endearing. 'Well, he plays his hand quite close to his chest.'

She cocked her head, and narrowed his eyes. 'Was he always like that?'

Charlie considered the question. 'I suppose he was always the most . . .' he searched for the right words '. . . self-contained of our kids.'

She nodded encouragingly, wanting him to say more.

'Yes. He never seemed to need us as much as the others did.'

'When I first got to know him, I wondered if there'd been some trauma – some deep upset in his past.'

'I don't think so. Not that I would necessarily know about it.'

'Oh, I don't think there was. That's kind of the point of Scott. I don't think he'd ever really put himself in the way of drama. Until he met me, of course!' She laughed.

'Precisely! He seems very glad he did.'

'I hope so.' Her smile was fond. 'I certainly am.'

He concentrated on buttering his teacake. He wasn't sure he was brilliant at deep-and-meaningfuls, although he really wanted to be. He had probably spoken more about relationships and feelings in his two days at the cottage than he had in the past ten years. He was certainly trying.

'What about the other two? They weren't like that, huh?'

'Not at all. Laura – she was always so close to Daphne. Not so much to me, I suppose. Fathers and daughters . . . I loved her to bits, always. But there was a sense that I got everything second-hand, through Daphne.'

'Uh-huh.'

'The real closeness was between the two of them. She misses her mother, terribly, still, I know.'

He realized he didn't know anything about Heather's mother. He might have asked, then, but Heather asked first.

'And Nick?'

He sighed. 'And Nick always wore his heart on his sleeve.'

'I like him so much.'

Charlie smiled. 'I do too.'

'He's so sad.' She shook her head, not meaning to sound asinine. 'I mean, of course he is. I didn't know him before, not really . . . but . . .'

'He was always so happy. You know, from a baby. Smiley. Daphne always used to say she couldn't get round the supermarket for people wanting to talk to him, even when he was really little. He used to just beam at them, and they were like moths to a flame . . . Some people are like that, aren't they?'

She nodded vigorously. 'Yes.'

'Carrie was the same, that was the thing. The lucky, lucky thing for those two. She had that glow about her. They were – they were an amazing couple, together. Powerful. It was like two and two made seventeen. So many friends, so much energy. They really were quite wonderful.' He could feel himself getting tearful. It was so bloody unfair. He swallowed hard on the lump in his throat, willing it away. Old men, damn it, cried so easily.

'Poor Nick. It'll take him a while to start to come back to life.'

Charlie looked at her sharply. 'That's how I see him. Not quite alive.'

'He's hibernating. It's how he'll heal. He's alive, I promise. He just has to rest his heart. He'll come back to you, the kids, to the world.'

It was quite a profound thing to say in a coffee shop on a sunny day to someone you didn't know very well about someone you knew even less well. Charlie was surprised.

It felt like she understood, not discordant at all. 'You sound like you know a bit about loss, Heather.'

She looked down at her mug. 'Not the kind Nick's suffered. But I've lost. We all have, by now, though, right? I'm nothing special. We all carry scars.'

Charlie nodded.

'If you don't, you haven't been doing it properly. Haven't risked anything.'

Ah, he thought. How true that was. How true.

Heather's voice was even gentler now. 'You must miss Daphne even more than normal at times like this.'

She was really going there, as Ethan might have said. 'My dear,' he put one hand over hers, 'you have no idea how much.'

She squeezed the hand. No words.

When they got back to the house, Scott came out, clearly having heard the car on the gravel. 'Had a good time?'

'Fantastic,' Heather offered. 'I gotta get these flowers in some water.' She jumped out, collected her basket from the back seat, slammed the car doors and hurried inside.

Scott went to the passenger side where Charlie was easing himself out.

'God, these seats are high – and I'm not quite as agile as once I was.'

Scott took his elbow, and Charlie let him. Once his feet met the ground, he smiled at his son. 'She's quite a woman, your wife.'

'Yeah?'

Charlie looked into his son's eyes. How strange it was. When your son was little, you crouched to get on his level.

Then he grew, and you shrank, until eventually, you almost had to put your head right back to meet his gaze. 'She's rather wonderful, isn't she?'

Scott broke into a wide, warm smile. 'I think so, Dad. I think so.'

'Your mum would definitely have approved.'

'Really?'

'She'd have loved her.'

Scott watched his father walk into the house. He swallowed hard, and blinked back a sudden tear.

33

The allure of the swimming-pool could be ignored no
longer. The younger kids had been begging for ages.
Eventually, Meredith took matters into her own hands
and went upstairs with them to change. They reappeared,
Arthur in a back-to-front swim nappy, armbands already
inflated and yanked on, just to wrist height. He and Delilah
were so excited that they were bouncing from one foot
to the other.

Nick admitted defeat and went to put on his trunks.
Scott said he'd swim too. Charlie demurred, despite the
pester power, but promised to go upstairs and change
into his shorts, then come down to the pool and dip his
feet into the water. No one had seen Laura for a while,
and Heather was apparently going to work on Hayley's
backhand on the tennis court. Hayley might have been
less keen on this activity in the midday sun if she hadn't
caught a glimpse of Lucy's hunky young electrician when
he'd parked on the drive. Liking the look of him, she'd
seized the opportunity to flip her ponytail and flaunt her
brown legs in her short white tennis skirt while he fixed
the floodlight. Life was a catwalk.

It was a big pool, for a private house. There was a set of
shallow steps at one end, and a small diving board at the
other, and halfway along one side a circular Jacuzzi pro-
truded. Nick activated the electric pool cover from the

wall while Scott pushed back the doors that opened one side of the pool to the garden. 'I've forgotten my goggles,' Meredith trilled, running towards the house. 'I'll just go grab them.'

Scott was examining the hinging system on the impressive doors. Fully opened, there were no piers or corners. They must have cost a fortune, but they really did achieve the inside-outside thing very well. 'Heather is taken with these doors.'

Nick thought of Scott's house in Haslemere. He'd only been there a couple of times. 'You haven't put in a pool?'

'Not yet. She's taken with the pool, too.' Scott smiled ruefully.

Nick laughed.

'We could have a pool at home, Daddy!' Bea chimed in excitedly.

'Where, darling?'

'In our garden.' She gestured at the Jacuzzi, arms echoing the shape. 'We have room for one of these!'

Nick tilted his head to one side. 'Not really.'

She put her hands on her hips defiantly. 'We could move the climbing frame.'

Nick kissed the top of her head. 'The one Daddy spent three days putting up? You love that climbing frame.'

Bea pondered the dilemma. She did love the climbing frame. 'Then we need a new house. With a much bigger garden.' The men laughed.

'You can go and live with Uncle Scott and Auntie Heather, if you like. They've got bags of room for a pool *and* a climbing frame.'

'Can I, too?' Delilah's eyes widened with excitement.

He ruffled his younger daughter's head. 'Oh, the loyalty. Charming, Lila.'

There was a sudden loud splash.

Arthur, undetected, had waddled down to the deep end, and jumped straight in.

His armbands had not been on properly, and one bobbed alarmingly to the surface, floating free.

For a second they all froze.

Scott was nearest. He didn't hesitate. Still wearing his watch, his shirt and his glasses, he ran full pelt a few metres, then dived in from the side, emerging seconds later with Arthur held aloft in his arms. The toddler wasn't in the least concerned, spluttering furiously, then squealing with delight as water streamed off him.

With his nephew under one arm, Scott paddled to the side where Nick took Arthur, standing him on the tiled edge. He pulled his son close, his heart racing from the punch of adrenalin. 'Mate, don't do that to me again.' Arthur giggled unrepentantly, too young to understand the admonishment, as Nick put his armbands on properly, then turned to his brother. 'Thank you.'

'No worries.' Scott heaved himself out and sat on the side, pulling his soaking shirt away from his skin, catching his breath.

'God, is that watch waterproof?'

Scott glanced at his wrist. 'To a thousand metres.'

'Thank God for that.'

'Aw, Nick. It's just stuff . . .'

Nick patted his brother's shoulder gratefully.

'Uncle Scott, you didn't take your glasses off.' This was Bea, her hand clamped across her mouth in a stifled giggle.

'Silly me.'

'Very silly,' Delilah piped.

'Oh, he's silly, is he?' Nick scooped up Delilah and, without taking off his own T-shirt, jumped in with her in his arms.

Bea whooped, and splashed in beside them, followed swiftly by Arthur, who marched once or twice on the side, then stepped in.

They all surfaced, water flying, laughing, happy. Charlie and Meredith heard the commotion from the pathway. Meredith flew past the old man, anxious not to miss any more of the fun.

It was a good sight. His two sons, still dressed but dripping, encircling his three youngest grandchildren and all of them laughing. Charlie's heart was full. This was what it was all about.

34

It turned out that 1 August was Hayley's birthday as well as Charlie's. He wished they'd said ages ago. Perhaps he was supposed to know: Daphne would have known. Heather, Hayley and Meredith's birthdays would all have been duly noted on the side bar of the calendar and in Daphne's ancient bulging Filofax, bought when they were first on sale, never to be missed or forgotten. In fairness, Charlie wasn't sure he'd ever been told. He was eighty, Hayley turning sixteen. She'd been born on his sixty-fourth birthday, on the other side of the world. Heather had made a big thing of saying, early on, that Hayley's celebrations were planned for later, when all her friends were back from their respective summer holidays, nearer to the start of term. Today must and should be all about Charlie.

As if Charlie might mind sharing. As if Charlie really cared that it was his birthday. Turning eighty was the hook on which he had hung the holiday, that was all: an excuse. Birthdays had never meant much to him, but since he'd lost Daphne, much like Christmas, New Year and every other so-called 'special day', they had merged into each other. All his adult birthday memories starred her, and without her to make more, he couldn't be bothered. He woke early, but stayed in bed, listening to Radio 4. He could hear people moving about downstairs. He knew they had something planned – and he would win an Oscar for looking touched, and feeling moved, but he would mostly be play-acting. He worked hard at hiding his uninterest in a world without her. It wasn't as dark as that made it sound – he wasn't suicidal, wasn't even waiting to die: that would be overstating it. It was just that his emotional range had been irrevocably changed when she died. The bandwidth of feeling had simply been restricted. He just knew he would never be as happy, or as excited, or as elated as he had once been with her, or, probably, as sad, lonely and bereft as her dying had left him. It just wasn't possible.

But they'd all come, ostensibly for today, to celebrate with him, so, for their sake, he was going to give it a damn good try.

You're not so bad, you silly old sod, he thought, as he swung his legs out of the bed to get dressed. There were plenty in far worse shape at his age. Even more who didn't make it that far. A bit blind, a bit deaf, nowhere near as strong as he had once been. Less hair on his head, more in his ears and nose, which, incidentally, were bigger than they had ever been. Skin, wrinkled. Muscles, stiff. Joints, achy. Brain, slower, no point denying it, even if he still did a crossword every day, and *The Times* Quiz, in which he occasionally scored double figures. But still going . . . still going. Daphne would be ten years older too, if she were here. How would age have treated her? 'They shall not grow old, as we that are left grow old. Age shall not weary them . . .' He didn't know why those words came into his head as he buttoned his shirt and stepped into his khaki trousers, but they did. Age sure had wearied him.

They were all waiting for him when he descended the

stairs. His family. Someone – he suspected Heather – had marshalled them all. There was bunting hung between the two big lights above the scrubbed table, which supported a pile of cards. And presents, wrapped in bright paper, tied with ribbons. There were balloons – how had they managed that? Helium balloons in loads of different colours, with ribbons tied on them, floating up against the ceiling, here and in the hallway. It really looked very jolly. Bea was front and centre, proudly holding a plate of muffins, with tapered candles in them. Someone must have lit them just when they heard him coming down. Nick hovered, crouched, anticipating spillage. Delilah and Arthur, holding hands, looked at their dad, awaiting his nod. When it was given, they started shouting the words to 'Happy Birthday' and everyone – even the teenagers – joined in. They made quite a chorus. It was almost overwhelming.

When they had finished, the smaller grandchildren clamoured for cuddles, eager to insinuate themselves into the centre of things. Bea did indeed spill muffins on the floor, and for a moment her bottom lip trembled with the promise of tears, but Charlie gathered her onto his lap, kissing her, and Heather quickly picked them up, invoking the five-second rule and gently stroking Bea's cheek.

He opened the cards far faster than he might have chosen, the little ones egging him on impatiently, and Hayley stood them up one at a time along the deep windowsill. Then his presents: wine, whisky, a book about Churchill, a linen shirt with a small print of bright flowers Daphne would have been proud of, tickets to a sold-out show ('and we'll take you to dinner afterwards, Dad – anywhere you like'), and to Lords for later that month. Some pebbles painted by the tinies to resemble ladybirds and bees ('To stop your papers blowing off your desk in the wind, Granddad,' Delilah patiently explained).

They'd planned the day, they said. There was to be a picnic, and they'd found some local cricket match, which would keep several of them out of the way while tonight was made ready. Heather was to stay behind ('not because I don't love cricket cos, wow, that is one exciting game') to oversee proceedings.

He was genuinely touched. While the others were clearing breakfast away, he sought Hayley out. He'd bought a card, and a small gift – some pretty-looking bath products in a set, modern and age-appropriate, not old-lady stuff – from a gift shop he and Heather had been in yesterday. He'd wrapped it in his room last night. He didn't have any idea whether she'd like the smell, but she looked pleased, as much at the thought as at the present, kissed his cheek and said he shouldn't have, so he was very glad he had.

They got back from the cricket at around five, in time to shower and dress for the evening. It had been a suitably gentle and happy afternoon. Scott had sorted out some really comfortable folding chairs, and he, Ethan, Charlie and Nick had watched a few overs of pretty decent cricket, although Charlie had drifted off for a few balls somewhere in the middle. Laura had read, and then slept across the picnic blanket, arms crossed on her chest, like a painting he remembered of Ophelia. Charlie was glad to see her rest. Hayley and Meredith kept the little ones amused with piggy-backs and roly-polys around the boundary, and, when they got bored of that, ice lollies and Disney on the iPad in the shade of Scott's big car.

When they got back, the caterer's van was parked in front of the house. Heather had banned them all from the long, thin room behind the pool until they were summoned, which they were, just before seven. She'd done a beautiful job. There were fairy lights wound around the oak posts of the building's frames, and the flowers she had bought the day before with Charlie had been supplemented with greenery from the garden and were arranged into pretty sprays all down the centre of the table. Tea lights glittered in mercury glass containers. The balloons had all been collected from the kitchen and allowed to float in the new space, and the overall effect was very pretty.

'It looks beautiful, Heather,' Charlie exclaimed, genuinely appreciative.

'Do you like it? I'm so glad.' Heather hugged him, delighted with the compliment.

'And don't we all look glamorous?' Even Nick was in a suit, and Ethan's white shirt was tucked in for once, trousers resting on his jutting hipbones, emphasizing his slender frame. Bea and Delilah had pretty dresses in sugared-almond colours with tulle skirts. Heather and her girls were a rainbow of chiffon. Laura looked as pretty as he'd seen her so far. She'd caught the sun, like Ethan, snoozing on the blanket this afternoon, and her slim shoulders were golden in a black halterneck dress. Her freckles – which she had inexplicably hated all her life – were out, and made her look five years younger. Charlie had on a bow-tie with his jacket. Daphne would have approved.

'Don't scrub up badly, no.'

'We need to take a picture.'

'I've set up a place, here.' Heather led them out onto the terrace where she'd put two benches that had been along the back wall of the pool. 'I figured the light would be good here, and if we put the kids up front, adults behind . . .'

They arranged themselves as she instructed, standing back to appraise them, telling the back row to leave a space for her between Scott and Charlie. Then, once they were as she wanted, she called one of the caterer's waitresses to come out and shoot the picture, and told them all to say, 'mozzarella'. There were four cameras, and the girl patiently snapped with all of them. Heather checked, rearranged, and they went again. Then she pronounced herself happy with the shot. She showed Charlie, who couldn't see quite as clearly in the small camera screen as he pretended he could. They were all just a bit of a blur.

'Gorgeous,' he said, though. He was sure it was.

'Can we get a bloody drink, now?' Scott mocked.

'You can. Champagne this way.'

When they all had a flute, and the children a cup of elderflower cordial, Scott raised his glass to his father. 'Happy birthday, Dad. Here's to you.'

'Hear hear!' they chorused, and drank.

'And thank you for all this.' That was Laura.

He raised his own glass. 'I'd like to drink to all of you.' He turned towards Hayley. 'Especially to you, Hayley, and happy birthday again, birthday twin. I'm so happy you and Meredith and your mum have joined the family. Delighted to have two new granddaughters. Really.' Both girls smiled at him, pink-cheeked. Scott put his arm around Heather and she grasped his hand. 'And I'd like to drink to your lovely mum and granny, my Daphne. She would have wanted, so very badly, to be here with us all tonight. She would have made a speech, and she'd have been so much funnier and more touching than me, so I'm not going to try to compete. You know, I think, how much she'd have loved it. I can tell you that she would have been very, very proud of each and every one of you.' He said each word slowly and carefully, scanning the gathering to make eye contact with all of them.

Laura's eyes had filled with tears, and he couldn't meet her gaze for long. He so didn't want to blub tonight.

Nick took up his toast, nodding briefly at Charlie. 'To Mum.'

Scott poured himself a glass. He'd pushed his chair back from the end of the table, and was watching everyone, suffused with a feeling of well-being and plenty of good red wine.

Heather was deep in conversation with Nick, their heads mirroring bobs of agreement. Ethan and Hayley were looking at Hayley's phone, while Bea and Delilah diligently collected streamers from the floor, draping them across the teens, who were managing to indulge and ignore them simultaneously. Arthur was asleep on Laura's lap; she was sitting within the crook of their father's arm, and Charlie was smiling beatifically as he surveyed the whole tableau.

It couldn't have gone any better.

Meredith suddenly appeared from under the table, the cloth around her head like a scarf. She'd been playing there with Nick's kids. Scott took her hands and she pulled herself up, then leaned against him. 'Had a good time, kiddo?'

She nodded enthusiastically. 'I like being in a big family.'

'You do?'

'I really, really do.'

Scott kissed her forehead. She looked up at him through her big blue eyes. 'Thank you, Scott.' Then rested her head against his shirt. 'I'm glad you're my dad.'

The lump in his throat was instantaneous. The tear he wiped away came just a moment behind it. She'd never said that before. He held her close. 'I'm glad that you're my daughter.'

Almost as if she sensed the magnitude of the quiet exchange, Heather looked up at them, and he held his wife's gaze, their eyes locked in understanding and emotion across the long table.

35

The caterer and her team had cleared up so effortlessly and silently that Laura barely realized they'd gone. The little kids had been in bed for hours, and the big kids, too, had crept away – there'd been talk of a Netflix horror film. Hayley seemed to have decided that she liked Ethan and was engineering spending time with him, and Laura was grateful to her. He'd looked less stricken today, she thought. He had resisted all notion of sunscreen, and his nose was sunburnt after the cricket.

Heather had excused herself on the second passing of the port, kissing Charlie as she passed his chair, and whispering a last 'Happy birthday.' He felt a rush of affection for her.

Perhaps it was always going to be maudlin – just the four of them left at the table with Daphne missing and too much wine drunk. A few minutes after Heather had gone, he pushed his chair back and stood up, reluctant to let the magical day end but suddenly exhausted and longing for bed. 'I've had a lovely day. Thank you all for all the hard work and effort.'

'One for the road, Dad?'

'The stairs!' He laughed, and shook his head. 'I don't think so. I've had quite enough. I'll start weeping, and you'll all rather I hadn't. I'd rather I hadn't. I'll quit while

I'm ahead. You stay.' He stopped and touched each of them as he left – shook Scott's hand until his son pulled him into a brief embrace, kissed Laura's cheek, put his arm around Nick's shoulders. His babies.

'And then there were three.' Nick filled everyone's glass.

Laura tried to put her hand across the top of hers at the last moment, but misjudged it and got port on her fingers.

'Oops. Sorry.'

She licked them. 'You're pissed.'

'So are you.' It was true. She had drunk more than she had in ages. She felt incredibly heavy and slow-moving.

When he'd charged everyone's glasses, Nick made them clink. 'Come on.'

'What are we drinking to?'

'Whatever you like.'

'Let's drink to three days down and not a cross word.'

'Bar set low, bro.'

'What about you, Laura? What do you want to drink to?'

'Let's drink to love and marriage.'

Her brothers eyed her warily.

At home, drinking alone, which she'd done rather too much of lately, Laura could let rage and hurt make her a bitter (then nauseous) drunk. She knew she was doing it. Here, she didn't seem to have the energy for it. Acutely conscious of Scott's happiness, even more aware of Nick's grief, it wasn't appropriate. Even through the champagne and wine haze she knew that. Her face crumpled, and she put down her glass without drinking from it.

'Laura?'

Her voice was more of a sob. 'I miss Mum.'

'Bloody hell.' Scott drank deeply.

'Mum would have known what to do about all of this,' she continued, sounding childish, even to herself.

'All of what?' Nick coaxed gently.

'Oh, all of it, the whole stinking mess.'

'Alex?'

'Alex. Bloody Genevieve.' Then another sob. 'Ethan.'

'What about Ethan?'

She'd forgotten, with the booze, that they didn't know. 'Turns out I'm not only a crappy wife, I'm a lousy mother too.'

'What the hell are you talking about?'

Scott wondered if it was too late for him to join Heather in bed, but when he went to stand up, Nick fired a warning glance in his direction and he sat back down.

That wasn't entirely fair – Laura and Nick had always been much closer, with a sibling shorthand and in-jokes he'd been excluded from. But he reasoned it wasn't entirely fair to leave Nick, now, to deal with her on his own either.

'I stopped watching . . . stopped making him my priority. I had one job, for God's sake. For months now I've been wallowing in self-pity and anger, using all my energy to hate Alex and fight him. Did you know he wants us to sell the house?' They didn't. She nodded slowly. 'Yep. Sell and divide the profits.' She waved away the statement as the diversion it was. 'Bastard.'

'Can he make you do that?'

'Yes. No. Probably. That's not the point. I wasn't, I haven't been prioritizing Ethan.'

'He seems okay.' Scott hadn't particularly noticed

226

anything. He wasn't an expert on the habits and behaviours of the teenage boy, but there hadn't seemed to be an unusual amount of grunting monosyllabic communication, and general squirming. Ethan was a bit Harry Enfield's Kevin, but that was all. Hayley and even Meredith seemed more grown-up, but wasn't that normal? Laura had always seemed more grown-up than him and Nick at the same age, hadn't she?

Laura rounded on him. 'He is *not* okay.' She shook her head slowly.

'Are you talking about GCSEs?'

Again the dismissive wave.

'No. I mean, maybe. I have no idea. We'll find out in a few days'

'What are you talking about, then?' Nick was contemplating the options. Drinking, drugs, tattoos, trouble with the law? He'd flirted with the lot of them, as the small yet ridiculous Bart Simpson on his left biceps still testified. Scott probably never had. Not Laura either, unless she'd done a great job in keeping it quiet. They were rule-followers, like Dad. He'd definitely been the envelope-pusher in their family.

Laura took a deep breath, and told them about Saskia, about Rupert, so furious. And Claudia wanting to do the right thing. About the awful limbo they were all in. And her teenage son sobbing in her lap, his heart broken, his faith in adults shaken, his future uncertain. She cried as she talked, snot and tears running down her face.

When she'd finished, the three of them sat still, slightly shocked. Laura blew her nose violently on her napkin, and looked at Nick. 'I'm sorry. You don't need this.'

'Oh, stop it.'

'No, you don't. You've got enough of your own crap.'

'That's not how it works, Sis. Mine's a rubbish situation, but it isn't ongoing. What's the medical term? Acute, not chronic? Is that it?' He gave a small, joyless laugh. 'I'm both. The worst happened. We've survived. I don't know how, but we have. We're still here. The world turns. I miss her. Every minute of every day I miss her. But it's done. The rest of it is the fallout. I'm too busy to wallow. I've no one to be angry with. I've just got to get on with it. Be mother and father, pay the bills, hold it together. I haven't got time to fall apart.'

'And I've had too much time.'

'Stop it. Will you just bloody stop it, Laura?' This was Scott, who had been very quiet until now, looking from one sibling to the other. Now he'd drawn himself up to his full height in the chair. His voice was louder and stronger than either of theirs. 'You said you missed Mum, right? Do you know what Mum would have said to you by now?'

Laura sat upright too, and pushed her hair back from her face.

Scott didn't wait for a response. 'She'd have told you to get a bloody grip.' Scott swallowed what remained in his glass and stood up. 'She'd have said you'd had long enough to be pathetic and victim-y. That it was time to stop bloody wallowing. You know I'm right. She'd have said she never really liked Alex. Neither, by the way, did the rest of us much care for the uptight prick. Even me, and I was the most like him. There's a bit of uptight prick in me too.'

Nick sniggered at the unintended innuendo. It broke

the tension just a little. Scott threw a glance of mock-fury at his brother, and Nick stifled the mirth and sat upright in his chair, accepting the near-reprimand.

'Don't think I like admitting that for a minute, by the way. Mum would have used her fridge-magnet wisdom on you and you'd have had a big hug and a speech made mainly in fucking aphorisms, and then she'd bloody well have expected you to pick yourself up, dust yourself off and get the fuck on with it. Focus on Ethan and this bloody mess he's in. Get your shit together. And you know it.'

The outburst was so out of character that Nick and Laura sat in stunned silence for a few seconds as Scott stood over them like a disapproving parent. Then he came and stood between them. 'I love you. Both. Very much. And I'm going to bed.' He kissed Laura's head, and very briefly stroked her hair, then went.

They watched him as he left the room. Eventually Nick and Laura looked at each other.

'That was a lot of swearing.'

'That was a lot of words – from Scott.'

The port and the shock and the truth of what he'd said made them childish. They bent their heads together and giggled.

'Heather really has unbuttoned him.' This observation triggered fresh guffaws. Crying was never far from laughing, Nick thought. And vice versa.

They pressed their foreheads together for a moment. Then Nick took Laura's hands in his own and held them. 'He's probably right, you know, Laur.'

'He probably bloody is.'

36

The rain started. Anyone studying the sky, or checking their iPhone, would have predicted its coming. The sky darkened suddenly, and a few plump raindrops gave way very quickly to a deluge. Charlie stirred a forbidden spoonful of sugar into his mug of tea and sat by the window, watching rain bounce off the path edging, and pool in the rose petals. He had never minded rain.

'That was summer, then.' Heather burst into the kitchen in gym kit, dripping, and wiped her face. Rain came down in heavy sheets, from a now positively leaden sky.

'My phone says it's just this morning. A clearing shower. Don't panic, Mr Mainwaring.'

'Who is Mr Mainwaring?'

Charlie laughed. He wasn't sure he could explain *Dad's Army* this morning. 'Long story, don't worry.'

Heather peered out of the window. 'Hope you're right. Scott's out in this. I do worry about wet roads – he goes so fast on that bike.'

'Laura too.'

She took a towel and rubbed her wet hair. 'God. We worry, right?'

'It's the price of love. That's what Daphne always used to say. If you didn't love, you wouldn't care so you wouldn't worry.'

'But life would be pretty empty and meaningless, right?'

'Exactly.'

She nodded, thinking. 'I like that.' Already the sun was shining again. 'Wow. That's bright. There'll be a rainbow somewhere.' She went to the front door and opened it. 'There is! Charlie, come look!' It was faint, but definite, framing the view. 'What a metaphor! I gotta get my phone and post this.'

Charlie smiled.

Laura had taken a large mug of coffee and two paracetamol to the garden. Her head was throbbing. She didn't mind when the rain started. It wasn't quite the warm rain of the tropics, but it was far from cold, and the drops were refreshing as they hit her face. She tilted it upwards, towards the sky, and let it fall on her.

She hadn't seen either of her brothers that morning. She wondered if they'd been processing what she'd told them about Ethan's predicament, whether they'd have any good advice.

Which was fine for a couple of minutes. But as the rain grew steadily heavier and harder, her clothes got wetter, and suddenly she wasn't refreshed but shivering. She tilted her head down, and wondered whether the greenhouse was locked. It was closer than the house, and quieter. It wasn't. She pushed open the door and went inside, just as the tempo of the rain went up a gear – 'stair rods' was what her parents would have said. The noise of the rain against the glass of the roof was nice. Inside it was warm, having held heat from the previous day, and it smelt musty and earthy – a scent that was unfamiliar but quite comforting. There were wide wooden benches on either side, cluttered with small terra-cotta and plastic pots, and gardening paraphernalia – balls of twine, secateurs, some seed packets. At the end, there was an old deckchair. Laura shook the sweatshirt she'd had around her shoulders and pulled it on, then curled herself into the deckchair, and listened to the rain's almost hypnotic rhythm against the panes. She pushed her thumbs into her temples trying to rub away the headache, subsiding now but still keeping time with her pulse.

The door opening brought a blast of cooler air. 'I seem destined to interrupt you in a reverie.'

Joe had a rain cape on – a vast billowing black affair with a hood.

'You look like a Weather Superhero.'

He raised his arms in a Popeye stance. 'At your service.' He pulled the hood down and ran his fingers through the hair at the front, which was wet.

'And I seem destined to be in your way. I'm an allot-ment crasher.'

He smirked. 'Weather Superhero and the Allotment Crasher. It sounds like a really bad film!'

'I've got a serious complaint to make – this is not the weather we ordered.'

'I should take it to the management.'

'I shall be writing a strongly worded letter, be assured. You cannot trap a disparate family group inside a coun-try house for a whole day. God only knows what might happen!'

'I see.'

'I'm kidding. I haven't actually seen anyone yet. Except

my dad – just briefly and only to grunt at. I'm hiding out. Again.' She pointed ruefully at her forehead. 'Hangover.'

'Was it worth it?'

'It was Dad's eightieth yesterday and we had a family party for him last night.'

'Ah.'

He had a very earnest way of looking at you. It wasn't quite a stare, but his gaze was more frank and curious than most people's. He met your eye. Not everyone did, not all of the time. And his eyes were warmer than most, too. As if he was predisposed to like you. It was disarming. It wasn't, she realized, how people looked at you in big towns and cities. Things were instantly easier, more comfortable between them than they had been the last time. She wasn't sure why. But it was nice.

'I should go.' He turned and put his hand on the door.

She wanted to stop him. 'Stay. Distract me.' God, why had she said that? She felt a blush rise across her cheeks.

'I'm actually running late.'

'Oh . . . yes, sorry.' She felt foolish.

'No. No.' He looked vaguely regretful.

'Going somewhere inside, I hope?'

He smiled. 'Yeah. Looks like it's easing off already, though.' It was. The quality of the light outside had changed, just in the time they'd both been in the greenhouse. Suddenly a rainbow appeared across the sky.

'Wow!'

'Must be a sign.'

'A sign of what?'

He shrugged. 'Guess that's up to us.'

Definitely flirting? Laura didn't know what to say.

'I needed to grab this.' He took a small bag off a shelf. It looked like a toolkit of some kind.

She smiled, in what she hoped was a nonchalant way. Who knew whether she'd pulled it off?

'I don't suppose . . .' He started a thought, turned towards the door, then back to her. Droplets of water shot off the cape as he whirled indecisively. He seemed to make up his mind at last, and moved away from her. 'No. No. Don't worry.' She wanted to ask him what he was going to say. But he'd opened the door.

'I hope the day gets better.'

'For you too.'

And then he was gone, leaving her feeling that it was a shame, that maybe talking to him in a dank greenhouse on a wet morning might have been exactly what she wanted to do. That talking to him, a virtual stranger, seemed easier than talking to almost anyone else right now. And then, almost immediately, that she was a complete idiot.

37

Nick knocked on Ethan's door. He didn't answer the first time, so he knocked again, a little more forcefully. This time, Ethan grunted, and he opened the door, a crack at first, then fully. Ethan was lying on his bed. The room looked like a jumble sale, discarded clothes flowing from every surface, and wet towels strewn on the floor. Nick laughed. 'This is even worse than ours. Don't let any of the women in here.'

'Wasn't planning on it.' Ethan smiled grimly.

'Looks like the rain is stopping.'

The boy shrugged a little, as if he couldn't care less, and hadn't even noticed it was raining.

Nick came into the room and closed the door behind him. 'Your mum says you're having a shitter, Eth.'

Ethan eyed him suspiciously. 'Has she sent you to talk to me?'

'Not exactly. I know she thought it might help.'

Ethan didn't speak. Nick sat on the other bed, pulling the pillows from the head to his back for support, and leant against them.

'What did she tell you?'

'That you're in love.' It seemed, to Nick, a good place to start.

'And the rest?'

Nick nodded. 'She told me what happened, yes. And

for what it's worth, mate, I think it stinks. What her dad said.'

The relief at not having to say out loud what had happened, the relief of his uncle's immediate support, took all the suppressed rage out of Ethan. Without the anger to keep him upright, his shoulders rounded and he began, to his horror, to cry.

He was glad Nick didn't move. He didn't want to be held like a child. For a moment or two, Nick sat, and Ethan fought to get himself back under control. Then Nick took out a handkerchief, balled it into a missile and threw it across the room to him. Ethan rubbed his eyes, and snorted into it.

'Keep it. Got loads. Done a bit of weeping and wailing myself lately, Eth.'

'Sorry.'

'Don't be. Means you're human.'

Ethan's breathing was settling down, but he could still only stare at the carpet.

'Tell me about her.'

'Saskia?'

'Yeah. If you want.'

Ethan smiled faintly. 'She's gorgeous.'

'I bet. Got a picture?'

Ethan picked up his phone and scrolled back through his photos. He held it out, and Nick came over. 'I like this one.'

It was a selfie. She must have taken it. She was looking straight at the camera, and Ethan was kissing her cheek. She was a good-looking girl, but it was Ethan's ease and confidence that made the picture memorable. 'Pretty. Really pretty.'

'She is.'

Nick went back to the other side of the room, and waited.

'Clever, too. Dead smart. Missed her help with revision, that's for sure.'

'You'll be fine.'

'She just got me. I got her. You know?'

Nick knew.

'I probably sound stupid, you'll probably tell me I'm too young, but I loved her, Nick.' He corrected himself. 'I love her, I mean.'

'Why would I tell you you're stupid, kid? Love is love, Eth. There's no right age. You say you love her, what sort of twat would I be if I told you you couldn't cos you're only sixteen?'

'Dad said it.'

Point proven, Nick thought. 'Well, the truth is, you're the only one who knows what's gone on between the two of you, right?'

'And now, because of her dad, her parents and mine do. By now maybe the police do. It's so bloody humiliating.'

'I get that. It should have been private.'

Ethan looked at him gratefully.

'I don't think he's going to take it any further, Eth. I'll bet you.'

Ethan sighed. Sitting there, he looked younger than sixteen. Maybe even too young for sex.

'Look. I'm a dad. I was also, once, a young boyfriend, so

I can see both sides. He loves his daughter. He wants to keep her young. He hates the idea she's having sex with someone. He hates the idea of being usurped in her affections. He hates her growing up. He's lashed out, that's all. He's threatened you with stuff because he can. Not because he's going to go through with it. It's a kind of revenge. Besides, if he was going to do that, he'd have done it by now. He'd have done it the first day, while he was still fuming.'

'I don't even care about the police. It's Mum and Dad who care about that. I don't give a shit. I care that he's split us up. He hasn't let her come anywhere near me.'

Nick ignored the idiocy of that: it showed Ethan's immaturity. If the police were involved, it would ruin him. But it wouldn't help to say so. Nick believed what he'd said about the father – he bet the moment had passed. But you never knew, and God help Ethan if the man did go through with it. 'He might relent on that too.'

Ethan snorted. 'Someone said she's going somewhere else for sixth form. Some boarding school. He's a bloody nutter.'

'I see.'

'Yeah. So. I might never see her again.' They were both aware of how melodramatic that sounded, but Ethan was past caring.

'Oh, Ethan.' Nick sighed.

Ethan looked directly at him. The tears had receded, and Nick could see that he was angry again. 'So you can't help me. Not really. Can you?'

'I can listen, for what that's worth. I can try to understand. I can keep you company if you want. Listen to Oasis with you . . .'

It had been Nick who'd got him into all the Britpop stuff. Ethan couldn't remember listening to music with his father, and his mum was strictly Radio 4 and Classic FM. His uncle had always had a stereo and records. He'd got really excited when Ethan had expressed an interest a few years ago, pulling albums out of the shelf where they were alphabetized, in his front room at home, exclaiming that Ethan 'had to hear' this or that song. He'd once declared that Ethan was the only other person allowed to put records on his old decks, being the only person who truly appreciated them, and Ethan, at twelve or thirteen, had swelled with pride.

The evocation broke the tension. Ethan half laughed, and Nick winked at him, then stood up. 'I can't fix it, mate. This is it. Life. Shits on you from a great height sometimes. It does on everyone. But other people help. Trust me. They do, if you let them.'

He squeezed his nephew's boyish shoulder, then left him alone.

38

By late afternoon, to everyone's relief, the weather had staged a miraculous recovery. The rain had acted as a mood oppressor, making the kids mope a bit, and the adults scratchy. The house shrank, when the gardens were out of bounds and the pool unappealing. By unspoken agreement, they'd quietly fled to different rooms. Nick's kids squabbled over Uno and waited for the downpour to pass. When it did, the August sun was strong enough to dry the stones on the terrace quickly, and its warmth seemed to make everyone unclench.

Laura didn't realize she'd avoided being alone with Heather until she found herself alone with Heather, not quite quick enough to think of a reason not to be. She acknowledged that she was jealous of her brother and his new wife. Of their shiny, polished happiness. Of their obvious joy in each other's company. Of Heather's relentless cheerful energy. And now of her closeness with the others. When, and how, had that happened? Was she on a charm offensive? She'd seen several tender exchanges between Heather and her dad. *Her* dad. Even Nick's kids, whom she'd known all their lives, seemed instantly fond of Heather.

Then again, why the hell wouldn't they? Something Daphne used to say, about there being two kinds of people, drains and radiators, kept coming back to her. Unfortunately, she knew which one she was at the moment.

And she knew which Heather was too. So it had seemed easier to avoid her, and the dark, twisty feelings she provoked. She'd turned down a game or three of tennis. But when she'd said yoga was more her thing, wouldn't you know it, Heather loved yoga too, and if Laura gave her just a minute she'd change and perhaps they could do some together on the lawn. She'd brought a mat. Of course she had.

Laura had a series of poses written on an index card, given to her by the teacher of the class she went to at home. Out on the lawn, in a corner under the shade of a large willow tree where she couldn't be seen clearly from the house, she unrolled her own mat and sat cross-legged, waiting for Heather, who appeared shortly thereafter, mat tucked under her arm, in perfectly co-ordinated peacock-blue leggings and a tight cropped top, with a racer back that showed off her golden, muscular shoulders and toned abs. Laura went through the poses on the card slowly and deliberately, trying to concentrate, Heather aping her moves. She was strong and supple, but Laura was too, she realized, and she felt proud of her ability to match her sister-in-law bend for stretch.

They ended in a child's pose, resting their bums on their feet, their legs spread, their faces on the mats.

'God.' Heather groaned. 'That feels good, doesn't it?'

'I love it.' Laura rolled onto her back, her eyes closed against the sun. Heather copied that move too, and lay with her hands behind her head.

'Thank God the rain didn't last, huh?'

'Mm.' Yoga made Laura feel still. Still and quiet. Not Heather, apparently.

'I'm happy we did this,' Heather said, turning her head to one side to look at Laura. 'You've been a bit wary of me.'

Oh, God, Laura thought. Directness. How terrifying. Her normal response would have been evasive, squirming denial. But, hey, when in Rome. 'A bit, yeah.'

Heather laughed. 'I'm so glad you admit it. Do you know why?'

'Do you?'

'Okay. If you like I can start. Maybe you thought I was a gold-digger. That your brother was a meal ticket. A rescue package for me and my two fatherless kids.'

'Wow.'

'Am I wrong?'

'Was he?'

'Do you answer every question with a question, Laura?'

Laura burst out laughing. 'Only if I'm trying to buy time to think of an answer!'

Heather smirked. 'He wasn't. I can completely, honestly see why you guys might think so, but he wasn't.'

Laura nodded.

'In actual fact, I was sure – I mean totally, utterly sure – that I was going to be on my own at least until the girls were grown-up, gone. I thought that was what I wanted. I thought it was best for them, and I knew it would be best for me. Their dad – he wasn't a good guy. I couldn't have stood having a parade of inadequate, not-good-enough – for them or me – men parading through their childhood. I had quite a fierce independent kickass thing going for myself and for them.

'In point of fact, I never had money. Didn't grow up with it, didn't marry it, first time round. Sure as hell didn't make it. Never expected it. Do I like it? Hell, yes. Who doesn't? I won't apologize for that. I won't say I'd have fallen in love with your brother if he'd been, I don't know, a road-sweeper either. I won't insult you. He's who he is because of who he is. Your brother. My husband. He's someone different from me, I know, but you must see what I see. Some, at least. He's . . . he's kind. And steady. Like a rock. Sounds dumb, maybe, but he's honourable. He's the best man I know. I've ever known. The most decent. He's never going to hurt me. He's always going to put us first.

'And I knew what you thought of me, when you met me, the first time, at my wedding. I always knew you were going to be the toughest nut to crack.'

She spoke fast, and quietly. Almost conspiratorially.

'That's quite a speech.'

'I practise in front of the mirror,' Heather deadpanned drily.

Laura couldn't tell whether she was joking or not, until Heather winked at her.

'Told myself I didn't care what you thought of me. My head hits the pillow and I don't wonder whether I'm a bad person. He's happy, I'm happy. Why *should* I care? Turns out, though, I do care. Damn it. I do care what you think.'

'Why?'

'I like you.' A shrug.

'And you want everyone to like you back?'

'You say that like it's a bad thing. But actually I'd settle for being understood.'

Laura sighed. 'I don't *not* like you.'

'Wow. Gee. Thanks.'

'Don't like myself much.' Laura felt herself hunch inwards.

'Okay. Why?' Heather had rolled onto her side now, and was resting her head on her hand. She had very, very pretty eyes, Laura thought. Even without makeup. She was very close. Laura didn't answer. She closed her eyes again.

'Because your husband turned out to be a schmuck who left you high and dry?'

It didn't surprise Laura that Heather knew everything. Or was comfortable to refer to it. It did surprise her that she didn't really mind. She'd been so private about it, so humiliated, for so long. 'Something like that.' She tried to straighten up.

'And that's your fault?'

'Maybe.'

'Bullshit.'

Laura didn't reply.

'Total bullshit. Only thing you did wrong was marry him in the first place. Scott says he was always bad news as far as he was concerned. But, hey, you were young. We've all screwed up. I hate, I mean, I *hate* when women blame themselves for men behaving badly. Men don't leave you because you put on ten pounds or got grey hairs or didn't want to screw him as often as you did before you had a kid. Men leave because they get bored and they leave because they can. And that's all on them, not on you.'

Laura smiled. Shyly at first. Then a little broader, with a nod.

Heather nodded back, her eyes narrowed to emphasize what she'd said. 'Okay, so newsflash for you here. You were wrong about me. I married your brother because I fell in love with him. Yes, he offered me a new life, security, a home … Love is a simple word, but there are complicated, different paths people follow to find it. But I love him, and he loves me, and I'm staying. Never been more sure of anything except what I grew up knowing – that I can survive on my own. It's knowing that that makes this work. If that makes sense. I'm here because I want to be, not because I need to be.

'I see you, Laura. I see that you're angry and hurt and I see that you feel shitty about yourself. I see it because I've lived it. And there's two widowers and a recently married bachelor in this family of yours. Just the one divorcee and I'm right here. You and me, we might have more in common than you think. You and me, we could maybe be friends.' She sat up, then stood in one easy movement, and rolled up her mat. 'And I'd like that.' She bent, a little awkwardly, and put her hand on Laura's shoulder, squeezing gently. Laura caught her hand with her own, surprised at herself and her response to the gesture.

39

He probably shouldn't have told her. She didn't, after all, need to know. Scott could have cut out his tongue. It had all been going so well.

If he was honest, he'd been rather enjoying being the most functional of the three of them. Maybe that wasn't very kind, but it made a change. For years, he'd been the anomaly: occasions like this, Christmas, Easter, for the longest time it had been Mum and Dad, Alex and Laura, Nick and Carrie. And Scott. He hadn't quite fitted. Scott, who didn't have girlfriends. Scott, who made a fortune at work – but who else understood what he did and, anyway, what did it matter how much you earned if you never had any time to spend it, no one to spend it on?

If he had been self-indulgent enough to recline on some expensive therapist's Corbusier lounger, he suspected he'd discover it went further back than that. Laura and Mum had always been a double act, tight. Nick was so much more like Charlie than Scott was and, if that wasn't enough, he was Mum's precious baby, too. Laura and Nick were closer. It was always him, vaguely on the outside, just different enough to feel a bit strange. He had never for a second doubted that his parents loved him. That they were proud of him. He just wasn't entirely sure they knew what to do with him. Perhaps he'd always been on a quest to please them.

But he wasn't self-indulgent enough to recline on an expensive therapist's Corbusier lounger. Heather had taught him, was teaching him, to be more open, more emotional . . . but he was still mostly comfortable doing that with her, through her. He'd been trying it out, though, on the others. The other day, in the pool with Nick and the kids, he'd felt a closeness he hadn't been aware of with his brother. After Carrie had died, he'd tried, but each time he saw or spoke to Nick, he was left with the feeling that he wasn't getting it right – that he hadn't said quite the right thing. But, when he'd scooped Arthur out of the water, and then they'd all gone in dressed and been silly and loving and fun, he'd felt very close to him.

He'd remembered something he hadn't thought about for years. A family holiday in Cornwall. Maybe Devon. There'd been a lot of those. They'd been on a beach with lots of rock pools, and Dad had bought them all nets and buckets, although Laura hadn't been that interested. Scott had been earnestly crabbing, photographing his catch with the Kodak camera he'd been given for Christmas. Nick had been following him, clad in his terry-towelling poncho and nothing else, while his trunks dried on the windbreak. His brother had been a shadow that summer, a little boy wanting to be bigger, and Scott had found him annoying. He'd fallen off a slimy rock into a pool that turned out to be quite deep, face first. Scott had jumped in after him, hooking him out by the hood of his poncho, splashing his camera. He'd worried he'd damaged the camera, and he'd lost a particularly interesting-looking crab. But he'd been proud of himself for 'saving' Nick. He hadn't hesitated.

The conversation after dinner had probably only happened because the three of them had had so much to drink, but he couldn't honestly say he was sorry it had. The next morning, when she'd first seen him, Laura hadn't said a word, but she'd come to him, where he was standing, propped against a cupboard in the kitchen, and leant her head very briefly against his chest, slipping her hand into his for just a second.

It had all been going so well.

Heather really was working her magic on all of them, exactly as he had hoped and believed she would. He'd watched her pick them off one by one – Charlie, Laura, Nick – talk to them with her own brand of warm, relatable straightness. And win them over. Even prickly, brittle Laura seemed to have softened in the last day. The kids were easy, of course, the easiest of all. They wanted to be mothered, and she was very good at that. Earlier, he'd watched them make jam tarts in the kitchen. She'd got them all in little gingham aprons she must have bought in town, and stood them on the chairs around the table, rolling pastry and spooning jam. If she'd deliberately put flour on their cheeks and photographed them for her Instagram account, Nick hadn't seemed to mind. Some people were very uptight about social media, and he'd thought his brother might have been too. He could almost hear him complaining about people living their lives through a lens under false pretences, or refusing to let his children be treated like catalogue models. Maybe he would have done, once. But not now. Some of that fight – that posturing – had gone out of him. Hashtag family.

Ethan was the only one he hadn't seen Heather charm.

Laura's explanation of what was going on at home had shone a light on his nephew's closed-off quietness. He knew Nick had spoken to him. He didn't feel quite that he could, although he'd been looking for an opening. And now he'd told her.

They'd been squeezed together in the middle of the vast bed in a soporific after-sex glow. He was new to the charms of quiet-cos-we're-in-a-busy-house-and-these-doors-don't-lock sex, and, somewhat to his surprise, he was a big fan. She'd laughed throatily when he'd confessed to finding it thrilling, the idea of being interrupted, gently scratching his chest through the greying hair, saying if he liked danger sex, she might have some other suggestions for him. He was immediately aroused again.

They were whispering about the others when he'd spilt the whole story of Ethan to her. As he spoke, he felt her back stiffen, and she stopped scratching his chest. She moved away from him in a sudden movement, and pulled the sheet around her, bringing her knees to her chest. The moment for more sex had most definitely passed.

'Oh, I don't like that.'

Scott was confused. 'Which part?'

'The underage-sex part.'

'Oh, come on, Heather. According to Nick she was only a few weeks off her sixteenth birthday.'

'Which, by the way, is still too young so far as I'm concerned. But she wasn't sixteen, was she? She was fifteen. *Fifteen*, Scott.'

'You're kidding, right?' For a moment, he thought she must be. Of the two of them, she was by far the most relaxed about sex. The most experienced, and the

most adventurous. Two minutes earlier she'd been stroking him and talking about the benefits of doing it in the
Jacuzzi. He was genuinely confused.

'That's younger than Hayley.'

'We don't know this girl. Maybe she seemed older.'

'And that's the point, is it? If she seemed older, it's fine.'
She was almost hissing at him now.

'No, I'm just saying . . .' Scott was struggling to organize his thoughts. This reaction had been so far from what
he'd expected. He felt wrongfooted.

'Eyeliner and high heels and miniskirts might make
you look older, Scott. They don't make your mind or your
body older.'

'I know that.'

'I'm not kidding. Look at my girls.' He heard the word,
the slight change of tone. 'Do you think *they* are doing it?'
She spat 'doing it'. Made it sound dirty.

'No. I mean, I don't know. Are they?'

'Of course they aren't.'

'I didn't mean Meredith.'

'Neither of them is.'

'But isn't it different? They're at a girls' school.'

'What difference does that make? You're just talking
about opportunity, Scott. If they were co-ed, do you think
it would be okay for Hayley to be sleeping with someone?
Without me knowing?' She was excluding him.

Scott tried to consider the matter. It wasn't easy to
think about, but he didn't feel outraged at the idea. No.
Clearly that wasn't what Heather expected or wanted to
hear. 'I don't understand why you're getting so worked
up about this, honey. They were going out. Boyfriend

and girlfriend. As Laura tells it, they really cared for each other.'

'Not enough to wait.'

'Is this some American purity bollocks?'

That was probably a mistake.

Her eyes sparkled with anger and she knelt up in the bed, poised. 'Don't do that. Don't do that. No. It's not some American purity bollocks, Scott. No. It's international morality.' She used air quotes, and in raising her hands, the sheet fell down, exposing her breasts. That seemed to make her madder, and she pulled it back up angrily.

'I think you're being ridiculous, if you don't mind my saying so.'

'No. Go ahead. We'll agree to disagree.' She shucked on her robe, which had lain discarded at the foot of the bed when she'd pulled him between the sheets.

He didn't know what had happened. He felt defensive on Ethan's behalf, but she seemed so genuinely upset by the story. He wanted to understand what he was missing. He took her hand. 'I'm sorry, baby.'

For a moment her hand stiffened and he thought she was going to snatch it away. But she didn't. The fingers softened, then interlinked with his own.

'I'm sorry. I know he's your nephew.'

'And I honestly think he's a nice kid.'

'I'm not saying he isn't. I just . . . I don't like to think about it, you know . . .'

'Who does?'

'I'm just saying, I have rather more sympathy with this girl's father than you seem to. If it was Hayley – if it had been Hayley – I'd have wanted to rip off that boy's head.'

'I get that.' He wasn't entirely sure he did, to be honest. It all seemed a bit out of proportion. But he was relieved that she was letting him hold her hand, and that her voice had returned to the modulation he was used to. Hissing Heather wasn't his favourite.

'And it changes how I feel about him, to be truthful.'

'Oh, honey. Please don't let that be how it is. He's in pieces. Laura's in bits too. He's got results coming up.'

'So has Hayley.'

'Hayley's fine.' He told himself this was just transposed anxiety. He knew Heather had worried about the girls making the transition to the English system. He knew she felt selfish. This wasn't about Ethan, not really. It couldn't be. She'd reacted like he was almost a criminal. A predator.

'I know. I know.'

He pulled her head to his chest and stroked her hair. She seemed calm now. 'You look after all of us, and you do it so brilliantly, I sometimes forget to take care of you.'

She snaked her arms around his back. 'I love you. I'm sorry.'

'Sssh. Nothing to be sorry about.' He kissed her and reflected that, just as he thought he was getting the hang of marriage, of real intimacy, perhaps he still had a long way to go. He had the uncomfortable feeling he hadn't really understood what had just happened, and wasn't quite brave enough to try to.

40

Ethan had only gone down to the pool because no one else was there. At first, he'd had no interest in swimming. He hadn't even had his trunks on. It was the peace and stillness he wanted. People were suddenly everywhere, in the kitchen, in the living room, on the terrace . . . Some ignored him, some seemed to goad him, some wanted to be sweet to him, and he didn't want any of it. Nick was getting ready to go for a run, and he and Scott were teasing each other about their relative fitness, like kids. Heather was cooking something, or at least pretending to cook something so she could take her stupid photos. Hashtag family! It was embarrassing. Granddad was reading the paper, like always, his head nodding as he dozed behind the pages, where he thought no one could see. He didn't know where his mum was, but he didn't particularly want to see her either. He could have stayed upstairs in his little room, but he was bored rigid by the four walls. His misery kept him mobile.

He took the cover off the pool to dip his feet in the water. Perhaps he'd like to swim after all. Just float, maybe. With the big glass doors closed, it was a bit hot. He had too many clothes on. The water began to look deliciously cool and welcoming. He might as well wallow while he wallowed. An adult might have stripped down to their underwear. Or skinny-dipped. No one was around, after

253

all. There were towels – Heather seemed to be drying and folding them all the time – in a stack on one of the loungers. No one need ever know. A sober teenager would never do that. Ethan padded up the path, then upstairs to get his trunks.

And, of course, he didn't put the cover back on. The same way he didn't put wet towels on the radiator, or dirty socks in the laundry hamper, or the lid back on the Marmite. He'd sloped back to the house to get something: he'd be gone for, what, three minutes tops? And he just hadn't done it.

At exactly that moment Meredith went into the toilet with Delilah, to make sure she washed her hands after she'd used the loo, and at precisely that time Arthur, who had been watching a cartoon with them, in his odd but customary pose of face down, bum in the air, thumb in on the rug, rolled sideways, a bit bored, and tottered outside, past his granddad, who had fallen asleep, his head back, his mouth open, snoring gently.

And because it had been so much fun, when he'd done it with Uncle Scott and Daddy, and because the water looked so nice, and because he had no real notion that the orange armbands, rather than his own natural buoyancy, were what kept him bobbing on the surface of the water, instead of sinking, Arthur stood starfish on the side and jumped in.

Ethan got back downstairs in his trunks, T-shirt slung across his shoulder, just before Meredith, standing on the patio from where she could see the open door to the pool, issued a piercing scream. 'Arthur?'

What followed seemed, to all of them, to happen in

heart-stopping slow motion. Ethan barged past his step-cousin, shoving her roughly against the door frame, and ran. Simultaneously, the adults within hearing distance appeared from the corners of the house and garden, Heather wiping her wet hands on an apron. Charlie, dozing on a reclining chair, sat up with a start, looking confused, then afraid.

Getting there first, Ethan side-stepped down the first part of the pool. Arthur had gone in about halfway towards the deep end, just where Scott had scooped him up last time. The exuberant projection of his jump had taken his small arms out of reach of the side, but, anyway, he was too young and too scared to think about making contact with the tiles. He didn't know how to save himself. For a second, Ethan was frozen by terror. Arthur was below the surface, face down. His arms were still in mid-flail.

He was dead. He had to be dead. With a wild sob rising in his throat, the spell broken, Ethan belly-flopped into the water with a loud crack, and lifted the small body out of the water in the arc of his movement.

Heather was there by the time he did so. She had made it to the side to snatch him from Ethan's hands, and she sat back in a single motion, sitting down hard, the little boy across her lap, his back arched. She murmured to him the whole time. Her eyes were wild, but she seemed calm, her movements deliberate and careful. 'Oh, no, baby. Oh, no, baby. No, you don't. Oh, no, you don't. Come on. You come back. You come back, you hear me? Daddy wants to see you. Your daddy wants to see you . . .'

While she quietly pleaded with him, she ministered to his tiny body, turning him first onto his side, rubbing his back, then rolling him over, pushing her knuckles into his sternum. It looked violent to Ethan. She put her head down to listen to his chest, his mouth. She shucked him off her lap, to lie on the floor, and bent down across him.

Ethan had pulled himself up and sat on the side, staring at them silently. He was shivering, or trembling. Meredith was crying, noisy, childish sobs. Hayley, who had been sunbathing on a towel at the other side of the garden, had come to the bifold doors at the commotion and had her hand across her mouth in horror.

Nick was at the door to the pool now. He shouted his son's name, once.

It took less than a minute, maybe much less, from the moment of Meredith's scream, for Arthur to splutter, cough, convulse slightly, so that water trickled from the side of his mouth, and then wail.

By then, Nick had slid onto the floor beside Heather, Ethan had stood up, Scott had arrived, and Hayley and Meredith had quietly led Bea and Delilah back into the house. Charlie stayed hovering by the door, his hands outstretched in a gesture of utter helplessness.

Nick pulled his son into his arms and rocked him. 'You're okay, guy. You're fine . . .'

No one spoke at first, letting the relief flood them and douse the flames of hot panic. Arthur's sobs subsided quickly, replaced by a persistent cough. Nick patted his back. Heather put her own hand there too, stroking him gently, looking intently at his face over his father's shoulder.

As the coughing slowed, Nick scanned the room. 'What the hell happened?' he asked.

'He fell in.' This was Ethan, staring at his feet.

'No shit, Sherlock. How?' Nick's voice sounded harsh.

Meredith had come back now. She was still crying. 'Is he okay? Nick? Is he okay?'

'Ssh.' Heather stood up, and went to her daughter. 'He's going to be fine, darling. He's okay.'

'It's my fault.' Her shoulders heaved, her face was stricken. 'I went to the bathroom with Lila. Just for a second.'

'It's not your fault.' Heather smiled at her, her eyes full of concern. 'It's okay, baby girl.' Meredith buried her face in her mother's chest, and Heather kissed her tenderly.

'I was asleep,' Charlie said, wringing his hands. 'He must have gone right past me.'

Ethan looked up. Heather met his gaze at once, and her eyes narrowed in a way he hadn't seen before. She was biting her lip. Nick's face, too, was furious.

'But why wasn't the pool closed?'

It felt like everyone was looking at him at once. Like he'd just been outed in an Agatha Christie novel. Granddad. Uncle Scott. Nick. Heather. Now Meredith.

The enormity of his stupidity and what it had almost meant hit him hard. He thought he was pretty much as miserable as he knew how to be, but it was like he was in a lift shaft, hurtling down to a new, dreadful low. 'It was me.'

'What the hell were you thinking, Ethan?'

'I – I wasn't,' he admitted. 'I just went to get my trunks.'

'You left the cover off and the door open while you went to get your trunks?' It was said more as an incredulous statement than as a question.

'I'm sorry.' Ethan preferred to stare at his feet, but he forced himself to drag his gaze up to meet Nick's eyes. He saw an expression and an intensity there he'd never seen before, and he almost physically shrank from it.

'You're sorry? Do you have any idea how idiotic that was? Do you have any idea what almost happened here?'

Ethan couldn't answer.

'Do you? Do you?'

Nick's words rained on him like blows. He actually flinched under their power as if they had been. He felt himself getting smaller.

'Nick.' Scott had stepped forward now, but it was Charlie speaking. 'Nick. Calm down.'

Nick stopped him with a raised hand. 'No, Dad. I won't calm down. Arthur could have drowned.'

'I know. But –'

Nick rounded on his father. 'No but, Dad. Don't defend him, not in this. He's not a kid. Is he? He wants to be taken seriously, then he goes and does this.' Nick was standing up now, still holding Arthur tightly. 'How fucking irresponsible.'

'I wasn't thinking –'

'You don't say.' Nick's contemptuous sarcasm penetrated further, even, than his anger.

Ethan felt like nothing at all. He wished his mum was there, then hated himself for the pathetic, pitiful desire to bury his face in her skirts, like Meredith was doing with hers right now. He was a worthless coward.

Nick turned his back on Ethan, and walked in the direction of the house, holding Arthur tightly to him. 'I'd better see the girls.'

Charlie smiled tightly, sadly, at Ethan. Scott touched him lightly on the shoulder. 'Better get yourself dried off, Ethan. Warmed up.'

Ethan nodded wordlessly.

Heather was following Nick out of the pool house, still concentrating her attention on Arthur. 'I don't like that cough, Nick. Don't you think you should take him to the emergency room?' She corrected herself unconsciously. 'A and E. To A and E. We don't know exactly how long he was in the water. And we don't know if he has any water in his lungs. That *can* cause a problem, if you don't treat it.'

Nick turned to look at her sharply. 'How do you know?'

'Water-safety course. With swimming lessons. When Hayley and Meredith were little. It's called secondary drowning, I think. And then on *The Affair*, on HBO a couple of years back. They had one. It's incredibly rare. But he's still coughing . . .'

'If you think we need to.'

Heather nodded decisively. 'Just to be sure. I'm certain he's completely fine. But you should hear that from a doctor, not from someone who did a course ten years ago or more. Right?'

Nick deferred. 'Okay. You're right.' He rubbed his face with his free hand. 'Christ.'

Heather squeezed his arm. 'It's okay. Look. You go and get Arthur dressed in something warm. You should change your shirt too – you're pretty wet. I'll come with you. I'll drive. Give me your car keys – we'll put his car seat in our car.'

'What about the girls?'

'Scott and Charlie can take care of them. My girls are here too, to help. They will be absolutely fine.'

He gave her a weak, smile, grateful for the direction. 'Okay.'

Ethan heard the gravel crunch. He went to the window in time to see the back of Heather's car turning out of the drive. He'd come straight up here. No one had been near him since. At some point Meredith had appeared on their landing, and stood briefly, glaring at him resentfully until he kicked the door shut against her. Dressed now, but still shivering, Ethan sat on the edge of the bed, with his face in his hands, willing Arthur to be all right. He was too shocked to cry.

He wanted to talk to Saskia. He wanted to talk to her so badly. And where the hell was his mother?

41

Never get into a car with a strange man. Except he wasn't strange. And this wasn't a car. It was a truck. A truck that was currently lost, and parked at a service station – the kind with a Little Chef, not the kind with a Harry Ramsden's and an M&S food hall.

'Have you heard of sat navs?' She was teasing.

Joe looked up from the road atlas, and smiled. 'I told you, I'm a Luddite.'

'So you spend a lot of time in lay-bys, then, do you?'

'I'm normally much better than this. You must have put me off.'

'Oh, my fault, is it?'

She arched her eyebrows. This was flirting, she realized. How absolutely ludicrous. And lovely.

She'd bumped into him by chance. Well, if it could technically be chance that she was walking beyond the garden in the direction he had vaguely pointed in, when they'd first spoken. She wasn't exactly looking for him, but she'd remembered the direction. Thankfully, he didn't seem suspicious that she was seeking him out. He had greeted her warmly – as though her being there was almost expected. Told her he lived 'over there' and pointed again. She had nodded, and exclaimed politely, which was neither acknowledging nor denying that she already knew.

'I'm always rushing when I bump into you,' he'd said,

although, to her, it seemed a very rural and laid-back interpretation of rushing. Everything about him seemed to be slower-paced than she was used to. She had the sudden thought that perhaps he was slow in bed, too. And shook her head, because it was so inappropriate and random and because she hadn't thought about being in bed with anyone in for ever. But the thought persisted. And she engaged with it . . .

'Where to?' A bit brazen. Had she had too much English summer sun?

'Oh, one of my other sidelines.'

'Sounds mysterious. People-smuggling?'

He'd laughed. 'Nothing so illegal. Pedestrian by comparison.'

'So tell me? Otherwise I'll have to make up all kinds of things.'

He shrugged his shoulders, then obviously decided to tell her. 'I work with wood. Specifically, furniture. I'm a trained joiner. I make my own pieces from scratch. But I also – Have you heard of upcycling?'

'Yeah. Making old stuff usable again, right?'

'Exactly. Taking unfashionable, or damaged, or just unwanted old stuff and making other stuff out of it.'

'Very twenty-first century.'

He smiled. 'I like to think I was into it before it became fashionable but, yeah, I guess. Sustainability, less waste, all that good stuff . . .'

'Very PC too.' Heather would be all over that, she thought. Immediately the prospect of Joe meeting Heather made her nervous. She was so pretty and youthful and sexy. She was thinking like a schoolgirl, for God's sake.

'If you like. For me, it's just better, the old stuff – better made, more substantial, higher quality. I can't bear it being thrown away and replaced with stuff that comes in a flatpack or from bloody Amazon.'

'Fair enough. A friend of mine moved house recently and she had two tables that didn't fit the new place, one a Victorian mahogany leafed table and the other an IKEA she'd screwed together fifteen years earlier. She was offered more for the IKEA one than the antique.'

'Exactly. That's crazy, right?'

'I did think so, when she told me.'

'And it can be very creative. I enjoy it – love it, actually.'

'Gardening, and furniture restoration.'

He nodded. 'That's me. Love what you do, never work a day in your life. So, I buy bits online from eBay, sometimes from house clearances, places like that, collect them, work on them, sell them on . . .'

'And that's where you're going?'

'Yep. Just north of Cirencester today. To collect an old Welsh dresser and a sewing table I bought.'

'Okay, then.' She prepared to let him go.

He did that hesitating thing he'd done in the greenhouse. Then seemed to decide something. 'Wanna come?'

She was surprised – it must have shown on her face. Was that what he'd been going to say in the greenhouse? A red spot sprang up on his chest, where the two top buttons of his shirt were undone, at her hesitation. 'Of course you don't. You're on holiday. You're walking . . . Stupid idea.'

'I'd love to.' For a second that was the answer she gave out of kindness, to cover his obvious embarrassment, to be polite. But only for a second. She wanted to go.

'Really?' He seemed gratifyingly pleased.

'Why not?'

They stood smiling at each other for just a moment longer than was normal.

'I'll throw in a cup of tea and a piece of cake if you help me lift stuff into the back of the truck.'

She giggled. 'Ah, an ulterior motive!'

'You didn't think I just wanted the company, did you?'

It was the lightness that was so intoxicating. That was how she explained it to herself. There'd been no light relief in her life for so long. Regular phone calls with Mel's gentle teasing and distracting stories from the pub: that was as flippant as it had got lately. Everything else was like wading through a treacly swamp, and she was tired of it. She wasn't going to see this guy after she left, so why not? It was harmless.

Laura had a horrible feeling that, as wretched as the last few months had been, there hadn't been nearly enough fun and lightness in her life before then either. It hadn't been a priority. She could, and probably would, blame Alex, but she'd been complicit. She wasn't a spontaneous woman. She might say she had been, more, when she was younger, but it wasn't really true. She was a planner, risk averse. And look where that had got her . . .

So it seemed to make sense, with just her phone and her sunglasses, to accept this invitation from a man she'd spent, oh, probably all of fifteen minutes with in total, to go and look at old furniture God knew where. She was still Laura, though, so she messaged her dad. Ethan, although his phone seemed to be spot-welded to his hand, rarely read her messages. *Gone out. Home for supper. Xx*

Eventually they'd found where they needed to be, Laura navigating with the ancient road atlas on her lap, both of them concentrating. It was oddly comfortable to be quiet together, the silence punctuated only by her directions.

En-route home, task completed, journey straight-forward, things were chattier. It had been vague between them until now but, by mutual agreement, they wanted to exchange facts, to know more about each other. They threw quick-fire questions at each other.

He'd grown up in Suffolk. Only child. His father had died ten years earlier. His mother had remarried a family friend and lived on the north Norfolk coast and played a lot of bridge. Lots of aunts, uncles and cousins. He'd done an engineering degree at university but he'd hated it – the subject, not the life. He'd lived and worked in London for a few years, but he liked his life better here and now, and he didn't miss the city.

His stock answer to the favourite-film question was *Goodfellas*, but his actual favourite film was *Moonstruck*, and his desert-island album would be *Diamond Dogs*. He liked reading, he said, and he loved cooking. 'And my one wish is for world peace.' He said this in falsetto, with a terrible cod-American accent.

'Sorry. I'm being nosy.'

'Me too. It's good. This is like speed-dating.'

'I wouldn't know.' She heard the flirtation in her own voice and, once again, was surprised by it.

'I did it once. A mate dragged me along. It was horrendous.'

'And this is like that?' But she was teasing.

'Correction. This couldn't be less like that.'

She felt herself glowing at the compliment.

'What about you? Same questions? Two minutes to answer.'

She laughed, flustered. 'Um. Um.'

'I'll have to hurry you.'

'Okay, okay. Big family. All staying in the house. Read English at uni. Should've read history. Or politics. Big crush on Norman What's-his-name on the BBC.'

'Really?'

'Really! Favourite film *Jack and Sarah*.'

'Never seen it.'

'It's lovely. Triple-hanky job. Richard E. Grant too.'

'Another crush?'

'You know it.'

'Music?'

'Radio. All sorts. Abba.'

'No one's perfect.'

'Oy!' She hit his arm playfully. 'Oh, and *Peaky Blinders*.'

'Cillian Murphy?'

'Tom Hardy.'

'You're incorrigible.' Joe laughed easily.

'You have to have a crush.'

'Jeanne Tripplehorn,' he answered. I look nothing like her, Laura thought. 'You.' He was looking ahead, at the road. 'Well, until I heard about Abba.'

'Ever been married?'

'Once.' He paused, and she wondered if she'd gone too far. 'To a woman named Rachel. We were married for three years. We've been divorced for seven or so.'

'I'm separated.' She had hardly ever said it out loud, and he hadn't asked.

266

'I figured.'

She stared at her hands on her knees.

'Are you okay?'

She turned to look at him, but he was gazing at the road ahead. She was touched by the simplicity of the question, and the tone in which he'd asked it. 'I think I'm going to be.'

She hadn't been home for supper, like she'd said she would be. They'd stopped at a pub with a big beer garden where they had wood-fired pizzas, carried on talking, and laughing. It was almost dark when he pulled into the driveway. He'd offered to drop her at the house, but she'd said she'd rather walk through the garden, not really ready for everyone to see who she'd been with, so she came in through the back, dawdling in the moonlight, puzzled, as she approached, by how still and dark the house seemed at barely nine o'clock.

'I had a lovely time. Thank you.' It was an oddly formal thing to say.

'Me too.' He took her hand, leant forward and kissed her cheek, very slowly and very softly, lingering so she could smell him.

She kissed his in return, quicker because she was suddenly nervous. 'Night.'

Scott was sitting alone in the kitchen in the quiet, with a glass of whisky. It was just getting dark but he'd only put on one sidelight. Laura could read the immediate change of energy in the house. No one else was around. Scott explained briefly. Nick and Heather had come back from the hospital an hour or so before she'd come in, and Nick had taken Arthur straight up, he said. Bea and Delilah were already asleep.

'Poor Nick. Poor Arthur. How the hell did that happen?'

Scott made no bones. 'Ethan left the cover off.'

'Fuck.' She'd had a sixth sense, the second Scott had said Arthur had fallen into the pool.

'It was just for a minute – he went upstairs to get his trunks.'

'Oh, my God. Where is he now?'

'In his room.'

'I'll go up.'

'Up to you, but I'd maybe leave him.'

A sharp remark about parenting advice bubbled into her throat but she didn't voice it.

'Everyone else seems to have retreated to their own space,' he explained. 'There were quite a few recriminations, quite a lot of shouting.'

'Of course.' She could imagine. The glow of a gorgeous afternoon was fading rapidly. All-too-familiar guilt flooded into its space. She should have been there, instead of gallivanting around like an irresponsible teenager. She felt old again.

'Hospital?' She was still struggling to understand what had happened. 'Was it bad? Is he okay?'

Scott patted her shoulder. 'He's fine. Heather thought they should just make sure – get him checked out. They had a longish wait in A and E, and he was tired and a bit overwrought. But he's physically perfectly fine. Don't worry. It's over.'

'Thank God.'

'Where've you been, Sis?' But his tone wasn't accusatory.

She sank into a kitchen chair and he poured Laura her own small tumbler of whisky. She drank it in one. 'Just out.' She hadn't the energy, suddenly, to explain. Hadn't Dad told them she'd sent a message? She'd come in high as a kite, as happy as she could remember feeling in ages, but the news had slammed her back down to earth. She was furious with Ethan, and sorry too. Maternal guilt seeped through her, irrational as it might be. If she'd been there, it wouldn't have happened. Ethan had needed her.

'Ethan.'

He wasn't asleep, but he lay still, kept his eyes closed.

'Ethan?' The whisper was a little louder, but he still ignored her. He didn't want to talk. Not now. He'd wanted her, badly, earlier, but she hadn't been there. And now he didn't. Didn't want her. Didn't want to speak.

She came into the room, leaving the door ajar so she could still see in the light from the landing. She sat very briefly on the foot of his bed, and put her hand across his ankle under the sheets. For a moment she just sat there, then she gently patted it, and stood up. She bent over and kissed his face. If she knew he was faking sleep, she didn't let on. She hovered for a moment, then sighed gently. 'I love you. It's going to be okay.'

And then she left him.

The next morning, when she deemed he'd slept long enough and might be ready to talk, she made them each a mug of tea, and carried it to the top of the house.

And Ethan wasn't there.

His bed was unmade, the floor was still strewn with his stuff. The rucksack he'd brought with him was there, spilling its crumpled contents onto the spare bed. His phone, of course, was gone, and she couldn't see his wallet. He was gone.

42

It would be hot later, but so early there was a chill in the air. Ethan pulled his hoody over his head, and yanked his sleeves over his hands, walking faster, until he was almost breathless but warmer.

It was just after six in the morning when he left, the rest of the house still asleep as he closed the front door quietly behind him, then walked into the town. He had his phone, fully charged, with headphones, a cap, a hoody and his wallet, which contained about thirty quid and some change, his rail and Oyster cards, and the emergency credit card Dad had given him. He was going to buy the ticket on that. Despite the stern talk Dad had had with him when he'd presented Ethan with the card, he either didn't check the statement that often or he had a different definition of what constituted an emergency. This definitely did. He bought a cup of coffee and a Chelsea bun from the café, ate it sitting in a bus shelter and got on the first bus that stopped. He had paid next to no attention on the journey there, and he didn't know the name of the town until he read it on the sign outside the library. He might have been predicted a good grade in geography, although he was far from sanguine about achieving it, but he had to put the name into Google on his phone to work out which way he was going.

He'd been thinking about it ever since they arrived.

What had happened yesterday had made up his mind. Everyone was furious with him, including himself. He didn't blame them at all.

Granddad had brought him up some dinner, fish and chips Scott had collected, and told him Arthur was fine, and that everyone was going to have an early night. He'd put a hand on his hair and asked, 'Are you coming down?'

Ethan had shaken his head.

'Maybe that's best. Let everyone calm down. It'll be better tomorrow.'

'Will it?'

'We all know, Eth, that it was an accident.'

'Nick's never gonna forgive me.'

'Of course he will. He was frightened, that's all. Scared. He's already —'

'Lost so much. I know.'

'Trust me when I tell you that this too shall pass.'

He always said that. One of his weird little pearls of wisdom. Was it from some poem, or the Bible, or something?

Ethan wasn't at all sure it would, though. He didn't see how. He ruined everything, didn't he? A Midas touch of crap. He'd nearly killed Arthur. His family would hate him. He hated himself. Saskia was gone. His mates had almost given up on him. Results would probably be a shitstorm of mediocrity. He might be called a rapist, for God's sake. It felt hopeless. He felt hopeless.

Mum had come in eventually, but he was too pissed off with her by then to want to speak to her, so he'd pretended he was asleep.

He'd slept badly, if at all, and by the time it was starting to get light, he knew what he wanted to do. At first it was just about not being *here* – about getting as far away from these people and this situation as quickly as he could.

The thought of where he might go came later, dawning on him gradually, hopefully, wonderfully. He wanted to see Saskia. He hadn't dared shower, in case he woke Hayley and Meredith. He'd pulled on a shirt and jeans, and he'd left. He wanted to message her and tell her he was coming, but she hadn't read any of his messages since that awful night. They'd probably changed her number.

He was in somewhere called Kidlington when his mum's message pinged up on the screen. *Where are you?*

He turned his phone over so he couldn't see it.

She waited five minutes. *Ethan?????*

Another ten minutes. *You're scaring me, Ethan. Please answer.*

I'm fine. Don't worry. Just needed some time.

This wasn't her fault. He didn't want her to be frightened.

OK. I understand.

He didn't reply to that one.

The next one was longer. If he opened it, to read the whole thing, he'd have to reply, so he didn't. He could see only the first part of the message on his screen.

Granddad told me what happened. I get that you feel horrid about it. You did a stupid thing . . .

He couldn't see the rest. Was she furious with him or protectively defensive? He'd rather she was furious.

When he was about eight, he'd stolen a packet of chewing gum from the local newsagent. The owner knew his mum because they went in there all the time and he knew how to contact her because she had some magazines on order. He'd held Ethan by the shoulder, in the days when you could touch someone else's kid and as long as you weren't hurting them it was sort of okay, while he dialled Mum's number. He needn't have done that. Ethan was far too frightened to run. He'd never taken anything he wasn't supposed to. He hadn't really understood why he'd done it then – it was the first time he'd done anything like that.

When she'd arrived, and Mr Cole had told her what had happened, she'd crouched, held both his arms and asked him if he had done it.

And he'd lied. He said he hadn't. He said he'd been going to pay for the gum, and he'd shown her the pound coin in his pocket.

And she'd believed him. She'd stood up and told Mr Cole that she believed him.

She was always on his side.

When she'd come to tuck him in that night, he'd been wide-eyed with wakefulness and fear, and he hadn't been able to bear the lie any longer, and he'd told her the truth.

And she was angry with him. Angry and disappointed, which was infinitely worse. The next morning she'd marched him back there and made him apologize, and there had been some kind of punishment he couldn't remember now. She'd done the right thing and he'd never stolen anything since. But what he remembered most was the way she'd spoken to Mr Cole when Ethan had lied and she'd backed him. He'd understood, in that moment, the full force of her maternal, mammalian urge to protect him. He'd seen it, again, the paternal variety, with Saskia's dad. He hadn't expected to see it last night and, no doubt, he would not have done. Perhaps it was that that he couldn't

274

bear. The thing with the chewing gum was the first time he had understood how it felt to disappoint his mother. He'd hated it. He had the feeling now.

He almost regretted leaving. He wouldn't call it running away, although he hadn't relished the thought of facing Nick and Heather this morning. Heather had looked at him with such ferocity. And Nick with such disappointment.

It was better for all of them if he wasn't there.

And he wanted to see Saskia.

It was midday when he finally got to her house. It was an immaculately neat and tidy semi. He hadn't been there for ages, but it looked like it always did. He lingered for a moment by the black railings at the front, his bravado wavering. When he'd played this out in his imagination, it was Saskia who answered the door. But maybe it would be her mother. She didn't work. He had to hope it wouldn't be her dad. He took a deep breath. Whoever answered the door, he had no option but to ring the bell. He couldn't call, and he was here now. But, still, he glanced up at the first-floor window of Saskia's bedroom, willing her to appear there and see him.

She didn't. He opened the gate, walked up to the glossy blue door, and rang the bell. Took one pace back, and realized he was holding his breath.

No one answered.

He wondered if he'd pressed the bell hard enough. He noticed his hand was shaking when he pressed again.

Still nothing.

A door opened, but it was the neighbour's house.

A white-haired elderly lady, barely tall enough to see over the beech hedge that separated the properties, stared at him suspiciously.

'Have you got a parcel?' Her tone was accusatory.

'What?'

She frowned, as if he were irritating. Spoke louder, and more slowly, like old people sometimes spoke to foreigners. 'Are you delivering a parcel here?'

'No. No.'

Her eyes narrowed, and she drew herself up formally. Behind her, he saw a Neighbourhood Watch sticker in the window. 'May I ask, then, what your business here is?'

He did his best to sound unthreatening. 'I'm a friend. A friend of Saskia's. From school. I've come to see her.'

Her tone and expression softened at Saskia's name. 'Well, then, I'm sorry, young man, but you've missed them.'

'They're out?' It seemed likely she'd know about the comings and goings. A 'twitcher', Mum would have called her. Always watching.

'They're away. On holiday. You must have got the day wrong, dear. They left yesterday.'

'Oh.'

'It's a long one, too. They won't be back for three weeks.'

'Okay.'

She realized she might have said too much. 'Can I say who was asking?'

He shook his head, and backed away.

'Young man?'

He walked through the gate and rapidly back the way he'd come.

Around the corner, he slumped against a low brick wall, close to tears of frustration and disappointment. He formed a fist and punched the wall. Stupid. Stupid. He looked at his knuckles, where spots of blood sprang from the inevitable graze, and sniffed hard.

A few yards away, a woman pushing a buggy eyed him warily, then crossed the road to continue on the other side.

Ethan wiped his knuckles on the leg of his jeans, wincing, then sank down to sit on the pavement, his shoulders hunched. And took his phone out.

43

Charlie had told Ethan to find a café, send the postcode and stay put. Then he had asked Scott to go and get him. He didn't want Laura driving, he said. He expected Laura to argue but she didn't. 'I'm not sure I'm what he needs, right now.' She'd laid her head on her father's shoulder, grateful for his taking control. Scott had agreed, not meeting Heather's eye. She'd walked out of the room.

'I'll come with you,' said Nick. Scott nodded.

They found the place easily enough. 'Not sure we should both go in.'

'Agreed. Want me to?'

Nick shook his head. 'Nah. Better be me. I yelled at him.'

'He deserved that. Besides, I reckon that was just the straw on the proverbial camel's back. Not your fault. The kid's had a bellyful.'

'I know. I'll go. You wait.'

'No problem. I can always make a few calls. Do me a favour – skinny cap and an almond croissant, if they have one. And don't take for ever. Good to avoid rush-hour if we can. And Laura will want us back.'

'Roger. Do my best.'

Ethan was sitting at the back, behind the cash desk, nursing a mug between his hands. He was staring into the middle distance, and Nick saw him first. The boy looked wretched. Approaching him, Nick touched his shoulder lightly. 'You scared us, mate.'

Ethan's shoulders sank a little – relief? Defeat? Nick couldn't tell. 'You okay?'

He rubbed his sleeve under his nose and sniffed hard. 'Not really. Yeah. I don't know. I'm sorry.'

Nick sat down. 'Whoa. Hold on. That's a lot of answers. Why don't you start by telling me what's happened? Did you find her?'

Ethan shook his head. 'No. She wasn't there. They're all away.'

'Well, that's good.'

'What?'

'It was daft to try. The last thing you need to be doing is pissing her father off any more than you already have.'

'Didn't think of that.'

'Didn't think at all, you plonker. Scared your mum, upset your granddad. Totally kiboshed Heather's Insta-breakfast.'

Ethan laughed, in spite of himself, but it was the kind of laugh that veered close to tears. Nick joined in, but Ethan stopped suddenly, his face close to crumpling. 'I could have killed Arthur.'

'And you didn't.'

'But I could've. And, besides, it's just the latest thing – I'm an idiot.'

'You're a kid. A kid coping with some shit. None of which is of your making. Why are you blaming yourself for any of it? I don't get it.'

Ethan couldn't immediately answer that one.

'I was much worse when I was your age.'

'No, you weren't.'

'Ask my dad sometime. Ask your mum. They don't know the half of it, really. But they'll still tell you I was all over the place. School, college, uni even. I didn't really grow up until I met Carrie, if I'm honest.'

'Really?' Ethan sat forward.

'Absolutely. I could tell you, but I'd have to kill you. More to the point, gotta get going. Scott's waiting outside, probably revving the engine. Time is money and all that. And he definitely didn't do any of that crap when we were young. He never really was young. Sort of born aged forty, if you know what I mean.'

Ethan sniggered.

Nick was glad he'd got the boy to relax a little. 'So can we get whatever you're drinking to go?'

'It's empty. Finished it an hour ago. Been nursing it so they didn't throw me out.'

'All right, Oliver Twist. You're killing me with this sob story. Let's get three hot drinks and a cake for the driver and get going. Come on.'

While they waited for the girl to make their coffees, Ethan touched Nick's arm. 'Thanks, Uncle Nick. I really am sorry. For all of this – especially Arthur.'

Nick put his finger to his lips. 'Enough. I know. Enough now.'

Late in the afternoon they all heard the car turn onto the gravel drive. The kids were watching *Finding Nemo*. The adults, except Laura, had been sitting in the kitchen, making small-talk. She'd been pacing in the gardens. Earlier, she'd tidied Ethan's room, folded all the discarded clothes into neat piles, then shaken out the duvet and pillows. She'd put a load of hoodies and jeans into the laundry downstairs, finding leftover detergent pods in a cupboard. She wanted to be busy. Heather had Scott on FindMy on her phone – she'd let them know he was twenty, ten and then five minutes away. Of course she bloody had. It wasn't fair, or nice, but in her misery Laura felt a flush of annoyance. Heather – perfect wife, perfect parent. Heather, Charlie and Hayley went wordlessly to the front door and out into the porch, although Laura wished they hadn't. Charlie's face was drawn with concern. She couldn't read Heather's as easily. Ethan slammed the car door, and walked past them all, his head down to avoid their eyes.

'Ethan,' Laura implored, her hand reaching for him, but he shrugged it off, and went into the house.

'Leave him for now, Laur,' Scott advised. Charlie put an arm around her shoulders, and squeezed gently.

'How is he?' she asked her brothers.

'He's embarrassed and angry and sad.' This was Nick.

'What did he say happened?'

'He'd gone with some idea of seeing Saskia. Only she wasn't there. She's away for three weeks, according to a neighbour he spoke to.'

'Poor kid.'

'He feels foolish. I think it was a combination of what happened here yesterday, and all the stuff from before.'

Charlie smiled gently. 'He's in a pickle. That's what your mum would have called it, and that's what it is. He's got himself in a state is all.'

'He and I have made peace about what happened with

Arthur. I know he was more cut up about it than any of us. I shouted because I was frightened.' He smiled weakly at Laura.

'I know that, Nick.' She touched his hand. 'Of course. Thank you for forgiving him.'

'No forgiveness necessary. Could have been me twenty-five years ago.'

'You're kind.'

'I'm honest. I feel for him, as far as the Saskia stuff is concerned. He misses her. And he's far more frightened than he's let on about her dad bringing a charge.'

'Then why the hell did he go looking for her? Rupert couldn't have been any clearer that he wanted Ethan to stay far, far away from her.'

'Because he isn't thinking straight. He knows that, really. I think he knows it's over, pretty much. He's just struggling to get his head around it.'

'Thank God they weren't there. But he spoke to someone?'

Scott nodded. 'A neighbour. But he didn't tell her his name.'

'Still, if she tells them . . .'

'Sssh. She won't. They're gone for weeks. She'll have forgotten.'

'I need to call Alex.'

'Do you, though? Really? What are you going to tell him? Nothing happened.'

Laura shrugged.

'Will he help?' Scott was logical, as ever.

Laura laughed weakly. 'Probably not.'

'Then save yourself the trouble. Like we said. No harm

done. Let Ethan sleep. Talk tomorrow. Maybe just wait for him to come to you, when he's ready.'

'When did you get so wise?'

'Perhaps I was always this wise and you just had me in a different pigeon-hole.' But Scott's eyes sparkled as he walked out of the room.

44

'He's out of control,' Heather hissed.

Scott closed the door to their bedroom, and moved towards her. When he answered, he whispered, 'He's my nephew, for God's sake.'

'And they are *my* daughters.'

And there it was. There it always would be. When she needed it to be that way, Hayley and Meredith would always be her daughters. He remembered their first conversation about Ethan.

Heather almost, but not quite, wished it unsaid the moment the words were out. She saw exasperation, then hurt pass over Scott's face, and the mirror pain of having caused it rippled through her own sternum.

She hadn't meant it. She hadn't. Except she had. She wondered briefly if she would ever be able to make him understand that the same distinction absolutely applied to their biological father. They were *hers*. She had grown them inside her own self, she had laboured to bring them into the world, and she had laboured ever since to keep them safe, to keep them right. She was their mother and she outranked anyone and everyone else.

And Ethan troubled her.

Scott's eyes examined her face. 'Where is this coming from, Heather?'

'What do you mean?' She didn't meet his gaze.

'It all seems just a bit . . .' he searched for the right word '. . . a bit disproportionate.'

Heather sank onto the edge of the bed. Her voice was very soft. He almost strained to hear her. 'You wouldn't say that if you knew.'

'Knew what?'

She shook her head.

'Talk to me, Heather. Knew what?' He knelt on the floor in front of her, and took her hands.

She looked at him with her big, wide eyes. Deciding.

He wanted to ask again, but he made himself keep quiet.

She seemed to make up her mind. She slid off the bed onto the floor beside him, and let him hold her for a moment.

'I think you need to tell me something. Please. Trust me and tell me.'

He made himself sound calm, held her chin with his finger to make her look at him, smiling reassuringly, as though nothing could be as bad as all that, although he felt oddly panicky.

'Something happened to me. I should have told you before.'

'You're telling me now.'

'I've never spoken about it.'

'Okay. Okay.' He clasped her hand tightly.

'When I was fifteen.'

He was frightened now. He almost wished, for a second, that he didn't have to hear this. Nothing that started in that way was going to be remotely okay. He felt a rush of protective love for his wife, and a lump formed in his throat.

'At a party. A party I was too young to be at, really. I had this friend . . .' She paused, shook her head a little. 'Anyway, I went with her.'

He nodded, encouragingly.

'And I knew almost right away that I shouldn't be there. They were college kids, all older. Drinking. Smoking. Cigarettes and weed. I was out of my comfort zone, you know. But my friend, she was really into it, and I didn't wanna leave on my own, because that didn't seem safe. It was late.'

He wanted to ask about her parents. Almost as if she knew, she continued: 'My parents, they thought I was sleeping over. Not that they were, you know, vigilant. They pretty much didn't seem to care where I was, what I did.'

He thought about the kind of mother she was to her girls. It went one of two ways, didn't it? You did what had been done to you or you did it so completely differently it was unrecognizable. You did it the way you wish it had been done for you.

A small sob broke her voice. 'I'm sorry.'

'It's okay.' He felt out of his depth. He wanted her to spit it out now. To see how bad it was.

She was struggling to carry on.

'Were you . . . ?'

The prompt helped. 'Raped? No.' The relief he felt was enormous. A surge.

'I guess I was assaulted. This guy, he – he touched me. He frightened me. He . . . I thought he was going to rape me. I think maybe he would have done, but someone

286

came in. He was drunk – really drunk. Maybe he wouldn't even have been capable of it.'

'Did you know him?'

She shook her head. 'I'd never seen him before and I never saw him again.'

'Did you tell anyone?'

Again, the small shake. 'No. I was embarrassed. I felt . . . foolish. I didn't want to talk about it . . . ever. I wouldn't have known who to tell. I actually never have. Then to now.'

'Heather . . .'

'It messed me up quite a bit. It was years before I could . . . be intimate with a guy, sleep with someone. I would start, you know, but all this weird stuff, these memories, would come back. I could smell him, cheap cologne, cheap cigarettes, booze. I could see him. I could feel how he felt. I could even hear the damn song that was playing when it happened. It was Journey. Something like that. A guitar solo.'

'Shit.'

'Even with the girls' father it was never really okay. I never . . . liked it. Sex. When we broke up, he threw it back at me.'

'But . . .' He didn't know how to say it.

She took his face in her hands. 'I know what you're going to say. But it's always been different with you. That was one of the ways I knew. I just . . . With you, I always knew you would take care of me, that you wouldn't hurt me. Do you remember the first time, with you and me?'

Scott nodded. Of course he did.

'I was waiting . . . waiting for all that crap to start up. It never did. You were . . . you were reverential. Does that sound ridiculous?'

'Not to me. I felt the same. I worshipped you from the start. I still do.'

'And so you fixed me.'

'You didn't need fixing.'

'We all need fixing, Scottie, in some way . . .'

He kissed her gently.

'I wanted to tell you at the beginning. I felt like I should. But what we had . . . it was so . . . I don't know, it sounds stupid. So pure. Clean. I felt better. I didn't want to dirty us up with it.'

'I wish you had.'

'And I'm sorry I didn't.'

'And Ethan?'

'I don't know. He scared me. That stuff with Arthur. The running away. What happened with that girl . . .'

'We talked about that.'

'I know it isn't the same but . . . all that irresponsibility. That loose-cannon thing. It scares me. It scares me that young men can get like that.'

She spun around, her face earnest. 'You see, I don't think the guy who did that to me at the party was "a bad guy". I bet you he's a responsible citizen now. Probably married, probably a father. Probably pays his taxes and coaches Little League and gives to good causes. I think he was out of control. I think he was colossally, dangerously out of control. That's the part that frightens me. I think good people do bad things, and I think bad people do good things.'

Scott understood.

'So I don't think Ethan is a bad kid. I think he's at risk of being a good kid doing bad things. *That*'s what frightens me.'

'I get it.'

'Do you? Do you?'

He held her close, like he'd never let her go, murmuring into her hair that he did. She relaxed and grew heavy in his arms, but he leant back against the bed, and held on.

45

Charlie slept fitfully, and rose early, troubled by the events of the last couple of days. Things had started so well, and he'd been so pleased. Now the cracks were starting to show, and he felt like he was losing control of everything, not succeeding in any of his objectives. He found Laura in the front garden, where the early sun was strongest. She was sitting on a teak bench, still in her pyjamas, her legs clutched to her chest, her dressing-gown wrapped tightly around her, her chin resting on her knees. He'd seen her through the window, as he came down the stairs, and ached on her behalf. He went into the kitchen to make two mugs of tea.

Outside, he put a hand on her shoulder. She laid her cheek on it. 'Hi, Dad.' Her voice was quiet, tired-sounding.

'Hi, love. May I sit?'

'Please.' She smiled at him, and took the mug he offered her. 'Thanks.'

For a moment, they were quiet, listening to the birdsong.

'Not for the first time, it must be said, I do so wish your mum was here.'

She didn't answer straight away. Then, 'Me too.' Laura's words almost caught in her throat. Emotion was terribly close to the surface.

Charlie turned his head and watched her precious face. 'You miss her almost as much as I do, I think.'

'Oh, Dad.' She slumped into his side, like a little girl.

He put an arm around her, making himself as strong and firm as he could. He thought she might be crying. 'Do you think she'd know what to do?'

Laura raised her head and smiled, but her eyes were full of tears. 'I think she'd know what to *say* . . .'

Charlie saw the distinction. 'She was like a sorcerer. That's how I thought of her. Or some kind of sage. There were times when I was in real danger of not being able to make a single decision without her – except at work – and I just deferred. Deferred like I breathed. Why wouldn't I? She was invariably right. And just wiser than me. She'd be doing stuff around the house, you know, cooking and cleaning, or we'd be walking . . . and she was always thinking, always problem-solving. Whether it was about one of you kids or something else. I swear to God, if she was in charge of the country, we wouldn't be going to hell in a handcart.'

She laughed ruefully. 'You're right.'

'When she was dying, I wanted to take notes.'

Laura stared at him. He never talked about that time. Never had. 'What do you mean?'

'While she could talk, before she got too addled by the morphine, she was still doing it. Thinking about things. Speaking her wisdom. I did – I wished I'd got a notebook with me.'

Laura remembered the hospice as if it had all happened yesterday. When she'd first been given the news that further treatment would only be palliative, that she was now terminal, Daphne hadn't wanted to go: she'd wanted to stay at home, and they had promised her that she could.

Macmillan nurses came for a while – wonderful, kind women, who'd made the unbearable seem almost bearable. In the end, though, she'd whispered to Laura that she'd been wrong – she didn't want to die in their home after all. 'He'll be staying here, your dad, and I don't want him seeing my ghost in every corner.'

They'd all dreaded the hospice but, of course, as everyone who used one seemed eventually to realize, the staff were calm and compassionate, in a peaceful place. There was a sense of safety about them. They knew what they were doing. She'd timed it well. Of course. While she remained at home, she was always able to get up, for at least part of the day, to wash and dress, to look and seem much like herself, to drink a cup of tea with visitors who knew not to stay for too long or ask too much. To take Ethan onto her lap and read to him so that he wasn't afraid of her. Once she entered hospice care, the will to normality ebbed gently away, and within just a week or so, she was sleeping more than she was awake, then unconscious more than she was asleep, and then, so gently that it almost came down to a change in the rise and fall of her chest, and the small change to the sound of her breath, not there at all.

She'd never seemed to be in real pain, not the kind they couldn't control, and Laura had been so very grateful for that. She wasn't sure any of them – Dad especially – could have borne to see her live from drug dose to drug dose, wretched with agony, as some people still seemed to have to die even in the twenty-first century. It was more that she had faded.

'What kind of notes?'

Charlie chuckled softly. 'Oh, all sorts. Recipes.' He lost himself in memory. 'She was worried I wouldn't eat properly. Reminders. Like I'd never find my way to the doctor or the optician or the dentist without her there to remind me. Random thoughts. What I ought to plant in the spring. How I needed to get rid of socks when they went thin, before they were holey. And she talked about you guys a lot. More than anything else. What she thought. What she wanted for you all. What I was to tell you.'

Laura smiled. It was very Mum. 'She was a control freak.'

Charlie agreed. 'Of the very, very best kind. She didn't want to leave you.'

'Or you.'

He laughed. 'Oh, she was quite fierce about that. Didn't allow herself an iota of self-pity, and didn't want me to. She said there was nothing less attractive than wallowing.'

Laura knew differently. Even in her last weeks and days, Mum had wanted to shield him. She'd cried, twisting a handkerchief, with Laura. Wished it was otherwise with Laura. Mourned for the old age she wasn't going to get with the man she adored. Issued instructions about Charlie to Laura. He had just never known. Laura laid her hand across her father's, keeping the promises she'd made all those years ago, and letting her dad speak his own truth about his dying wife.

'She said we'd had a good run, her and me. That she couldn't bring herself to be angry about leaving me.' He was close to tears. But he shook them away. 'But, my God, she was angry about all of you. About not seeing Ethan grow up, or Nick have children, or Scott get a blooming girlfriend.'

'I wonder what she'd make of us all.'

He leant forward, and whispered, 'She'd be extraordinarily proud of each and every one of you.'

46

Fran's car was already at the farm when Nick pulled into the car park just on ten a.m. He spotted her by the entrance. She was wearing a red and white spotted dress, with a colourful scarf in her hair, like the girl in the wartime propaganda posters – 'We Can Do It'. It suited her. He discovered that he was pleased to see her. It had been ages, when they were used to seeing each other so regularly. And when she saw him, and smiled broadly, he was relieved as well. He opened the back door. Bea and Delilah slithered out excitedly, seeing their friends, impatient while he released Arthur from the car seat, then retrieved the buggy from the boot.

She watched him walk towards her, and spoke as soon as they were within earshot.

'Hey, everyone! How are you? Gorgeous day, huh?'

Kissing and squealing and hugs. So far so entirely normal. So far so entirely lovely.

Nick let Fran sort out tickets, then navigate the entrance and a visit to the loo. Carrie might have raised an eyebrow at his submissiveness, but he'd have told her to cut him some slack.

At the farm it was easy to be carried along by the myriad activities on offer, and there was no time for proper talking. Petting zoo, pony rides, tractor safari ... The kids chattered incessantly and pulled them in different directions. Fran stayed on the grass with the buggies and the smallest kids while Nick took the big ones to the top of the wobbly slide and saw them into the hessian sacks in which they whizzed, shrieking, to the bottom. He watched their stuff when Fran climbed into the chicken enclosure with their offspring to look for eggs. They both grappled with the sunscreen and the squirming children, who didn't want to stand still long enough to have it applied. Fran did her own face and looked at Nick, eyebrows raised, until he held out his hand for some.

At lunchtime, they congregated around a picnic table. Nick bought chips and ice-cold juice boxes from the small restaurant, while Fran unpacked a coolbag she'd brought with her: cheese sticks, crudités and cocktail sausages. They made several attempts to start a proper conversation, then laughed at the continual interruptions, and gave up. He would have quite liked to tell her what had happened, with Ethan and Arthur, and the fallout, but the kids were omnipresent.

When they'd finished the savoury offerings, Bea begged to be allowed to buy ice creams for everyone from the van thirty yards away. Nick gave her a ten-pound note, and he and Fran watched as she led the others in a straggly line to join the queue. She kept turning to look back at her dad for reassurance. He nodded and waved.

Fran waved too. 'She's a born mum, that one.'

Nick frowned. 'Maybe she thinks she has to be.'

'Hey. I don't think so. She always was, way before . . .' Her voice trailed off, then came back. 'I remember her, from when she was tiny, wanting to look after the others, clucking over them. Don't you remember how she used to speak for them?'

'Maybe not a mum – a union leader!'

'Well, that'd be okay too,' Fran joked. 'Girl power!'

'Absolutely.'

They weren't looking at each other – they were facing the kids, ever vigilant.

'So, how's the big family thing panning out, then?'

Nick considered. 'Some and some, to be honest.'

'Okay.' Fran sighed, and picked at the leftovers. 'Not exactly all happy families, then.'

There was more, of course, but Nick felt exhausted at the thought of talking about it. He gave a grim laugh. 'Who'd have 'em?'

Bea had completed her transaction at the van, and had arranged her charges in a circle on the grass to eat their ice creams.

'That's adorable. You should get a picture.'

Nick picked up his camera and zoomed in on the group, firing off a series of shots with the telephoto lens. 'And how about you? What's going on?'

'The space has been good.'

He was glad she wasn't evasive with him.

'He's moving out while we're here. Not stuff, just clothes. We've not got to sharing-out-the-records stage yet. It's him who won't be there when we get back. I've got to tell them.'

'You haven't yet?'

'Nope.'

'Shouldn't you do that together?'

'I wondered that. He says he can't. He wants me to

explain it, and them to have a bit of time to get used to it, and then he'll come round, once we're home, and they can ask him questions and things, you know, be reassured that he's not going far. That he and I are okay in a room together, at least.'

'Do you think they'll get it?'

'Can't decide. Sometimes I think they're too young to understand. I tell myself kids are resilient and adaptable.'

'Both of those things are true.'

'I know. And it's not like he's died.'

The words hung in the air.

'Sorry, Nick. That was incredibly insensitive.'

He put up his hand to stop her. 'No. Don't worry. It's okay.'

A tear rolled down her cheek. She brushed it away, angry with herself. 'I'm so sorry.'

'Hey.' He turned to look right at her. 'Stop it. Don't you dare say sorry to me. You have been the single most helpful, most present, most kind person to me and the kids since Carrie died. You could never, never need to say sorry to me. Do you hear me?'

She nodded.

'And no. He hasn't died. And that's good. Good for the kids. But that doesn't mean this isn't hard for you all. And I'm here. I'm gonna be here. I'm not sure I can be as helpful to you as you've been to me, but I can try, can't I? I want to. You know, in some ways, it's a relief.'

'What do you mean?'

'Well, it's all been about me, hasn't it? Poor tragic Nick. You know, at the house, with my sister, my nephew and my dad, who also, by the way, lost his wife, it just makes me realize. What happened to me was shitty. But shitty stuff happens all around. Not just to me. It's nice to think about other people for a change. It feels . . . normal. Does that make any sense at all?'

'It does, actually.' He had turned back to where the kids were finishing. Arthur was wearing more of his ice cream than he'd eaten. 'Wet wipes?' Fran rummaged in her bag.

'So we're good?' He'd wondered if they were going to talk about what had happened that night after supper, but now wasn't the time.

'Yeah. All clear.' There didn't seem to be a subtext in it, and for that he was grateful. He wasn't ready to think about it, and she seemed to feel exactly the same, unless what had happened had been nothing at all and she didn't know there was anything to think about.

She smirked at him. 'My pity party for a while. That's what you're saying.'

He smiled back. 'And you'll self-pity cry if you want to.' Fran was walking now, towards the sticky fingers and mouths. 'But you've got to lay off the wine boxes, mate. Promise?'

'Shan't.' She threw the word over her shoulder, not turning.

47

Hayley and Meredith were lukewarm, at first, at Heather's suggestion that the three of them drive into Cheltenham for lunch. It was sunny again, and already very warm. The day seemed more suited to lounging than driving. The promise of shopping was the clincher. Hayley was too self-absorbed and slothful, and Meredith probably too young, to read their mother's slightly brittle, bruised mood, but it wasn't lost on the adults in the house, especially Laura and Scott.

Laura was glad she was going. In front of Charlie, Heather had invited her but Laura had known from her tone she didn't mean it. A woman understood. Charlie smiled benevolently at Heather, when she offered, and Laura felt a childish frisson of envy and possessiveness. He was *her* dad.

She was confused about how she felt. She'd been wrong about Heather, she knew that. Unfair. But now whatever fledgling friendship had been established between them was besieged by maternal hackles, raised.

Scott was glad too, if he was honest. Things weren't back, yet, on an even keel. She wasn't relaxed with the others in the house, as she had been. She'd been stepping warily around Laura, avoiding Ethan. What worried him more was how she'd been with him, after the time they'd spent sitting on the bedroom floor, after she'd told him what had happened to her. He'd had questions, but the time hadn't seemed right to ask them. He'd felt incredibly protective, full of something between impotent anger directed towards a punk of a kid from decades ago and sadness. She'd retreated again. She'd gone quiet and it troubled him. Maybe she wished she hadn't told him. He tried to fight the feeling that she was suggesting this shopping trip to avoid him. He'd offered to drive them, but had been rebuffed. She'd blustered more noisily than necessary, and with a forced gaiety that convinced no one he'd be bored and cramp their style.

Heather didn't talk much on the way. Plugged into their respective devices, the girls didn't notice.

Radio 4 was playing in the front, as usual. Melvyn Bragg and some dry historians talking about an obscure nineteenth-century courtesan. But Heather wasn't really listening. She was processing. Something had clicked in her brain when she'd told Scott what had happened when she was young. She had never spoken about it before to anyone. Having done so now changed several things. It cemented in her mind how deeply she trusted her husband – and how much she loved him. How safe she felt. It unlocked, somehow, why she felt so protective and so easily triggered about her own girls. Those two things about her had run along parallel tracks in her brain, but now they had crossed, and her parenting made more sense to her. It was hard to explain, but perhaps saying it out loud had taken the power, the trauma, out of it. She should have done it years ago. She should have shouted from the rooftops the moment it had happened, of course. She shouldn't have felt shame or even fear. She shouldn't have let it cast a shadow over her life. So it wasn't that it had happened she regretted. It was how it had affected her. What she felt now was a small, powerful sense of freedom.

In Cheltenham, they busied themselves on the main shopping street for a few hours. Trainers and books for Meredith, clothes and makeup for Hayley. An armful of particularly glorious apricot roses and some interiors magazines for Heather. Some colourful garden games for the little ones back at the house. By two o'clock, Hayley and Meredith had realized they were ravenous, and they found an Italian restaurant. The girls ordered pizzas, which they devoured while their mother pushed a garden salad around a plate and nibbled at the edges of a garlic flatbread. They'd finished before she was a third of the way through. The waitress approached the table, and made to back away again, seeing that she had so much food left on her plate. Heather beckoned her.

'I'm done, thanks.' She beamed at the woman to let her know she wasn't going to complain.

'You're eating less than normal,' Meredith observed.

'As if that's even possible', was Hayley's wry aside.

Heather looked at them sharply, and put her fork down to stir artificial sweetener into a large glass of iced tea. She'd read all the books she was supposed to read about how not to infect your daughters with the food nonsense you yourself subscribed to, but they weren't stupid. They knew she stayed as slim as she was through concerted effort. 'I don't care for the dressing. That's all. You can bet I'm having ice cream.'

She meant sorbet. And she meant three spoonfuls. But they all knew that.

'Are you okay, Mum?' asked Meredith.

'Of course I am.'

'You're not.' Hayley cocked her head on one side. 'So don't pretend you are. You didn't kiss Scott goodbye when we left. Not properly. It was a peck. Did you guys fight?'

They both fixed their wide eyes on her.

'No.'

'Really?'

'It's none of your business.'

'So you did?'

Meredith's face registered real anxiety and Heather felt a stab of guilt. She didn't want either of them to feel anything less than totally stable and safe. Not ever. She leant forward and pinched Hayley's cheek. It was meant to be an affectionate touch but it seemed harder than that, like a reproach. Hayley flicked away the gesture in annoyance. 'You're too smart for your own good, you know that?'

'I'm going to the bathroom,' Meredith announced. She'd lost most of her American vernacular, as her sister had, within days of attending an English school, sensing that it was an irritant to their new classmates, but when the three were alone together, it crept back. 'Two scoops chocolate and one raspberry for me, please.' She skipped off.

'So what's wrong?'

Heather took a deep breath. There wasn't time now to tell it all. Meredith would be back in a minute. It had taken a lot out of her to tell Scott. It felt incredibly strange to have another person know her story, after all these years. She wasn't sure she ever wanted Hayley to know. Her aim was to teach her everything she needed to know to keep herself safe – so safe – without ever having to hear what had happened to her mother.

'Was it about Ethan?'

'Why would you ask me that?'

'You don't like him, do you?'

'That's not fair.'

Hayley shrugged. 'I feel like you don't.'

'Do you?'

'I didn't think I would. But I actually really do. He's a nice guy.'

Heather nodded.

'I mean, I know what happened with Arthur was really bad. And I know there's all this drama . . . but when you speak to him, he's just a sweet boy. Smart too. He's sad.'

Heather smiled at her. 'And you've spoken to him a lot, have you?

The omnipresent shrug. 'Quite a lot, I suppose. He's the only person my age here, you know!'

'Do you know many English boys his age?'

Hayley narrowed her eyes suspiciously. 'A few.'

'How?'

'Mum! Really! I have friends with brothers. There are guys at parties. Around.'

'Anyone special?' She tried to keep her voice casual, but she wasn't sure she succeeded.

'No one. I'd have told you.'

'Would you?' She sounded sharper than she meant to.

'Of course.'

'And your mates? Do they have boyfriends?'

'Some, yeah. Why all these questions, suddenly?'

'You're growing up. Sometimes I don't notice it because I see you all the time.'

Hayley looked quizzical.

'Do you know how I found out you'd learnt to roll when you were a baby?'

'No. How?'

'You rolled off the bed. I was changing you, turned around to get something – a wipe maybe – and when I turned back, thud, you were on the floor.'

'Wow.'

'I was behind the curve. That's the point I'm making. It's kind of been that way ever since. I just don't wanna be behind that particular curve.'

'The guy curve?' Hayley's tone was amused.

'The guy curve. I want you to be able to talk to me, to tell me anything.'

'I will. I can. I said so to Ethan. When we were talking.'

'And you think I'm being unfair to him?'

Hayley smiled. 'Yeah. I do.'

'Okay, then. I'll try. For you.'

'Good.' Hayley proffered a spoonful of sorbet. Heather smiled and took it from her, just as Meredith skipped back from the loo.

As she stirred sweetener into her cappuccino, Heather looked from one daughter to the other. 'How are you both doing?'

'What do you mean?'

'I mean, how are you? Really.'

Meredith laughed. 'So serious, Mom. I'm fine. I love

305

Bea and Lila and Arthur so much. I want to see them all the time after the vacation. I really hope Nick will let me babysit them sometimes. I mean, we're cousins, right?'

Heather nodded. 'That's right.'

'And Charlie is so nice. And Nick. And the house. I love the pool. All of it is cool.'

She had ice cream on her chin. Heather passed her a napkin, and turned to Hayley.

'And you?'

'It's been way better than I thought it might be. It's nice, feeling like you're part of a family. We've never really had that. I didn't know I missed it, but when you're sur-rounded by it, and watching them – Scott and Laura and Nick – doing their sibling thing, and Charlie just loving everyone, it's really nice. I like how they've included us. It feels good.'

Heather smiled.

'You like them, right?' Hayley seemed desperately keen for Heather to say yes.

She felt a pang. 'I do. I really do. I mean, I love Charlie. What a sweetheart. Nick is funny. More like Scott than either of them think, I reckon.'

Hayley nodded. 'Laura takes a bit of getting to know, but she's not in a good place. And, yeah, they're pretty great.'

Heather took their hands. 'I love you, my girls. You're brilliant, you know that?'

'So can we go back to Zara and get that jacket I liked, if I'm so brilliant?'

48

It was late in the afternoon when Ethan sought out his mother. It had taken huge reserves of patience for Laura to give him space. She'd taken a book outside to read, but it lay unopened beside her on the bench. She'd laid her head back against a cushion, and closed her eyes, letting the late-afternoon sun warm her face. Her mind wandered back to the time she'd spent with Joe. It seemed much longer ago than it was, but the reminiscence was clouded by the persistent feeling that she should have been here. With Ethan.

He slid onto the bench beside her while her eyes were still closed, but she knew, with some inexplicable maternal instinct, that he was there. She waited for him to speak.

Eventually he did.

'Been a shitty couple of days.'

She opened her eyes, and looked at her son. He was sitting forward, shoulders hunched, gaze fixed on the ground.

'I was an idiot and nearly hurt Arthur. And then I was an idiot and made a right show of myself.'

'Stop saying "idiot".'

'Mum! I. Was. A. Fucking idiot.'

'Okay. You can say "idiot" about the pool stuff but not about the rest.'

He smiled tightly.

She sat up. 'Can't defend you on the pool. But it happened, and you've owned it, and you didn't hurt Arthur. He's fine, love. And no one thought you meant to do it, and everyone knows you'll never, ever do it again. So park that.'

'Okay.' Ethan nodded slowly, decisively.

'Okay? Really?' She looked at him pointedly.

He nodded again.

'Running away —'

'Don't say it like that. I'm not a kid. I didn't "run away".'

'Sorry. I don't mean to treat you like a kid.' How on earth did a parent *stop* treating their kid like a kid? How had Mum and Dad made that change? Gradually? Reluctantly? Or was there always a single moment when you looked at your child and saw an adult – fledgling, maybe, but the unmistakable outline of a grown-up?

'Sorry.'

'What?'

Now he shook his head in something like despair. 'I don't know. The two things just sort of collided in my mind. I didn't want to stay, because I knew everyone was totally pissed off with me. And I didn't blame them. And I just thought that if I could talk . . .'

'Talk to who? To Saskia?'

'Oh, God, I don't know. To Saskia. Her mum. Maybe even her dad.'

'Oh.'

'I wanted to explain myself. I was lying up in that bloody room in the eaves, pretty much hating myself, and

I just got – got really panicked. About what he said to me about what he could do.'

'Ethan . . .' Her heart ached for him. She'd known, the second she'd seen Rupert's face, what real danger he posed. Was she wrong not to have spelt it out to Ethan from the start? She'd been protecting him, but she couldn't, could she? She hadn't.

'And something else, too. I just got afraid that he'd have persuaded her, you know, that I'd . . .' He couldn't say the word.

He was blinking hard now, and she knew he was trying not to cry. She didn't want to scare him off but she couldn't help herself: she put a hand on his leg. When he didn't shrug it off or brush it away, she moved a bit closer.

And a dam broke.

His words were hard to hear, almost lost in the heaving sobs. 'I couldn't . . . I couldn't . . .'

'I know, Eth. I know you. I know.'

He almost collapsed onto her chest. He was too big, really, ungainly in her embrace. She felt winded by the weight of him. But she put her arms around him and held him as though he were a small child again, as if he'd scraped his knee falling off his bike, or woken from a nightmare, although this was far harder, and let him cry.

Eventually, after a long time, he was still, and calm. He sat back, still close to his mother, and rubbed his face with the sleeve of his shirt, his arm pushing his hair back from his forehead.

'I know it's over, by the way.'

She didn't look at him.

'I've known for a while.'

Laura had known, of course, almost from the minute Rupert had burst into her house, but she didn't know that Ethan knew, too. Not really.

'It's ruined.'

'Sweetheart . . .'

'We couldn't get past it.'

She didn't want to tell him he was wrong.

'But it wasn't what he said. It wasn't like he said.'

She pressed his hand. 'I promise you I know it wasn't, my love.' She had to keep saying it. He needed to know she believed him. Believe that she believed him.

Some vestige of the old familiar rage that had been eating her for the longest time reared again in the pit of her stomach. How dare he – that ghastly man – how dare he do this to her boy, make him feel like this? Whatever had happened between Ethan and Saskia – and no one really believed they would stay together beyond A levels, or university, or into their twenties – their memories of their relationship should be positive. For the experience to be tainted by Saskia's father wasn't fair, and the injustice gnawed at her. She didn't know how to fix it – how to reverse the effects of someone else's careless words and agenda. But she would try.

She felt the lioness stir, and begin to prowl, within her. She felt strength returning. The steel in her spine she'd been aware of in the last little while was building volume. Rupert had better watch out. Claudia might have persuaded him to let it go, but if she hadn't, Laura would fight him. This was her son – his future. Never get between the mother and her cub and threaten the young. Alex had better be careful too. For the first time in ages she almost relished the thought of getting home, getting back into the lawyer's office, getting the divorce moving so that she would be free of him. Free. Strong. She'd got it wrong – moping about happiness. It was the wrong way around. Free and strong must come first. Joy would surely follow.

49

Joe was in the garden when Laura showed up, hoping he would be. The other night – before the Arthur stuff, and the Saskia drama – when he'd dropped her off, there had been a moment, she was certain, when he had thought about kissing her mouth, not just her cheek, and she had considered letting him. It hadn't happened, but it had been in the air – the possibility of it.

It was odd – it had happened only two days ago. It felt like longer.

There had been a strange dynamic in the house. Maybe it was her. She was restless. She'd picked up a book, but read the same page three or four times and retained nothing. The kitchen was sparkling clean, much more so than hers at home. She tried a couple of yoga poses, but couldn't settle to that either. Something was up between Heather and Scott, and she felt it had to do with Ethan, although no one had said anything. She and Heather had gone backwards: those moves towards closeness they'd made the other day, lying on the mats under the tree, seemed never to have happened. Heather had taken Hayley and Meredith out, and Scott was pacing around anxiously.

She should have been there. But she couldn't quite feel guilty about the time she'd spent with Joe. And she was back now. This part was so much nicer than the other. Was it selfish to want more?

Today he kissed her cheek, lightly and swiftly, before either of them had time to think about it. It was platonic, except that it wasn't.

There was no pretence this time that she had stumbled across him randomly, or that he just happened to be there. It was clear to both of them that they'd sought each other out. They sat side by side on the bench, not quite touching.

'How's it going?'

She exhaled sharply. 'How long have you got?' she half joked.

'All day. If you like.' He wasn't joking. 'What's up?'

'Nah. Not to worry. Parent stuff – don't want to bore you.'

'Okay. I won't give you a cheesy line about how you never could. Bore me.'

She laughed. 'For which I am duly grateful.' He gave a small, ironic bow from the waist. She'd much rather talk about him than about her. 'You said you were married. You never said whether you'd had kids.'

'No kids. I would have liked some. One, even. It was Rachel, my wife. She said she wasn't ready.'

'Right.'

'What she meant was she wasn't ready to have them with me. She has three now. Two boys and a girl. Oliver, Archie and Amelia, if the Christmas card she sends me every year is to be believed. The first was born less than a year after we split up. Closer to nine months, actually.'

'God, I'm sorry. That's rough.'

'It's okay.' He gave her a broad smile. 'I'm glad she didn't have them with me, if she knew it wasn't right.'

Laura had the strange thought that she couldn't imagine what had made Rachel think he wasn't good father material. She couldn't imagine someone wanting to cheat on him either. 'It's not too late.'

He looked amused. 'For what?'

'For kids. How old are you?'

He laughed. 'Forty-three. And I know it's not. The thing is, with me, it was never just an urge to have kids. It was always tied up to being with the right person to have those kids.'

'And did you think she was? The right person?' He looked at her sharply. She blushed. 'I'm sorry. I'm being too personal.'

'It's fine. I like it. You're direct.'

'Nosy.'

'Straightforward. I wish more people were. My tolerance for bullshit is very low, these days. I wasn't sure she was. That's the truth of it. Rachel and I met and married quickly. I was thirty-three or so, and all my mates were getting married, getting mortgages, getting serious. She was a few years younger, but she definitely drove it. Not to sound pathetic, but I let her. Like a lemming. Truthfully, I knew the day I married her that I wasn't a hundred per cent in it.'

'You did it anyway.'

'Cowardly, I suppose. Church was full, champagne was on ice, honeymoon was booked. Then again, I didn't know whether that was normal or not. I loved her. I just think you should probably only marry someone you can't imagine living without. And I wasn't there.'

'You could be talking about me.'

'Really?' He turned to her.

'I wanted to be married. I wanted desperately to be a mother. I think we differ there. Alex – my husband, my ex – I loved him. But on the day, when I was in the big white meringue of a dress, it wouldn't have been true to say I couldn't imagine living without him.'

She remembered being in the back of a Rolls-Royce with her dad on the way to the church. It had rained – nothing dramatic, just a persistent chilly drizzle that fell all day from a leaden sky. The photographer was conciliatory, telling her weather like that made a good light for photographs, but in truth it had felt, if not ominous, then slightly . . . dampening. Daphne had gone ahead, and her brothers were already on duty, showing guests to pews and handing out orders of service. Bridesmaids huddled in the vestry in their puffed organza sleeves. Charlie hadn't trusted his voice – she'd appeared in the living room, and his eyes had filled with tears when he'd seen her, and the tears hadn't been far away in the back of the car. He tried, several times, to say what she thought would be profound things to her, but each time emotion interrupted, so he was reduced to holding her hand tightly in his, patting it with the other, and smiling. Perhaps he'd been going to ask her if she was sure, if she could imagine a life without Alex, and if she had answered that she could, perhaps he would have told the driver to keep going, past the church where 150 people were waiting.

How different everything would have been.

But there would have been no Ethan. And that was unimaginable.

'Why did you do it, then?'

'Same as you. I believed. I wanted to believe.'

'Was he a good husband?'

Laura thought about it for a moment. 'On paper.'

'Ouch.'

'Until he wasn't.'

'What happened?'

'Genevieve.'

He sucked air between his teeth. 'Okay.'

'He's a cliché made flesh. She's young, all tits and teeth, high heels . . .'

'God.'

'. . . and I've been so angry. More angry than hurt.'

'Aren't they two sides of the same thing?'

'I just never thought it would happen to me. I had a vision, you know, of my life. Of my marriage. I never thought I'd end up alone, at my age, starting again.'

'I don't think anybody does.'

'You're all right.'

'It took a while. Perhaps we're a pair of incurable romantics.'

'Oh, I'm very much cured of anything romantic, believe me.' She hoped she hadn't sounded bitter.

'That would be a tragedy, in my opinion. I mean, how old are *you*, Laura?'

'Older than you.'

'Not an answer.'

'So . . .'

'So . . .' He had come close to her now. 'Come and have a drink with me.'

'When?'

'Tonight. Tomorrow. I have no other plans.'

'Where?'

'Mine. You know where.'

'Why?'

'Because I'd like it, and I think you'd like it too.'

Their faces were as close as they'd been when they were saying goodnight in the cab of the van. She could hear his breathing. And she sensed the lioness again, pacing.

She wanted to kiss him. The tiniest incline of her head would see her lips meet his. The same for him. She hadn't kissed anyone but Alex for twenty years, more maybe. And she hadn't been kissed by him in a long time. And she hadn't realized until just this very moment how much she had missed being kissed.

50

The next morning, Hayley decided she'd given Ethan as wide a berth as he needed, and went to look for him. He was in the small snug at the back. Without a television or a view out to the garden, there was little competition for the space, and he'd been hiding out there without being bothered much since he'd got back. He was lying across the sofa, his gangly legs hanging off the end, his arms behind his head, the ever-present Gallagher brothers on full blast in his ears. She could hear the beat in the still room.

He looked up when the door opened, and Hayley thought she saw relief replace irritation on his face when he saw that it was her and not one of the grown-ups. She shut the door behind her. 'You okay?'

Ethan grunted a sound halfway between a yes and a no, translatable only by a fellow teen.

Hayley slid into the chair next to him, and pulled her legs up to her chest, hugging them and resting her chin on her knees.

He took his headphones off, but didn't say anything else. Hayley figured it meant he was listening, at least.

'Quite the drama, you caused.' Not unkindly said.

'Yeah. Sorry about that.'

'No need to be.'

He shrugged.

'It could have been me, you know.'

'What?'

'Me who left the cover off. I do shit like that all the time. We all do. We're kids. Could have been Meredith.'

'But you didn't. Meredith didn't. It was me. You're just being nice.'

'Just being real. I know it seemed like Mum was just making more drama – making Nick take Arthur to the hospital and all that. It's just how she is – nothing personal. You shouldn't think it was about you. She's . . . a *thorough* parent. I suppose it's partly how she's wired. Partly because she was on her own with us for so long. She's a worrier. A bit of a neuro.'

'Mine too.'

'Maybe they all are. She's drummed all this stuff into us all our lives – I'm allergic to nuts. Mildly, to be honest. It was worse when I was a kid – I'm meant to be growing out of it – but she goes on and on and on about it, like I don't get it. That's just one thing. Then there's wound care. She's big on wound care. Makes us sneeze into our elbows. Heads. Never mess with a bang on the head. Get it checked out.'

Ethan smirked.

'You know, when we moved here, she was thrilled we wouldn't be able to learn to drive until we were seventeen. It was sixteen in New Jersey. One more year of not worrying like crazy, she said. She's nuts.'

They sat quietly for a moment. Hayley's monologue had made the silence companionable, though.

'I get my provisional licence in a couple of months.'

'Cool. I'm pretty terrified, to be honest. Driving a stick shift seems really hard.'

'A manual car?'

'Yeah. All the cars in America are automatic. Practically all . . .'

'Do you see your dad?' Ethan stared ahead.

If she was surprised by the gear change in conversation, Hayley didn't let on. 'Not really. I mean, we barely did even when we lived in the States.'

'Is that okay?'

Hayley shrugged. 'We were really, really little, when they broke up. He was never around much.'

'Don't you want him to want to see you?'

Hayley considered. 'I don't think about it much.' She paused. 'I really like Scott. He's great. I mean, I'm not saying he's a dad to us, or anything.'

'He's your stepdad.'

'Yeah. But he doesn't push that. He's like . . . a great friend. Good to talk to, you know. Really kind. Makes awesome pancakes.'

'That's cool.'

Hayley nodded. 'Yeah. What about your dad?'

'My parents only broke up this year.'

'I think I sort of knew. How was that?'

'Shitty. And a relief.'

'Right.'

'Shitty because Dad moved out. He has a new girlfriend, a new flashy house, all that. He really, really hurt my mum. She's been in bits pretty much ever since. And a relief because they weren't happy. Things had been crappy for a while. Quite a while.'

'Like fighting, and stuff?'

'Fighting, sulking, some world-class passive-aggressive chat . . .'

'Sounds grim.'

'Yeah.'

'Do you see him?'

'He says I'm welcome to go there whenever I want. But it's weird.'

'Weird how?'

'Weird because she's always there. Genevieve. I think she lives there, and they just pretend she doesn't. Like, the master bedroom is full of her stuff. And the shower has all this girly crap in it. If she has her own place, I feel like she's hardly ever there. Weird because I know it hurts Mum when I go. It feels disloyal.'

'I get that.'

'She's really young. Like I don't even know if she's thirty. It's a ridiculous age gap. He's such a fucking cliché. It's embarrassing.' He didn't say that she was attractive. And sexy. And that that confused him even more. He didn't want Hayley to think he was a pervert.

'So I don't go that often. And he doesn't invite me, anyway. He says to think of it like it's my home, but I don't.'

'That's tough. I'm sorry.' He looked at her for the first time. She smiled. 'We're cousins now, kind of, right?'

'I guess.'

'So we could hang out, you know, after this holiday. If you like.'

He smiled back. It was the first genuine, unguarded smile she had seen him give. 'I would. Thanks.'

Hayley nodded, as though a deal had been brokered. She made a fist and gently punched his leg, then stood up.

'Wanna hit balls on the tennis court? You can use Scott's racquet.'

'I have to warn you, I'm pretty rubbish.'

'That's fine. I'm a really good coach.'

Ethan laughed, which made Hayley glad, and stood up. 'You're on.'

51

Nick and Charlie sat with the sun on their backs, and their feet dangling in the pool. Nick was in shorts, but Charlie had had to roll up his chinos and take off his socks, and Nick had had to put his arm out to help his father sit on the edge. Nick's legs were tanned and muscular, while Charlie's had a bluish-white hue, and gnarled varicose veins. His father's legs made him sad, marking his age and his increasing frailty more clearly than his animated, familiar face ever did. But it was what Charlie had wanted, to sit, dangle his feet and be near his grandchildren. Meredith was in the pool with Bea and Delilah. Arthur was napping inside, Heather listening for him. She said she was happy pottering in the kitchen. The small girls were deliriously happy in the company of their new cousin, splashing and giggling, climbing out of the pool to walk round (they preferred to run, but Nick kept admonishing them – 'Slow down, slow down'), jump in, and repeat, over and over again.

'God, what I wouldn't give for a fraction of their energy!'

'You and me both, Dad. They're the proverbial Duracell bunnies.'

'They're amazing.' Charlie shook his head in fond wonderment.

'They'll be spark out by seven thirty. Sleep for twelve hours.'

'Lucky devils. All so simple, isn't it, when you're that age? Eat, sleep, play. Eat, sleep, play.'

'I'm so glad we came. Thanks, Dad, for all of this. They're clearly loving having all the family around.'

Charlie touched Nick's arm. 'I'm so glad.'

'It's a year tomorrow.'

One date Charlie hadn't forgotten. He hadn't needed Daphne to fix that one in his mind. He would remember the phone call, and Nick's voice at the other end of the line, for as long as he lived. It was the worst call he had ever taken, in a long life with a fair share of horridness, and the very worst news he'd ever had. The very worst.

A lot of that was shock. You didn't expect it. It came from so far out of left field, and it hit you so hard, news like that. His beloved son had lost his wife. His young, lovely, loving wife. His adored grandchildren had lost their mother. In an instant. On an ordinary day.

He'd stood alone in the hallway, staring at a photograph of Daphne, sinking onto the stairs, because he'd felt his legs start to give way beneath him, trying desperately to think of the right thing to say, realizing there was absolutely nothing, that letting Nick cry, and listen to him crying, was all he could do. The time for rallying would come, but for that moment, it was all. It had been 364 days ago, but it might have been yesterday.

'They're good, right?' Nick's voice broke. Charlie knew what he was asking.

'They're very good. They seem very good indeed. You're doing wonderfully.'

Nick exhaled at the reassurance.

'And how are you, my boy?'

Nick smiled at his father. 'Ah. More of a work in progress.'

'Understandable. A year is nothing. Nothing at all.'

'Thank you for saying that. Sometimes people give me the impression that a year is long enough for me to have got myself together, sorted.'

'People who haven't lost what you've lost. Only those people could even think that, let alone say it.'

'Exactly.'

'I've been a work in progress since the day your mother died. I think I've progressed as far as I'm ever going to, to be honest. I miss her every day. Sometimes every hour of every day.'

Nick almost laughed. 'A guy in the pub – a mate, or a sort of mate – a few weeks, maybe couple of months ago, he said I should get back on the horse. Back on the damn horse – get back out there. Can you believe it? He'd been drinking. He was all arm around the shoulders, home-truths time. He said I needed to "get back out there, find a new mother", find myself a new wife. That I shouldn't wallow.'

Charlie blew out his cheeks. 'Wow.'

'Wow indeed.' Nick shook his head.

'And did this sensitive soul have a suggestion as to how you might do that?'

'Online. Tinder. Or Bumble. Or something . . .'

'Oh, yes. Of course.' Charlie was incredulous. 'Why didn't I think of that? I could have replaced your mother.' He clicked his fingers, like an impatient customer summoning a waiter. 'Do they have a site for silver surfers?'

Nick smirked. 'I'm sure they do.'

'Bumbling?'

Nick laughed. 'I'll write a profile today. "Charlie. Compos mentis. Own teeth, if you don't count crowns. Still vaguely continent. Seeks . . ."'

'Replacement wife.'

'Replacement wife.'

Charlie nodded slowly, and the levity passed.

'Can I ask you something, Dad?'

'Anything, son.'

'Do you suppose that if you'd lost Mum sooner, much sooner I mean, you'd have married again? Wanted to, even?'

Charlie thought about it. 'I know what your mother would have said. If you lot had been small, I mean. She'd have said I should.'

'Is that what *you* think?'

Again, Charlie was slow to answer, trying to get it right. 'If you force yourself into something, it won't be right. You have to give yourself time. I don't think you can do it for the children. They're okay. They have all the love you give them, all the love all of us, their other grandparents, the friends the two of you had, can give them, and that's enough for now.'

Nick nodded vigorously as though his father had said exactly what he had wanted to hear.

'But . . .'

Nick turned to him.

'. . . but I don't think you should close yourself off to the idea completely. You shouldn't want to spend the rest of your life alone, Nick. She wouldn't have wanted that for you because she loved you, and I don't want that for you because I love you too.'

'There'll never be anyone as right for me as she was.'

'Of course you feel that way. But it isn't true. It would be different.'

Nick's eyes had filled with tears. Instinctively, unthinkingly, Charlie tried to hold him, although it was awkward on the side of the pool.

Bea, on one of her running walks from steps to deep end, saw the movement. 'Are you okay, Daddy?'

Nick sniffed, pushed his father away, not unkindly, and pinched the top of his nose fiercely. 'I'm absolutely fine, darling.'

Bea stopped and put a wet hand on his shoulder, peering at his face.

'Hey, you're getting me all wet!' He diverted her with a theatrical shake. She giggled, and forgot.

'Might have to get into my trunks and come in, now you've *soaked* me . . .'

'Oh, yes! Come in! Come in! Please! You, too, Granddad!'

Charlie laughed.

Delilah added her pleas: 'Yes! Granddad! Come in!'

Nick stood up, and helped his father stand on the pool edge. 'I think we'd better do as they ask!'

The mask was back. It had slipped for just a moment.

Charlie had the clearest memory of Daphne, and music played in his head. She'd particularly loved a Nanci Griffith song – 'Talk To Me While I'm Listening'. He could hear the refrain in his head now, hear Daphne telling him that was all you could do with your children – talk to them while they were listening.

52

Charlie had made a speech at the smart luncheon (they'd laughed at how putting 'eon' on the end of 'lunch' made it smart) he and Daphne had held for their twenty-fifth wedding anniversary. The speech had been short and touching and funny, and he'd spoken without notes, standing behind Daphne's chair. He'd had a hand on her shoulder the whole time, as if she was a talisman, and at various points she'd put her own over it, patting supportively. Scott remembered it very clearly. He'd been impressed by his father's ability to extemporize, reminded of the impressive man he'd always seemed to the outside world. The substance of his father's words had been his own notion of what made a marriage work. Never go to sleep on a quarrel, he'd said. It wasn't an original thought, he had acknowledged. His own mother had told them at their wedding a quarter of a century before, and she'd been told the same thing at hers. But it was good advice, he said. He made everyone laugh with a story about a fight they'd had as newlyweds, something about shoes and carpet squares. Scott didn't remember the story but he'd always remembered the advice.

He and Heather hadn't exactly gone to sleep on a quarrel, but they'd hardly been right either. They normally chatted while they undressed and brushed their teeth. He liked to watch her put hand cream on her elbows, and comb her hair back from her face – those intimate rituals were precious to him. She'd been quiet. She had put out her bedside light and lain down with her back to him while he was still reading, and when Scott had leant over and put one hand on her hip, she had patted it just once. He'd read more, listening to her breathing slow. When he was sure she was asleep, because she'd shifted position onto her back, he'd rolled towards her, to look at her lovely face, as if staring at her sleeping might provide him with answers, or move them towards reconciliation. They'd slept, at first, perilously close to their respective edges, an ocean of crisp sheet between them.

And in a way it did. Across the night, they'd migrated closer together without even meaning to, and he awoke with the dawn to find her pressed to him. He knew she was awake because her hand was moving gently through the thick hair on his chest. He turned towards her, and stroked her velvety smooth, soft back. She shrugged her shoulders a little, then made a familiar small sound, and put a leg across his thigh as his hand moved lower, slowly stroking each vertebra of her spine, until it got to the small hollow right at the base, and what was usually the point of no return with Heather.

That morning was no different. He loved the swift, lithe athleticism with which she tilted her narrow pelvis and was suddenly straddling him, her full weight on him, and he loved the way she shivered when he ran two hands, one down each of her slender flanks, his thumbs skimming the sides of her breasts, to cup her bum.

After she'd lain there just long enough to achieve the desired effect for both of them, Heather put the heels of her hands on his chest, and pushed herself up into a sitting position, raised and then lowered herself onto him in an easy, practised movement. She smiled, almost triumphantly, as though she'd won some prize, and began the almost excruciatingly slow, teasing rise and fall they both loved.

Part of him wanted to stop her – he needed to talk to her about what had happened. But not the greater part. This was better. Way better . . .

Afterwards, before they dozed back to sleep, because it was still very early, they did talk, and it was easier because of what had gone just before: some equilibrium had been restored.

'I'm sorry, Scottie.'

'I don't think you've got anything to be sorry for. I didn't know . . .'

'And that's what I'm sorry for. That part feels like a lie. Leaving that out when we were first . . .'

'I don't have the right to know every single thing about you, Heather.'

'But I want you to. I trust you. I love you.'

He held her close to his chest. 'I love you too. And I'm glad I know.'

'I am too.' Her voice was muffled. 'And I'm sorry for being so hard on Ethan. That wasn't fair.'

'No.' He wasn't about to tell her it was. She'd misjudged Ethan, even if he knew what had motivated her to do it.

'Hayley put me straight.'

'She did?'

'She put Ethan's case. Very eloquently. Made me see I

was getting him wrong. She doesn't know, of course, why I flipped.'

'And you didn't want to tell her?'

'Not yet. One day. So I'm sorry. I was wrong.'

He kissed her for an answer. She was so straightforward. He loved her for it. He was, still, a very lucky man.

53

Laura knocked on the door at Joe's place, surprised by how jittery she suddenly felt. God. She almost turned around and walked back in the direction she'd come. She'd been so sure he wanted her to come. Now she'd forgotten why. Would he think she was tragic? He didn't answer quickly. Maybe he was with someone . . . Maybe she was wrong about all of it, had stupidly misinterpreted everything. Panic set in. She took one, two, three steps backwards, and was on the verge of spinning and running away when he opened the door.

He'd showered. His hair was wet and water had made it darker. There were rivulets running down into the open neck of his white shirt, not tucked into the dark denim jeans. His feet were bare.

If he was surprised, he didn't seem it. A less insecure woman might have noticed how his eyes opened wide and twinkled when he saw her, might have known that the broad smile signified genuine pleasure at her presence.

'You came.'

She shrugged. 'I came.'

She stepped backwards again, but he moved forward, across his threshold, keeping the space between them the same.

'Are you coming in?'

'No. No. You're home . . .' What did that even mean?

He smiled wryly. 'Which is how I can ask you in.'

'I mean I should get back.'

'No, you really shouldn't.'

'I shouldn't.' It was as if something else was working her voice.

'So come in.' He stepped back into the dark interior, and left the door open wide.

The room had a masculine sparseness – the work surfaces were devoid of clutter, almost minimalist. There were no photographs, just a couple of landscape watercolours framed on the walls. No ornaments. But everything was clean and neat. The space was calm, like he was. One wall, though, was entirely full of books, floor to ceiling on sturdy oak shelves. Large heavy ones at the bottom – the kind about art or animals or exotic locations – up through hardback biographies and history books to paperbacks at the top. She scanned the spines – Nevil Shute, Ian McEwan, Mark Billingham. A complete mix, in complete order. There was a deep old cognac-leather armchair in front of the shelves, worn and cracked, with a tall Anglepoise lamp behind it. Three books were piled on the arm, and on top of them a folded pair of tortoiseshell reading glasses she had never seen him wearing. It looked stylish – almost like it had been posed for a magazine or something.

It was a good space.

He watched her taking everything in.

'Alphabetical. By genre. Wow. That's a little . . .'

'OCD?'

'OCD. Yep.'

'What can I say? I'm a neat guy.'

'I'm a messy woman.'

'Don't believe you.'

'Oh. Believe. Total slob.'

He was still watching her. Watching her mouth as she spoke.

She hadn't expected to be here. She was suddenly acutely aware of herself. He seemed so still and cool and calm. That quality she'd always noticed was magnified indoors. By contrast, she was hot, possibly even a little sweaty, and she couldn't seem to breathe quietly.

She forced herself not to witter into the silence.

'So. That's sorted, then.' He laughed. 'I'm a little bit OCD. You're a little bit messy. Laura Harcourt.'

He was closer now, although she hadn't been conscious of him moving. His tone was light, but still challenging.

Something in the way he was looking at her and speaking to her made her want to say something real and true about herself.

She repeated her own name. 'Laura Harcourt. Not sure who she is any more. That's the thing. The whole pathetic thing . . .'

She could feel tears in her eyes. 'Not a wife, barely a mother. Nothing useful to offer society. Lousy daughter. Too busy being pissed off to be a decent friend. Not even good company.' Her shoulders dropped.

'Not true. I enjoy your company.'

She almost snorted.

'Don't do that.' He took another step towards her. Laura might have backed away, had she not already been leaning against the wall, close to the books. 'Shall I tell you who I think you are?'

Silence was her answer. Her heart raced faster still.

'I think you are a beautiful woman who hasn't been told she's a beautiful woman nearly often enough, and certainly not recently enough. A clever woman who hasn't had anyone to spark off lately. A funny one, with no one to make laugh. A sexy one . . .'

God, if it was a line, it was nothing short of genius.

Closer. A step at a time. Barely moving. His voice was calm, his breathing slow. Just that spot of red on his chest gave him away, just above where the blond hair grew, and just below that pale hollow at the base of his throat, where she could see his pulse. She loved the spot of red. It seemed to prove to her that this meant something to him. That she did. She reached out and touched it with one finger.

This time there was nothing safe or careful about the contact. They both knew it was different.

Something snapped in her. It felt like a guitar string. Ping. The tension gone. She launched herself at him, and kissed him. His stubble scratched her face. He took her shoulders in his hands and pushed her away from him. For a dreadful moment she thought she'd horribly mis-judged him. But he just wanted to look into her eyes, and then, with a small, triumphant smile, he wanted to be the one who initiated the kiss. He brought his hands from her shoulders to her face, and held it on a tilt, his palms cov-ering almost all of it, his fingers in her hair, while he kissed her back, hard.

It had been such a long time. For ever. Laura had

perhaps thought, certainly considered, in the middle of the long, lonely nights, that this part of her was dead. That she might never feel like this again. But lust flooded back, like a tsunami. And you never really forgot how it worked.

Then again, she'd never done it in a leather armchair, until now. She couldn't remember Alex ever being so keen to be inside of her that he hadn't taken his trousers off, so that her heels, clasped around his back, felt denim, not flesh. He'd pulled her dress over her head, but he hadn't bothered to take off her bra, just pulled the cups aside, not gently, to get at her, and it was as sexy as hell to be only partly undressed. His skin was warm, and soft, except for his hands, which were as rough as she'd thought they would be, calluses adding to the sensations as he stroked her everywhere he could reach. The leather was strangely cool and hard against her skin. But it all felt good. So, so good. He kept his eyes open and he kept them on her. She looked away at first, because it was too much, but it got easier to meet his stare. When he cast it over her body, she was surprised to feel not self-conscious but powerful.

Alex had been a quiet lover, even in the early days. Joe was the opposite. He spoke to her at first, murmuring that she was beautiful, that she felt so good. Later he seemed happy to abandon himself to noises. His grunts and groans were hugely affirming to her. She felt . . . desired. When he closed his eyes at last and lost himself in the rhythm, pounding into her, there was something magical about his oblivion, and it carried her along with him. And when he collapsed heavily onto her, his breathing ragged, his mouth open against her shoulder, and his heartbeat fast, she threw her head back and laughed triumphantly, the sound neither strange nor discordant.

He spoke first. 'Christ. My knees.' He reached behind her and pulled a cushion from under her.

'I'm sorry.' She tried to move, but he held her still. She realized he was still inside her, more intimate now than in motion.

'Don't you dare be sorry.' He deftly slipped the cushion under his knees on the floor, one arm holding her firmly against him. 'You've got absolutely nothing to be sorry about.'

She laughed again. 'That was –'

'Bloody fantastic.'

She flushed with the compliment. He thought it had been fantastic. Not just fantastic – bloody fantastic. 'I was going with unexpected.'

His face was on her chest, and his voice was muffled, and still a little, gratifyingly, breathless. 'You mean you didn't come here with the express intention of seducing me?'

'That's what happened, is it? I seduced you?'

Their tone was playful. Sex had moved them on a level.

'Absolutely, your honour.'

They were still and quiet for a few moments, catching their breath. His head was on her chest. She had one hand across his shoulder, while the other smoothed his thick hair.

'I don't do this.' She heard the wonder in her own voice.

He lifted his head and smiled kindly, briefly at her. 'Neither do I.'

And she believed him.

Another minute. Then he said, 'I'd like to stay here for ever, but I've got to move', and groaned softly. He handed her dress to her as he stood up and shucked himself back into his jeans. It was thoughtful of him – she felt suddenly vulnerable and very, very naked as his flesh left hers. He walked over to the kitchen part of the room, away from her, and she watched him move while she tidied herself hastily. His back was broad, with well-defined muscles, chestnut brown from the sun. He was the best-looking man she'd ever been with. She remembered Alex. Pinky-white, ever so slightly sunken-chested and hairy. There was a second when she felt disloyal, then remembered her loyalty was no longer required. And almost giggled.

'Drink?'

'Please.'

'Glass of wine?'

'Mm.'

'White? I hate rosé.'

'I do too. White sounds great.'

'Sauvignon Blanc or Chardonnay?'

'I'm easy.'

He raised an eyebrow. She blushed.

'I don't mind,' she corrected herself.

He took a bottle from the door of the fridge, uncorked it, and filled two large glasses he took from an open shelf beside the sink. Holding them in one hand, he grabbed a blanket that was folded over the arm of the sofa in the other. 'Come and see.'

The sun was setting. She hadn't realized the time.

The view from the back of his place was uninterrupted

big sky. The sun was going down behind a line of trees far away across two empty fields. There was no breeze, and the air was still wonderfully warm. One wide bench, more like a daybed, faced the sky, and he inclined his head in its direction. The others would wonder where she was. Let them. Someone else could make the sodding salad. Her mobile was inside, on the bookshelf where she'd put it before he'd kissed her, and she felt no inclination to get it.

He sat on the bench, and motioned for her to sit between his legs, resting on him. He spread the blanket around both of them, handed her a glass, took his own, and put his other arm around her. 'It's going to be a good one . . .'

That was all he said, and it didn't require a response. Laura relaxed into him, and watched the sun, feeling perfectly contented. His chest rose and fell beneath her, and her own breathing slowed naturally to keep pace with that movement. Without her trying.

It wasn't love. She wasn't a kid and she wasn't stupid. But there was tenderness in it, and gratitude, for the sense that each had filled a need in the other. And, most of all, there was peace. At this moment, there was no past and no future. Just the 'present' her yoga teacher talked about. No need to 'refuse to engage' with her thoughts. She wasn't having any. She felt almost liquidly languid, and she knew it was because – for good or for now – the anger had gone. 'Shavasana.' She said the word almost to herself, under her breath.

'What?'

'Shavasana. It's a word my yoga teacher uses.'

'What does it mean?'

She laughed quietly. 'I think the literal translation is "corpse pose".'

'Sounds great.'

'It's the best bit. It's basically you lying completely still. We do it at the end of a class. For five minutes, a few more maybe. Part relaxation, part meditation.'

'Why?'

She rested her head on his shoulder, tilting her face towards the last rays of the sun. 'It rejuvenates the body, mind and spirit.'

He nuzzled into her neck, planting soft, dry kisses in tiny touches on her skin, and whispered, '*Namaste.*'

54

Nick woke up on 6 August with two of his three children in bed with him. Only Delilah was missing, the others having migrated at some point between his coming up around eleven, and five, when he first woke, pushed unnaturally into the top left-hand corner of the bed by a starfish and a dervish. For a long while, he watched them sleep, forcing his breath into the peaceful, gentle rhythm of theirs, and smelling their familiar, sleepy smell. A year. It had been a year. They'd been only his for 365 days. But she was here, their fierce and fabulous mother, of course, in their precious faces, in their hairlines. The whorls at the napes of their necks were all Carrie, and so were their long eyelashes, and their smooth, golden skin. She was here, in the echo and the memory of everything she'd ever said about them and what she wanted for them. She would always be here.

He wanted her to be as alive and vivid and real for them as she was for him, but he knew she wouldn't be, and the thought brought tears to his eyes in the bed where he lay between them. She had loved them so.

Last night at dinner he'd sought his family's advice about the anniversary. The kids had been in bed. Bea was the only one who knew what today was. He wasn't even sure how she knew, but she'd mentioned it a couple of times in the last few weeks, and a couple more in recent days. She'd announced it to him, in the hearing of her siblings, at bedtime, after he'd read them a story. Hearing the fact in her small voice had almost floored him.

He hadn't known what to say.

Charlie's eyes had filled with tears. 'Anniversaries are hard. You can't ignore them.'

'Especially not where Bea is concerned. It's pretty obvious that would seem strange to her.'

'But I don't want to churn them all up either.'

'You may not be able to stop that, Nick.'

'I know. But there's a difference between that and initiating it.'

Heather had been quiet, but now she was ready to speak. 'Nick. Tell me to butt out if you want to . . .'

Nick smiled. 'No, Heather, please.'

'I've never been in your position, so I –'

'I'm really hard to offend, Heather.' He laughed.

'He is. I can vouch for that. I've been trying to for bloody years.' Scott wasn't sure what Heather was going to suggest, but he wanted to encourage her.

Heather spoke a little more boldly.

'So. You don't want to ignore it. You don't want them to be upset. So let's do a thing. A little celebration of her. Give them a chance to talk about her. Look at some pictures. If we do it at breakfast, then distract them, get on with the day. If they come back later on, want to do more – especially Bea – then fine. You may find they don't.'

Scott squeezed Heather's shoulder reassuringly, and looked at his brother. 'Not a bad idea, Nicky.'

Nick looked at Heather's kind, open face and felt a rush of gratitude for her. 'That might work.'

She beamed. 'Okay, then. Got some work to do. Scott – you can airdrop, right? And, Nick, you have your laptop, yeah?'

Charlie grinned at Nick. 'Let the woman work, I say.'

And so the inaugural Carrie breakfast came to be. When Nick, carrying Arthur, and trailed by Bea and Delilah, came down the stairs, the table was laid for their mother's favourite weekend breakfast – round pancakes with bananas and maple syrup. Scott's laptop was somehow hooked up to project images onto a white wall – how the hell had she done that? The pictures that usually hung there had been taken down – and a series of images and short videos of Carrie was playing silently. Nick was almost transfixed. There she was, Carrie. Laughing, fooling about, blowing kisses. As he watched, the pictures traced a journey. An impossibly young and pretty bride. An expectant mother cradling her bump proudly. A new mum, tired and triumphant. In the swimming-pools, on the sofas and at the parks of their life together.

The children saw the pancakes before they saw the wall. 'Pancakes! Yippee! I love pancakes.'

Delilah clambered onto a chair, and reached across to the large serving dish in the middle, picking one up in her hand and taking a bite.

Then, 'It's my mummy!' Bea froze for a long moment, every adult in the room watching her face, then clapped her hands. She pulled on the wooden chair where her sister sat, angling her to see the wall. 'Look, Lila. It's lots of pictures of Mummy. That's you, in her tummy. I know, because that's me, holding her hand. See?'

'Aw. Look!' Delilah didn't stop eating but her eyes, too,

343

were fixed on the wall. Bea helped Arthur into his chair, little mother that she was. 'Wait a minute, Arthur. Keep looking. You'll be in a picture in a minute.'

Heather glanced from the children to Nick, clearly nervous as to how he might react. He tore his gaze away, and looked, dew-eyed, back at her. He didn't trust himself to speak, so he just hugged her tightly. Over her shoulder he saw Scott, who nodded, then patted his chest above his heart. Charlie picked Arthur up, and sat down with the little boy on his lap, pouring syrup and cutting a pancake into toddler-sized pieces, but it was difficult with tears in his eyes.

Laura stepped forward and did it for him, then moved to where Heather was leaning against the door. 'You're a bloody star, do you know that? A bloody star.'

55

Laura told herself she intended to apologize to Joe, and that was why she was wandering towards his place. To take the blame for what had happened, and to smooth over what would seem to them both now, surely, an embarrassing episode. It was more adult, she said to herself, to seek him out, to tackle the inevitable awkwardness head on. They were here for a couple more days – she was bound to run into him. She wanted him to know she didn't expect anything from him. Or hold what had happened against him.

She'd never had a one-night stand. What an admission. She almost had, once, at university. She'd been pissed and taken some guy back to her room, thinking that everyone else did it, but her flatmate, Lou, had hammered on the locked door long enough to get rid of him: she said she knew Laura would be really cross with herself in the morning if she went through with it. She was right, of course. Laura had always been too careful. She'd have agonized and analysed and effectively sucked out of the encounter whatever illicit pleasure she might have had in it.

So did what had happened with Joe count?

She hadn't gone there expecting it so much as daydreaming about it, so that when it had it was almost like it had been happening to someone else. What had surprised her the most was the tenderness afterwards. He'd wanted her to stay – he'd been kind and considerate and affectionate.

But that didn't mean it wasn't a one-night stand, did it? A one-night stand with a good guy. There were still good guys.

Whatever her reasons for seeking him out, though, she couldn't not.

He was in his workshop when she arrived, adjacent to the house, two barn doors open, and the sound of a machine making his whereabouts known. He didn't hear her come in. He was wearing a conker-coloured leather apron over jeans and a T-shirt, goggles and a mask. He was working on the table they'd picked up the other day, sanding off layers of paint and varnish to reveal the pale wood underneath.

For a while she just watched him work. He was unbelievably sexy in concentration. Then she stepped two, three paces around the edge of the room until she knew she was in his line of vision. When he saw her, he switched off the machine, pushed the goggles onto the top of his head, and pulled down his mask. Beneath it he was smiling broadly. He looked pleased that she was there. 'Didn't hear you come in!'

'I didn't mean to interrupt.'

'You're not. I'm due a break. I'm happy to see you.'

'You are?'

He walked towards her. 'Of course.'

When he drew level with her, he put one hand on the back of her neck and kissed her. It wasn't a polite kiss, or a friendly one. It was hungry. He smelt of sawdust and, just a little, of clean, fresh sweat.

'I was hoping you'd come. Give me a sec to get this clobber off.'

'You don't have to stop on my account. I don't want to hold you up.'

Again the smile. Laura wondered if he knew exactly how sexy it was. She figured, at his age, he must do.

'No, I want to.'

With the apron and the safety gear put neatly on the workbench, he came back towards her. 'I'm glad you're here. Come and have some tea with me.'

She let herself be led into the house. He filled the kettle and switched it on, took mugs down from the thick oak shelf behind the sink. 'How are you?'

'Good. I'm good. I wanted to say, you know, about the other day . . .' She felt like an awkward teenager, blurting. He came to stand close to her, and the feeling got worse. And better.

And then, before her agonizing and awkward explanation or apology, or whatever it was, could continue, they were kissing, and his arms went around her and moved lower, firmly pulling her into him, and the kettle boiled, and no one wanted tea any more . . .

'That went well,' she said, much later. 'I came to apologize.'

He murmured into her neck, 'Apology accepted.'

She pushed him away, with no conviction whatsoever. 'I'm serious. I don't know what I'm doing.'

'You're pretty good at it.'

'And you're determined not to let me be serious, even for a minute.'

He sat up, shoulders back, assuming a sober countenance. 'Sorry. Serious. Go.'

It was her turn to smile. 'We don't know each other.'

'What would you like to know? I'm an open book.'

'I don't know . . . How did you get here?'

'In the existential sense?'

'No. The actual sense. I know bits and pieces but I can't fit any of it together.'

'And that bothers you?'

'A bit.'

He sighed, but he was still smiling.

'Okay. Fair enough. It's pretty simple. I stepped off the conveyor-belt. I was oh-so-conventional at one point. University. Good job in the City. Made my old dad proud. Saw a gap in the market. Started a business. Financial services. Please don't make me tell you about it. Sold the business a few years later, made a few quid. Professional life going well, personal life down the tubes. Don't spend too long trying to figure out whether the two things are linked, but I suspect she waited to leave me until I was worth a bit. She took half, but it was half of quite a lot. I wasn't Gordon Gecko or anything, but it was enough. I hated having to let her take it, and I hated myself for hating it. I woke up one morning in my empty bed in my Canary Wharf flat and realized I didn't need to stay there. Had nothing left to prove to myself or anyone else in that arena. Wanted something different. Came here. Didn't do a lot for a year or so. And then I got bored. I'm not a do-nothing type of guy. There's only so many books you can read. So I took on the garden for Lucy and Col. Started the upcycling. That's where you find me. And now I have a life I truly, truly love.'

She'd never heard him speak as much in one go before.

'Is that the kind of thing? Helpful?'

She nodded.

'Your turn?' At her expression he laughed. 'Come on. Fair is fair.'

Laura took a deep breath. 'Okay. Okay. Well, I guess the difference between us is that I was shoved off the conveyor-belt. I'd climbed on voluntarily. Early twenties. Married the first guy who asked. Thought I'd be happy just because I wanted to be. Had Ethan, who is the light of my life, and pretty much the only reason I don't consider myself to be a total failure. Gave up work, gave up too much of myself, if I'm honest. Homemaker. Then he left me for a younger model, just like in all the books and films. Took me out at the knees. That's where you find me. Trying to get up off the mat.'

'It's a good sob story but, frankly, I'm not sure I'm buying it.'

'What do you mean?'

'Because that's not who I see. You've told me most of that already.'

She laughed.

'I'm serious now.'

She blushed.

'Look at me, Laura.' She met his gaze. 'You're not that woman.'

And she almost believed him. 'I don't know what woman I am. I mean, my world has shifted on its axis. Everything around me is different. I know I need to adapt. But am I finding myself, or reinventing myself? That's the question.'

'Are you getting nearer an answer?'

She smiled. 'I think I might be.'

56

The cinema had been Heather's idea. The latest Pixar film was showing at the local multiplex. She'd persuaded Hayley, who in turn had cajoled Ethan, who said he'd only agree because there was no chance anyone he knew would see him going into a kids' film. Which was only partly true. Films like *Toy Story* and *The Incredibles* had played on a loop in his house for years.

Meredith, Bea and Delilah hadn't needed any persuading, and neither had Charlie, who recognized a nap opportunity when he saw one. When Laura, Scott and Nick had been young, cinemas had served gin and tonic and let you smoke in certain rows and he'd never had to be asked twice to take them, in exchange for nine holes on a Sunday morning. Now that cinemas offered nachos and people talked through entire features, he wasn't quite so keen, but he wanted to be with the kids while he could. Nick stayed behind with a sleeping Arthur, and Scott agreed to drive them on condition he didn't have to go in. They all fitted into his big car.

'So what do you think your mother's up to, Eth?'

Ethan shrugged at his uncle's question.

'A sudden passionate interest in gardening?'

'Or gardeners?' Hayley giggled.

'Oh, God. I don't know! I'd really prefer not to think about it.'

'Fair enough. Leave Ethan alone,' Charlie chided.

Scott raised one hand in surrender. 'Okay. Okay. I was just saying . . .'

'Well, don't just say!' But everyone's tone was light and teasing.

'Well, I think it's nice if Laura's found . . .' Apparently Hayley couldn't decide on a word to end with.

'A new hobby?' Heather supplied. 'Me, too. You go, girl.'

'Really. Please. Enough,' Ethan implored, but he was laughing now too. He'd noticed, like everyone else, that his mum was sneaking off. But she was different when she was around. Good different. Lighter. Brighter, somehow. And he liked it.

Charlie insisted on paying for the tickets. Heather countered that she'd buy snacks, and the group huddled for a while at the Pic 'n' Mix. Ethan showed the girls how to maximize space in the cup with shrewd loading, and made Delilah squeal by brandishing a long jelly worm at her.

Heather watched him. He was just a kid after all. A sweet kid.

Once they'd paid – the snacks coming out more expensive than the tickets themselves – Heather and Charlie waited with Ethan and Hayley in the foyer while Meredith, who cherished every opportunity she was given to have sole charge of the little girls, took Bea and Delilah to the toilets.

Ethan took a sweet from his tub, threw it into the air and ducked to catch it in his mouth.

'Let me try that,' Hayley said, taking one from his pot, and tossing it upwards from an open palm. Before she had a chance, Ethan grabbed it. 'Oy! You!' she admonished.

'Nut – you nut!' Ethan showed her the chocolate-covered peanut in his hand. 'Aren't you allergic?'

'Gosh. Yeah. Thanks.'

'Thank you, Ethan,' Heather interjected, keen for him to know that she'd seen what he'd done.

'You're welcome. No problem.' Ethan dismissed her thanks with a brief wave, but Charlie saw the briefest flush in his grandson's cheek and, not for the first time in the week, felt a rush of gratitude towards his daughter-in-law.

57

Nick took a coffee out into the garden and reread Fran's text from the day before. He should have replied yesterday. It was selfish of him. He hadn't called Carrie's parents either, and he'd do that now. If it was selfish, he felt entitled to it. He hadn't had the room, yesterday, for other people's grief. He barely had the capacity to absorb it today. But yesterday had been for him and the children. Carrie's parents were out, or not answering the telephone. He left a stilted and awkward message – it wasn't the subject matter for an answerphone, and he hadn't prepared anything. He knew yesterday would have been wretched for them.

He dialled Fran. She answered on the third ring.

'Fran? It's me?'

'I know. Caller ID.' She sounded glad that he'd called, and he was a bit relieved.

'I'm sorry I didn't reply yesterday.'

'No need. I didn't expect you to. I just wanted you to know I was thinking about you all. And about Carrie.'

'And I appreciate that. I appreciated it, I mean. How are you?'

'Oh, we're fine.' She sighed.

'Having fun?'

'Well, the novelty of camping has well and truly worn off, I can tell you that. I'd be dreaming of my own bed, if I could sleep deeply enough to dream.'

'Not comfy?'

'Not comfy enough. The walk to the shower block has become slightly longer every day. So now it's like setting off to climb the north face of the Eiger in your dressing-gown with a sponge-bag.'

Nick laughed. She always made him laugh.

'And I'm never eating sausage and beans again. Particularly if the sausages are carcinogenically charred. Which they have been. And I've sworn off wine boxes. And Uno. Fucking Uno. Excuse my language.'

He was so with her on Uno. He'd often wondered when they'd be old enough to be taught proper card games. 'Weather's been good, though, right?'

'Don't try to console me. If it had rained, I'd have been less hot and sweaty and rash-y, and I'd probably have had a legitimate excuse to throw the kids and the crap into the back of the car and head home.'

'It's nearly over, though, isn't it? Your glamping ordeal?'

She harrumphed. 'Glamping, my arse. That, my friend, is Alastair Campbell-worthy spin.' She famously, vocally, viscerally hated Alastair Campbell, for reasons she could happily explain at length after three glasses of anything. 'But, yes, tonight. I'd go earlier, but the kids have welded themselves to some poor unsuspecting family from Nottingham, and are refusing to leave until tonight.'

'You'll beat rush-hour traffic at least.'

'Will you stop with the consolation, Mr Silver Linings?'

Nick laughed. 'Okay, okay.'

Her voice was serious now. 'And how are you? Really? How was it?'

'It was okay. I was dreading it, to be honest. Not sure why, really. It's just another day without her.'

'It's a milestone, that's why.'

'I suppose. I've done every date without her now.'

'Exactly. I get why it loomed large. It did for me too.'

'But everyone was great. Got it right. Didn't ignore it. Didn't let me wallow. It was nice to be with them.'

'I bet your dad engineered it that way.'

Nick hadn't thought of that. His mother definitely would have done so. He hadn't thought of his dad planning the holiday to cover the day. Perhaps he had. Nick felt a sudden rush of affection for his father. Not just for Charlie the father, but for Charlie the husband, and for the new bond their histories had bound around them.

'The kids? How were they?'

'Not bad. Bea was obviously sad. Lila was sort of taking her cue from Bea. If that makes sense. Arthur . . . oblivious, more or less. We did a little ceremony. It was my sister-in-law's idea.'

'The new one?'

'The new one. The only one. My actual sister's been a bit busy – and a bit AWOL.'

'How can you be AWOL on a family holiday?'

'Not easy, but she's managing it. Anyway, it was Heather's idea. It was thoughtful of her . . . and it was nice.'

'I'm glad.' Fran paused, but Nick had nothing more to say on the subject and she didn't push. 'I got a bit maudlin, in my tent prison. I've never deleted our chat, the one Carrie and I had. You know, WhatsApp. On my phone. I went back and read all our messages.'

'Aw, Fran.'

'Daft, really. It took bloomin' ages. It's no wonder I've got RSI in my thumbs. There were millions. Arrangements, in-jokes, pictures, gossip, bitching. All of it's there. It made me incredibly sad. It made me remember how in each other's pockets we were . . . the enormity of the hole she's left in my life . . .'

'I do know.'

'Sorry. Sorry. Listen to me.'

'It's okay.'

'It's not. I shouldn't –'

'It's not a competition, Fran. I loved her, you loved her. We've both lost something precious.'

'Ain't that the truth.'

After that there wasn't much more to say. It was what it was. Nick wanted to get off the phone. As he'd suspected, the weight of Fran's grief was too heavy, even down a telephone line, without her face in front of him. He didn't want it.

As if she sensed it, Fran spoke, her voice brighter. 'Well, I can hear one of my precious darlings calling me. Better go.'

He hadn't heard anyone. 'So we'll get together, once you're back, right?'

'Sure. We'll fix a thing.'

'Okay. Definitely.' He didn't know what.

And she was gone.

58

Charlie was at a tea party. He was, in fact, guest of honour at a very exclusive tea party. Bea was maître d', Delilah acting as waitress, and Arthur a somewhat disruptive fellow guest who kept running across the picnic blanket, sending everything flying. The tea was terrible, weak and watery, but he'd never have said so. The fairy cakes were better, but then Heather had baked them. He wouldn't normally have chosen to wear a gem-studded tiara so early in the afternoon, and he wasn't at all sure that Essie's Watermelon, borrowed from Heather, was quite his manicure shade. But it was a five-star Trip Advisor review from him.

This, to him, was what being a grandfather was all about. He only wished he could do more of it. And that their granny was here too.

When Ethan was born, Daphne had been ecstatic to become a grandmother. She had a friend in the village who refused to be called 'Granny' or 'Grandma' or 'Nanny' – it made her feel old, she said. Daphne thought she was ridiculous. She couldn't wait.

When Laura had gone into labour, just a day or two before the due date, she'd called them, even though it was one a.m. Daphne had answered, sleeping lightly in anticipation. He'd heard, next to Daphne in the bed, the edge of panic in Laura's voice, higher and louder than normal. Daphne spoke to her calmly and soothingly, firm at the same time. It was the alchemy of her parenting, the balance only she could achieve. He'd observed it, failed to emulate it, envied it. Now he was just grateful she knew how to do it. For a moment, she just breathed in and out, slowly, in time with her daughter.

Laura hadn't known how she'd feel, whom she'd want to be with her, until her waters burst dramatically on the bathroom floor, and the first strong contraction tightened ominously across her belly, but she knew then that she wanted her mother. Please could they come? Please? Alex had taken the phone from her at that point, but he didn't sound any less keen.

It was all the encouragement Daphne needed. Charlie knew that for weeks she'd been half waiting for such a call. They were up and dressed and in the car within fifteen minutes. At the hospital within an hour. By the time they arrived, Laura had been admitted, and the contractions, which had obviously been rumbling all evening, were coming faster and more fiercely.

Alex was almost pitifully grateful they were there. Charlie remembered feeling an unfamiliar surge of affection for his son-in-law, grey with worry, so out of place in the ward. He hadn't been at the birth of any of his own three children, and he was glad. It hadn't been at all the thing in his day, thank God. Alex, it seemed, a modern father, had no choice. But he let himself be taken for a cup of tea, and a walk around the grounds of the hospital, relieved and grateful to leave Laura, her mess and her pain with her mother.

Laura had been fully dilated in a fairly swift three and a half hours. She had relaxed once her mother had arrived. They'd even been joking, the low, conspiratorial laugh he'd been hearing since Laura was a teenager.

And then things had deviated from the smooth path they'd all thought they were on. Second stage deep transverse arrest. Charlie had never forgotten the medical term. The baby was stuck. By now, he and Alex were back from their walk. Alex came in and out of the room, ostensibly to give Charlie updates where he sat on a row of interlocked plastic chairs. Charlie could see that he needed to move.

Things got frightening quickly. People who had been relaxed and even quite slow started to move at speed, and that in itself felt alarming. The foetal monitor taped to Laura's bump registered that the baby was distressed. His heart rate was too fast. The midwife called for an obstetrician, and the handsome young houseman advised that they needed to take Laura to theatre. Alex was taken away to be changed into scrubs. Father only in the theatre.

Charlie and Daphne had sat on the hard chairs in the corridor outside the double doors Laura had been wheeled through. Charlie had tried to take Daphne's clenched hand, and she had unfurled her fingers to reveal Laura's narrow white gold wedding band.

'They'll be all right, won't they?'

'She'll be all right. I don't know about the baby. I don't know.' Her confidence had deserted her. She didn't want to promise him something she couldn't, and she was too frightened to protect him. He had come to rely completely on her certainty. He felt lost without it.

It had all been all right. Mother and baby safe. Groggy from a general anaesthetic, sore from an incision, Laura was exhausted and relieved. Ethan was six pounds nine ounces of red, blotchy, bawling baby, with a shock of dark hair. And Daphne was in love. The intensity of her feeling for her grandson had surprised even Charlie, who knew more than most about the ferocity of her love for her own children.

How she would have adored these other little people, the ones she'd never got to meet.

Lucy came round the corner, stopped short when she saw them. 'I'm so sorry . . . I knocked at the front but no one answered.'

'Not at all.' Charlie chuckled.

'I didn't mean to disturb your tea!'

'You can have some,' Bea announced.

'Well that's very kind of you,' Lucy crouched to Bea's level, 'but I'm rather late for my own tea. It's waiting for me at home. I just came to say hello to your granddad.' Over Bea's head, she whispered, 'Just to make sure all was good – you're off the day after tomorrow, I know.'

'Oh, yes. It's been wonderful. Let me . . .' Charlie made as if to stand up.

Lucy put her hand up. 'No. You stay there! Please! It can wait. I'll catch up with you in the morning.'

'Granddad, you haven't finished!' Delilah was indignant, hands on tiny hips.

Lucy backed away, smiling. 'Quite right, Granddad. Finish your tea! Just adorable . . .'

'Please have a cup.'

Lucy smiled. 'Well, okay, then, you've persuaded me. Can I have tea with two sugars please?'

'Sugar is bad for your teeth.'

'You're quite right.'

'So just one.'

Lucy laughed. 'One. Thank you.'

Charlie mouthed, 'Thank you', over Delilah's head.

'A pleasure.'

'Let's go and find a real biscuit for Lucy.' Bea grabbed her sister's hand and they skipped off towards the kitchen.

Charlie cleared his throat. 'It really has been wonderful.'

'I'm so glad. Have you been able to . . .' Lucy paused.

'Fix everyone? That's more or less what I said I wanted to do, isn't it? In your garden?'

'Well, you obviously wanted to spend time with them.' She was being tactful.

'I think you felt everyone needed to spend some time together.'

'And I really didn't know how it would go. But it's been great. I should have known you can't fix people. Only time and themselves can do that.'

She nodded, understanding.

'But family matters. Family reminds you of who you are. Where you've come from. Family always loves you, even when you don't love yourself. Even when it doesn't like what you're doing or how you're being . . . Families aren't perfect. But they're what you've got. Whatever.'

'Wise words.'

'I think, I hope, we've all remembered that.'

'Something to build on.'

'I hope so.'

'They're lucky to have you.'

She'd said that before. In the garden. He'd replied that they'd been lucky to have their mum. This time he answered differently: 'And I'm lucky to have them.'

59

Laura woke up in Joe's bed. She'd left the house early, before anyone, even Heather, was up. She was in her running kit as an alibi, in case.

She'd woken him, of course. He'd answered the door, tousled, rubbing his eyes, topless, with a pair of track pants worn low on his hips.

She loved that he didn't make any small-talk. He just smiled his slow, sexy smile, accepting her presence without question, and pulled her into his arms to kiss her. The novelty of being desired was almost overwhelming. It made her feel weak, grateful, tearful. And sexy as all hell.

Inside, the door closed against the world, he took in her get-up. 'Are we going running?'

She laughed self-consciously. 'A disguise.'

'Thank God for that. I can think of far better ways to work up a sweat.' He'd pulled her to him again, his hands sliding inside the Lycra.

'What a line!'

'Is it working?'

'It's working.'

And then they'd drifted off, back to sleep. When she woke up, it was after nine. Joe lay on his stomach beside her, still asleep. She studied his still face for a few moments, taking in the morning stubble across his cheeks, the fine lines at his eyes, the arch of his brows. Then rolled onto her back, and stretched. The sun was streaming in now, through open windows without curtains, and she luxuriated in being there, in the birdsong, in the sun, in his bed.

Beside her, Joe stirred. 'Good morning. Again.'

'Mmm. Morning.'

They rolled together, so that they lay facing each other. Joe rubbed his nose against hers. 'This is becoming a habit.'

Laura smiled. 'It takes two weeks to form a new habit.'

'Oh, it does, does it?'

'It does. I read it somewhere. And I'm leaving the day after tomorrow.'

He put one arm across her hip possessively. 'I might not let you.'

Laura felt a shadow of sadness pass across the light mood. She rolled onto her back, and breathed out slowly.

Joe sat up, and leant over her. 'Can I make you breakfast?'

'Breakfast?'

'Meal eaten at the start of the day. Breakfast. Avocado on toast? Maybe with a poached egg. Some roasted tomatoes. Coffee? I know what you city types like.'

'Sounds like a restaurant. You're full of surprises.'

'I hope so . . .'

She was grateful to him for ignoring the question of the day after tomorrow for now. This, this here, was like a bubble. A bright, warm, safe, sexy bubble. It would have to burst. Life was like that. She didn't want to burst it yet.

'You can have it in bed, if you like.'

'Well, in that case . . .' Laura laughed delightedly and

pulled herself up to sit against the headboard, sheet tucked decorously under each arm.

Joe stood up and pulled on his track pants. He had a truly great arse. She resisted the urge to lurch forward and kiss it. What the hell was happening to her?

Eventually, unwillingly, Joe took her back from his place to the house, through the field, down the track and up through the vegetable garden. It was only a seven- or eight-minute walk, but it took longer: they stopped often to kiss like kids with nowhere to go, her back against a tree.

Insatiable. She rolled the word around her brain silently. Insatiable. She could have done this all day. She wanted to do it all day. It had never been like this with Alex. Never with anyone. How truly sad to get to her age before she'd felt it. How inexplicably wonderful to feel like this right now.

She didn't want to go straight into the house, so she sat for a while in a sort of reverie to the side of the tennis court. She half expected to be discovered there by Heather, out to bang balls around, but it was Ethan, his appearance in the garden unexpected, who found her first.

'Hey.'

'Hi.' He sat down next to her. 'All right?'

'Yes, love. I'm very all right.'

'You've been with that guy again, haven't you?' His tone was not accusatory. 'The guy who does the gardening. The one you went out with the other day.'

She was shocked, and didn't answer him straight away.

'The one you thought we didn't know about, except we all do.'

'All of you?'

Ethan laughed. 'Well, I don't think Bea, Lila and Arthur are really tuned in, but everyone else, yep.' He was evidently enjoying the moment. 'It's okay, by the way. No one minds. Not that it's anyone else's business. But they don't.'

'And you?'

Ethan shrugged shyly. 'If you're happy, I'm happy.'

'That's my line.'

'Well, it works both ways. Are you? Happy?'

She sighed. 'I feel a bit daft. It's just a bit of a holiday romance. I'm acting like a kid.'

'I think you're a little happy.'

'You do?'

'Hey, you two!' Now it was Heather who appeared, in her impeccable whites, Hayley trailing behind a little less enthusiastically carrying a tube of yellow balls. 'How are *you* doing?'

The arch of her eyebrows, and the emphasis on 'you' confirmed what Ethan had already said. Laura smoothed her hair self-consciously. 'Good. You?'

'All good here. Just gonna play a quick set. Need to do something to exercise off all this cheese and wine and cake we've been having, huh?' And she definitely winked.

60

Heather was reading on a lounger on the terrace, her hair tied in a high ponytail, wearing enormous dark glasses. She looked about twenty, Scott thought. 'Coffee?'

'You read my mind.' She smiled at him briefly, then went back to the book. 'Sorry. Good part.'

Scott laughed. 'It must be – you've been still for, like, an hour.'

Heather wrinkled her nose, to acknowledge that she'd heard him, but didn't look up again.

In the kitchen he made two coffees, noting that there was only one unopened sleeve of capsules left. Just as well they were going home soon.

Back outside, Heather's book was on the floor beside the lounger. It had been replaced by Arthur, who had obviously climbed on and distracted her. He was sitting astride her, with one plump toddler leg on either side of her lap, and they were doing 'Incy Wincy Spider' together, the novel forgotten. Heather's face and voice were animated, and Arthur rewarded her efforts with a raucous belly laugh every few seconds. She tickled his tummy, and he threw himself violently backwards, but she caught him, and as she pulled him upwards, he put his arms around her neck and clung to her. Heather's eyes closed, and her arms held him tight. When she released him, Arthur kissed her square on the lips, a wet, noisy smacker, his hands holding her face still so he could, and it was her turn to laugh.

Then, as quickly as he had come, Arthur was off again, sliding impatiently down onto the patio, with one quick pat on the behind from Heather, and tottering off in the direction of his sisters, who were sprawled on a checked blanket a few metres away on the lawn with their dolls. He was intent on disrupting their quiet game. Heather didn't pick up the book straight away, watching him go with a fond smile.

Scott put down one of the coffee mugs on the small wicker table next to her.

'He's a sweetie, isn't he?'

She nodded. 'Thanks, honey. He sure is. I could eat him . . . Let's have one. Let's try and have one, at least.'

The thing was, they'd completely ruled it out, really early on. They'd had a two-martini dinner at a little neighbourhood joint a few blocks south-east of the office, where they served crab cakes and celeriac *rémoulade* to die for, and decided, mutually, brave on gin, that kids were not going to be a part of the picture. Hayley and Meredith were enough for Heather, she'd said, and he'd told her that they would be enough for him too. Believed it. Been a little relieved, even, if he was honest. Children – at least children for whom he was responsible – frightened him a little. Teenagers – ready-made – seemed, to him, a good compromise. He'd thought he could relish the daydream of college graduations and weddings and driving licences, but the idea of nappies and tantrums and sleepless nights made him anxious. He was obsessed with Heather – consumed by her, by the physicality of her – and jealous of the idea that a baby would come between them, annexing her glorious body, her time and her love. He was too selfish for that, he'd thought. He'd only just found her. He didn't want to share her. He'd never told her that. He'd been slightly ashamed of feeling that way.

Something had changed. It had changed almost across these ten days. Maybe it was Arthur and Bea and Delilah, and seeing her with them. Maybe it was what she'd told him. He felt closer to her now than he ever had, against an unexpectedly lovely tableau of familial love. The ties that bind felt less like the ropes of bondage and more like lifelines now. This was good. Something had changed.

But it was Heather who'd said it. He might not have been brave enough. She pushed the enormous sunglasses up onto her head, so he could see her pretty eyes, and he was surprised to see that they were shiny with tears. She was gazing at him, her lips pressed together, bright and worried, searching his face for a reaction. Not at all sure of him.

He didn't know why not.

'Yes.' He blurted it out.

'Yes?' She stood up excitedly.

Scott pulled her to him, held her tightly, and spoke into her hair, and then into her mouth, kissing her passionately. 'Yes. Yes. Yes.'

Hayley, passing, curled her lip disdainfully at their public display of affection, oblivious to the momentousness of the exchange. 'God. Get a room, you two.'

61

'So what are we all going to do today, then? Last day and all that.' Nick poured tea from the pot into a mug and leant against the windowsill.

His children were already seated around the table, eating Rice Krispies. 'A picnic! A picnic!' Bea and Delilah bounced in their chairs at the kitchen table, banging their spoons.

'Rounders competition.' This was Charlie.

'Rounders *and* a picnic.' The smallest people amended their chant.

Charlie chucked the girls under their chins. 'Sounds like an excellent idea, my darlings.'

'Rounders is softball, right?' Heather asked.

Meredith nodded. 'More or less. We play it at school.'

Laura peered into the teapot, and topped it up with water from the kettle. 'Do we even have the stuff for rounders?'

'We certainly do.' Charlie smiled. 'Bats, balls, even some little plastic cones for the bases. They're in that cupboard in the boot room.'

'How many of us are there? Enough for two teams?'

'Plenty. I've asked Lucy and her husband to join us. When she came round yesterday to talk about check-out she mentioned they'd be around. I thought it would be fun.'

'So you've been planning this, huh?' Laura winked at her father.

'Might have been.' He was pleased at the reception his idea was getting. This was just what he wanted. Everyone involved.

Bea was counting and muttering names under her breath.

'How many of us are there, then, sweet Bea?'

'Ten. No, twelve, with Lucy and Col. If you don't count Arthur.'

'Arthur . . .' This was Arthur, disgruntled at the idea of not counting.

'We have to count Arthur. He needs to run for his old granddad. You can do that, can't you, Arthur, old chap?'

Arthur nodded enthusiastically, without much understanding of what he was agreeing to.

'That's settled, then. Rounders and a picnic.'

'Have we got what we need for a picnic?'

'We've got loads of crisps and biscuits and cheese and stuff. Tomatoes.'

'Lashings of ginger beer?'

Heather looked puzzled.

'Seventies childhood cultural reference. Don't worry.' Scott slung an arm around her shoulders. 'Why don't you and I pop to the deli, grab some stuff?'

'I'll go and tip the youths out of their beds.'

'I might . . . ask a friend. To come.' Laura spoke into the room, half hoping no one would hear her in the cacophony of breakfast and planning. But they did.

Nick, halfway to the stairs to rouse Ethan and Hayley, raised an eyebrow. 'A friend?'

Laura hated the pink blush she could feel rising. Everyone was looking at her.

Charlie put his arm around her, protective. 'The more the merrier, sweetheart. You ask your friend.'

'Yes, ask your friend . . .' Nick's voice lingered on the word more than his father's had, but the amused tone was just as fond.

Laura paused, desperate for the family chaos to wash over the awkward moment.

She didn't have to wait long. 'That's fourteen.' Bea looked exercised. 'If Auntie Laura brings a friend, there will be fourteen people, which makes two teams the same size.'

62

The caterer had come in again for the last night, although it had all been a lot more casual than the evening of Charlie's birthday celebration. There were three interesting salads of the kind you could never quite be bothered to make for yourself, two baguettes, a chicken and mustard casserole, and some very superior, chef-style chicken nuggets for the children. And two pillowy pavlovas for dessert. All left for them to help themselves.

Charlie had put all the booze everyone had brought on the kitchen island, declaring that the bar was open, because who could be bothered to take half-drunk bottles of anything home?

They were all in the lightest mood, happy, sunkissed, relaxed.

Charlie, expansive with happiness, had asked Lucy, Col and Joe to join them, but the three tactfully claimed to have good reasons why they couldn't. He watched Joe say goodbye to Laura, around the corner, where they thought no one could see them. They spoke for a while, heads close together, and then he kissed her on the lips, tender and gentle, stroking her cheek, the other hand holding hers. As he walked away, their arms extended, fingers still entwined, lingering a moment. Laura turned back, wistfulness on her face, and he wondered how it would play out, the fledgling thing between them.

Inside, someone put an iPod on shuffle and the kitchen was suddenly full of eclectic music. Laura bumped hips with Nick, who took her hand and spun her in a pirouette under his arm, one way and then the other. When Duran Duran's 'Hungry Like The Wolf' came on, the three siblings sang the chorus into imaginary microphones, giddy with instantaneous nostalgia, to an audience delighted and horrified in more or less equal measure.

Heather had made a pitcher of martinis. Scott referred to it as 'neat gin with vermouth wafted over it', and told the old New York joke about martinis being like breasts – one wasn't enough and three was one too many. Nick poured a large one for himself, and a slightly smaller one for Ethan. 'That'll put hairs on your chest, kid.'

'Ew.' This was Hayley. 'Who wants hairs on their chest?'

'Don't knock it till you've tried it.' Heather giggled, slipping a hand inside Scott's shirt.

'Oh. My. God. Gross.' Meredith hid her face in her hands, but she was giggling too.

Ethan took a sip from his glass, and immediately coughed. More laughter ensued.

'I wanna try it.' This was Hayley. Ethan handed her his, and she sipped gingerly. 'Mm. Nice . . .' Sipped again. Ethan rolled his eyes, and took the glass from her.

'Don't even think about it!' But Heather's tone was light as she passed Hayley a compromise glass of white wine. Hayley hesitated, then cut her losses and took it, clinking glasses with Ethan.

'Selfie?'

He frowned, but then put his arm around her shoulders,

raised his glass into the shot and leant in as she held her phone at arm's length.

'Hashtag family.' But the sting was gone from the humour, leaving just a new, tentative, gentle mocking. It wasn't lost on Heather, or on Scott and Laura.

'What is it with you kids, anyway?' Nick asked. 'Why does everyone have to be waxed and smooth all over – men and women?'

'Nick!'

'I mean it. It's weird. You all want to look like Morph, for Christ's sake.'

'Who in hell is Morph?'

Laura tried to google Morph, the smooth and hairless Plasticine man from their childhood television. Got, instead, a gimp suit on a sex-toy website, which created more hysterical peals of laughter.

Heather made mocktails for Bea and Delilah. Bea was brave, and took a bite from an olive, but spat it out straight away, brushing frantically at her tongue to get rid of the taste.

Somehow, among the noise and the chaos and the banter, plates and cutlery were collated, the table was laid with napkins and water glasses, and the caterer's platters were carried over.

Charlie stood in the corner, and watched them all, with a huge lump in his throat. This was what he had wanted. This was what he wanted to capture like a photograph and remember for ever. This . . . this. Daphne was here in the room. He knew it.

It wasn't the moment for toasts or speeches. Calling for silence so he could speak mawkish words, invoke their dead mother, thank them for being here or seek thanks for facilitating it risked breaking the spell. And the spell was so lovely. He spoke in his head instead, just to her. *Here we all are.* Her lovely face was so vivid in his mind. *I've done it, darling. I love you. I miss you. I wish you were here with us.*

63

Home. Laura had to push the door hard, nudging ten days' worth of post out of the way, to open it. She put her suitcase at the bottom of the stairs, and stooped to gather up the pizza-delivery fliers and unsolicited catalogues. In the kitchen, she filled the kettle, and put a mint teabag in a mug. There was no milk for a builder's tea – she'd ordered an online shop but it wasn't coming for a couple of hours. Ethan had made straight for the stairs. 'Throw your washing onto the landing, love.' You weren't home until the washing-machine was going. Just like Mum. Not quite as bad. Mum would have stripped you in the kitchen so she could have a full load. She smiled at the memory. The pot of basil she kept on the windowsill was half dead, and she put it under the tap while the kettle boiled, then opened the back door and the window: it was stuffy in there after ten days all locked up.

When she had left, everything had been different. She had a muscle memory of that angry, tense, brittle person who had spent hours sitting at the kitchen table in despair and impotent rage. A shiver of sadness rippled through her. She wasn't going back there. She was drawing a line. Then. Now.

She took the mint tea to the table, and started to separate the post into recycling and opening piles. Mostly, as ever, it was bills and bank statements. There was a letter, with unfamiliar handwriting on the envelope, no address on the back. She opened it, scanned to the bottom of a second page of writing, and felt her heart beat faster when she saw Claudia's name. She put the letter on the table, as if it were too hot to hold, and sat back in her chair, then took a deep breath and picked it up again. Read it once, fast, scanning the lines. Read it again, more slowly, saying each word out loud to herself in her head. Put her face in her hands and wept.

Dear Laura

I thought a great deal about the conversation you and I had in the café that day. I'm glad we met. If we hadn't it would have been easy for me to never consider your son, a fact I am not proud of but need to acknowledge.

Everything you said was right and fair. Ethan did nothing wrong, and nor did Saskia. Rupert did. He had no right to barge into your home and speak to you and to Ethan in the way he did. It was wrong, and it was wrong of me to defend him to you. I'm sorry.

He will not be taking anything to the police. This will go away for ever for Ethan, but only if he and Saskia break up. Really break up. Rupert can't get past it. I have tried. But he can't.

Saskia is going away. You might remember my saying how much he hated the idea of her being at boarding school: that tells you how high emotions are still running for him.

This is the best that I can do.

He is a difficult man, but he's my husband and Saskia's father, and I am sure you will appreciate that family is everything to me.

Saskia understands. You need to make Ethan understand. I hope it won't be too hard for him. They haven't seen each other for ages now. I do hope that some of the intensity they felt has passed. They are, after all, so very young.

I realize, reading this back, that it sounds very Shakespearian and dramatic. I'm sorry for that. But it is for the best, I'm sure. I hope you understand.

I wish Ethan all the best: I honestly do.
Claudia

He already knew it was over: the conversations they'd been having, in the last couple of days, made her feel confident that he didn't see a future. He'd guessed, hadn't he, that Saskia would not be coming back for sixth form? She sensed his starting to move on. She'd even thought, once or twice, that he was slightly surprised at feeling okay.

And now the threat had gone away. She exhaled deeply, and let relief flood through her. The three a.m. fears of what could potentially happen to Ethan had had her in their grasp for weeks, even though Alex, Scott and Nick had told her it wouldn't happen – that an angry father was striking out in the only way he could. The risk to her boy's future had seemed immense, the injustice of it staggering. She felt almost giddy with relief, standing in the kitchen gazing out at her parched, neglected garden. She imagined the conversation that had gone on between Claudia and Rupert. Laura wondered what threats and bargains Claudia had had to use. It was a strange, discordant thought that Claudia was stuck in a difficult marriage, and she wasn't. It wouldn't have been easy for her, convincing him, not so much not to do anything but to stop threatening to do something.

First she needed to share the news with Ethan upstairs. Maybe they'd order Domino's, to celebrate – open a couple of beers. He'd be low-key, with her, she knew. And that was okay. Alex would need to know too. She'd text him. And he'd be happy to hear it. But then, she realized, she would come downstairs, pick up the phone, and tell Joe it was all going to be okay.

'Cocktails at lunchtime? Who even are you? Where is my beloved, risk-averse, jolly-sensible friend?'

Laura had ordered before Mel arrived. It was a long-standing date, made before the holiday. Mel cherished the occasional day in town. They might see an exhibition, do a bit of shopping. A film even. But lunch first. Two passion-fruit martinis were waiting on the table.

She stood up and hugged her friend. 'So, so good to see you.'

'You too, love.' Mel threw her handbag strap over the chair's back, and ran her fingers through her unruly hair. 'Am I late?'

'You're always late. Actually, you're fairly early on Mel time.'

Mel giggled and blew her a kiss, unrepentant.

Then, hair tamed, seat taken, she narrowed her eyes and looked hard at Laura's face. 'You look . . . you look fab.'

Laura didn't do what she normally did – brush away the compliment. She beamed at Mel and accepted it. The truth was, she sort of, almost, knew she was right. She'd seen herself in a shop window on her way here. And there'd been a subtle but definite change. What had been scrawny a few weeks ago was somehow slender now. She was golden from her time in the sun, not pale and drawn as she'd been before she'd gone away. And she was a bit bouncier, more upright, happier-looking. Something like a sparkle twinkled in her eyes. She'd been surprised, then pleased. She was even more pleased that Mel had noticed it.

Mel raised an eyebrow, then narrowed her eyes. 'Wait a minute. Something's different.'

Laura felt her cheeks go pink.

'You've . . . unclenched.'

'Charming.'

'Okay. You've unfurled.' Mel made an expansive gesture in the air with both hands.

It wasn't something. It was everything. Mel could see the lioness.

It was Ethan being okay. It was realizing that the idea of Alex being with Genevieve suddenly wasn't gnawing at her heart. It was knowing she had found the voice she needed to go ahead with the divorce – a more equal partner to Alex in ending their marriage than she had been during most of it. That maybe selling the house where she had been so unhappy would be all right after all. A new beginning.

'You've been shagging!' Mel's reductive but accurate diagnosis was triumphantly delivered. A man at the next table heard, and stared at them. Mel smiled broadly at him.

And it was that too.

Laura smiled shyly, avoiding the frank appraising gaze of the eavesdropper. 'It's obscene that you can tell,' she whispered.

'Aha. I knew it!' Mel exclaimed. 'Cheers to that.' She picked up the martini glass and raised it. 'Here's to that.'

Laura clinked, and sipped.

'Tell me all.'

For the first time in God knew how long, she had only good news to impart to her long-suffering friend. She leant in, conspiratorial. Mel rubbed her hands in glee. 'What do you want first?'

'Filth, obvs. All the filth.'

Laura laughed at Mel's delighted smile, and started to talk.

64

Nick headed north, not east. To the farm. He'd got through, finally, to his parents-in-law. He asked them if he could bring the girls and Arthur for a visit. He had a couple more days, he said. Ed had called Maureen to the phone.

'Of course, Nick. Please. We loved it when you were up here at Easter. It feels like ages ago. You don't even have to ask. You've never had to ask. We'd love to see you all.'

Nick had been relieved that it wasn't awkward.

The kids had been thrilled when he told them. They didn't want to leave the holiday house, or the pool, or Meredith and the others. Granny and Granddad seemed a more exciting prospect than home.

At the farm, Ed and Maureen had rushed out when they heard the car, Maureen crouching so Bea and Delilah could run straight into a hug. Ed swung Arthur into his arms, the little boy giggling delightedly.

'We wanna see the cows.'

'And the sheep!'

'And the chickens . . .'

'All right, all right, all right.' Ed had laughed. 'All right?' he'd asked Nick.

Nick nodded, smiling. 'Fine.'

'He'll take them.' Maureen hooked her arm through Nick's. His three children headed off down the yard with their grandfather without a backwards glance, Arthur on

Ed's shoulders, Bea and Delilah either side of him, Delilah holding his free hand. For a second they watched them go. Maureen patted his arm. 'You come in the house and have a cold drink.'

The cool kitchen was a welcome respite from the shimmering heat. The walls of the farmhouse were ancient and very thick. The old Rayburn was off for the summer. Maureen poured him a tall glass of water, making small-talk about the heat, and how little rain there'd been but, thank goodness, there was a load in next week's forecast.

Nick accepted the drink gratefully, and sat down at the pine table.

Carrie was everywhere. Not in photographs, although there were several of those. In memories. He could see her now, sitting at this table, one knee clutched to her chest, an oversized moth-eaten cardigan she was too sentimental to part with sliding off one shoulder, pulling a rasher of bacon apart with her fingers, even though her mother had always told her off for eating like that. Over by the huge double Belfast sink, blowing bubbles over baby Bea's head as she sat in five inches of warm water. Warming her feet by the fire after a bracing walk.

It hurt. But it was good too.

'We're so happy to see you, Nick.'

'I'm sorry. I've stayed away too long.'

'You've had so much to deal with.' Maureen was an eager peacemaker. 'We upset you. We didn't mean to.'

'Ssh. It's okay. You were right.'

Maureen didn't reply. Nick wanted to try to explain. 'I think I held out for so long because acknowledging I needed help, appreciating that I needed to make real changes to the way we lived, meant I had to admit she was never coming home. That sounds ridiculous. Of course she wasn't. But in some really ridiculous way it felt disloyal, filling her place. I wasn't ready to move on. Does that make any sense at all or do I just sound pathetic?'

Maureen's voice was very quiet, her gaze middle-distanced. 'I stand in her old bedroom sometimes and pretend she's just out.' A small, joyless laugh. 'And she hasn't lived here in years.' She looked at him. 'So, no, you don't sound pathetic.'

Nick put his arms around her, and she laid her head on his chest. They stood like that for a while. He felt her cry softly, then calm. Eventually, she pulled back, and smiled. 'We miss you, Nick.' He knew. 'So, sit down here, and tell me all about you all.'

65

Results went live at seven a.m. It wasn't at all like it had been in Laura's day. She'd been camping on the Isle of Wight with mates, and had come home late on results day to a letter, opened with Charlie and Daphne hovering anxiously, ready to celebrate or console as required. Ethan could have gone to school, to line up with his classmates and rip open a brown envelope with everyone else watching, including a reporter from the local newspaper. He'd chosen the more private, electronic way.

He hadn't slept much, and certainly not at all since five. She'd heard him pacing, wide awake herself. So they'd sat over the laptop together in the kitchen, making small-talk and watching *Frasier* on Channel 4, with Ethan tapping refresh every few minutes. Eventually, a different page appeared, and he could access them.

He took a deep breath and she held his free hand.

And it was good. A mix of numbers and letter grades she hadn't quite understood until he'd painstakingly explained it to her. But really good. More than enough to proceed with the A levels he'd chosen, far better than he'd feared. Laura let out a triumphant whoop, and Ethan didn't shush her.

They had Bucks Fizz and chocolate croissants for breakfast, and when Ethan texted his dad, Laura hadn't minded at all.

After they'd texted back and forth about Ethan, Alex, emboldened, perhaps, by her civility, had asked Laura if she wanted to have lunch with him. She wasn't ready for that, but she'd agreed to coffee at a place near his office.

She'd been waiting when he arrived. It was weird. You spent decades with a person, and then you weren't with them, and it was so different. You knew them inside out and then not at all. He was wearing a jazzy tie and a matching pocket square in bright pink. He'd never have bought them himself. The Genevieve effect. She wondered whether it suited him, and decided that it did, rather.

We'll be better off apart, she thought. It was quite a simple, but profound thought.

Apparently he couldn't decide whether or not to kiss her but went with a fleeting touch of dry lips on her turned cheek. All she could think about in that moment was Joe's open mouth against hers, his breath hot on her skin. Up close, Alex didn't even smell like her husband any more.

They ordered coffee, and talked a little about Ethan. Their son didn't want him to know anything that had happened on holiday, so Laura didn't tell him.

When the barista brought the two coffees and put them on the table, Laura changed the subject. 'So, I know we're supposed to do all this through lawyers, but I thought we could be adult enough to do some of the figuring out on our own.'

Alex looked wary. 'Okay . . .'

She ignored his reticence. 'I've been thinking about the house. You're right. I'm going to sell.'

Alex raised a hand to stop her. 'I don't need you to do that now.'

She ignored the gesture. 'I've got three estate agents coming round in the next few days. Two nationals, one local. I've thought about that online one, the one with no commission, but I'm not sure. You happy with that? Once I've got three valuations, we'll choose one – the middle one probably, no point in being greedy, but no need to low ball it either.'

He looked alarmed. Laura couldn't help enjoying his expression. 'September isn't a bad time to go on the market. Second best time after spring, I gather. I'll get the bread baking, coffee brewing, all that. People will want to be in by Christmas, so with a bit of luck, we'll get offers within a few weeks, a month or two.'

'You've been busy.'

'I know you're not going to screw me over with the settlement, Alex. I know you're not a sleaze. You're not, are you? A sleaze who'd try to cheat a woman he spent twenty-odd years with? The woman who supported him while he built a successful career, who raised his child?'

Alex blustered. But she hadn't finished.

'Men count on women like me being on our knees when they leave us. After all, when you're broken, you don't fight. And I *was* broken. I've been as low as I've ever been. For a long time. Too damn long.'

It was gratifying to see a shadow of guilt cross his face.

'But I've been angry too. And I can still be angry. If – and please listen carefully to this, and believe it – if you do this the wrong way, I'll resurrect all that anger, and I'll use it against you.'

He tried to speak. 'Hey –'

It was her turn to put up a hand. 'I've got a good lawyer

now. The law is clear. And it's fair. But I'll get a better one if I have to. I'll get a man-hating, furious ball-breaker of a woman lawyer. I'll get a forensic accountant.'

The colour had drained from Alex's face. 'There's no need for that.'

'Okay then.' She'd finished.

'You know me, Laura.'

'No. I don't. I knew you.'

Outside, away from him, she took out her phone and called Joe.

'How'd it go?'

'I said it all – all that stuff I wanted to get out.'

'How'd he take it?'

'He listened. I think.'

'Good for you. How do you feel?'

Laura paused. 'Good. I feel good.'

Joe laughed his rich, warm laugh. 'I'm happy for you.'

'I've got to do it now. Get on and sell the house. I might be homeless by Christmas.' She laughed. Her heart was racing.

'No, you won't. You'll come and stay here, with me.'

66

'You okay with tuna for supper, Ethan?' Heather stood in the doorway of the TV room, in an apron, her hair piled on her head.

'Yeah. Sounds great. Thanks.'

'Asian or Mediterranean?' She made her hands like scales, weighing up the options.

'Either is fine. They both sound good.'

'Sure?'

'Asian,' Hayley answered. She looked at Ethan. 'That's my favourite. Lemongrass, soy, ginger . . . sticky rice . . .' He nodded appreciatively.

'Coming up. Scott's on the six fifteen – miracles will never cease – so we'll eat around seven forty-five, okay? There's snacks if you're hungry.' She'd winked at him, and headed back to the kitchen.

Heather was totally normal with him. Really nice, actually, which was a relief. He knew she'd been the most upset – of all the adults – by the way he'd been back in August. They'd got it on track, he'd felt, by the end – that last day or two had seemed okay. Better than okay. But he'd had a residual worry that once everyone was back home, away from Granddad and from the unabashed sentimentality of the end of the holiday, she'd remember that she didn't like him very much. There was no sign of that, though.

'You are so spoilt.'

'I could deny. Not gonna. We are pretty spoilt.' Hayley giggled.

'Your mum used to work, though, right?'

'Yeah. Really hard.' She stood up. 'I hope you aren't implying that being an Instagram influencer is not a proper job?' They sniggered. 'I'll go get us some Cokes and chips.'

'Crisps,' he corrected.

She stuck out her tongue at him, and went off to forage.

Left alone with the remote control, Ethan flicked around the channels, looking for something to watch. They had thousands. He liked being here and not just because of the superior satellite cable package. It had been Hayley's idea. They'd been talking on the phone a bit, since the summer. It was cool. When he'd said he was probably going to his dad's at the weekend because Joe was coming to see his mum and he wanted to clear out, she'd suggested he come to her house.

He'd been wary at first, but Hayley had taken the phone into the kitchen and asked her mother, right there and then, with him on the line. So when Heather had said yes, he knew she had said it without pressure or cajoling.

Heather had picked him up from the station in the big Audi. He'd offered to wait and come with Scott, but she'd said it was fine to come straight from college. He finished at two on a Friday – his timetable was much lighter this year, now that he was only doing four subjects. She'd picked him up and they'd driven together to collect Hayley from her school.

The place was amazing – a building like a stately home, long driveway, loads of sports fields. Hayley spilt out in a sea of navy blue uniforms, Meredith, too, although she only came up to the car to collect a duffel bag of stuff – she was going to a sleepover. It was good to see her. She'd called him 'cuz'.

Hayley asked about Saskia, whether he'd heard from her (he hadn't), and whether he missed her (he did, but not unbearably). She didn't probe.

During the week, they might FaceTime or text every few days. He was the only member of the family who knew she'd met a boy, the older brother of a school friend – Kurt – when he was home from boarding school at half-term, that they'd been talking and were planning to meet up in the Christmas holidays at a couple of parties. Hayley had told him about the party where she'd drunk too many VKs, been sick in the flower borders and had had to be put to bed in the family's guest room. She knew he thought he might like a girl called Amelia, who'd joined the sixth form in September. She was the only person he talked to, now, about his fears of getting involved. Mum had been amazing about Saskia – he was grateful for that – and they were much closer now, maybe closer than they'd ever been. But it still felt weird to talk to her about girls. The thing he was most grateful about after that whole awful business had ended was that he could reclaim a normal degree of teenager's privacy about his love life. Hayley was safe, and she was good to talk to. Family, but not quite. Close, but not too close.

67

Laura felt ridiculous. And excited. And ridiculously excited. She glanced down at her chest and saw the hives she'd known would be there. Her nerves, like her tears, disfigured her. Thank God for the scarf.

This was no way for a middle-aged woman to behave. And yet she was a middle-aged woman, and she couldn't stop herself. She didn't want to. She hadn't waited for someone at a railway station for years. And here she was, at Paddington, in the middle of a Saturday morning, waiting for Joe. She felt like a kid. She'd arrived unnecessarily early, had had a coffee, been to the loo twice (once to make sure she didn't have a latte moustache), wandered in and out of the few shops available, then tried and failed to read a magazine in WHSmith. Someone must be playing football this afternoon – she didn't know the team, but loads of men in the same shirt were milling about. A few scruffy kids moved sullenly between groups, scrounging coins, and a promotional company was pressing small cans of coconut water on passers-by, who mostly seemed uninterested. The train was running late – he should have been there ten minutes ago, and he wasn't due for another five. She'd have been there for forty-five. Now she was leaning against a rail and watching the comings and goings, trying not to feel emotional. That bit at least wasn't new – airports and stations always made her weepy, if she let them. She had palpitations, for God's sake! A busker was playing Neil Young and Ed Sheeran songs. He was good, and an elderly couple were swaying in time, their heads bobbing to the music.

She hadn't seen him in a while. Never here. They'd been messaging. A lot. If texts and WhatsApps were modern love letters, they were vastly inferior to their predecessors, but his were better than most. She found herself rereading the chain of messages all the time, scrolling back through. There were photographs – sometimes they sent pictures of themselves or of what they were doing that day. The odd video. Sweet, short 'good mornings' and 'sleep tights', and longer 'chats' about Ethan. And they'd talked on the phone, for hours and hours. She'd gone out and bought those absurd white stick things you could shove in your ear so you could speak hands free, and she talked to Joe while she did all kinds of other things – stomped across the park, changed the duvet cover, drove to the supermarket, made chilli, watched TV. Fell asleep.

And now, after the missing and the longing, he was there, walking towards her, a holdall over his shoulder, looking different, dressed for winter in a pea coat with the collar up, big smile across his lovely face, his eyes fixed on her. That thing happened where all the other people melted away, and it was just him, coming her way. It was like a boyband music video.

And there was something else as well. Lust. Unfamiliar, powerful, good.

When he got to her, he dropped the bag, and pulled her into him. Her hands went inside the open coat, to where she could feel his ribcage, warm and solid, and his big arms were very tight around her – her whole frame remembered that instantaneous feeling of being safe and . . . home. Exhale. Relax. Rejoice.

For long moments he just held her. And then he kissed her, hands on her face and in her hair, and the kiss was deep and long and hard and possessive, and she felt engulfed and almost overwhelmed. His stubble was rough against her cheeks, his teeth were against hers. A most definitely inside kiss outside, because they were both oblivious. He pulled back and looked into her eyes. 'God, it's good to see you. I've missed you.'

'You too.'

And then he kissed her again. Daphne would have called it a knee-trembler.

Eventually, they stopped. When she opened her eyes, a few people were staring. A middle-aged woman looked almost envious, a teenage boy in that footie shirt more repulsed. Joe picked up the bag, and slung one arm around her shoulders, keeping her close to him, and they started walking towards the exit.

'What are we doing?'

'I have absolutely no idea.' She was giddy. She laughed. 'What do you fancy?'

She'd fed him the line and he took the bait. 'That's bloody obvious.'

'No, I mean what would you like to do? Are you hungry?'

'Maybe. I could eat. We could get a drink.' He looked down at her. 'I don't care. I really don't care what we do. I'm just stupid-happy to be back with you.'

They went to the pub. The nearest pub to the station.

Joe went to the bar to get drinks, and Laura couldn't take her eyes off him. It seemed so unlikely that she'd be there, now, doing this, with him. But she was.

He slid into the booth beside her, and they clinked glasses.

'I. Have. Missed. You,' Laura said. 'A lot.'

He nuzzled into her neck, murmured, 'I don't know how but I do know, Laura, I've known for ages, maybe even from the very start, I absolutely know that you and me need to be together. Somewhere. In the same place. All of the time. Here. There.'

She was shocked.

'Say something.'

Words failed her. She hadn't known until he said it how completely and exactly it was what she had wanted to hear him say, what she'd wanted him to want. How would she even have dreamt it would be?

Joe, anxious now, was misinterpreting her silence. 'You think I'm insane.'

'No, no.' She took his hand. 'I think you're lovely.'

'But . . .'

Laura laughed. 'There's no but, Joe. No but at all.'

68

Nick wove his way from the bar to the table Fran had chosen for them, a beer and a glass of white wine in his hands, a packet of pork scratchings under his arm. They clinked, said cheers and drank.

They'd come together – Nick had picked her up – and they'd done all their small-talk in the car. Now, they both fell quiet. The pub was busy: a lively crowd was watching a big football match being broadcast from the huge screen in the corner. The two of them seemed subdued by comparison.

Nick didn't know where to start, but he was very clear on where he wanted to end up. Fran gave a sad, closed-lip smile that didn't reach her eyes, and started it for them both.

'We'd better talk about the elephant in the room.'

He considered a lame joke about pachyderms and their football-team allegiances, but he didn't want to be cowardly. He wouldn't pretend he didn't know what she meant, either. They'd had a good stab at it, meeting up on the holiday, but the weird-kiss moment between them all those months ago was hanging in the air. He so badly didn't want to hurt her, and he was, in truth, a bit scared of losing her as a friend. But he needed to say this.

'You know it wouldn't be right, don't you? Letting anything happen between us?'

Fran stared into her glass of wine for a moment, then lifted her gaze and met his. 'Yes. I do. Really. I'm just sort of in denial.'

He took her hand. 'Carrie is what we have in common.'

She pulled it away, picking up her glass, but she didn't drink from it. 'Missing her is what we have in common.'

'And you and me together just won't fill the space. We can't.'

'I know.'

'I need to be clear. I wanted to kiss you that night.'

'I wanted it too.' That smile again.

'I think I maybe wanted more. But if I'm brutally honest, Frannie, it wasn't *you* I wanted. It was someone.'

A tiny laugh. 'That *is* brutal.'

He hadn't intended it to sound that way. 'I don't mean it like that. You know I don't. I was sad and lonely and we'd had a good night.'

'Me too.'

'And the Carrie thing. You were her best friend, Fran. Her *best friend*. You knew her so well. I'm betting you know stuff about me and her. Our life together. Like I know stuff about you. And you've been so incredibly brilliant.' He felt emotional now. He heard it in his voice. 'I don't know how I would have managed, in the beginning, without you.'

She started to shake her head as though she didn't want to hear it.

'No. No, Fran. I need to say it. It was exactly because you knew her so well that you knew what to do. You were so brave. You got me through those horrendous early days and weeks. You.' Fran's eyes filled with tears, and he knew Carrie was very close to them both then. He reached for her hand again, and this time she let him hold it. 'You helped more than I can ever express to you. And I will always, always, be profoundly grateful for that. And I want your friendship. If we can get past this weird stuff – this understandable, sad, lonely confusion . . .'

Up on the plasma screen, someone scored, and everyone cheered. The two of them looked at each other while the celebrations subsided.

'We can.'

'We can?'

'Of course we can.' She didn't quite look at him when she said it, and Nick knew he couldn't push. It wasn't up to him.

'It was just a moment, for God's sake.' It wasn't. He knew it and she knew it. It was a possibility that he at least had let swirl around his head for weeks. A temptation. A solution. It wasn't just a moment. Not for him, and not, he suspected – he knew – for her. But that didn't matter now. And they couldn't help each other to get past it.

They might be able to be friends. They could stay close, or drift apart. It wasn't up to him. He had to let her decide, and accept her decision. He knew what he would choose.

69

He'd always, from a boy, hated going to doctors. Hated hospitals too. The smell, the look, the way you avoided everyone's eye.

All three of the children had been born at home, so he didn't have those glorious, life-affirming memories to counter the dreadful ones. Broken limbs, painful minor surgeries, terminal diagnoses . . . They were anxiety-inducing places to him. He'd heard someone on the radio say that modern anxiety stemmed from human beings' caveman origins: we were always alert for tigers, and because there weren't any tigers for most of us, we made unnecessary worries our foe. Doctors were Charlie's tigers. Even Dr Stephens, and he really liked Dr Stephens. If he'd played golf, or lived on the same street, the two men could have been friends. He'd been seeing him, at the practice, for almost nineteen years. They were almost friends. The older you got, the more time you had to spend there. There were pills and blood tests and chest infections that didn't seem to clear up without a prescription, and moles that suddenly looked like a map of the Isle of Wight and had to be excised. There was nothing much to recommend growing old.

Dr Stephens was no spring chicken himself. He had to be over sixty. Maybe even sixty-five. Charlie hoped to God he died before Dr Stephens retired. How awful to have to get to know a new doctor. 'How've you been, Charlie?' He looked up as Charlie came in, then turned to the ubiquitous computer screen, calling up his catalogue of woes.

Charlie sat down heavily in the chair adjacent to the desk. 'Not so bad.'

'I'm not looking for the polite answer.'

'Not giving you the polite answer. I'm okay.'

'How's the cough?'

'No worse.' Which was almost, but not quite, true.

'Any swelling? Legs or ankles?'

'You'll tell me.' Charlie pulled up his trouser leg and stuck his leg out to prove he could lift one independently of the other. His ankle was thicker. He knew it was. Dr Stephens leant forward, pressed the flesh with his thumb, observing how the oedema blanched, then returned to the usual blotchy white-pink. He sat up, and Charlie let his trouser leg fall.

'And how about in yourself?'

'Not confused, if that's what you mean. I know what day it is, who's prime minister. My car keys weren't in the fridge when I looked for them this morning.'

Dr Stephens laughed. 'You're on the ball today.'

'And every day.'

He unfurled the cuff of the blood-pressure machine. Charlie obligingly unbuttoned and took off his shirt, resting his left arm on the corner of Dr Stephens's desk. Neither man spoke while he took the readings and made a note of them. Charlie tried to think of white sandy beaches and gentle tropical breezes, but he failed.

'You know,' Dr Stephens's conversational style was

laid-back, chatty, 'patients like you are the worst. You know more about what's wrong with you than I do.' That wasn't true, but Charlie knew enough. 'And you're the stiff-upper-lip generation. Dangerous combo.'

Charlie smiled. 'The day you tell me there's a cure, I'll open up like a clam.'

There it was – the whole truth. There was no cure. There were palliative therapies, there were decisions to be made about interventions, there were things that could make him more comfortable when the time came. But there was nothing , not a damn thing, that could be done to stop congestive heart failure killing him in the end. He'd known that for a couple of years now, and the chances were that in a couple of years more he'd be gone.

He'd meant to tell the kids. He'd planned to, while they were all away together, but the right moment hadn't presented itself. He'd been more their father, it seemed to him, in those ten days than he had in the previous ten years. The tipping point he'd hated so much – the one where they cared more for him than he for them – had briefly, gloriously, tipped back in that pretty house in the countryside. It would have been a lousy time to tell them. He'd liked how it felt. Damn it, he didn't want to tell them. Then or now. He hoped they'd never need to know. He had to die of something. It would be no one's idea of a tragedy, not at his age. Better to keep it to himself.

Daphne had said to him, near the end, her voice smaller and quieter than it had ever been, that she was sorry she was going first: she hated him being the one left behind. He didn't. Even in his misery, he was glad. Living without her had been hard. Relentlessly lonely and sad. He couldn't have borne the thought of her living without him, however much he could acknowledge that she'd probably have made a better fist of it than he had.

He was going to enjoy the parts of what was left as much as he could. Spend more time with the kids, if they'd let him. And when the right time came, they would know if they needed to. And it was all right. There was a peace to it.

'So I'd be wasting my breath if I tried to talk to you about options?' This was a well-rehearsed double act by now, and Charlie always went home feeling dignified and respected.

'Pretty much. Not yet. Not yet. I've got my next consultant appointment booked.'

The doctor shook his head ruefully. 'Good to see you, Charlie. You take care.'

Charlie buttoned his shirt, and left, smiling warmly at the cantankerous receptionist and the timid-looking new mother in the waiting area, then gratefully stepping outside into the crisp, cold air.

70

'Ethan! Breakfast!' Laura put a plate with toast, scrambled egg and two rashers of bacon on the table, then sat down adjacent to it to nurse a vast mug of tea. She smiled at her son's heavy tread on the stairs. He lurched into the kitchen, wet hair flicked back, and slid into the chair.

'Cheers, Mum.'

She pushed the ketchup across to him. Ethan didn't eat anything without ketchup.

He smiled. 'What you up to today?' That was new, since the summer, asking about her day.

'Well, the second I've got you out of my hair, I'm whizzing round with the Hoover. Second viewing later.'

'The people with the twins?'

'They're keen, I gather. The agent thinks they're measuring to see if their furniture fits.'

'And that's a good sign?'

'I reckon. He reckons, too. They might make an offer this afternoon.'

Ethan was eating heartily. He nodded his approval.

'You sure you're okay with this?'

He swallowed his mouthful and rolled his eyes. 'For the ten-thousandth time, I'm fine with it.'

He seemed truly fine with all of it. With the house being on the market. With Joe being a regular visitor. With school. Even with his dad. He saw Alex less than before, but seemed happier and more relaxed now when he got back from those visits. Alex appeared to be making what for him would be a Herculean effort to be what he might refer to disparagingly as 'present'. He'd taken him to a football match. And gone to watch Ethan play in one. The painfully bloody obvious stuff he should have been doing all along. Not just since he left them. Laura was glad. She'd never wanted Ethan to be estranged from his father, except in the early, darkest days, and she wasn't ever going back there. He'd even confessed, a little shyly and cautiously, a few weeks ago that he'd had an okay chat with Genevieve. That maybe she wasn't quite as bad as he'd thought. Laura felt proud he wanted to tell her that, because it meant he knew, too, that she was moving on.

And she was. She didn't want to double-date, and some tiny, twisty part of her might always hope that Genevieve and Alex didn't work out, but she could think of them together and not get palpitations now. She was at peace with the tiny, twisty part. She was entitled to it. What mattered was that that part lived in a box, and she controlled the lid.

Ethan came first. He had risen to the surface, where he belonged, of her psyche and her consciousness. For now, he had to. These were crucial times. Practically and emotionally. In two years he'd be going to university – at least, that was what he planned. She tried not to push it, although she assumed Alex would be horrified if he chose a different path. They'd cross that bridge when they got to it. It seemed unimaginable that he'd be leaving home. But it would come, and come fast, she knew, just as she knew it would be years more before he left for good. For now, he was stable and he was doing well. And that meant everything to her.

They hadn't talked about Saskia in ages. There wasn't a new girl, so far as he'd told her, but he was hanging out with a big gang of guys and girls – some old friends from school, and new people, too, who'd joined the sixth form, filling the spaces left by Saskia and others. There were gatherings and parties, and often their kitchen was full of kids messing about, laughing and eating everything in sight. When that happened, Laura would say hi, and chat for a few minutes, then slope off to the living room to watch TV, or upstairs to her room to call Joe, content to hear them, and to know Ethan was safe and seemingly happy. She worried, because she was his mother, that it would be hard for him to start something with someone else – but Joe and Scott and Nick, her triptych of male wisdom, had told her he'd be fine in time.

She was glad he was spending more time with his uncles. They were better men than his father – stronger and wiser and less selfish.

Ethan gestured to the pile of papers on Laura's left. 'So if we get an offer, we can go and see some of these, can we?'

She'd held off viewings. She dreaded finding something she loved when she wasn't in a position to make an offer. But she'd signed up with agents, and they kept sending things. 'Yeah. You going to come with me, are you?'

'When I can. I mean, I've got college . . . Maybe I'll just do the second viewings.'

She smiled. 'Checking for your en-suite, eh?'

'Something like that. Got one at Dad's, you know.' He was only joking, and they both knew it.

She hit his arm playfully. 'Don't start that crap with me!'

'I'm kidding! I'm hoping for somewhere a bit more homey than Dad's boutique hotel.'

'I've never been there.'

'Trust me. It's all very . . . anonymous. You'll need a shed,' he added.

'Why on earth would I need a shed?'

'Not you.' He looked at her like she was being obtuse. 'For Joe. He'll need somewhere for all his projects.' He was teasing, his voice light and kind. But it was, she figured, his way of letting her know that he was okay with Joe's presence. Okay, even, with that presence becoming more permanent.

'Oy.'

'You know you want to.'

She laughed. 'We've only been going out for a few months, Eth. We're taking it slowly.'

'You're not getting any younger, though, Mum, are you? Better crack on, I reckon . . .'

'Cheeky sod.'

He took a last bite of toast, and pushed his chair back from the table before he'd finished chewing. Which didn't stop him planting a quick kiss on the top of her head as he left. She brushed her hair, checking for egg, and went back to her sheaf of house details, smiling to herself.

71

Nick shut the front door behind him, and breathed in the frosty air, the quiet stillness of the early morning. Winter mornings like this – the infrequent fiercely cold and dazzlingly bright kind – were his favourite. Carrie had always been a summer woman. His golden girl, a glorious thing of freckles and coconut oil and stargazing. He was a winter man. Log fires, Irish whiskey, white trees.

Behind him, inside, his three children were laughing, happy and secure. The arrival of Susie, the young, giggly Australian nanny, in September, had revolutionized his life: he couldn't have made a luckier choice. She had swept in on a tide of optimism and energy and 'no worries' enthusiasm for life, and all three of the children had fallen hard for her almost at once. It had been nothing short of transformative. It was better. Better for him, better for them. She lived in from Monday to Friday, and at her boyfriend Mike's at the weekends. During Nick's working week, she was there for breakfast and tea. When he came home, it wasn't to dried-on cereal in bowls still not stacked in the dishwasher. Bags were packed for school. The laundry was folded. He didn't miss the sock-pairing, or the lunchbox packing. Or, at least, he didn't miss trying to get all of that done in the tiny periods of time he had to do them in. When he came home now, it was just him and them, not a to-do list a mile long. He could slip off his shoes, and perch on a bean bag in Bea's room, and listen properly to Delilah telling him about her day, or hear Bea's reading, or just submit to Arthur's embraces without watching the clock.

When he'd settled them down, his evening was his own. Free from domestic drudgery, he was sometimes sadder than he had been – there was space and time to feel all the things he hadn't had time for before. When you flopped onto the sofa with a glass of wine and you weren't knackered, you missed the person who was supposed to be flopped beside you. But he knew it was healthy. He let it happen. He knew he was healing.

Weeks were for working, weekends for them.

Now that he was less exhausted by the end of the week, less strung out by trying to do and be everything, he was more imaginative about Saturday and Sunday. They'd seen more of Charlie, more of Ed and Maureen, more of old university friends with children of similar ages in pub gardens, National Trust houses and adventure playgrounds. They'd drive down to Scott's, Bea and Delilah ecstatic to see their beloved Meredith. Even Ethan was around more.

Life was bigger than it had been since Carrie had died. And happier.

He saw a lot less of Fran. He wasn't at the school gates. They had gently stopped being each other's person. And it was okay. He didn't want to stop being friends, but he did want to stop being each other's crutch. It could never have worked. He'd seen her husband a couple of times, and wondered whether they were trying to make it work, but he was wary of asking.

This morning, he had a meeting north-east of Shoreditch. It wasn't a part of London he knew well, so he left wriggle room and found himself there early. With a few minutes to spare before he was due, he stopped at a tiny café for a coffee to go. It was one of those hipster places, with a blend of the day and healthy snacks. There was a longish queue of blokes with beards, and young mums with babies in slings and pugs on leashes. The pug was definitely the dog of choice in this neighbourhood. The girl working the big chrome coffee machine looked a bit like Audrey Tautou, with a heavy fringe, and a nose stud.

She smiled as she handed him his coffee. Her front teeth overlapped slightly.

'Nice glasses.'

'Thanks.'

'I like your style in general,' she added.

Nick laughed nervously. 'Thanks.'

'You're welcome!'

Turning, he stepped out into the street, and headed left, towards the office he was visiting. Carrie would have teased him mercilessly at being so pleased with the compliment. Then she'd have winked and said the girl was right, and that he was a catch. And she'd never do that again. And he was going to be okay.

72

Heather was reading a copy of *Country Life* from April 2016 and sipping water from a small plastic cup when Scott strode into the waiting room.

'Sorry. Damn train. Sat for ages just outside Woking. Why is it always bloody Woking? As if people are queuing up, desperate to get to . . . Woking?'

She patted him reassuringly to quell the Woking rant. 'Don't worry. You're here in time.'

Scott put his overcoat and briefcase on the chair next to him, and loosened his tie. 'Are you okay? I haven't missed anything, have I?'

She smiled. 'Absolutely fine. And no, no. Relax. Actually, I'm desperate to pee.'

He gestured towards the Ladies, fifteen metres or so down the corridor on the left. Heather patted her belly. 'Gotta have a full bladder.'

He nodded vigorously. So much to know, so much to learn. He'd been to Foyles the day after she'd taken the test, the positive test that had changed everything, and bought no fewer than eight books on pregnancy and childbirth. He had one that explained the development of the foetus in extraordinary detail, one that explored how you kept your relationship healthy through the process, one on hypnobirthing. *What to Expect When You're Expecting* obviously. Another called *How to Grow a Baby and Push it Out of You*. Heather had laughed at him when he'd unpacked them that evening onto his bedside table.

'Seriously?'

'I've got an analytical mind. Logical. Numerical. I need to understand it all.'

'Jeez. It's in, it's coming out. There. That's what you need to know. The rest is up to the doctors.'

'Midwives.'

She wrinkled her nose at the correction. 'Sorry. Midwives.'

He was reading his way through the pile each night. Occasionally he read something out to her, but mostly not. If Heather found herself thinking that she had *actually* done this before, and more or less knew what was coming, she was kind enough not to say so. She found him rather charming like this.

And now she was twelve weeks and four days (he kept a tally in his phone) and this was the first scan. He was terrified. Heather, by contrast, seemed extraordinarily calm. She beamed at him, and he took her hand.

And then they were called in, and Heather was on the bed, and the gel was being squeezed onto the small mound of her stomach, and the strange wand was being man-oeuvred across the gel, and then the screen flickered for an agonizing moment. And there he was. Or she was. He didn't think he honestly cared which. A grainy grey blob with an oversized head and a tiny pulsating heart. Their baby.

And he couldn't speak.

73

Heather hosted. Of course. There was never any question, really, that she would. Her house was made for it. Charlie couldn't possibly – everyone agreed on that. Laura and Nick were grateful that the mess and fuss and organization could be someone else's problem. And, of course, it wasn't a problem to Heather. It was an Instagram wet dream, certain to garner a shedload of new followers.

There was a small herd – no kidding – of wicker reindeer, lit up with fairy lights, in the front garden, and a massive lit star, which suggested the Messiah Himself might be found beneath it and the Three Kings would be along any minute, adorned the side of the barn carport. By the massive front door, a tableau of ancient sledges and vintage ice skates sat on the York stone steps, and the wreath above the brass bee knocker (idea stolen from the Cotswolds house in the summer) was three-quarters of a metre wide, all white roses and pinky hellebores and trailing ivy. It smelt Christmassy. Heavy on the cinnamon, maybe, but allowances could be made. It was Heather's national scent, after all.

In the hall there was a tree that had to be twelve feet tall, all decked out in silver and green, and another, wide and fragrant, in the kitchen, dressed all in white, a collection of gifts in matching paper, with tasteful ribbons, arranged around the bottom. Easily twenty perfect white poinsettias in zinc pots ran down the middle of the long table. Each chair was tied with a hessian and lace ribbon and sprigs of winter herbs. Names were written in Heather's calligraphic writing on die-cut place cards. It was like walking into a magazine. It certainly urged you to go home and change into something that might make you worthy of such a setting. Jeans and a jumper that proclaimed you'd been more nice than naughty didn't really do it justice.

Except that they knew now that Heather liked things to *look* perfect, but didn't necessarily expect them to *be* so. And that knowledge was tremendously liberating. Making things look lovely was her pleasure, not her test for her guests. And, crucially, that she'd already taken about a thousand photographs before they'd arrived and started messing everything up.

In the end, they were a bit more like a Christmas advert than any of them might have thought they'd be. Or a feelgood Richard Curtis movie that warmed your heart even as it curled your toes. Starring Joe as the handsome stranger in the Fair Isle sweater, his arm slung possessively around Laura's shoulders while he chatted easily to Scott and Charlie. Featuring Hayley and Ethan, huddled together in a corner, watching something evidently hilarious on an iPad, and Meredith, dancing with an overexcited Bea and Delilah in a froth of tulle and sequined ballet pumps, as Arthur toddled behind them, grumbling at not being able to keep up. With a guest appearance from Heather's small bump, barely visible beneath a retro kitchen apron with a prancing reindeer pattern, and a platter of carrots roasted with thyme sprigs.

At the long, exquisitely dressed table, wine was poured, turkey was carved, crackers were pulled by crossed hands and hats worn rakishly. Jokes were told and groaned at, mottoes read with nods, gravy boats passed and pigs in blankets fought over.

And at some point during the proceedings, each one took a moment to look around the cacophonous room, at the dysfunctional, disparate, blended, broken family gathered at the heaving, Instagrammable table, and to be glad, almost to the point of a lump in the throat, that they were all there.

74

Later, at home, in the silence, Charlie closed the curtains, and switched on the two lamps at either end of the sofa, and then, despite having illuminated the space, wandered into the kitchen and went through the same ritual there, lowering the two roman blinds behind the work surface, and pulling the large curtains that covered the French windows that led out onto the patio. As he did so, he saw his neighbour's mulberry tree, resplendent in its Christmas fairy lights, and thought of all the families in all the houses, eating chocolates and drinking Baileys in front of the TV, and was suddenly very glad he'd been with his own family today. Turning back into the room, he opened the fridge for no apparent reason. He wasn't at all hungry. He might never be hungry again after the lunch he'd eaten.

Just as well. There wasn't an awful lot of what might constitute a meal within its white walls. Eggs. Some questionable bacon. Half an onion, a tub of butter, and most of a two-pint container of milk. He knew what Daphne would do. An omelette. In five minutes flat. Which would taste delicious. He could make an omelette – of course he could. He'd been feeding himself since she'd gone, and he wasn't exactly wasting away. His cholesterol and sugar readings would tell you that. But hers would have tasted far nicer. She'd have done it whether they were hungry or not, because in the world according to Daphne it was supper time and you had to eat something, regardless of the size or timing of your lunch. He'd probably have poured them a glass of wine while she busied herself adding a pinch of salt and pepper and a handful of herbs to a bowl of vigorously whisked eggs.

All the while she'd talk about the day. He would listen and he might add some of his own thoughts, but mostly his pleasure would be to listen to her opinions about their children and grandchildren. She'd have seen and heard so many things that had passed him by. Nuances and glances and stuff he never had noticed and never would. When she'd slid the omelette effortlessly out of the pan and onto warm plates, he'd take knives and forks from the drawer under the microwave, and they'd sit facing each other at the kitchen table, him pointing at the garden, her towards the hall, like always. They'd clink glasses and drink to their family, and to each other, and there would be a lingering glance of pride and love before they turned their attention to the food. And the omelette would be delicious, and he would finish it, even though he'd declared himself not hungry just twenty minutes earlier, and she'd make two mugs of tea while he stacked the plates, cutlery and wine glasses in the dishwasher.

They might watch a bit of telly with their tea. The news, perhaps. She liked to listen to the Queen's Speech, and she wouldn't have heard it earlier, because who the hell had heard anything much earlier, with all the kids running around? Nothing past the headlines, because Daphne never wanted to hear sad news on Christmas Day and the weather forecast was largely irrelevant. Later, in bed, he'd watch her put cream on her hands, her elbows and her neck, sitting up in bed, the sight and the smell so utterly familiar to him that he could play it like a film in his mind, and then he'd hold her for a while, kiss her goodnight on the mouth, hear her say, 'Sleep tight, darling', and they would separate to sleep.

My ordinary, everyday, extraordinary life. My ordinary, everyday, extraordinary wife.

Tonight there would be no omelette with wine. No cuddle in bed. No 'Sleep tight, darling.' She wasn't there. Except she was. He didn't feel as sad, now, as he felt grateful. He felt very calm, and peaceful. He had been the luckiest of men. Nothing in the present, or even in the future, mattered to him now as much as the past did, and tonight the past seemed gloriously close at hand.

He could hear her voice.

He thought about the day. About Laura and Scott and Nick. About all of their babies. He remembered Candlewood, in the Cotswolds, and how everything had changed there. They were all right. Everyone was okay, or they were going to be.

Upstairs, Charlie climbed into bed, and lay on his pillows, his face turned to where Daphne's own precious face had lain for so long. He could hear her voice. And what she was saying was 'Well done, my love. Well done.'

Acknowledgements

I am so very lucky to be supported in what I do by some very fine people. My grateful thanks go to Jonathan Lloyd, Lucy Morris, Hannah Beer and everyone else at Curtis Brown. At Penguin, I feel very grateful to be published by Maxine Hitchcock and Louise Moore, whose expert advice and kindness is matchless. Thank you to the incomparable Hazel Orme, who improves every page, to the brilliantly efficient (and patient!) Beatrix McIntyre, who shepherds manuscript to finished book so very well, to Ella Watkins and to all the other wonderful Penguins.

And to David, Tallulah and Ottilie: I love you.

Other People's Husbands

COMING SUMMER 2021

Read on for a sneak peek . . .

May Bank Holiday weekend, 2002

Perfect, golden days. How many of them did you truly live in a year? Or a lifetime?

This had been one.

Georgie pulled her sweater around her, and leant her head back on the cushion, reflecting that she felt so happy she could cry. After everything she and Phil had been through, to be here, now, with these people, feeling this way . . . it seemed absolutely miraculous to her. She looked around the firepit at the others, determined to remember every detail.

She was tipsy, of course. Georgie felt delightfully woozy. And woozily delighted. Someone had pulled a CD player to the open kitchen window behind them, and there was music now. 'Dancing in the Moonlight'. And they were.

The weather had been spectacular – the May Bank Holiday showing off, staying warm into the evening. There'd been rounders on the beach, sandy sandwiches and fizzy drinks kept cool Enid Blyton-style in rockpools, crabbing and sandcastles in the afternoon, adults snoozing in turn. And then a straggling, sun-kissed parade to the ice-cream van halfway up the hill towards home. Splashy baths for the kids, and enormous gins for the parents, before the men got serious about the business of grilling sausages and burgers. And then, sated, and pink-nosed, the kids had sprawled in front of a Disney film, and were eventually marshalled into various beds and settled top and toe onto sofas.

And so now the grown-ups were sat around the firepit, sharing scratchy blankets that smelled of mildew and moth-balls. In the absence of light pollution, someone who knew about stars was pointing out the constellations, and a few people pretended, good-naturedly, to listen.

It felt, to her, like she'd been initiated into this club. If she was honest with herself, even though this was May, and she'd known these people since the previous September, she'd had imposter syndrome until this weekend. She wasn't, couldn't be, entirely sure she and Phil belonged with this gilded group. They were very ordinary people. She'd always thought so. It wasn't a pejorative. Not dull or boring, she'd hoped, but ordinary nonetheless. She'd had what were almost crushes on these women she'd met at the school gates, and slowly and carefully got to know over the last few months.

Glossy Sarah, so in control, but then she had taught at the school for years, and she knew everybody and everything. She was the leader, the planner. She seemed so perpetually sussed. Her husband Dom was equally together and organized. Even the man's hairline was exquisitely neat, and his blue linen shirt didn't seem to have wrinkled all day. Phil, also in linen, looked like an unmade bed: it was the way she liked him, but still . . .

Natalie and Kit were so arty and bohemian. They'd started the dancing, and it was definitely bordering on the dirty kind. You felt almost like you shouldn't watch. Natalie had the kind of untamed curly hair that made women like Georgie try perms, the sexy kind.

Annie and Rupert – the Hawtreys – so posh they were almost aliens. Easily the grandest people she'd ever known. This house, this effortlessly glorious coastal home they were all in now, had been in Annie's family for generations. She'd spent summers here all her life. This weekend – this extraordinary, pinch-yourself weekend – was just normal for her.

Flick was wild and funny. Her husband Andrew was the only one who'd seemed distracted today – his mobile kept ringing and she'd seen him several times circling by the groyne, speaking on it. Flick just teased him, and he didn't seem to mind at all. They'd been married less than a year. You could see the newlywed sparkle between them – the tenderness. His proud eyes followed her everywhere she walked.

Vanessa and Ross seemed intellectual. They'd met at Cambridge, she knew. She imagined all their other friends were professors and junior government ministers and book editors. Georgie was pretty sure she wasn't smart enough to get into a serious conversation with them. She wasn't quite as sure who made her feel that way – was it them, or did she do it to herself?

But here she was. Here they were, the three of them. Her, Phil, and Liam, curled up now under a crochet blanket on an ancient green velvet chaise at the foot of the bed in the room they'd been given. Liam, her beautiful and precious little boy, with his ginger curls and his dusting of pale freckles, was, it seemed, her golden ticket into this particular club.

They wouldn't have been her friends at school or university, these women – she was sure of it. She'd have envied them, imitated them, admired them, maybe even despised them.

It was different for the guys. Guys didn't evaluate. Men didn't keep score. Not in the same way, she didn't think. They might have all been on the same football team, or propping up the same bar, and it would have been easier for them to be friends. They'd fallen, it seemed, into a quick and easy, matey friendship. If they had less in common than their wives – maybe if they *only* had in common those wives and their children and their postcodes – it didn't seem so obvious.

It was always more complicated for the women. Over a few months, via dozens of playdates, a hundred cups of tea, and a Christmas fair committee all this had happened, and now they were a gang. She'd even used the word, talking on the phone to her mother, turning down an invitation to stay for the Bank Holiday. 'We'd have loved to, but we're away with the gang.'

And there were years to come. Years and years. These children would grow up together. And these people were going to be her friends. Hers and Phil's. She wanted to savour every moment, but at the same time, she couldn't wait. And it could only get better, right?